THE VALLEY

NANCY BAILEY

UNLEASHED
publications

ANDERSON, CALIFORNIA

Published in the United States of America by UNLEASHED PUBLICATIONS.

First Edition

V-051118

ISBN-13: 978-0692862926

✳ Created with Vellum

DEDICATION

DEDICATED TO:
My Mom, Lois Holloway, who supported and inspired me until this book
became a reality.

MAIN CHARACTERS

Craig Michaels – (Federal Bureau of Land Management, International Exchange and Gas Division)
Wife: Linda
Twins: Nate and Brianna (19)
Son: Caleb (6)
Craig's mother: Lois
Linda's mother: Joliene
Linda's brother: Duane
Richard Carter - (Craig's friend and co-worker)
Wife: Tracey
Son: Chad (12)
Daughters: Sara (7) Cassie (9)
Richard's father: Darren (physician)
Brock: (lab assistant)
Dr. Savi: (head of lab)
Professor Heileich: (researcher)
Jason: (diner owner)
June: (waitress in diner)
Leon: (Director of the International Department of BLM)

MAIN CHARACTERS

Jeanette: (wife)
Jacque: (Canadian BLM director)
Twig and Slick: (brothers and vagrants)
Ralph: (father)
Jeremy: (son)

THE VALLEY

PART I

CHAPTER 1

HORROR BEGINS

On the second day of March, at 6:15 in the morning, Professor Gustaf Heileich took Michelle's hand as they stepped onto Amtrak's slippery platform. Glistening ice fog floated through the air, the wind was crisp, but nothing could dampen the professor's spirits —not today.

He adjusted his wife's scarf, covered her ears, then tilted her chin. "Why are you so nervous, sweetheart? You know how long I've waited for an opportunity like this."

She took a half step back, gave him a long look then brushed a loose hair from his collar. "You look very handsome, and you'll make a great impression on . . . whomever you're meeting, but how could I not be nervous? There's too much secrecy. Unless it's a life or death situation, why would a branch of the Federal Government—or any other professional organization—call a person after midnight, and tell them to catch the six thirty train—that very morning? It makes no sense."

"I admit it's a little bizarre, but where's the harm? This can be a make or break opportunity. Missing a few hours sleep is a small price to pay."

He took a quick glance around then whispered. "Homeland Security chose *me*, Michelle. They chose *me*. If they like my work, they may offer me a permanent position. Instead of teaching math, I'll be doing research—my favorite field—and we could look forward to some generous paydays."

"Sweetheart, you love being a Professor, and we're doing just fine. Suddenly, you're off to some secret meeting at an undisclosed location. It just doesn't set well."

"I know, and I don't mean to make light of your concerns, but *I* think it's exciting. The secrecy adds a layer of intrigue, and to top it off, someone in a trench coat, and dark glasses is picking me up at Denver's train station. Imagine that?"

"You're not funny mister, and you sure aren't James Bond." She yanked on his tie and pulled his head down.

"Answer me this. Why did they tell you to leave your cell phone at home?"

"I'm not sure, but they must have their reasons."

Michelle's voice rose slightly. "They're separating you from your GPS so you can't be tracked. That's their reason."

When he burst out laughing, she popped him on the arm. "This still isn't funny. The girls and I will be here on this platform, at 4:30 sharp. If you're late, you will be met by four unhappy women."

They walked hand in hand to the steps of the coach then he wrapped her in his arms, pulling her close. "You're getting just a little dramatic, aren't you? When I get back we'll go to dinner. Let the girls pick the place."

A long, shrill whistle drowned out her answer. He hugged her one more time, gave her a passionate kiss then turned, and with an extra spring in his step, climbed on board. He smiled and blew her one more kiss from his window seat.

The clacking wheels grew in intensity as the monster gained momentum. The couple kept eye contact until the train rounded a curve, then Gustaf's eyes were drawn from his beautiful wife to the deep green forests, and majestic snow covered mountains. He smiled, envisioning all the possibilities this day might afford. "*I wish she could catch some of my excitement,*" he whispered.

The Professor's train pulled into the Denver station at 10 a.m. When he descended the stairs a handsome young man approached, with hand extended.

"You must be Professor Heileich."

"Well, yes, I am. How did you know?"

"You look the part, you're carrying a briefcase, and I have a picture of you."

Heileich laughed. "Then you must be Brock. I *don't* have a picture of you."

After other pleasantries, Brock led the way to a dark SUV with tinted windows. He opened the trunk and took out a black mask.

"I hope this doesn't offend you sir, but the location of the lab must be protected. You'll need to wear the mask for about ten minutes. It's for your protection, as well as ours. I'll tell you when to put it on, and when to take it off. I'm sure you understand."

The professor didn't understand. In fact, was a little stunned, but reluctantly agreed.

Brock drove from the parking lot onto the boulevard and said, "Its time."

Heileich wanted to object. He wanted to say he could be trusted, but he pulled the mask over his head, covering his eyes. He wanted to drink in the sights of the city, but for the first few minutes, honking horns, short bursts of conversation, and distant sirens was all he heard. After the third turn outside noise was faint. *This venture has been a little quirky so far, but if this day turns out like I hope, it will be a small price to pay.*

Brock slowed, then stopped. The professor started to remove the mask, but the young man said, "Not yet, sir. I'll tell you when."

Brock waited as some type of door opened. When it clicked into place they moved forward. All sounds of the city disappeared, and the air felt heavier.

This must be the place, but I'm surprised it's this close to the city.

The car moved forward again, then stopped as another door, sounding much like the one on the Professor's garage, opened.

"It won't be much longer, sir. Thank you for your patience."

Heileich heard crunching under the tires—certain they had replaced a smooth blacktop surface with one of ice and snow. He swayed once again as Brock rounded a sharp curve.

"You can take it off now, sir. Sorry about that."

Heileich was temporarily blinded by the brilliance of the glistening snow. It never occurred to him to bring sunglasses.

"Open the glove box, sir. There's dark glasses in there."

When his eyes were protected, he looked around. All signs of civilization had disappeared. They were on a narrow, ice covered two-lane highway, lined with high fences, heading in the direction of a large snow-covered mountain.

He whispered, "Those fence posts blend so well with the snow, they're almost invisible. They look like tall crystals."

"What did you say, sir?" Brock asked.

"Nothing really. Just admiring the scenery."

He wanted to ask questions, but exactly one month earlier, when he met with a Mr. Canberra from DHS. He was given a stack of documents to sign—*if* he accepted the assignment, agreeing to abide by all the conditions, fully understanding he could face arrest and/or imprisonment if he failed to do so. Mr. Canberra stressed, several times, the assignment was Top Secret, and if it fell into the wrong hands, it could disrupt national security. His report was for a Dr. S's eyes only, unless the good doctor gave different written instructions.

Four large huskies, looking much like wolves, tracked their movement for the first mile. "Brock, why aren't they barking?"

"They only bark at vehicles they don't recognize. There's an intricate alarm system on the fence posts. Their bark triggers it . . . uh . . . keep that bit of information to yourself."

Heileich laughed. Laughing felt good and relieved some of his growing apprehension.

At marker 6,800 feet, his breathing became labored, but the beauty of the area, and a few deep breaths made his temporary discomfort tolerable.

"You know, Brock. I've never seen a bluer sky, or whiter snow than we have in Colorado. We truly live in a winter wonderland."

"Yes, sir, I agree, but I travel these mountain roads so often, I don't appreciate it as I should."

Thirty minutes later, Brock stopped. "Sir, we are approaching the lab. Please cover your eyes for about ten more minutes, and again, I will tell you when to remove it."

When the professor's eyes were covered Brock veered from the main highway, drove a little further, waited for a gate to open then drove forward—about twenty feet, the professor estimated.

"You may remove your mask, sir."

The door they faced was made from the same material as the fence posts. It too blended with the snow, making it appear invisible. After Brock drove forward, and the door closed, he pulled into a designated parking spot, bearing his name on a red and white placard.

Heileich was amazed. This was a garage, sunk into the side of a mountain, full of white vans. He could contain himself no longer. "This is not what I expected, Brock. Where is everybody?"

"Only twenty people work here, on any given day. These vans transport them, and materials, up and down the mountain. This lab is not open to the public. There is no reception center here. We keep the location secure. I'm sure you understand."

Heileich hesitated, "Well . . . yes . . . I suppose I do."

Brock led the professor to an elevator then pushed the sub-level 3 button.

"I've never seen an elevator with 3 sub-floors."

"Our lab is unique, and cost several million dollars to construct. We develop antidotes that reverse evolving microbes from viral strains, which means we're working with some pretty wicked stuff. Nothing can escape this facility. We've taken every precaution."

Heileich nodded, as an involuntary shiver travelled up his spine. *Something about Brock's constant reassurances remind me of Richard Atten-borough, in Jurassic Park. He kept repeating that no dinosaurs could escape because, "We spared no expense."*

When the smooth elevator came to a flawless stop the doors slid open with barely a whisper. The professor caught his first glimpse of the well-lit corridor, but instead of stepping forward—he stepped back. The hall was lined with seamless, highly buffed grey walls, flowing without interruption into an equally shiny floor. It created the false illusion of a deep liquid pool. He whispered, "If I leave this elevator, will I be swallowed?"

Brock said, "Sorry about that, sir. I should have warned you about this corridor. It's made from non-porous material. If an infectious agent is accidentally released, it can be quickly eradicated. There's a lot of nasty stuff in this place."

"I'm sure."

Half way down the corridor Brock stopped and unlocked an office door. He ushered the professor to a large oak desk, then handed him a document.

"This letter gives me permission to review your reports before we disturb Dr. Savi. I have everything prepared for your power point presentation. I'm sure you understand."

Heileich raised his eyebrows, still thinking of Jurassic Park. He read the letter, checked the logo, and said, "That's fine. Maybe I won't be so nervous the second time."

As Brock viewed the impact and graphic study, displayed on the screen, a broad smile erupted across his face. Heileich thought, *how can he find humor in the carnage of a deadly viral attack?* He wanted to say something, but again, said nothing.

The presentation lasted one hour and ten minutes. When it was over, Brock said, "Good work, sir. This is the information Dr. Savi needed. You must be getting hungry. Wait here. I'll be right back with lunch."

He returned with two hoagie type sandwiches, potato chips, apple juice, and brownies.

When they finished eating, Brock asked, "Are you ready to meet Doctor Savi?"

"Yes, I believe I am."

Heileich followed Brock down the rest of the fifteen-foot hall. It ended in front of a glass sliding door. Bold black lettering read: Viral Research Lab-Bio Hazard Material-Restricted Entry.

"Brock, don't we need to suit up?"

The young man laughed as he removed a gold key card from his pocket. "There's no need. Live specimens are rarely brought to this portion of the lab. When they are, they're fully contained. We take advance precautions including inoculating the staff, and quick access to antidotes—well for most strains. Nothing to worry about."

Brock slid his card through the designated slot. After a series of clicks the door opened automatically.

"Dr. Savi will meet us in the rear portion of the lab. It's right down here." Heileich followed to an unmarked door, which Brock held open for him. "Doctor Savi, I want you to meet Professor Heil..."

"Out! Out! Get him out! There's been a spill!"

The professor froze in place. Dr. Savi lunged at a large red button, located on a white pillar, in the middle of the room. An ear piercing alarm pulsated throughout the whole facility.

Brock screamed. "Get out, sir. Get out!"

The professor tried to move but his legs were like gelatin. He stumbled backwards, slid down a wall as the soft scent of vanilla invaded his nostrils then filled his lungs. His briefcase slipped from his hand hitting the floor with a thud. With all the strength he could muster, he inched toward the door, blood escaping from every orifice, engulfing his collar, his shirt then oozing down his expensive grey suit. It reached his belt before spilling onto the floor, leaving a gruesome trail of crimson. He trembled, grabbed his chest and looked toward the door.

Tears, mixed with blood, made paths down his face. He reached the threshold with the tips of his fingers then whispered, "Why?"

Brock knelt beside him. "I'm sorry, man. I'm sorry—and after all you did for us."

The professor touched Brock's hand then grabbed his pants leg. His voice was barely audible. "My research—was it for this? Promise you'll destroy it. Promise. Tell my wife—my kids . . ." He was gone.

Brock stood like a stone, showing no emotion as Dr. Savi grabbed the professor's legs and pulled him back, making room for two men, dressed in protective gear, to enter. They loaded the professor's limp body onto a cart and within seconds were out the door. Brock hesitated then decided to follow the sound of the clipping wheels down the corridor to a door marked INCINERATOR. He stepped back when the scorching heat hit his face, and watched as the men, without hesitation or ceremony, tossed the distorted body of this husband, father, and victim number one, into the all-consuming flames.

When the incinerator door slammed, Brock stumbled back to the lab. He scooted around another crew who were methodically covering the professor's blood spill with chemicals. He backed onto a tall stool and watched as the remainder of the horrid scene, streamed obediently into the drainage tank. All evidence of the professor's demise was gone—except for his briefcase—and the memory.

When the second crew left the area, Brock, still shaken by the unexpected turn of events, stared at Dr. Savi, then an involuntary smile spread across his face. "Wow! That was really something. You said it was fast, but I had no idea. People won't know what hit them."

Dr. Savi said, "That's the beauty of the thing. We'll wake our sleeper cells—then, with no guns, no bombs, no noise, we'll move swiftly across this nation, and beyond, with our silent, deadly emissions. Now, let me get down to business. Where's his research? There's no time to waste."

Brock used disinfectant wipes to clean the professor's brief case before placing it on the counter. "It's very impressive. His impact study charts, and graphs, cover this whole country, plus southern

Canada." Brock laid his hand on the smooth case. "I'm sorry you missed his presentation, but I think you'll be pleased."

Dr. Savi said, "I've waited five years for this day. The professor's information was the final step. If it's as thorough as you say, we can set the launch date. Are you sure he showed no one else his work?"

"I'm sure, sir. Our computer—well the one I gave him, is in the briefcase. He was convinced the Department of Homeland Security commissioned him, and he knew his research was Top Secret."

"Good! Good!"

"Dr. Savi," Brock asked, "how did the virus get into this part of the lab? I thought . . ."

"A transport problem, boy, that's all. Now leave me while I familiarize myself with his work. We may be ready for North Dakota in a few short weeks. We can't afford any mistakes now."

Brock threw his black leather jacket over his arm then looked around one last time. *Too bad the professor didn't live long enough to see his impact study play out. Soon, people will have something else to think about besides their pathetic, insignificant little lives.*

Michelle kept her promise. She, and three little girls, stood in the frigid weather on the platform of Fort Collins train station. They watched as the 4:30 train rounded the curve. Five-year-old Beth's yell could be heard above the whistle. "He's here, Mommy. Daddy's here."

CHAPTER 2

A LITTLE DINER

*B*LM supervisor, Craig Michael's, pulled into the parking lot of Jason's Diner. He shut off the engine and laid his head on the steering wheel. He was not antisocial but dreaded going inside—too tired to engage in unnecessary conversation, but they were hungry, and in need of a break.

He, and his co worker, Richard Carter, had just completed a grueling three week assignment, in Southern Canada. Reuben, North Dakota was their first stop after crossing the Canadian border.

Craig said. "I believe those were the longest three hours of my life."

"Yes, and we've just begun. Seattle is a long way from here," Richard said.

"Don't remind me. One step at a time. That's all I'm good for. Let's eat."

A small bell jangled when Richard pushed open the diner door, and Craig cringed. To his ears it was a gong, plus a signal for all the patrons to turn and stare.

Richard offered a polite nod, but Craig stared straight ahead.

The diner was quaint, well cared for and *very* bright. Yellow gingham covered four windows—and eight tables. Adding to the decor, was an oversized sunflower clock hanging directly above the counter. Craig noticed the coat rack was a mixture of straw hats and helmets, surmising the majority of the customers were farmers or oil well workers.

He shaded his eyes and whispered, "Ninety-nine percent of these patrons are men. You would think that Jason guy could tone it down a little. I'm not in a yellow mood, and my sunglasses are in the truck."

Richard laughed. "You're never in a yellow mood, but it doesn't seem to bother anyone else. This is a nice place. The windows are clean—no dead flies in the sills. Tracey would love it."

Craig knew that was true. Richard's wife cleaned and sanitized everything, including their three children.

A young blond waitress, dressed in a bright canary uniform, hurried from table to table. She looked their way and smiled. "You gentlemen have a seat. There's an empty table near the end of the counter. I'll be with you in a minute."

Their table sat against an outside wall, in full view of the kitchen. A young man stood at the grill skillfully turning several eggs, flipping pancakes and filling plates.

Richard stretched before folding his six-foot, four-inch frame onto the padded chair. "

June grabbed a fresh pot of coffee, two menus and approached their table. She turned over the heavy brown mugs and said, "Good morning. You guys look like you could use an eye opener."

Craig nodded. *At least the mugs aren't yellow.*

"Good morning to you, and if that coffee tastes as good as it smells, we'll be taking some with us," Richard said.

"Don't worry, it does. It goes so fast it has no chance to get old. What brings you boys to this neck of the woods?"

Craig kept his eyes on the menu and said, "We just came down from Canada."

"No wonder you look so tired. That's a long old road, and not much to see."

Richard said, "You won't get any argument from us, and we're hungry. What do you recommend?"

"Jason's pancakes, of course. They're world famous."

"Well, I better have some. Throw in some bacon, hash browns, and a couple of over easy eggs, and I'll call it good."

"Make that two," Craig said, still looking down.

"You won't be sorry. By the way, if you don't mind me asking, where are you guys headed, and what type of work . . .?"

"June! Your order's up."

When she walked away Craig put his head in his hands and moaned. "She has too much energy for me."

"Yes, but she's cute, spunky, and a perfect match for this job. Cheer up buddy. Tomorrow night we sleep in our own beds. *That* cheers *me* up."

"Right now, it's the only thing that keeps me going." Craig said. "One more motel, then home."

Richard stirred cream in his coffee then laid the spoon across a napkin. "Leon says we have three weeks off. I hope he's right."

"So do I."

Their work for the Federal Bureau of Land Management, International Exchange—Energy and Gas Division, took them all over. On rare occasions they flew to worksites, but for the most part they drove. They had just completed an impact study for a section of the Canadian/American oil pipeline. Three weeks of long days and short nights. They were eager to go home, but dreaded the remaining drive.

They sat quietly for a few moments enjoying their coffee while unintentionally eavesdropping on a myriad of conversations. Craig looked up just in time to see a small red headed boy smiling at him. He smiled back and gave the boy a low wave.

"That little guy reminds me of Caleb, especially with that crop of red hair."

"You must remind him of someone too," Richard said. "He keeps staring at you."

June delivered their food, filled their coffee mugs then floated away. She was right about the pancakes. They were delicious. Craig finished his last bite just as the little diner's bell sounded for the fourth time. A dark haired man entered, surveyed the room, then chose a stool directly under the ceiling fan. He did a quick survey of the room, careful to meet no ones' eyes.

June smiled his way. "Good morning. I'll be with you shortly."

The stranger said nothing.

June delivered steaming plates to a table of four then hurried back to the kitchen for a new bottle of syrup.

Craig heard Jason say, "I think we just set a new record. Three strangers in less than thirty minutes. Not bad."

"I know, and that new guy is pretty cute, plus—there's no ring on that left hand."

Jason laughed. "You don't miss a thing do you girl?"

June grabbed the coffee pot and approached the stranger. She handed him a menu, said good morning for the second time, and for the second time, he didn't answer. Before she could turn over his mug, he covered it with his hand.

"I haven't seen you before. Are you visiting someone in the area, or just passing through?"

He kept his eyes down, ignored her question, and tapped a picture of blueberry-topped pancakes.

"Good choice," she said.

He placed the menu in her hand, waved her away as if he was shooing a fly.

Craig clinched his fists and wanted to say—or do something, but June was certainly experienced enough to handle a jerk like that. She clipped the man's order on the spindle, and gave it a forceful turn.

Craig caught Richard's eye. They had no intention of eavesdropping, but could hear every word.

Jason laughed. "What's wrong girl? Did you strike out?"

June threw a dish towel his way, and whispered back, "He's just plain rude, and that's too bad. I could get lost in those dark eyes."

"That guy looks a bit like an Easterner. He may be from India or Iraq or someplace like that. Why don't you ask him?"

"Are you kidding? Two rejections are enough."

"You're not used to that—are you? Wonder what brought him here?"

"Someone probably told him about your great cooking."

"Now, why didn't I think of that? Maybe he'll go home—wherever home is, and tell all his friends about Reuben North Dakota's only diner. Our little community of 350 might become world renown."

June laughed, then headed off with a water pitcher in one hand, a coffee pot in the other. She went about her business, filling glasses and mugs. She called all the regulars by their first name. In return she was treated with a great amount of respect.

Jason called her back to the kitchen to pick up the stranger's meal and said, "This should soften him up. He's probably just hungry."

June backed out of the swinging doors and whispered, "We'll see."

She slid the warm plate across the counter to the unfriendly guest. "Will there be anything else?"

Again, offering no reply, he turned his plate, picked up his knife and fork, cut a bite, and started eating.

Craig sighed deeply as June rushed back to the kitchen. She threw her pen and pad on the counter, and crossed her arms.

"I've met some rude people in my life, but I have to say, he tops them all. This is the first time I've ever been totally ignored. It was embarrassing. You take him the ticket, okay Jason?"

"Sure, whatever you say. Now get back out there and take care of our patrons who *do* talk to you. Don't let that guy spoil your day. Maybe he'll make it up by leaving a large tip."

"Yeah, right. We'll be lucky if he pays his bill at all."

The stranger concentrated on his meal until the last bite disappeared. June watched him place his fork on the plate's edge then followed his eyes to the diner's clock. The time was 7:35.

She shook her head. "That's one strange guy."

∼

Craig pushed back from the table and handed Richard a twenty-dollar bill. "Would you pay for that young woman, and her little boy's break-fast? If there's any change, tell June to keep it."

Richard laughed. "Oh! Maybe there is a soft bone in that body somewhere." Craig grunted, and went into the men's room.

Richard paid for his and Craig's meal with the company credit card, handed June the twenty, and told her what it was for. She tried to give him the change but he told her to keep it. She said she would give it to Tommy's mother.

"She's raising Tommy alone," June said. "He's a sweetheart. Thank you for doing this. She'll appreciate it. Can I take care of it now so she can thank you?"

"Are you kidding? Craig would kill me. By the way, we both appreciated your great service. And, if you don't mind, fill our thermos, give us two cups to go, and be sure to compliment the chef."

Richard paid cash for the coffee, and again told her to keep the change.

CHAPTER 3

DEATH RELEASED

*C*raig was standing next to the Toyota Tundra, staring across the parking lot when Richard joined him. A misty rain was falling, but the sky was filled with threatening dark clouds. Craig tossed Richard the keys then climbed into the passenger seat.

Richard shivered in the dampness, pulled his jacket from the back seat, and adjusted the truck's temperature. As he pulled out of the parking lot he asked Craig what he had been staring at.

"There was a pullout, a few miles back. I saw a black SUV roll out of a silver tractor-trailer. I couldn't make out the company logo, but I'm pretty sure that same SUV was parked across from us. It must belong to the guy at the counter. I should have asked him what company he's with—or maybe not. If he ignored me like he did June, I might have yanked him off that stool."

"Watch that temper boy. I don't want to be stuck this far from home trying to explain to Linda why I'm making bail for you. It might be time to dye that red hair."

Craig laughed, "No worries. I have better things to spend my limited energy on."

Heavy rain began to fall and Richard turned the windshield wipers up another notch. "Why were you so intrigued by the big rig?"

"If you kept your eyes open for more than five minutes at a time, you would have noticed that portion of highway was not conducive to big rigs. It just felt like a strange combination and frankly, the most interesting thing I saw for a hundred miles."

"Well, Sherlock, they could be rich farmers checking out their crops, or oil executives."

Craig said, "I suppose so." He put his seat back, grumbled at the raindrops, plopped his head onto his pillow, and closed his eyes.

June walked away from the cash register just in time to see the stranger remove something from the left pocket of his jacket. She followed his eyes as he glanced at the ceiling fan. He moved one stool to the right, then removed a seal from a small container, then dumped the contents onto the counter. He looked down, smiled then returned the pieces to his pocket.

One of the farmers yelled, "Hey, buddy, what is that stuff?"

The stranger kept his position and said nothing.

June heard the same farmer murmur, "I suppose it's some kind of ritual or something. I don't know much about those people."

She asked Jason to throw her a towel then said, loud enough for the stranger to hear, "The guy at the counter dumped out some kind of liquid. It smells like vanilla."

Then she turned to the stranger. "I'm going to clean this up, and I would very much like for you would leave. Your breakfast is on me."

When she took the first swipe he grabbed her hand. "Leave it."

"Oh, so you can talk." June narrowed her eyes. "May I also assume you can hear? Turn me loose!"

His dark eyes narrowed. He yanked her forward then loosened his grip. June stumbled back a few paces just as Jason came around the end of the counter. He threw his cooks hat on the floor, clenched his fists, and tightened his jaw. Beads of sweat popped out on his forehead, but before he could land a punch, four-year-old Tommy dropped his fork. It hit the edge of his plate then plunged to the floor. Blood was dripping from the little boy's nose.

"I don't feel good, Mommy."

June grabbed some napkins as Tommy's mother took him from his chair. She sat him on her lap and pinched his nose with a napkin then laid her head on top of his.

Tears came to June's eyes when she saw blood dripping from his mother's nose, too. June heard her say, "You know what sweetie—I don't feel good either."

As if on cue, agonizing groans began rising from every patron in the diner, except for the stranger. He slid off his stool, walked to the window, flipped the sign from Open to Closed then turned off the dining room lights. Once again, the friendly little bell jangled, this time announcing a ghastly departure. June saw him standing next to his car staring at the diner's large window.

Jason yelled, "June! Call 9-1-1. Tell them to hurry. We need help fast."

June ran to the phone as painful seizures and bloodletting wracked the young, old, and everyone in between. They thrashed around on the floor, as if trying to escape from their own bodies. She wiped her nose as she punched in the numbers.

The dispatcher said, "9-1-1. What's your emergency?"

In a fading whisper she forced her plea, "Jason's Diner . . . Reuben. We're bleeding . . . I . . ."

She fell back into Jason's arms and they slid down the wall together. The last sound she would ever hear was, "June! June! Are you there? What's your..."

CHAPTER 4

ESCAPE

*B*rock unlocked his SUV and smiled, satisfied with his success. As with Professor Heileich, death came quickly. Brock threw his jacket on the passenger seat then headed south. His deadly rampage had just begun. *If the good doctor is satisfied, I get to do this again. Lunch crowd, here I come.*

Five miles south of Reuben he pulled off the highway and placed a call. "It's finished, sir. The poison was ingested within seconds. It was not a pretty picture, but everyone succumbed in less than ten minutes."

"And you, Brock? Did you feel any effects?"

"No, sir, I'm fine. The antidote is still protecting me. Are you on-site?"

"Yes, we parked behind the grain elevator. When you drove away we blocked the diner's driveway, documented the scene, and measured the integrity of the residual. We're leaving the parking lot now. Allow us to catch up, before you enter the next location."

"Will do. By the way, there were two government guys in the restaurant. They headed south just before I released the virus. They're driving a Toyota Tundra with a fancy canopy. Its red. I have their plate number."

"Good, good, but nothing we can do about it now. Keep the number just in case. If your next stop is a success we'll launch the full attack at noon—Mountain Time. Now, I must go over the material we just collected."

Ten minutes later, Brock met a state patrol car, then an ambulance, with red lights flashing and sirens blaring. They were approaching from the South. Brock pulled over in mocked respect and smiled. *If you only knew what was waiting for you.*

CHAPTER 5

EMERGENCY-BROADCASTING SIGNAL

*S*hortly, before exiting onto State Highway 2, Craig was awakened again, by a second set of emergency vehicles. Richard pulled over, waiting for them to pass.

"Were they heading north too?" Craig asked.

"They were." Richard said. "I suppose with all the farming and drilling in the area, there's bound to be a lot of accidents."

"I suppose so, but if they need two sets of emergency responders it must be serious."

A hundred miles over Montana's eastern border, close to Glasgow, they stopped for gas. Craig purchased two hamburger deluxe meals from a small diner, and filled their thermos. Richard moved to the passenger seat, consumed his last bite, and said, "I'm taking a nap."

"You know what you remind me of, don't you?"

"No, what?"

Craig glanced his way. "An old hound dog."

"What do you mean?"

"After every meal, you curl up someplace and go to sleep. I'll use your nap time to catch up on the news. If I get really bored, there's always talk radio. Those opinionated clowns are irritating, but at least they keep me awake."

Craig did most of the driving on all their work assignments—because he wanted to, and because Richard had a tendency to doze at the wheel without some type of stimulating medication.

Craig adjusted the seat, turned on the radio and pushed, Seek. After allowing several cycles to roll through he said, "What's wrong with this thing? All I'm getting is that annoying squeal. Even the satellite stations aren't working."

Growing more agitated by the moment, Craig struck the dash, and turned the volume down. "It'll be a long ride if my only entertainment is your snoring. Hand me the MP 3 case, please. I'll listen to a John Grisham book."

Richard flipped his seat upright. "Wait a minute!" He turned the volume back up, and listened for a second. "That's the emergency broadcasting signal."

Richard switched back and forth between satellite, FM, and AM stations until he heard an announcer say, "This is not a drill. We just received news that portions of our country are under attack. Please stay tuned to this station for updates as information is being gathered."

Craig said, "What is going on?"

"I'm not sure, but it's affecting all the stations. It must be widespread."

Richard scrolled for several minutes until he heard another announcer say, "Information is coming in, but it's sketchy. The AP wire is going crazy. A national emergency has been declared. We're being told that hundreds of people are dying from an unknown source. The scary part is, the attacks are happening in many places at once—North Dakota, Maine, Boston—too many to name right now."

Craig felt blood shooting to his head. Richard was white as a ghost.

"My producer just told me, some type of deadly airborne chemical is doing the killing. How it's being spread is unknown. It has components similar to those in Ebola, only deadlier. He tells me people bleed out and succumb to death within minutes of exposure. The first reported incident occurred at a small diner in western North Dakota. Twelve people, including a small child, died this horrible death."

Craig glanced Richard's way.

The announcer went on. "Two sets of emergency responders reported they were on scene, but died before they gave a report. The second incident occurred in a restaurant 50 miles south. Emergency responders were lost there as well. Disease and containment teams just landed at both sites. The area around the restaurants is quarantined. Those are the only two sites we have updates on. As soon as we know more, we'll report it."

After a long pause the announcer said, "We just learned the names of the first two locations, in North Dakota. The first was Reuben. The second was Clairton."

Craig jerked the wheel so hard the truck left the highway. The right front tire caught a groove of gravel and he battled to gain control. When the truck was stable he glanced at Richard who was gripping his seat belt with both hands.

"You don't suppose? They couldn't be talking about that little boy —and June?"

Richard's eyes were wide. "Who else could it be? The town wasn't big enough to support two diners."

The radio announcer went on. "Stand by for an important announcement."

After a short pause, which seemed like a lifetime, a man's voice filled the air. "This is Joseph Manning, director of Homeland Security. I have with me, members of the Centers for Disease Control and the World Health Organization. We urge you to notify your friends and family. Encourage them to stay close to any device that gives news updates."

Manning repeated the same information the radio announcer had given, then said, "Soft targets such as malls, hospitals, and office complexes are falling prey."

Craig said, "Bunch of heartless cowards!"

Manning continued with the gruesome report. "In enclosed settings, the poison is spread through ventilation systems. Small drones with pay loads have been seen spraying populated open areas such as military bases, campuses, and city streets—too many locations to name. When this substance becomes airborne it spreads at an alarming rate. Isolation is critical. Stay away from public arenas. If you're listening from your home, collect clean water and ration your food."

Craig took a quick glance at Richard. "He's not being specific with the locations."

"Probably because there's too many."

Both men felt numb as Manning drummed on. "All businesses in the Mountain, Central, and Eastern Time Zones must send their patrons home and close immediately. Western Montana, northern Idaho, Oregon and Washington should stay on alert. No attacks are reported in those regions—at this time—but we have no reason to believe they'll be spared."

Craig took his first real breath. "Thank God. Now, if we can just get home in time."

"There's no way to soften the remainder of this report," Manning said. "If you come in contact with this substance your chance of survival appears to be zero. Don't attempt to go to the hospital. They can't help you. There's no antidote, and no country—or terrorist group—claiming responsibility. All citizens are to shelter in place. If you're traveling, you may face serious delays. Road blocks are being set up on all major exchanges, and until further notice, all forms of public transportation are frozen."

Craig and Richard exchanged glances, and Craig increased his speed.

Manning wrapped up his report. "The CDC is labeling the deadly element QD–13. That's all I have to report at this time, and you should be aware, multiple news outlets are no longer broadcasting, but we will make every effort to find those that are, so keep searching your channels."

The radio returned to the annoying squeal, and Craig pulled over. His head was woozy. He felt as if he might pass out. After slumping against the window for a minute he jerked open the door and climbed out of the truck. Compared to what they just heard, the pouring rain felt mild. He kicked the front tire a couple of times then paced like a caged animal. *At best, we can't make it home until early morning.*

Richard joined him then dropped to his knees and threw up. He was shaking so hard he was unable to lift himself off the ground. "What if the Seattle area's attacked before we get home, or we run into an infected area?"

In a gesture, not common for Craig, he knelt beside his friend, placed a hand on Richard's shoulder and helped him to his feet. "It sounds like we're already in an infected area, and you know the answer. We'll get home even if we have to walk. Let's get back on the road. We're getting soaked. I need to call Linda. You need to call Tracey."

CHAPTER 6

REALITY SETS IN

*C*raig kept the windshield wipers at their highest peek, and the speedometer in the low eighties. Richard lowered his window, drinking in the cool spring air.

Craig fumbled with his phone a moment then tossed it to Richard.

"Would you call Linda for me? The blue tooth is not working. I better keep my hands on the wheel."

Richard punched in the number then handed it back to Craig. On the fifth ring he said, "She's not picking up, and she never listens to her voice mail. Send her a text—please, and ask her to call me?"

Craig's thoughts went crazy. *What if our area has already been hit, but hasn't been reported?* He felt his eardrums might burst from the pounding of his heart. *This is ridiculous. Get it together man.* He took a few deep breaths, then glanced Richard's way, whose phone was resting on his shoulder.

"Are you calling Tracey?"

"I started to, but I wanted to reach Dad first. I hope he's already made contact with her, but I can't reach him. He was scheduled to work today, but hospital's calls are going straight to an automated service. I sent him a text."

Richard started to punch in Tracey's number—again— but instead, he laid the phone on his lap and looked out the window.

"Are you okay?" Craig asked.

"I just remembered, Tracey was taking the girls to brunch then the mall. Why today, and why the mall? You heard what Manning said about public arenas. What if she doesn't answer?"

"Take a breath, buddy. We've got to face facts, no matter what they are. Manning said it hasn't hit Seattle, yet."

"*I hate that word yet.*"

Richard's phone buzzed. "Thank God! It's Tracey." He stiffened, then swallowed hard before accepting the call. Craig gave him thumbs up.

The only word he got out was, "Sweetheart…" Her voice was so loud Craig could hear every word.

"Richard, we were in the mall. An urgent message came over the loud speaker and said to leave quickly through the nearest exit. People went crazy. Sara was shoved away from me. Her little shoulder was slammed into a wall. Cassie got to her first, but she was knocked down too, and her hand was stepped on. It's already black and blue. I thought both girls would be crushed. They might even have broken bones."

At that point Tracey sobbed so loud Richard was almost shouting. "Are you out of there?"

"Yes, we are—thank God. Two soldiers saw what happened. One pushed people away, while the other picked up the girls. Richard, they held them—and ran interference for us all the way to the car. They were a God send."

Richard's body began to quake. He covered his eyes and asked, "Where are you now?"

"We're in the car. Before the soldiers walked away they made sure we were locked in with the motor running. Then when we were inching along in the string of traffic, a man ran up and started pulling on the door handle. He banged on my window with something! He cracked it! His eyes were wild, Richard. He looked crazy. We were terrified."

"You didn't…"

"Of course not," Tracey said. "Thank God those same two soldiers saw him. They ran back, dragged him off our car, held him until we turned onto the Boulevard. We finally made it to the freeway. It's packed. People are tailgating and cutting me off. They're acting crazy, plus, it's raining very hard. I turned the radio on to find out what was going on. You'll never believe what I heard."

Richard let out a long breath. "Yes, I would. Craig and I heard the same thing. We don't know any more than you do, but thank God, *no* attacks are reported in the Seattle area—yet."

Craig thought, *"There's that word 'yet' again."*

"Where are you, and when will you be home? What should we do?"

"We're in Eastern Montana and can't possibly make it home until early morning. I want Dad to join you, but I haven't been able to reach him. Please go to Craig's, and don't make any stops. As soon Dad calls me, I'll tell him where you are. He'll check the girls out. He'll know what to do. Don't leave Linda's house until I get there."

"I won't," Tracey said. "I don't want to be alone with the kids right now, but I want to get away from all these crazy people."

"Where's Chad?"

"There's no school today so he's helping Linda with the animals."

"I would feel better if he was with you. Is that Sara I hear crying? Let me talk to her then Cassie."

"That would be good. Here's Sara."

"Hi, Daddy. Where are you? Would you come and get us?"

Richard clinched his fists, looked out the window, and swallowed hard. "I wish I could, baby. We're driving as fast as we can."

"My arm hurts, and there's blood on my shirt. Cassie's hand is all swelled up."

"Don't worry. Mom will clean your shirt, and put ice on Cassie's hand as soon as you get to Caleb's house. Can you be really brave for Mommy right now?"

"Yes, Daddy, I promise. Do you want to talk to sister?"

"Yes, I do."

"Hi, Dad," Cassie said. "Where are you?"

"Hi, big girl. Craig and I are still in Montana. We plan to be home early in the morning. Can you be brave for Mom too?"

"Of course, I will."

Richard said, "You girls hang onto the phone, and call me anytime your Mom says it's okay. Now, let me talk to Mom again."

"Thanks for talking to the girls. They needed to hear your voice… me too. Love you, sweetheart."

"Love you too. Is traffic moving any better?"

"Yes, it's slow, but smoother. I better go. We're about five miles from Everett. I'll call you when we get to Linda's."

Richard laid the phone down and turned toward the window, again.

Craig's heart was breaking for his friend. He had never known a more dedicated husband and father.

A couple deep breaths later Richard said. "I guess you heard, I'm sending them to your house. I hope that's okay?"

"Sounds good to me. We'll both feel better if they're together. Would you try Linda again, and give me the phone?"

Linda answered on the fourth ring with a cheerful, "Hi Babe."

"Thank God you're home! Have you been listening to the news?"

"No, I haven't seen or heard any media today. We've been outside all morning in the rain. We're soaked. I left my phone in the house. Brianna's horse got out again. Chad and I ran her down while your mom manned the gate and…"

Craig cringed and stroked his chin, "Linda listen! I don't mean to cut you off, but I have something really important to tell you, and then I need you to do exactly what I say. Okay?"

"What's wrong, Craig, you're scaring me?"

"Richard and I heard breaking news on the radio. Some type of viral or chemical terrorist attack is taking place. Reports are sketchy, but we know it's killing lots of people, and most likely heading west."

"Craig, what are you saying?"

"It's not what I am saying—it's what I know. We just heard an emergency announcement from the Director of Homeland Security. The Centers for Disease Control, and the World Health Organization were with him. It's not contained in one single location, and people are dying within minutes of contact. No attacks have been reported in the Seattle area—so far. Are the twin's home?"

Linda gasped. "No, they both had labs at the university. Wait, I have a text message from Brianna. She said they just heard the news about a terrorist attack, and they're headed home."

"That was thirty-three minutes ago."

"Try to reach them as soon as we hang up. You should also call your mom and ask her to come to our house."

"I have a message from her too." Linda said. "She's on her way."

"Once they get there, don't let anybody leave for any reason."

"You didn't mention Duane."

"Call him too—if you must."

"Craig!"

"Sorry. Of course, you should call Duane. He's your brother."

"Has Richard talked to Tracey?" Linda asked.

"He just hung up. She's on her way to our house, too. He asked her to stay with you until we get home. She and the girls were in the mall when the announcement came. They were nearly trampled. The girls will need some medical treatment. Hopefully, they'll be there shortly."

"I think that's a great idea. What about Darren?"

Craig cringed as a large flash of lightening hit off to his left, followed by a loud crack of thunder that shook the truck.

Linda said, "What's going on?"

"We're driving in a bit of a storm. It gets a little loud once in a while. Now, about Darren. Richard left messages all over, but he hasn't responded. As soon as he does we're hoping he will join you too, but right now keep the national news on. They will broadcast as long as they can stay on the air. This is just breaking, and no one knows exactly what we're dealing with. Listen for the emergency sirens, keep the doors locked, and don't let anyone in except our immediate families . . . unless . . ."

"Unless what?"

"Unless one of them is sick."

"Craig, this is too much."

"I know, sweetheart. I've put a lot on you, but you can handle it.

Let us know if anything in the area changes. We're on Highway 2, several hours out."

"Craig, what if you can't get home?"

"Oh, we'll get home. Don't worry about that."

"What are we going to do? Will be able to stay here?"

"Try not to worry. Richard and I have plenty of time to work on a plan."

"I'll try. Should we start packing?"

"Yes, even if our area is not attacked, by the time we get home, I wouldn't feel safe to stay there. Our window of opportunity may be short, so the more you get done the better. And Linda, think essentials, long term and survival. When everyone gets there, lock the driveway gate. Have Nathaniel hook up the fifth wheel and pull it under the canopy. Have him fill the water tank, and…never mind. He knows the routine. Just have him get busy."

Richard tapped Craig on the shoulder, and pointed at the speedometer.

Craig said, "Whoa," and took his foot off the pedal. His speed had reached ninety-two miles per hour.

Linda asked, "What's going on? Is everything okay?"

"Yes, its fine here, but things could get crazy where you are. You're not going to like this, but I want you to load the .22 rifle—and the larger pistol. It's a .45 caliber. The ammunition boxes are marked."

"Craig, are you kidding me? Do you think we may actually have to defend ourselves—with guns?"

"It could get that way real quick. Keep your eyes and ears open. I can't stress that enough. Big Ben will help you. If anyone's hanging around he'll be barking."

"Okay, but stay safe. I want you to get home in one piece."

"I'll do my best. Be sure to keep the television and radio on. We're getting reception, so far, but many stations are off the air. When you guys are all together and locked in, it will take a lot of stress off of us. Listen babe, I have another call coming in. We'll talk again shortly. I love you."

"I love you too."

CHAPTER 7

A WORD FROM LEON

*C*raig answered on the third buzz, happy to hear a welcome and familiar voice.

"Craig, this is Leon. Are you guys still on the road?"

"We are," Craig said.

"That's what I was afraid of. I hope you're listening to the radio."

Leon Haden was not only their boss—and friend, he was Deputy Director of the BLM. His office was in Washington, DC.

"We are, but Leon, this is crazy. How can something like this happen, and who's behind it?"

"No one knows for sure, but it's killed thousands of people, and the attacks continue."

Craig said, "Hold on, let me put you on speaker."

"Hey, Leon."

"Hi, Richard."

Craig went on. "We're in Montana on Highway 2, just passed Malta."

"Well, keep moving, and don't stop unless you're forced to," Leon said. "The attacks are scattered throughout the nation, except in the direction you're headed. "

"Let's pray it stays that way," Richard whispered.

After a brief silence, Leon said, "That's exactly how I am praying. As soon as the eastern seaboard was attacked, the West bound highways were flooded with frantic people—until road blocks were set up. Those people were nothing more than easy targets. The current directive is for everyone to shelter in place."

"That explains why we haven't seen much traffic," Craig said.

Richard said, "Leon, you could not guess where we ate breakfast this morning."

"Where?"

An involuntary shudder travelled through Craig's body as images of little Tommy, and June shot through his mind.

"In Reuben, North Dakota."

Leon's gasp was spontaneous and loud. "Where the first incident took place?"

"Sure sounds like it. Not long before we left, a guy came in, sat at the counter and spoke to no one—not even the waitress. There was just something about him, besides his rudeness. We weren't too far down the road when two sets of emergency vehicles flew by. Maybe those are the responders who lost their life. You know. The ones mentioned on the news."

"Did you see what the guy was driving?"

"Craig said he wasn't sure, but there was a black SUV in the parking lot of the diner when we pulled out. He was pretty sure it was the same one he saw rolling out of a semi a few miles north of Reuben.

"It had Colorado license plates," Craig said, "but I didn't get the number."

"Well, it might still be our first lead. I'll pass it along. Someone from Homeland Security may be calling you."

"Was there no chatter?" Craig asked. "This thing had to take a lot of planning—and expertise. If it's a terrorist attack you would think they would be gloating and making their voice heard all over the world?"

"I agree, but so far no group has claimed responsibility. That's why some of us think it could be homegrown—but only time will tell."

Craig and Richard glanced at each other. Craig said, "Okay, just keep us posted."

"Is your family with you?" Richard asked.

"Jeanette and I were in Connecticut when it hit. I got called back to Washington. She came with me. Our kids were already with her mother at our cabin, in Big Bear. We thought they would be safe, but..."

The line went silent for a moment then Leon struggled when he said, "We haven't been able to reach them for the past few hours."

Richard and Craig exchanged glances. "I'm sorry, Leon." Richard said. "Maybe their cell signal was disrupted. Keep trying. Are you and Jeanette in a safe location?"

"I hope so. We're in the White House bunker. It's been quiet so far, but not at the Capitol. they were in an emergency joint session. There's a good chance we no longer have a congress. We could be next."

Leon cleared his throat before describing the rest of the gruesome scene.

"I have no idea what will happen if we're hit, and it penetrates this chamber. Our surveillance cameras keep sweeping sites that have been. There's no sign of survivors. Bodies lay where they fell. Some on the floor of the House. Others in their office or corridor. There's so much carnage. We don't even know if a containment crew is available, or how long the killing agent is lethal. A lot of questions—very few answers—hold on. Something new is in."

Leon's line was open. Craig and Richard heard voices, but could not make out what was being said.

Craig prayed Leon's something *new*, would not prevent, or hinder them from getting home. Every rotation of their tires was taking them closer. *What will we do if that rotation stops?*

Richard stared out the window, tapping his fingers on his knee. "I wish he would hurry. I feel like a caged animal, banging against all sides of my pen."

Craig shared the same fears, but kept them to himself. He saw no reason to add to Richard's anxiety. He said, "No matter what he's finding out we're not giving up. We're going home."

Five minutes later Leon came back on line. "We just got two pieces of really bad news."

Craig and Richard groaned before sharing a quick stare. Richard whispered, "Now what?"

"Most state capitols have been attacked, and massive numbers of illegals are rushing our borders."

"Why?" Richard asked. "Shouldn't they be running the other direction? Where's the Border Patrol?"

"That's what we were just talking about. Our source tells us the enlisted military, National Guard, and Border Patrol were ordered to stand down. They were needed else where. The president said he would give reorganization orders shortly, and will address the nation in a few hours."

"In a few hours? Why not now?" Craig asked.

"I can't answer that. His advisors want him to do a *reassuring* talk to calm people down, but he won't. He keeps reminding them he's Commander-and-Chief, and wants detailed reports before he speaks."

"Doesn't he realize..." Craig started to ask? "Never mind."

Leon said, "As soon as you know what your plans are let me know. If you're going to Canada, I need a list of everyone you're taking, and their birthdays. You're the only two with top security clearance. Make sure everyone else has a photo ID, birth certificate, and just for good measure, other proofs. This will sound harsh, but you can only take close blood relatives. Don't have anybody meet you at the border."

Craig said, "We won't. Our crew is large enough already—probably fourteen."

"You may get some static if they think it's too large," Leon said. "As far as we know, Canada hasn't been attacked so you can be sure their borders are being rushed. It will be swarming with Mounted Police with guns drawn—ready to fire."

"We'll do our best. Thanks for the heads up," Craig said.

"Listen guys, I have to go. Everyone here is under scrutiny. It's a little eerie. I hope it's just a feeling, but frankly—I don't know who to trust, and I don't know who the real enemy is."

"No problem. Thanks for everything, Leon," Craig said. "Keep us posted—when you can."

Craig laid his phone on the seat. "That president may be Commander-and-Chief, but I think it's in title only."

"Forget about the president. We need to concentrate."

"I know, I know." Craig slapped the dash board. "Just remind me not to vote for that guy, if he runs again."

"Well, unless he's declared king or dictator, he can't. And, if I remember right, you have never voted for him."

Craig gave a halfhearted laugh. "Maybe I'm smarter than I look. Okay, enough of that. You're right. We need a plan. Have you come up with anything?"

"Actually, taking refuge in Canada, or heading up the Alcan Highway to Alaska, just might work, but I do have another thought running around in my head—hoping you'll talk me out of it."

"I can't unless I know what you're thinking. What's up?"

"Well, remember that isolated BLM site, east of the Selwyn Mountains?"

"Yes, I do. I also remember the very long weeks we spent there. You're kidding, right?"

Richard was silent. Craig said, "You're *not* kidding."

"I know how it sounds. That's why I'm hoping you shoot me down, but not before we look at the pros and cons. It could be a safe place to wait out the attack."

Craig took a long pause before responding, "Yes, my friend. That's true, but how do *you* propose to sell it to the family? We would be living in total isolation, surrounded by rugged mountains, wilderness, populated with wolves and bears—not to mention very long, and very cold winters. It's a pretty extreme idea, and definitely not appealing."

Richard said, "The possibility of a sudden, painful, bloody death, might get their attention. And, I will not be in this alone. You'll be persuading right along with me."

"Fat chance. Lest you forget, you and I didn't drive to that location.

We took a helicopter. I don't suppose we could do that again," Craig said, as he glanced Richard's way.

Richard said, "There's connecting roads. I saw them from the air. Well—they looked like roads. They began at the Selwyn State Park and went right past the valley."

"Let me think about this for a while, okay?"

CHAPTER 8

PLANNING CONTINUES

*C*raig stared straight down the highway in silence. Road signs flew by as he kept the accelerator fixed between 70 and 80, depending on how straight the road was, and how well he could see through the downpour. At times, the windshield wipers barely kept up. He caught sight of an unmanned, self serve gas station, with a covered canopy and flipped a U-turn, pulled under the shelter, and put his seat back.

"Let's fill up the tank then I'm changing my shoes and socks. I'm tired of wet feet."

"Good idea," Richard said, then pointed to the front of the facility. "There's a coffee vending machine over there. I'll fill the thermos."

When they finished, Craig put his seat into position, and closed his eyes. "I know we discussed that valley after the 9/11 attacks, but man that's extreme, and I'm not sure I can get my head around it. You might as well give me your spiel. I've got nothing."

Richard said, "If we're able to cross the border, we can check out Providence, Benton Creek and Fort Wilson first, praying one of them will work, but if they don't, we'll need to head for the valley. Alaska is always a consideration, but we could get trapped on the Alcan Highway without a chance to retreat."

Craig pulled back onto the highway. He liked Richard's ideas, but decided not to respond until he heard everything.

Richard reminded Craig of the three large, and connected Quonset huts. He was sure they would still be there. It would have been way too expensive and time consuming for the BLM to dismantle, and haul them away.

"We won't have beefsteak and lobster, but there's enough natural food available to keep a party our size alive—and we should be able to grow a garden. We could survive."

"Sounds like you've already moved us there—but I'm intrigued. Pull up a map of that area. Check out the roads."

While Richard poured over the map, Craig kept his eyes on the rearview and side mirrors. "It's too quiet. I don't see a car anywhere."

"Well, Manning told people to stay in their homes. They may be too scared to move, or like Leon said, the highway might be closed behind us."

Heavy rain continued to fall. Craig was hoping for a break, but the storm remained their constant companion. Flashes of lightning lit up the sky, and claps of thunder rattled the truck. He prayed they would be able to stop if they rolled up on a stalled vehicle, or a washed out portion of road. They kept the radio volume at a comfortable level, cringing at every update. The virus was not only moving in a Southerly direction, it was beginning its trek, west. In spite of all the bad news, Craig was thankful they had a connection with the outside world.

Craig appreciated Richard's careful map search. The more solid their plan was, the better. He finally turned the radio down, and asked Richard to place a call to Linda. He needed to hear her voice again, but would never admit it. For all his gruff talk, anger outbursts, and effort to—stay in charge, Craig knew he would be nothing without his wife. She was the love of his life and his stabilizing force.

When she answered, Richard handed the phone to Craig. Linda gave a good progress report, but he could tell from her forced laugh, and effort to keep the conversation in a positive light, she was nervous.

"You're doing great, sweetheart. If you keep up this pace, we'll be ready to go. That will give us a chance to help the others."

She said, "I've been trying to watch every update. The last one said the viral attacks are headed this way, but only inside facilities like malls, hospitals, and large business complexes. A couple hours ago I saw a video taken by a father. He was filming his young son shooting baskets. The little boy stopped and stared at the sky. He told his daddy to look at the little plane that was coming their way."

Craig was sure she was trying to bite back tears. What horror had she seen?

"The dad turned his camera toward what turned out to be a drone," Linda said. "I don't think anything happened to them because he was able to send his feed to social media. Shortly after that, a large hospital was hit in Little Rock. We have so many family members in that area. I pray they're okay. If it was the drone, how could such a small thing carry enough chemicals to do that kind of damage?"

"They worked until they got just the right blend to make it spread. That's all I can guess," Craig said.

She paused again, and in a voice so soft he could barely hear, she said, "Get home safe. I love you. If we're still here when the virus hits —well, it would be easier to face it with you than without you. Every time we say goodbye I wonder if it's our last."

A lump grew in Craig's throat. He had the same fears, but swallowed and whispered, "I'll see you in the early morning hours. You can count on that. You call as often as you like, and I'll do the same. I love you too."

When Richard called Tracey, Craig had to smile at his friend's portion of the conversation.

"Yes, sweetheart, we'll make it home."

"Yes, we're working on a plan."

"No, I can't give it to you now."

"Why? Because we haven't worked out enough details."

"I love you too. Can I talk to Dad?"

When Darren answered, Richard put it on speaker, but before he could utter a word, Darren launched right in.

"Son, I agree we should be here together, but some of us need to go home and pack. If the virus hits before you get back, we may not be able to leave."

"Dad, do whatever you like, but wouldn't it be wiser to wait until we get there so I can go with you? You know what comes out of the woodwork in situations like this. Someone could be ransacking our homes right now. In fact, you need to take charge. Don't let anyone go anywhere. This is not a movie. It's a nightmare. We can't control it and we can't manipulate the plot."

The line went silent. "Dad, are you there?"

"Yes, I am. You just set me back a little. I've never heard such forceful language come out of your mouth. I'm glad to help Linda and Nathaniel load, but my mind is on all the things I need to do at my house—if we have to leave. Don't worry, I'll crack the whip around here if I need too."

Richard and Craig heard a short giggle in the background. "You may have to start with Linda and Tracey. I'm assuming that laugh came from them."

"You got it, but a nice sound to hear in the middle of all this doom and gloom. I think they like me taking orders from you."

The line was silent for a moment then Darren said, "Listen, son. I don't say this often enough, but I love you. Stay safe."

Richard swallowed hard. "We will. Craig and I both feel relieved you're there. Love you too, Dad."

"I think we better finalize some plans. Dad's taking charge, but we could still have a mutiny."

"I would love to, but lest you forget—and I will keep reminding you—we did not drive into that valley. We made the trip in a helicopter."

"I wish, but with the number of people we have, the supplies we need, it would take a lot of trips, plus—all flights are cancelled."

Craig said, "Well a guy can hope can't he? Back to the real world. Tell me what you think? Are the roads passable? Can we drive all the way to the valley?"

"It depends on what you mean by roads, and passable," Richard said. "We would follow Highway 77 to 7, which would take us to the Selwyn State Park. According to the BLM map, they have a secured gate located in the Northwest corner. Our master key will fit it. Once we pass through the gate we'll be on Canadian BLM property, approximately twenty-five miles from the valley."

"Does the map give you the condition of the road?"

"It's not totally clear, but it looks like the first few miles have a gravel base, and fairly straight. That portion ends at the Cripple Creek gravel pit. From that point I'm afraid it's logging and fire roads, except for one short stretch next to a string of telephone poles."

Craig took a deep sigh. "Well, the good news is we'll have nothing but time. We could take advantage of the gravel pit and build a road— I suppose, but back to the bottom line—is it doable? We'll not be traveling in jeeps. We'll be pulling fully loaded, heavy trailers."

"I believe it's doable. We can camp as often as we need. If it takes a week to get through a bad area, who cares as long as we're safe?"

Craig shot Richard a glance. "You're kidding, right? You really think no one will care?"

Richard laid the map down. "We'll get to the family later. Right now, I want to know what you think? If we do this thing we have to present it with a united front."

Craig was honest. He hated the idea, but because of the severity of the current threat, which continued to spread, the valley seemed to be their best option.

"Okay, let's do it. At least you've given us some direction. I had nothing. When we're through with all the tears and hysteria, we'll finish packing and hit the road. And— thanks."

Richard gave him a long look to which Craig quickly responded, "No! I'm serious! Thank you. You've worked out a master plan."

"Well, let's hope it is masterful—and pray it works."

Craig said, "I'll let Linda know what we need, and we'll get the rest of you home to pack, as soon as possible, but I don't think we'll dump out all the details of our plan—yet."

Richard nodded and smiled.

CHAPTER 9

THE VIRUS SPREADS

*C*raig adjusted his position, hoping to take pressure off his back. He watched road signs whiz by, and counted down the miles. Both men remained stunned at the limited traffic.

Earlier in the day, they saw several law enforcement cars heading east, but never west. Only seventeen rigs had overtaken them, all driving at dangerously high speeds. Craig wondered what they would do if they rolled up on an accident. How would they handle it?

Richard startled him back to reality when he asked, "What if the virus beats us to Canada?"

"I don't think it will—yet. You heard what Leon said. This appears to be an attack on America. Not only that, it has all the markings of a takeover. If it's not, whoever's behind it is missing a golden opportunity. America and Canada together would be a huge undertaking. I keep wondering—how did these heartless beasts manage to produce such a large volume of—whatever they're spreading?"

Richard shrugged then poured he and Craig some coffee.

They rode in silence again, and Craig's thoughts turned to his family. *Mom is confined to a wheel chair, most of the time. Caleb's only six. And, my beautiful, spoiled Brianna. She demands a well-ordered life. Will she ever forgive me for disrupting it, no matter what the reason?* He cringed at the thought.

He wasn't worried about Brianna's twin, Nathaniel. He would do well. He loved new adventures. Then Craig's mind went to his wife, Linda. *She's my rock.*

Craig's job took him away from home an average of 300 days a year. It was Linda who kept the family together. She was the voice of reason and wisdom, and to his constant amazement, always in his corner. Craig's heart was pounding again. The distance they still needed to cover seemed ominous. *We must get home. We must.*

Richard interrupted Craig's thoughts. "By the way, do we have to take Duane?"

Craig laughed. "You know Linda won't let us leave him behind. But, if he wasn't her brother..."

"I was afraid you'd say that. Having Linda for a sister might be his one redeeming value."

∼

Every news update grew more sinister. The silent killer was wreaking havoc on police stations, hospitals, news agencies, transportation centers, and neighborhoods.

When Craig reached over and turned the radio off, Richard said, "What's up man? We need to hear the updates."

"I know," Craig said. "I just wanted a short break from all the carnage. We'll turn it back on in a minute, but have you thought about how many drones it takes for such a wide spread attack? I didn't know *that* many existed."

"I didn't either, but I did hear that China is mass producing them, and some retail companies plan to make deliveries with them. Obviously, they can carry a payload. Several pictures I saw showed a hundred, plus, in one area. The way they're being used now is more than plausible."

Craig said, "I had no idea. I'm glad you keep up on the news. It wears me out."

Craig turned the radio back on. Darkness was overtaking them, and every community they flew past looked like a ghost town. They rode in silence for a long while listening to updates, until east of Kalispell, Craig saw flashing lights and a sign—ROADBLOCK AHEAD.

"Oh, great. Time to pray, my brother, and be forewarned. We won't be letting this keep us from moving forward."

A rain soaked officer glanced at their Federal Government license plate, as Craig rolled to a stop.

"May I see your registration, and driver's license?" The officer asked.

Craig nodded, but decided not to say anything. He would let the officer do his job and see what happened.

When he asked why they were on the road and where they were going, Craig told him who they worked for, that they had just completed a job in Canada, and were on their way home to Everett, Washington.

Craig chose not to mention where they re-entered America. The officer, satisfied everything was in order, warned them to stay alert then pulled aside the sawhorse. Craig barely started to roll when Richard asked him to back up.

"Back up? Why?"

"Just do it. Please, and roll your window down."

The officer stepped next to his patrol car, and placed his hand on his weapon. Craig had no idea what Richard was doing until he heard his compassionate friend ask, "Is anyone relieving you, or giving you a break? Do you have food and drink?"

The officer was taken back, took a deep breath and said, "No, to all your questions. I have nothing. Division sent me here six hours ago. I can't reach anyone at the station. I'm not sure what to do."

Richard reached into the back seat. "Here . . . take these."

He handed the officer a 12-ounce bag of chips, several cookies, a small bag of peanuts, 1 bottled water then poured him a cup of coffee.

"This isn't the best in the world. We filled our thermos from a vending machine, but at least it's hot."

"I don't know what to say, except thank you."

Craig nodded his head and Richard said, "No problem. Take care, and if I were you, I would head home."

Craig felt guilty. *Now, why didn't I think of that?*

Richard was dozing when they crossed the Idaho-Washington border. Craig leaned forward in his seat, slowed—then braked hard, causing Richard to jerk upright. "What's going on?"

"There's a fire in the middle of the highway. Whoever set it must be using some kind of solvent to keep it going. A fire that size is not possible, as heavy as this rain is."

When he rolled a little closer they could see a man standing beside the flames, furiously waving his arms. Craig stopped a few hundred feet back.

Richard said, "This can't be good. Look off to the right at the bobbing heads. Those clothes look orange to me. They must be escaped prisoners."

The guy in the road continued to wave. His white undershirt, and orange pants were drenched in the downpour.

Craig said, "Get the spotlight ready. Roll down your window and when I say go, sweep it from side to side as fast as you can. I'll blast the horn and gun it. I'm not worried about rolling over the fire. I just don't want anyone to hop on. Maybe we can distract them long enough to get by."

"What if the guy in the road *doesn't* jump for cover?"

"Just control the light when I say go."

Craig crept forward then yelled, "Now!"

Richard swung the blinding light back and forth as instructed, and Craig laid on the horn. He did not have time to count, but ten or more men stumbled toward the highway. The man in the road jumped to the side just in time. Craig rolled over the hot embers, and fiery logs. One flew over the truck and rolled off the canopy.

They both watched their side mirrors then Craig yelled, "Get down!" Several bullets riddled the canopy and one pinged off the back bumper.

When they were out of bullet range Richard let out a large sigh, "That was too close for comfort. The sad thing is, they're probably not all bad guys—just trying to get home."

"That may be true. But, if we stopped, we could have been robbed, maybe left for dead, or be the ones standing in the middle of the road. If they're good guys, they'll have to find another ride. We're in no position to help them, or anyone else."

CHAPTER 10

HOME AT LAST

The remainder of the trip was long and stormy, but the Seattle area had not been attacked. At three in the morning, Richard sloshed through puddles to unlock Craig's driveway gate. When he climbed back in the truck Craig pulled forward, and heard Big Ben offer a few welcome barks. The front door flew open, and eight family members filed out on the covered porch.

Richard gave a weak wave. "There they are."

"Yes, I see that," Craig whispered. "Are we ready for them?"

Tracey met Richard at the bottom of the steps. "I'm so thankful you're here. This is a nightmare. What are we going to do?"

"Let's get inside. I'm really tired of this rain. Give us a chance to gather our thoughts, then we'll talk," Richard said. "How are the girls?"

"They're banged up and sore, but at least there's no broken bones. We gave them some pain med, and they're finally asleep. Sara woke up twice, crying. They'll be glad to see you."

Richard wrapped his arms around his wife. "I'll be glad to see them too."

Craig and Linda embraced, at the top of the stairs, but said nothing.

51

He ushered the family inside, knowing Tracey's question was on everyone's mind. He saw Duane dozing on the couch. *That figures.* The three younger children were in bed, but just as he closed the front door, Caleb came running down the hall, straight into his arms.

"Are we moving, Daddy?"

Craig turned his back on the family and held Caleb close. Tears filled his eyes as images of little Tommy swelled in his head. He was thankful for Caleb's warm body and the pounding of his little heart. *I will do everything in my power to keep him from that barbaric death.*

Craig swallowed before he dare speak. "Well, sort of—but first we have a lot of work to do."

"I'll help you, Daddy. I already packed my stuff—see?" Caleb pointed toward two large cardboard boxes, and five plastic grocery bags, propped up against the end of the couch. The head of two dinosaurs, and one kangaroo poked out of the largest box. A Spider Man's helmet hung precariously over the edge of the other. Two large yellow trucks, a scooter, and plastic building blocks sat in front.

Craig rubbed Caleb's head, "Yes, I do. Thank you buddy, I appreciate that, but right now you can help most by going back to bed. You need plenty of rest because, in a few hours I will have a lot of jobs for you. I want your muscles to be really strong."

Caleb dropped his head and shuffled toward the bedroom. "Okay. Good night, Daddy."

Duane opened his eyes, gave Craig a weak wave then sat up. Linda whispered, "I'm really scared. It sounds like we don't have much time. Do you guys have a plan?"

"Be patient a few minutes, sweetheart. We do, but it'll take family cooperation."

"I'm listening."

He squeezed her hand, looked over the room, then directly at Richard. "Why don't we all sit down and Richard will tell you what we've been discussing? He explains things a lot better than I do. And—

listen to everything he says before you comment. While he's talking, keep in mind, the virus could be here any minute. If we don't get out in time, there's a good chance we'll be trapped, and God forbid, we all know what that means."

Richard leaned forward in the recliner. "Thanks buddy, I feel a little like Daniel, just before he was thrown to the lions . . . not that you guys are lions. I'll do my best."

Before he had a chance to say anything, Duane blurted, "The virus is no place near us. It could be eradicated in just a few days. Why can't we stay here until we see what happens? Could it really be that bad?"

Craig bit his lip before meeting Duane's eyes. "Bad? You've been listening—just like we have—*moment by moment,* to the worst *bad* we've ever known? No one understands why this area hasn't been hit, but from everything we've heard, it's just a matter of time."

Duane folded his arms and flung himself back against the couch.

Richard continued. "Here's the deal. Our situation calls for strong measures, so please be quiet and listen."

A gasp came from Joliene so Craig jumped in. "Believe me, we've had plenty of time to talk about options, and we're convinced we've come up with a logical plan, so give Richard a chance to tell you what it is."

Richard stared at the floor then looked up.

"We're fairly close to Canada's border. If we're allowed to cross— and Leon's helping us with that—we will seek refuge in Providence or Benton Creek or areas beyond. If that doesn't work, we don't think it would be good to head to Alaska. We could get trapped on the Alcan Highway, so we have an alternate, and more daring plan. Remember our assignment in the Selwyn Mountains?"

"I do," Tracey said. "You hated it, and couldn't wait to get home."

"That's true, but if the virus spreads into Canada, we would have to keep moving, so those mountains are looking better and better. We both think they're isolated enough to give us long-term protection. It would be a reasonably safe place. We can't travel around like vagabonds, and if we don't get out in time, we could be DOA"

Craig stood up, and aimed his glare directly at Duane. "Before we go any further, do any of you have a better option? If so, this is the time to speak up."

The whole room was silent. Craig glanced back at Richard. "Go ahead."

Richard said, "We need to work together, and head north—tomorrow. Correction—I mean today." He shrugged his shoulders and slid back into the chair. "That's all I have to say—right now."

Craig knew Richard's words hit hard. His audience resembled zombies—white-faced and wide-eyed. No one twitched until Darren spoke up.

"Wow, Tracey's right, this is a living nightmare. I agree we can't stay here, but an isolated valley? That's a little over the top, isn't it?"

Joliene, Linda's mother, was next. "How can we possibly get ready to go in such a short time? What if we forget something important?"

"Look, we're all intelligent people," Craig said. "If we put our heads together we can do this." He plopped back into a chair and turned to Lois.

"Mom, you lived in Alaska, and you're a great organizer. Could I talk you into heading this thing up? I'm out of words."

"I'll give it my best shot," Lois said. "I do have lingering memories of Alaska—the winters are cold and very long. I'm also familiar with the sections of Canada you mentioned first, but no matter where we settle, that far north, we'll face frigid weather, and when I say frigid, I mean frigid. Keeping that in mind, let's get started."

Richard ran back to the work truck, brought his laptop in, laid it on the stand next to her chair, then pulled up the notes he compiled through the night.

She said, "This is great. We've already packed a lot of this stuff, but there's things here I never thought of. This will be our master. Good job."

But, instead of jumping into action, a solemn mood settled over the room. To Craig, it looked like everyone was shrinking. He walked over to Richard and quietly said, *"Playtime is over. This is not the time for complacency."*

But, when he looked again at the bewildered faces, he had an addi-

54

tional thought—It's *also not the time for more frustration*—so, he softened his tone and simply said, "Listen guys, we know this whole scenario is mind boggling, but if it helps, even if we end up in the mountains, we won't be leaving all civilization behind. You'll have your tablets, computers, and all sorts of power sources. Richard and I are linked to the BLM satellite. As long as it's functioning, we can use our cell phones. We'll be able to track the virus—and like Richard said, when its safe we'll come home."

Lois asked Craig, "Do you think we can do some shopping before leaving this area?"

She said no matter where they settled, especially for an extended stay, a group their size would need a lot of food.

Craig didn't like the sounds of it, but he saw her point and said if the coast was clear, when they were close to moving out, they could try.

Darren spoke up, "And, make sure your cell phones are charged, and on your body. We need to see, or hear, every update."

"If the virus is anywhere close," Craig said, "head back here. If that's not possible, head north toward the border, but don't try to cross. Just park on the side of the road."

"Good idea," Richard said. "And wherever you make a purchase, use your credit cards first, if possible. It won't be long before all transactions will be cash only, if they're not already. Speaking of that, we stopped at an ATM just before midnight, and again right after. We all need to gather as much cash as possible. It will be vital."

"Well, that's not an issue with me," Duane whined. "I have a few dollars in my pocket and *none* in the bank. My check doesn't come until next week. If I need money we'll have to wait for it."

Joliene took his hand. "Don't worry son, we're not leaving you behind because you have no money."

Before Craig could respond, Linda's narrowing eyes struck him down. He cleared his throat and went on with his spiel.

"Be sure to gather all the toilet paper you can find. I'm not sure how our forefathers survived without it, and I don't want anyone to tell me, so bring what you have and buy plenty more."

Craig's mother, Lois, was sixty-nine. She understood hardships after losing her husband, and suffering two severe strokes, but Craig knew she was tough, and it was time for action. He leaned over and whispered in her ear while the room was a buzz with nervous chatter.

"Mom, get this crew moving. I'm counting on you."

"I'll do my best."

Lois clapped her hands, looked first at Richard then Craig. "I have one more question for you guys. If we settle in the valley, we know we'll run out of supplies. Will we be able to restock?"

This was the question they were dreading.

Richard said, "When we say this valley is isolated, we mean isolated. The closest town is about fifty miles away."

"That's not so bad," Darren said. "Makes me feel a little better."

Craig said, "Well, it's actually under fifty miles, but driving conditions may not always be conducive to frequent trips. Richard can show you the valley on his computer. You can get an idea of where it is, in relation to the nearest town."

The only site available was a winter view, depicting isolation, snow, and an absence of roads. Craig waited for reactions, and as expected there were several gasps. Duane was first to comment.

"Are you kidding me?"

Tracey was next. "I don't see *any* civilization close to that valley, and the town you mentioned looks really small. There's snow —everywhere."

Craig gave adequate time for gasps and shock then said, "Okay. You're no longer in the dark—and that area is not *always* covered in snow, but at least you have an idea of what we may be up against. Trips to the market will be few and far between. That's why we have to work hard on this end—and fast."

For a few moments, words were replaced by wide-eyed stares.

Craig said, "Come on guys. None of us wanted to hear this, but it's the truth. If we work together we can make it. Now let's get busy.

Time is wasting. Finish your lists. When the children wake up, don't forget to take their suggestions too."

Richard stood up. "I need some coffee. Dad, will you join me in the kitchen? I want to talk to you on another matter."

Richard stopped at the coffee maker, selected a dark roast pod, and pushed the button. "Do you want me to fix you an herbal tea?" His dad said no, so when the final drop hit the cup, Richard joined him at the dining table.

"What's on your mind, son?"

"We need your help. How can we handle the family's prescriptions and other meds? Can we get enough for a few months? Can we get refills in Canada?"

"I already thought about that. I'll get a list from everyone then try to reach Jesse at Holloway's East Side Pharmacy—if he's still in town. I know he'll accept my script, especially under these circumstances. I will also collect all the medical supplies I can locate."

Darren put his head in his hands, and began speaking through his fingers. "Man, what are we doing?"

Richard laid his hand on his dad's shoulder. "I'm sorry, but as we keep saying, we didn't create this mess. We just have to figure out a way to survive it, and pray we have enough time."

Craig was in the family room with the others. Richard and Darren reentered just in time to hear Lois say, "Ladies, be sure to gather personal items—you know what I mean. And Craig, meat won't be a problem, will it?"

"Meat?" Tracey said. "Why won't meat be a problem?"

Richard didn't move a muscle.

Craig jumped right in, "Because, there's moose, caribou, mountain goat, fish, wild boar…"

Tracey interrupted him and looked right at Richard. "He's kidding right? We don't know how to dress out fresh game."

Chad spoke up, "Wow Dad, will you teach me to hunt?"

Nathaniel said, "Me too."

Tracey's glare shut Chad down before his dad could answer, and Nathaniel was careful not to meet his mother's eyes.

Richard folded his arms, then made a tight fist. He stood stiff as a statue. Craig knew his friend was near the breaking point so he jumped in, with a tone that was a little too sharp.

"Look, there will be hardships, and yes, a life style we're not used too, but we won't be living like early pioneers, or barbarians. We may have only one chance to get this right, and yes—we will be killing animals to eat, and when this horror ends—if we have meat left over —we'll give it to a food bank."

Tracey stared first at Craig then Richard, looking as if she might cry. Her long blond hair framed her face as she stared at the floor. She stood very still and said nothing.

Richard moved next to her and lifted her chin. "It may give us a chance to live. It seems like we need to keep driving that point home. If we don't have to go as far as the valley, this is all a moot point—but right now, it's all about survival."

Lois wheeled around and struck the table with the palm of her hand, startling everyone. "Listen, are we going to keep talking, or get to work? We heard the news. We know what's coming. If we don't want to get trapped, let's quit wasting time debating. Focus people."

Craig hit his forehead with the back of his hand. "I can't believe we forgot—Richard reserved a mid-sized rental truck from the U-Haul business up the street. They promised to leave the key on the inside of the rear bumper. Nathaniel, will you drive him over there to get it? We should have plenty of room for everything."

"Well, good job," Lois said. "We could even use it as a shelter if we needed to. Now, what about the animals?"

"We'll take the two young calves and a few chickens." Craig said. "The other will have a better chance to survive, if we let them go."

Brianna gasped. She had been silent to this point. "Dad, what about

Millie? I can't leave her behind. If you let her go I may never see her again."

"Sweetheart, we can't take your horse. There's no room in our livestock trailer. We have a young bull and heifer. They're both healthy. She could give us milk, and if they make it through the winter—we might have a calf in the spring. I'm sorry."

Brianna moved closer to her mom, turned her back on her dad, and began to cry. Craig started to approach, thought better, and said, "Look at the television! According to that chart, the virus moved a hundred miles closer since we've been talking. We have to stay on track."

"Wait, wait!" Duane was waving his arms as if he were fighting off a swarm of bees. "This is ridiculous! We can't just move away from our homes, and go off in the boonies to live. I already told you, I don't have any money. I can't buy gas for a trip like that. There must be another option."

Craig stepped forward until he and Duane were nose to nose. "There is one other option, Duane, and you're free to take it."

"I knew it. What is it?"

"Nothing is stopping you from making your own plan. You don't have to go with us. You can stay here and take your chances, and frankly, I wish you would. We need everyone on board. Do I make myself clear?"

Duane took a step back and glared.

"Now," Craig said, "we have a lot to do, so make up your mind. If you're not going to go with us, please leave—and do it right now. We've already spent an hour discussing this. You're wasting valuable time."

Gasps could be heard throughout the room, and Brianna's cry turned to a wail.

Duane grabbed his coat and headed for the door. "Well, I think I will. This is crazy. Who wants to go with me?"

Joliene was right behind him, "Son, don't go. We can make this work." She turned and glared at Craig. "We need to stick together."

Through her sobs Brianna said, "Daddy, this is not fair. We can't leave Uncle Duane and Millie."

Craig's heart raced in his ears. He covered his crimson face with both hands, and instead of screaming, he lowered his voice and wrapped his arms around a resistant Brianna.

"Sweetheart, Richard and I did not create this fiasco. We're simply trying to figure out a way to survive it. Like I already said, if anyone has a better option, spell it out. Tell us how to go—and stay at the same time."

Brianna melted in her dad's arms, and through deep sobs she said, "I'm sorry, Dad. I'm sorry."

He led her to the couch and helped her sit down. Duane was standing in the open door when the emergency broadcasting signal caught everyone's attention. Flashing across the screen was more Breaking News.

CHAPTER 11

PREPARING TO LEAVE

*L*inda turned up the volume. Tom Cox, a familiar broadcaster known for his crisp and arrogant nature, spoke one simple phrase in shaky, broken tones, "We're going live to bring you a special message from the president."

"It's about time," Craig muttered.

"A little respect," Linda whispered.

President Maurer was seated behind a makeshift desk—hands clasped tightly together. Deep shades of grey circled his eyes. An untidy flag was his backdrop.

"Fellow Americans, I address you in these early morning hours with a heavy heart. You must be aware our country is under a well-organized attack, and you may have already heard much of what I'm going to say."

He paused a moment then went on. "Our country is under a well-organized viral attack. No country, or group has claimed responsibility. Symptoms are much like those of the Ebola Virus, but deadlier. It ravages the body and death comes in less than ten minutes. The first reported attack took place in North Dakota, spread rapidly across the eastern seaboard, then in all directions, simultaneously hitting hundreds of locations."

Linda and Tracey turned at the same time and stared at their husbands. Craig gave Linda thumbs up, but said nothing. Richard stood straight as a statue and did not look at his wife.

The president continued. "Forty-five of our fifty states have reported massive deaths. Pandemic level six was reached within the first few hours. The death toll is estimated to be in the millions. All forms of public transportation, including airports, are frozen. No flights are allowed to enter or leave this country. I am fully aware this decision will cause hardships for many, but I had no choice. I must use all means at my disposal to slow down the spread of this killer."

He looked down, and took a deep breath. "Many large cities and military bases have been hit as well, as soft targets. There are too many to list. Because of the danger, we're unable to send recovery teams to take care of the fallen. My heart grieves with those of you who have already suffered loss."

The president wiped his eyes and swallowed hard. "As soon as our Fort Winton lab receives blood samples, and identifies the viral properties, they will work around the clock to produce an antidote."

Someone off camera placed a glass of water on the president's table. He took a quick drink then continued.

"I know many of you are wondering where to go, and what to do. We have no answer. We cannot set up shelters. One infected person would insure the death of the whole facility. You must develop your own plan. Ration your supplies and keep a media device active at all times."

He shuffled in his chair, sat straight up and pointed at the camera. "As the situation grows more direr, non-violent people can certainly turn violent. Home invasions *will* become rampant. Carjacking's *will* take place. You must remain alert, and ready to defend yourself if the need arises."

Craig noticed that everyone was fixated on the screen, but only Duane was leaning forward over a recliner, squeezing his hands together. *Maybe this is what it took to get him on board.*

The president said, "Even if we found an antidote in the next few hours we could not produce enough vaccine to protect our whole nation. We must identify these terrorists, and stop them. They *will* be brought to justice. If you have information that can help us, call the number at the bottom of the screen. At the end of this broadcast, a map will display the forward movement of the virus, and a general update will be given every thirty minutes, as long as we have means. When this is over we will gather up the pieces. We *will* prosper once again. God Bless the United States of America."

A map of the states spread across the screen. Green blotches showed affected areas. A large black arrow pinpointed the virus's forward movement, which was north west.

In a manner of seconds the feed was lost. Dancing specks of grey bounced across the screen. No one moved until Duane shut the front door and Lois clapped her hands.

"All right you guys, we all heard the same thing. It's heading this way, and our window of opportunity is growing shorter. Get those lists made so the rest of you guys can go home and pack. We need to hit the road."

Richard lightened the tension when he slapped Darren on the back. "Well, I've made fun of you in the past for hoarding groceries, but now I think they'll come in real handy."

"Yes, unlike you Baptists who took all your food to potlucks?" He rubbed his belly, "Although, I do have to admit, I enjoyed the meals you invited me too."

Tracey pulled Richard aside. "Did you have any trouble on the way home? The president said the breakout started in North Dakota. Well?"

He stroked her hair as if it were fine silk. "We did okay. God protected us, smoothed out the road, and here we are. I'll give you all the details when we catch our first break. Will you wait until then?"

"I think I already have the answer." She grabbed him and buried her head in his chest.

He hugged her tight. "Now, are you ready to get busy?"

She nodded, and hugged him one more time.

Craig and Linda were getting ready to take a load to the travel trailer when the telephone rang. She looked at the caller "Oh no, Craig, it's Elaine."

He put his hand on her shoulder. "Be careful what you say. We have all the people we can handle right now. Don't offer our assistance, and don't give our plans away."

"Craig, that's terrible. How can we turn off our hearts?"

Lois spoke up, "Linda, Craig's right, and Elaine is not the only friend we have in this area. We can't help everyone." She motioned around the room, "These people are our immediate responsibility."

Linda shook her head in disbelief, and picked up the receiver, leaving the speaker on. "Hi, Elaine."

Elaine's high-pitched fervor reverberated throughout the room. "Linda, did you hear the president's speech? I'm scared to death."

"Is Phil there with you?"

"No, he's in Denver visiting his sister. I've been trying to call him for hours, but his phone just keeps going to voice mail. After what the president said about Denver—you don't suppose? Oh Linda, Phil can't be dead. I…" She broke into sobs.

"I'm sure he's fine. Just keep trying. Cell phone signals are probably pretty sketchy right now."

Elaine asked, "What are you guys doing? Are you leaving?"

Craig mouthed the word, "Don't."

He hurt for his wife, and he didn't want her to lie, but they had all the people they could handle.

Linda frowned and said, "We're still working things out. Where's your son?"

"He's on his way."

"Do you have a plan?"

"He says we'll head for our cabin at Mt. Baker. He thinks we'll be safe there. I just hope Phil gets home in time to join us. Do you think he will?"

"I don't know sweetie, but you know he'll try. Johns pretty smart—you can trust him. Take plenty of food, water, and warm clothing, and don't forget your medicines. I hate to hang up, but our family has to get our plans nailed down, too. Take care of yourself, and God bless you."

"You too, and give those precious kids my love. Lois and Craig too."

Linda placed the phone back on the cradle, and stared at the floor. Tears streamed down her face. She turned toward Craig. He lifted her chin, and wiped the tears with his fingers.

"Now see, they have a plan so try to let it go. Mom's right. We've lived here a long time, and you've been very kind to a lot of people so this may be the first of many calls. Decide now if you really want to talk to anyone else."

Linda laid her head on his chest and sighed. "I don't think I will. I can't take it. I've had my kick in the pants. Let's get busy."

Craig was happy to see everyone, including Duane, spring into action. Operating on pure adrenaline they loaded food, clothing, supplies, tools, weapons, electronic devices, crafts, books, medicine, seeds, utensils, and more. Within an hour Craig's family was packed.

Shopping assignments were handed out at eight forty-five, a.m. Richard left with his dad to gather medicine and medical supplies. Linda and Lois would stay behind with the kids.

Lois told the shoppers not to be shocked by long lines filled with frustrated, people. "They will act uglier than you can ever imagine."

Tracey and Joliene were standing at the door waiting for Duane, but he went the other way and plopped down on the couch.

"I'm too tired for long lines, and mean people. Besides, there's no virus in this area, It's still miles away. Why would there be a run on stores?"

Craig decided to let the comment go, but Linda didn't.

"Duane, when stores and warehouses are empty, no one will restock them. The sooner your team gets to the market, the better chance you'll have to buy food. Now come on. Get up and get going."

With a big sigh, Duane grabbed his jacket then held the door for Tracey and Joliene.

~

The next three hours were a nightmare. Tracey was thankful she and Joliene shared the same Seattle Union bank. After waiting thirty minutes to reach the ATM machine, she was able to make her full withdrawal, but Joliene was shorted twenty dollars. The machine was empty of cash.

Tracey looked out the side mirror. "Poor people. I hope they have better luck somewhere else."

When they arrived at the, CUT COST BOX STORE, Tracey was forced to park three blocks away. Duane let out a loud groan when he saw the line of shoppers stretching around the full length of the store. A large sign instructed them to submit a shopping list to the next available attendant and receive a number. Each shopper was allowed one cart. An attendant would do their shopping, make substitutions if necessary, and all transactions were cash only. When their number was called they were to drive to a designated area, pay for their order and wait for an attendant to load their items.

"Thank God Lois gave us a shopping list," Tracey said, and quickly divided it into three parts. They moved ahead slowly, shivering in the early morning drizzle.

When they were half way up the line, people ahead of them began dispersing.

"What's going on?" Duane asked.

Two men in army fatigues hurried up to them and said the store was out of stock.

Tracey was shocked. "You've got to be kidding. We wasted all…"

Before she could finish speaking, three security guards ran around the corner of the building, grabbed the men in fatigues, and wrestled them to the ground. After a brief scuffle, the disruptors were secured in handcuffs, pulled to their feet and shoved toward the store.

The younger guard yelled, "Stay in line folks. We're not out of stock, in many items. When we're ready to close the store a representative will let you know."

"Thank God," Tracey and Joliene said together.

Duane leaned against the side of the building. "I'm exhausted."

"You can't give up now. The line is moving at a pretty good pace,"

Tracey said, as she checked her cell phone. *Today it's true . . . no news is good news.*

Forty-five minutes later their numbers were called. Tracey brought the truck around, turned the heater on high, and watched as their purchases were loaded.

At twelve thirty in the afternoon, Craig opened the gate for the three weary shoppers. He told them his family would load the new items so they could go home and pack. He reminded them to get their ID's, and be back by three o'clock. Darren had finished packing when he and Richard were out. He volunteered to accompany Joliene and Duane.

Richard's family filled their truck canopy and fifth wheel in ninety minutes. When they were ready to pull out, Tracey asked Chad to buckle the girls up in the truck.

"I don't want them to see me put the cat out."

When she finished, and before pulling the front door closed, Richard and Chad stood with her, taking one final look. As Richard turned the key, Tracey's head fell to her chest, and tears ran down her cheeks.

She asked, "Will we have a home to come back too?"

Chad took her hand. "Of course, Mom. No matter what happens, we're together."

Richard said, "That's for sure, so lock the door, and lets hit the road."

CHAPTER 12

TWIG AND SLICK

Fifteen miles north of the Washington-Oregon border, on the Interstate 5 corridor, Bill Weyland unlocked the front door of his Uncle's convenience store. It was five a.m. He opened the safe, placed money in the cash register, moved a few boxes of stock out of the isles, then piped in his favorite rock C.D.'s. A full hour went by, and his only customer's were three camping rigs purchasing gas at the pump. None came inside. Bill thought it strange, but enjoyed the free time. Two hours later he turned on the radio, unprepared for what came next.

The announcer was saying: "One poor victim captured the gruesome scene on his cell phone. Dead bodies—scattered over the floor of an airline terminal. He posted it on social media. We picked it up from there, and can only assume he is dead, as well. Our nation has never seen anything like this. Untold numbers of people are falling victim to a deadly virus. No one knows where it will strike next. We're under attack folks. We're under attack."

Bill stared at the radio visualizing what the announcer was portraying. "A deadly virus? Is this some kind of sick joke?" His fingers shook as he punched in his Uncle's number.

"Yes, Bill. What's up?"

"Listen, I'm going home."

"What do you mean you're going home? You've got the morning shift, and I don't have a replacement."

Bill shouted into the phone, "Of course, you don't have a replacement! Are you listening to the news? People are dying all over."

"Are you talking about that virus thing?"

"Yes, I'm talking about that virus thing. The next person who comes in here could be sick. I'm scared and I'm leaving."

"For crying out loud, it hasn't even reached our area, and you know many business's have already closed. This is my chance to make some real money. Would you at least stay until I get there?"

"Okay, but I'm locking the door."

Bill hung up the phone, flipped off the lights and was putting on his coat when two hitchhikers walked in.

"We're closed." Bill said. "You'll have to go somewhere else. I'm locking up."

The taller one set his backpack down and the other said, "Come on Slick, you heard him. They're closed. Let's go."

"We ain't going nowhere. We came here to shop, and that's what we're going to do. In fact, the first thing we're shopping for is the money in his till. Get back there, and hand it over, son."

"Slick, what are you doing? We ain't never robbed nobody before."

"Shut up, Twig. We ain't never been so short of money before. Get us some food."

Bill leaned against the counter. "I'm not giving you money so get out of here. I'm going home before someone shows up with the virus."

"Boy, I don't know what virus you're talking about, but I'm going to count to three, and you better be putting that money in my hand."

Bill lunged toward him, "Oh, yeah, or what?"

In a quick, calculated move, Slick backed up, slung open his trench coat, and flipped up his rifle. Twig yelled "No!" But it was too late. Slick fired.

Bill grabbed his chest, stumbled back, and fell over a rack of chips. He tried to speak, but no words came out. His head fell to the side, and he was gone.

Twig, bent over the young man and shouted, "Slick! What have you done?"

"Shut up and lock the door! We need food and supplies. Check his pockets for keys . . . and money."

Slick motioned toward a parking area, right of the gas pumps. "I figure he owns that jeep."

As Twig removed Bill's keys, tears welled up in his eyes. "I'm sorry, boy. I'm so sorry."

Slick walked over, and hit Twig on his shoulder blade with the butt of the rifle. Twig flinched in pain.

"Get going!" Slick said. "If someone heard that shot, the cops could be here any minute."

Twig took one last look at Bill's body, followed his brother to the door, then locked it.

CHAPTER 13

THE TRIP BEGINS

*C*raig looked at his watch. It was three forty-five p.m. Packing was complete, lists reviewed numerous times, and the caravan was lined up in Craig's long driveway.

He said, "Okay. I know everyone is exhausted, but we need drivers. I believe we'll start with Richard, Darren, Nathaniel, Duane . . ."

Duane whined, "I can't drive right now. I'm too sleepy. What if I run off the road?"

Craig gritted his teeth. "Linda, will you drive for your brother—so he can catch a nap?"

She agreed, then he turned to Brianna and took her by the hand. "Let's do this together."

They walked to the barn where Millie was waiting to be fed. She neighed when they entered the side door. Brianna fed her a carrot then laid four others on the edge of the feeding trough. Craig propped the stall door open, filled the trough with grain then fed the remaining fowl. He was thankful the calves and chickens were already loaded.

He used large wooden blocks to prop open the barn door and corral gate—thankful the rain blended with his tears. *This is no way to treat my daughter.*

When he finished, he placed his hands on Brianna's shoulders as she patted Millie's golden head one last time. They walked hand-in-hand back to the house in silence, but before they opened the back door, Craig whispered, "I love you."

"I love you too, Dad."

When they entered the family room, no one asked any questions. Craig's voice was soft when he said, "Well, this is it. We're finally ready. I'm assuming all of you have your ID's?"

Satisfied with their nods he said, "Let's hit the road. Our first official stop will be the Canadian border at Sumas. It's approximately 83 miles. We stay on I-5 until we reach Burlington, then change to highway 9. We'll rotate drivers periodically, so if you're not driving, use these next two hours to rest."

Richard said, "Lois, you're the matriarch of this crew. I think we need some prayer. Would you honor us?"

"Of course, I will. Let's hold hands."

She stood silent for a moment, then prayed, "Father, You never lose sight of us, but I for one have to admit, this is a crazy situation. Please give us faith, courage and a double portion of wisdom. It's hard to understand how such a horrific thing has happened, but I'm not surprised. Our great country has walked away from you, and I'm afraid you're bringing us to our knees. I pray this wake up call will rush this nation back to you. Now, go with us on this journey. Keep us safe, fed and warm. Keep our fellowship sweet, and our trust in you strong. In Jesus name—Amen."

A quiet amen, resonated around the circle then Craig said, "Okay! Load up!" He held the front door open until everyone was out, took a quick glance around then made sure both locks were secured. *I wonder if our home will be here when we return—if we return?*

Craig took the lead, and Richard was last. When they hit the freeway, his two-way radio buzzed. "Yes?"

"Craig here. The traffic is spread out better than I expected. You would think more people would be heading for the hills, or Canada, by the droves."

"They would if they were smart, but maybe they can't, or maybe *they're* the smart ones."

"That could be, or maybe they're waiting for Daddy Government to step in."

"I wouldn't be surprised."

Craig signed off, but Richard said, "Listen up everyone. You're all in my view. Spread out a little in case we have to stop suddenly for some reason. We don't want to rear end each other."

An hour later Richard called Craig. "I'm getting pretty sleepy. I'm not asking for a relief driver, but a few miles north of the border, there's a Forest Service Camp. Can we stop and get some rest?"

Craig squawked back, "Sounds good to me. I'm about to drop."

CHAPTER 14

UNFRIENDLY BORDER

*C*raig and Richard were familiar with Canadian borders. They crossed them frequently, and always with ease. Craig was not overly concerned. He was sure their papers were in order, plus Leon sent other necessary documents ahead, so the crossing should be smooth. He was too tired to consider anything different until they were a half-mile from the border. Traffic slowed to a snails pace then came to a complete stop. The scattered, steady line of traffic heading south, away from the border, worried him. *That's not good. It can only mean they were not allowed to cross—God help us.*

The border was bathed in blinding floodlights. Vehicles were forced to form three lines between two-foot high, concrete or boulder barriers. Many vehicles were being turned away through an opening in a circular drive. Heavily armed Mounties wore face masks and rubber gloves. Their uniforms were covered in plastic. Craig thought they resembled an army of aliens, and there was no way possible to slip past them. When it was Craig's turn, he drove forward and got out of the truck. One of the officers shouted, "Are any of these other rigs with you?"

"Five of them, sir."

Richard stepped out of the rental, intending to join Craig, but a Mountie saw him, extended his rifle and yelled, "Stay where you are." Richard raised his hands then climbed back into the cab, and cracked his window.

The officer asked Craig how many people were in his party. And if everyone had proper identification?

Craig handed him a stack of paperwork. "There are fourteen of us and yes, we do. Here are most of our documents. The rest were sent on line from our Bureau of Land Management, International Exchange and Gas Division. Those items are listed on this yellow sheet."

The officer grabbed the sealed packet and slipped it under his rain cover. "Is anyone in your party sick?"

"No sir, that's why we're seeking refuge in Canada. We're attempting to escape the virus, and we should be entitled to cross."

The officer narrowed his eyes and stared at Craig. *He looks positively evil*, Craig thought.

"No one is *entitled*," the officer said. "No one is granted free access. After, we look over your documents, match them to your group, and confirm the computer entries, then—and only then, will we decide *if* you are *entitled* to cross."

"Yes, sir."

"*If* you are cleared you will pull into the gated area on the left. You will park by the shrubs. Every member will line up in front of their vehicle, be matched to their documentation, and checked for illness. Each vehicle will be searched for stowaways." Motioning for Richard, he said, "You two come with me."

Craig counted thirty-five Mounties on-site. He wondered how many others were ready to jump in? Were all border crossings the same? He and Richard stared at the large amount of vehicles being turned away, forced back to frightening and unknown futures.

The officer escorting them, turned toward a conversation coming from a white mini van. A young mother, probably in her early thirties was driving. She had three small children on board, and was in the lane next to them. Her voice grew more intense as she pleaded with two of the Mounties.

"Please don't send us back. My husband's mother lives just a few miles past the border. Take pity on my children, please? If I can't enter, please take them to her!"

"I'm sorry lady. We have our orders. Canadian borders were closed as soon as we heard about the virus. You have no acceptable identification—and we do not transport anyone—anywhere. Turn your automobile to the right and exit."

She laid her head on the steering wheel and burst into tears. When she raised it again, her eyes narrowed, and she took a long look at the gate. As if reading her mind, one of the Mounties raised his rifle and pointed it at her head.

Craig said, "Oh dear God! Will they really shoot her?"

She yelled a few superlatives, put the van in gear, and peeled out to the right. He heard one of her little boys' say, "Mommy, I thought we were going to Grandmas' house?"

She said nothing, took the exit and sped onto the blacktop. Craig and Richard saw three little blond heads stretching to look back, and watched until she was out of sight.

Tears came to Richard's eyes, blending with a myriad of raindrops. He whispered to Craig, "Is this what society has come too? It will take a long time to get that image out of my head."

Craig grunted then kicked around some loose rocks.

Darren stood with Tracey, Chad, and the younger girls, just outside his truck under a picnic table's awning. It was inadequate to protect them from the blowing rain, but it was where they chose to be. They watched in horror as the van sped away, heard every word the desperate young mother spoke, and the confusion in the children's voices. Cassie and Sara buried their head against their mother and sobbed.

"What if that happens to us?" Tracey whispered. "What if they don't let us pass?" He squeezed her hand, then knelt down by his granddaughters. He pulled them to his chest and let them cry against his shoulders.

He nodded toward the highway, "I don't know. We'll just have to wait and see. We can't blame them for being cautious. The line of cars hoping to cross keeps growing."

Tracey said, "If we get turned back, where will we go?"

"Don't worry about that. We'll put our heads together and figure something out."

Chad slipped his arm around his mother's waist. "Let's get out of the rain, Mom. We're getting soaked."

The Mountie led Richard and Craig to a guard post, and handed their paperwork to the commander in charge. He was sitting rigid in front of a computer screen. He slammed their documents down, then looked up long enough to meet Craig's gaze.

With a slight French accent he growled, "What is your destination, and how long do you plan to *visit* Canada?"

Craig simply stated, "Fort Wilson, sir. We hope to stay there until its safe to go home."

The commander muttered, "You and a thousand others." Silence hung heavy as he checked their passports and ID's. Then he turned to his computer screen. Neither Craig nor Richard moved an inch, fearful to call unnecessary attention to themselves.

Craig's legs were turning to rubber. He was sure another twenty minutes passed before the commander began stacking their paperwork. His heart began to race. Their immediate future lay in this unfriendly mans hands, no matter how thorough the documentation was.

After returning their paperwork to its large folder, the man handed it back to Craig. "You and your party will be quarantined until approximately six o'clock in the morning."

Craig started to object, but Richard elbowed him. Craig understood the meaning.

"Pull your vehicles into the fenced area on the left of the drive. We will secure the gate. If you, or any member of your party shows any sign of illness, you will be turned around. Do you understand?"

Richard said, "Yes, sir, we do. We need some sleep anyway. Thank you very much."

Craig's caravan joined the large number of vehicles already in the compound. He led his group around the outer edge of the fence, facing the exit, and prayed they would be heading north soon.

When the search and inspections were complete, Craig took a deep breath, and looked at Richard. "I feel like the weight of the world is off my shoulders. What a relief! Let's get some rest. You look exhausted."

"You too. See you soon." Craig turned and walked toward his fifth wheel. He took one final look at the long line of cars being turned away. Only a few were placed in other isolation compounds located across the road. He whispered, "There, but for the grace of God…"

Linda laid dry clothes on the bed for Craig. Lois, Nathaniel, Brianna, and Caleb were already buried deep in their covers.

It was nine thirty when Linda turned off the lights. "Good night you guys."

Nathaniel and Brianna said, "Good night Mom." Caleb was asleep.

Craig pulled back the covers, punched his pillow a couple of times then stretched out. "This feels good."

Linda said, "Good night, sweetheart," then kissed his forehead. "I love you."

He muttered some unintelligible words without opening his eyes, snuggling deeper into his blanket. Sleep had been too long coming.

At six fifteen, the following morning, a Mountie knocked on their door. Craig stumbled past Linda to open it. She and Lois were up early, preparing a couple of large egg casseroles and biscuits, for the whole party.

He said, "Good morning."

The Mountie nodded. " You, and your party are cleared to cross if you pass my final inspection. Has anyone become ill?"

"Not to the best of my knowledge, but I've only been in contact with my immediate family."

"Have everyone in this trailer line up outside in five minutes. The rest of your group will join you."

Linda asked, "Is it okay if we eat breakfast before we leave?"

"Yes, ma'am. Just don't be too long. You never know when someone might show up sick."

"That's a good point," Craig said. "I think we'll eat farther up the road."

The Mountie tilted his hat, and Craig heard him knock on each of their party's doors, and order every family member to line up. Amid all the moans and groans the straggly crew poured out, most with bare feet. It only took a couple of minutes for them to become rain soaked. The officer was satisfied, so he gave Craig an orange pass then walked back to the guard shack.

Craig yelled, "Load up just as you are, pajamas and all."

He was met with more moaning and groaning. Duane muttered, "I can't believe he won't let us change clothes."

Darren heard him. "He has his reasons Duane. Just get in your truck."

They were underway in less than ten minutes, and when Craig exited the gate he saw more families being turned away. Senior adults, infants and every age in between, were denied refuge in Canada. Tires squealed, accompanied by a few choice words he would rather his family not hear.

Richard buzzed Craig on their radio. "Thank God for our connections. What are those poor people going to do? Its like they've been issued a death sentence."

"Try not to think about it. It will drive you crazy." Craig said. "Start thinking about the task ahead. That will keep your mind busy."

CHAPTER 15

SEARCHING FOR A HOME

Twenty miles north of the border, Craig led his caravan onto a side road near a grocery store. He drove for another half-mile before finding room for all their rigs to park. He opened the living room slider, and Linda warmed up the breakfast food. As exhausted as they were, Craig noticed moods were lighter. Crossing the border was a great victory. Skies were cloudy, but rain had subsided, at least for the moment.

After breakfast, Craig led north on Highway 97, also known as the Alaska Highway. They spent the night at a wide spot just off the road and arrived in Providence the following day at 11:30, in the morning. Every street was packed with poorly parked cars, trucks, campers, and careless pedestrians were on both sides of the highway. *I hope they're all headed for Alaska.*

Craig was certain they would find no place to settle in this area, but kept his promise to make an effort. He, Richard, Linda, and Tracey borrowed Darren's cab over camper. They searched for almost three hours for a place to settle before returning with the disappointing news.

"Tomorrow we'll head to Benton Creek," Craig said. "If we have no luck there we'll try Fort Wilson."

He chose not to mention the valley again until all other options played out, but he knew from radio updates, the situation in America was growing more dire by the moment. Massive areas were under attack, and death tolls were overwhelming.

Benton Creek was as disappointing as Providence, and when they arrived in Fort Wilson, a day and a half later, Craig turned on the radio. The latest update made him shudder. Silent, undetected drones were sweeping Canadian borders, as well. They were able to make a five-mile inland sweep in many portions of the country. Hundreds of Mounties and civilians died before they knew what hit them.

Craig asked all the family to join him next to his truck, then asked Duane to take the younger kids into the fifth wheel. He said he would fill him in later.

When Duane walked away he looked over his shoulder and snipped, "According to the radio, Craig, Seattle hasn't been attacked. We should have stayed there."

"Just take care of the kids, Duane. You had an option. You should have taken it." *And why didn't you?*

When Craig gave the report there were no tears or gasps, just silence. It was too ghastly to take in. When Richard recovered his voice he said, "I was wondering why the influx of traffic slowed, but refused to ask myself any questions."

Linda asked, "Does this mean what I think it means? Are we headed to the valley?"

Craig said, "I'm afraid so. Those drones are being launched from America. If Canada is under attack, too, the valley looks like our safest option. I'll give Duane an update then we'll load up."

"You're right, son," Lois said. "The farther we get from the border, the better I'll feel." Darren and Joliene agreed. Tracey said nothing. She just clung to Richard's hand.

When the others walked away, Craig turned to Linda. "Will you do me a favor? When we stop to talk about our plans will you duct tape Duane's mouth? I can't take much more of his negativity."

"Craig! That's awful!"

"Sorry, but he needs to get on board. At least—tell him to give me his concerns in private."

"That sounds better."

CHAPTER 16

SELWYN STATE PARK

*C*raig led the family to Highway 77, then to 7. Traffic was light. More so than Craig expected. The following day, he was relieved to see a sign reading, *Selwyn State Park Exit 10-Miles*

He waited to enter until dark, and was disappointed to see three RVs and one camper van, scattered throughout the large area. He was hoping for none. Deeper in the park the trees grew thicker and the brush was thicker. The group campsite was in that area. They parked on black top close to a large fire pit. He hoped the BLM map was correct and the gate was close by.

Before stepping out of the truck he said to Linda, "I know this will go against your nature, but we must avoid the other campers—as much as possible. We have to slip through that gate unseen. Can you help me pass the word?"

Linda said, "Sure. I totally understand."

Numerous patches of snow, and brisk wind were not a surprise to Craig and Richard. They both knew spring weather, this far north, was several degrees cooler than Seattle weather. Caleb and Sara ran straight to the patch closest to the camp. They made snowballs and threw them into the brush until their gloveless hands turned beet red. Chad and Nathaniel gathered wood and built a roaring fire. Soon their smoke floated through the air covering the scent of wet leaves and pine trees. There was not much chatter, just a lot of stretching and walking.

Craig and Richard were eager to find the gate, test the key, and get a glimpse of the road . . . or trail. Duane reluctantly allowed them to use his truck, but made it clear he would not unhook the trailer. Craig shook his head and while he was unhitching, his brain searched for any scenario that would allow him to leave Duane behind, without losing his relationship with Linda and his mother-in-law.

Four roads led to the rear of the park. After dark, Craig and Richard drove up and down each one looking for the gate. On the third pass at a bend in the blacktop, Richard saw a small reflection off to the right.

"Back up. I think I see it."

They pulled away tangled brush, exposing a small sign attached to the front of a heavy iron barrier.

GOVERNMENT PROPERTY – NO TRESPASSING

"This lock is pretty rusty," Craig said.

Richard treated it with graphite, but the key would not turn. He gripped it with pliers, and after a couple of tries he felt it twist. Both men sighed in relief. Craig treated the hinges with oil before pushing the large gate open. It groaned a little, but the sound was so slight no one was close enough to hear. Richard held the gate open as Craig drove the front of the truck through. The roadbed was red clay, mixed with a limited amount of gravel. The area his headlights exposed looked passable, but a few hundred feet ahead it curved to the left.

Craig said, "We'll need to do some exploring tomorrow with your Dad's ATV's. Its good you suggested he bring them. Let's put this thing back the way we found it and clean up our tracks."

"I'm glad the gates where it is. We have to get away discreetly,"

Richard said. "Our closest neighbors are those two guys in the sleeper van."

"Let's hope they leave before we do."

"Craig, regardless of what we discover tomorrow, we should hang around a couple of days. We need a break."

The next morning, Craig filled his coffee mug and went outside. The sky was covered with grey, banked clouds. He hoped it wasn't going to snow. Bad weather could complicate their travel plans, and the last thing he wanted was more complications. He asked Nathaniel and Chad to help he and Richard unload Darren's ATVs, then asked them to take the younger kids for a ride. Craig wanted the other campers to get used to the sound of these machines before they were used to explore the road beyond the curve.

When the ATV rides were finished, Darren yelled over his shoulder that he and Chad were taking a walk. Fifteen minutes later they ran back into camp. Craig was sitting by the fire helping Caleb and the girls roast marshmallows.

"What's the hurry, guys?" Craig asked.

"We found a fast moving stream not far from here," Darren said. "We came back for our fly poles."

"Great. Take Nathaniel too and catch enough for dinner."

"We'll do our best," Darren said.

Lois was pleased when the other ladies appointed her as the head cook. When the guys came back to camp, toting a five-gallon bucket of plump, flopping fish, she helped clean them. There was more than enough for at least two meals. Caleb helped her roll them in corn mea. Joliene watched over them while Lois, on the other side of the grill made fried corn bread and heated some baked beans. It was an inexpensive, yet tasty meal to feed this bunch.

After dinner, Lois said to Linda. "It makes me sad to see Cassie and Sara watch Caleb run and play with Big Ben. Their Momma told them to stay seated by the fire while she cleans up."

Sara was entertained by sliding her feet back and forth in the mud. Lois was sure the little girl would pay later. Cassie picked up her book, taking advantage of the flickering flames to illuminate its pages.

Later that evening, Craig was sitting next to the fire. He took a long look at the large group and felt his chest begin to tighten. He was afraid he was having a heart attack, but after a few deep breaths he felt better, and hoped his discomfort was only a surge of apprehension. He took Linda by the hand and directed her toward the road. When they were out of earshot, he stopped and turned her around to face him.

"Sweetheart, I think I need some prayer."

"Okay, but what's wrong, other than the obvious?"

"The obvious *is* the problem. I believe we're doing the right thing, but I don't really know what we're getting ourselves into. I wish we could find a place to settle, closer to civilization, but if winter catches us in these trailers they will all freeze up. Then what?"

Linda took him by the hand. "Let's sit in the truck so we can have some heat. I'm getting cold."

When they were settled, Craig said. "We'll not be able to avoid a harsh winter in this part of the country. Are we up to it? What if there's a real emergency? How will we handle it?"

"You, my friend are diving into God's business. He's the only one who knows the future, and emergencies can happen anywhere, even in the safety of our home. Remember when Brianna was thrown from the horse? Do you think it was an accident you decided to close the corral gate early that day? If you hadn't, there is no telling how long she would have laid there."

"That's true, but an ambulance was available to take her to the hospital. We would not have that luxury in the valley."

"In our twenty-two years of marriage, I have never seen you this unsure of yourself. America has never experienced a crisis like this, but it was not a surprise to God. We're not prepared or capable of handling a lot of things, but we can do what you asked earlier. We can bathe this whole venture in prayer."

"I know. Do you suppose Richard and my assignment to the valley was ordained by God? Was He showing us a safe place to ride out this attack?"

"Well, we'll find out, but wouldn't it be a good idea to lay our questions out in front of Him—right now?"

Craig agreed, and they spent the next fifteen minutes praying for every member of the family, asking the Lord for safety, wisdom and understanding. When they finished, Craig said, "I do feel better."

He pulled Linda close. "Truth is, there is not much I can't do when you are beside me."

Early the next morning Craig turned on the radio. Three stations were broadcasting from America. He was happy to hear there had been no new attacks for the past twenty-four hours. He thought it might be a good time to take a trip to Wilson Creek, postponing the exploring mission until later in the day. His hope was to see what was available, buy more supplies, fill gas cans and propane tanks. They could also inquire about a place to live. Richard, Tracey and Brianna accompanied him.

Just past the city limits sign, they spotted a little diner on the right. It was called Rosie's Place. Various types of rigs lined the road on both sides of the highway. This had become a familiar sight. They waited 30 minutes to be seated, and when they were led to their table everyone turned to stare. Craig felt a cold chill. He whispered, "This brings back some bad memories."

Richard nodded.

The waitress showed them to a table, apologized for the limited menu then launched into a well-rehearsed speech.

"We've had more visitors than usual lately. People are running from the virus. Some think they can settle here, but we're overrun."

Her not so gentle message was *Keep moving. There's nothing for you here,* did not fall on deaf ears. Craig recognized it as just another sign that the valley was where they belonged, but he still had to ask if she knew where they could buy some hardware, gas, propane, and a few groceries?

"Well, my dad owns a hardware store, a quarter of a mile up the road on the right. He carries propane, if he's not out. One block past him, on the left, is the grocery store. It has a gas pump. You can't get lost. Everyone is low on supplies. We barely have enough to take care of our locals. It will stay that way until its safe for our suppliers to travel. Most of our goods come from America and Eastern Canada, you know."

Tracey smiled, said thank you then looked at her menu. "I'm glad she didn't ask where we're living. Deceit takes a little practice, and I don't like it."

Richard frowned, nodded in agreement and took a sip of coffee. "This is good, but nothing like the coffee we had in Reuben."

They arrived back at camp early afternoon with more supplies than they had hoped for, plus full gas and propane tanks, but to Craig's horror, the two men from the sleeper van were standing by the fire talking with Darren and Chad.

They wouldn't give away our plans on purpose, but they could let something slip. Craig offered a half-hearted hello then reluctantly shook their hands.

Slick introduced himself, and his brother Twig, but gave no explanation for their unusual names, and Craig did not ask. When the ladies came out of Craig's fifth wheel he handed each a bag then quietly asked them to take the children back inside, and stay there. Slick smiled in their direction until the fifth wheel door closed.

Craig's jaw tightened. He felt like smacking the smile off the man's face.

Twig said, "Come on, Slick. Let's get going. These nice people probably got stuff to do."

Slick said, "Shut up! If they get tired of us they'll let us know."

Richard did not trust Craig to respond so he said, "Actually guys, we *do* need to get settled, but thanks for introducing yourself."

Twig said bye, then turned to walk away. Slick took another long look at Craig's fifth wheel. "You have a good day. You sure got some pretty women folk."

When the coast was clear Craig said, "After meeting those hillbillies, I'm really eager to get going. That Slick guy makes my skin crawl."

Craig and Richard made sure there was no one in sight before rolling out the ATVs. They didn't start the engines until camp was out of sight. They hated to undo all the brush then clean up after themselves, but it was important to see more of the road they would face tomorrow. They found it to be rough, but possible.

Craig said, "I just pray it doesn't get any worse. It's going to be a bumpy ride."

After dinner, the family stayed together in Craig's unit. Richard started the generator, and soon a movie spread across the television screen. Tracey made popcorn, and for a couple of hours Craig envisioned this as a family vacation . . . a time when mosquitos, sunburns, and snack shortages were their biggest concerns.

Before daybreak, Craig woke everyone up, encouraged them to be very quiet lest they wake up other campers—especially those two in the sleeper van. As he was getting his fifth wheel ready to travel, he heard footsteps approaching from behind. "Aren't you forgetting something?"

"What's that, Duane?"

"You didn't hitch the trailer back to my truck."

Richard heard the comment and rushed between the two men. "Duane! It would be a really good idea if you took care of it yourself."

Duane did not budge, so Craig by passed Richard, took Duane by the shoulders, turned him around and said, "Now."

Duane fell over his own feet as he walked away, and once again Richard moved between them, facing Craig. "Down, tiger. He's going."

"Is this what we have to look forward to? It's a good thing his sister is my wife."

They watched Duane for a moment then took one more walk through the campsite. Craig turned in the direction of the highway.

"I pray we're making the right decision."

"I don't see we have much choice. We can't settle in Wilson Creek. The town's people wouldn't let us anyway—at least not at this time, and if there's a viral attack in this area we would be trapped, or dead. We can't stay in this park for the same reasons."

"I'm sure you're right. We can always keep checking back . . . weather permitting."

"Listen Craig, I know we're doing a lot of this, but before we drive away, I want you to lead us in prayer."

"Me? Why me?"

"Because you're the leader, that's why."

"Who made that declaration?"

"I did—just now. Face it Craig. You're a lot tougher than I am. You command respect. When you bark, people listen. You just proved that. When I bark, someone tells me to sit down."

Craig laughed. "Linda and I talked about this last night. We need a lot of wisdom, and it sure won't come from me. It has to come from God, so . . . since I'm the leader . . . rather, the shafted leader, I command *you* to round the family up, and lead us in prayer."

"Oh, I see how this is going."

When everyone was accounted for, Richard prayed, "Lord, thank you for helping us get out of Seattle. Thank you we were able to cross the border before it was attacked. We've been traveling in safety, and we know the rest of this trip may get pretty rough, so be with us. Help us stay alert, use the wisdom You will give us, and when we get to our destination, help us get things set up. And please . . . be with all those people standing in the wake of the virus. Be especially with that young mother and her children who were turned away at the border. I can't get them out of my mind. It could have been us. In Jesus name—Amen."

Tracey hugged Richard, and there were tears in her eyes. "Thank you, sweetheart."

Craig stood still for a moment letting the prayer resonate in his heart then said, "Okay, load up as quiet as possible and we'll hit the road."

CHAPTER 17

THROUGH THE GATE

*A*s soon as Richard's big truck cleared the gate, he helped Craig wipe out tire tracks. Chad and Nathaniel stayed on the park side, repacked the entrance with branches and brush then pulled the gate shut. When it snapped, Richard shuddered.

"Are you all right, Dad?" Chad asked.

"I'm fine, son. I just got a chill. Let's hit the road."

Craig and Richard were familiar with the first five miles, and the next three were similar . . . bumpy, but tolerable. Craig sat relaxed until they were about seven miles out. He suddenly sat straight up and tightened his grip on the wheel.

Lois asked, "What's wrong, son?"

"What's going on?" Linda asked, from the back seat.

"The road changed from pot holes to pea gravel."

"It does feel a lot smoother," Lois said. "We quit bouncing all over the place."

"Yes, but this type of gravel has a tendency to do its own thing. It can roll under the tires like marbles, and take you where you don't want to—Oh no!"

Brianna, next in line behind Craig, was pulling the camp trailer. From the side mirror, he saw her unit rolling slowly to the right toward the deep ravine. He knew better than to slam on his brakes. His truck would do the same. It seemed an eternity before he could come to a complete stop, then he tore open his door, ran back to Brianna yelling, "Don't try to correct it! Put it in park! Put it in park! Unfasten your seat belt!"

Her truck was less than ten feet from the drop off when Craig reached her. He jerked open the door, and yanked her to safety before anyone else knew what was happening. Her truck continued rolling at a snail's pace, dragging the trailer behind it. It was less than five foot from the drop off. Nathaniel and Chad reached Craig first.

Craig yelled, "Nathaniel, grab a chain!"

He took it from Nathaniel's hand, threw an end toward Chad and yelled, "Hook it to that tree," pointing to a large spruce.

Craig hit the ground, rolled between the truck, and trailer, and hooked his end around the truck axle.

Before the chain tightened, the right front tire was half way off the road. Had it gone any farther, and without the chain, the weight of the trailer could have plunged the whole unit over the edge.

Brianna's knees were weak and all color was drained from her face. Craig was worse. He wrapped his arms around his daughter and they stood in the middle of the road shaking. Linda came running.

"Bri, are you okay?"

"I'm fine, Mom. Wow, that was scary. I was getting closer and closer to the edge. My brakes wouldn't stop me—then I froze. Thank God no one was riding with me."

Linda put her hand on the door handle of the truck as if she was guarding it. "It's my turn to drive. You ride with your dad and grandma."

"Mom, let Duane do it. Nathaniel's driving his truck. You don't…"

"This is not up for discussion. Go with your dad."

Craig was still shaken, but when he saw Linda biting back tears, and trembling, he laid his hand on her arm. She left it there for a second then gently pushed it away. Nothing he could do would redirect her attention from the wayward truck. She watched in silence as he, Richard and Chad, unhooked the trailer, winched it back, then did the same to the truck.

Craig suggested they take a short break then called Richard aside. "What's on your mind?"

"Maybe we should unload the ATV's and find out what's ahead?"

Richard disagreed. He thought they should keep moving forward, even if they had to inch along. "If we have to repair or build a road, that's what we'll do—not to mention the gas we'll save."

"Those are good points. If we're uncertain we can always walk ahead and scout it out."

Craig looked down and kicked at the pea gravel. "I should have recognized this stuff before we drove over it."

"We're all okay. That's all that matters," Richard said. "I think we've roughed it up enough to make it safe, but why don't we take it one rig at a time?"

Craig agreed, and Richard, before he passed the word along by radio, laid his hand on Craig's shoulder. "I'm sorry this happened, but you're doing a great job. Now, let's forge ahead and reach that valley."

"Okay, let's do it."

Linda was quiet for the rest of the day.

It was hard for Craig to believe things could get worse, but a couple miles down the road they transitioned onto what looked like an old logging trail. He cringed. They parked the units and, as Richard suggested they walked ahead to see if it got better, or—God forbid—worse. It did. It was a terrible road. They shoveled dirt in ruts, placed loose rocks over the large holes, but they were still jerked and thrown around in violent thrusts.

Craig suggested his mom put a pillow between her head and the window. Brianna had already moved Caleb's booster to the middle of the seat, and let him use her neck pillow.

"Dad! This is exhausting." Brianna said. "Every minute feels like an hour."

"That's for sure," Lois said.

"I agree. Let's take a break."

Craig rolled to a stop near a sparse forest on his right and an open plateau on the left. Across the plateau—off in the distance—he saw a range of snow-covered mountains, capped in a heavy blanket of white clouds. It was a beautiful scene, and a grim reminder of how isolated they were.

He opened Lois's door and said, "Mom, let me help you out. You need a break as much as anyone else."

"Thank you. I'm pretty sure parts of my body may never work again."

Richard walked up, stretching his arms toward the sky. "Well, that was fun. Maybe, we should have used those ATV's, as you suggested."

"Maybe, but would we still have turned back? You know the answer. We're doing what we needed to do."

Richard said. "I'll just be glad to see that valley. At least it should be an extended stopping point."

"I sure hope so."

Thirty minutes later Craig yelled, "Load up." He closed his ears to the sea of mumbling, grumbling as he helped his mom back into her seat.

At noon, he led the caravan onto a graveled opening by a lake. He announced they would camp overnight, and half the next day. The large hot campfire did little to push back the frigid air. Everyone chose warmer clothes. They used a large portion of this reprieve to rest, and put dislodged items back in place.

Shortly before pulling out the next afternoon Craig overheard Tracey ask Richard if the road would get any better.

"We're really taking a beating," she said.

"Just hang in there a little longer," Richard said. "We're not far from the valley. Keep reminding yourself of why we're doing this."

Tracey said, "It sounds like you're telling me things *will* get worse."

"We don't know for sure so why don't we get everyone together and look at the map and—"

She cut him off and shot a sideways glance at Craig. "I know you selected *him* as leader, but it's *you* I want to hear from." Darren, Duane, Joliene, and Linda approached.

Craig wasn't sure what to say, and looked to Linda, but she shrugged her shoulders.

Richard, clearly frustrated by the situation, turned from Linda and walked past Craig waving his cell phone. "I'm going to try and reach Leon."

Tracey was tapping her foot. "Craig, what have we gotten ourselves into? This is more than we can take. Now tell us the truth. How much worse is it going to get?"

Duane took a step forward. "Yeah, that's what I want to know. I'm bruised all over. Are you sure there isn't some other way to get to this valley?"

Craig bristled. Duane always managed to push his buttons.

"If you remember, Richard explained this trip in great detail. He told you it would get rough. Why are you so surprised? We've all talked and prayed about it. There is *every* possibility it will get worse. I just don't know. Richard and I made this trip in a helicopter so we've never..."

Duane gritted his teeth then let out a burst of air. "You've never what? You flew in on a helicopter? You mean you've never driven these God-awful . . . awful . . . whatever they are. They certainly aren't roads. How could you do this to us?"

Craig slanted his eyes and tightened his fists. "As I said before, if you had a better plan you should have taken it, but right now, we have no other option. We've come this far, and we have to forge on. If we don't make it all the way, we'll set up camp wherever we get stuck. Regardless, we're in for the long haul. The valley is less than ten miles from here. At the rate we're going, we could make it tomorrow, or the next day."

Richard came around the end of the fifth wheel, and motioned for Craig. "I'll be right back," he said.

He whispered to Richard, "You may have saved Duane's life. He makes me so angry."

"Forget about Duane. We have bigger problems."

"What now?"

Richard was visibly shaken. He took Craig's arm and led him to the back of the rental truck. "I've got some really bad news. Leon didn't answer, but there was a recorded message. All divisions of federal, state and local governments are sheltering in place. The virus has reached every major city."

"Including Seattle?"

"Yes, the report said it happened as soon as the heavy rain stopped. Drones showed up by the dozens and swept all the populated areas. How and what are we going to tell this family?"

"Well, they're already angry, so lets just lay it on the table then pick up the pieces later. They deserve the truth."

"I'm the one who heard the report. Do you want me to tell them?" Richard asked.

"No, I can handle it, but this will be the hardest news we've faced so far." He put his hand on Richard's shoulder. "Are you all right man?"

Before he could respond Linda and Tracey came around the truck. Tracey said, "What's going on? Richard you're white as a ghost."

He said, "We just got some news we didn't want to hear."

Craig took Linda's hands. "It's the virus. It made it's way to all major cities—including Seattle."

Both women were speechless. Tracey buried her face in Richard's chest. He laid his cheek on top of her head, and held her tight.

"Those poor people." Linda said. "Thank God we got away."

"I'll talk to Mom and tell her what's going on," Craig said. "She can take the three little ones inside and give them a snack . . . if that's okay with you guys?"

He started to walk away, but Linda stopped him. "Will you please forgive me for the hateful way I've been acting. I'm sorry I was so hard on you both. I'm done complaining, and I'm all in. We'll finish this trip together."

Craig smiled. "I wasn't worried about you, sweetheart, you're always in my corner, but thanks."

Chad and Nathaniel were standing in an open area throwing a football back and forth. Joliene and Darren were walking together and stretching. The three young ones were chasing Big Ben around. Duane had his arms folded across his chest. He was obviously pouting.

When Craig gave his mom the news, she took it like the strong woman he knew her to be. Craig helped her and the children climb into the fifth wheel with the promise of a snack.

When he shared the news with the rest of the party, he was met with gasps. Brianna cried silently in his arms. He held her for a few minutes then hit the side of his truck.

"Load up! I think we're keyed up enough to move on. Let's finish this trip folks. We've left civilization behind. We should be safe. If you see anything flying overhead—duck."

"That's not funny, Craig," Duane said. "You shouldn't joke about something so serious."

Craig pretended not to hear and was grateful when Joliene changed the subject. "Don't you think someone should thank God that our families got out in time?"

"I'll do it," Nathaniel said.

Craig placed his hand on his son's shoulder. "Go ahead."

"Lord," Nathaniel began, "I'm not sure why you spared us, but thank you. So when things get tough, remind us of what You have already done—Amen."

Forward movement was slow, and Craig stopped often. The BLM map had accurately identified the road changes, but not the graphic details. Craig wondered if they would have attempted this venture if they knew then, what they know now.

Three and a half miles from the valley they had to climb a mountain that skirted the rim of a deep canyon. Craig thought these places would make a Mountain Goat quiver. The trailers twisted and groaned, but kept moving. Every advancement felt like a victory. The animals cried out, the chickens squawked, and Big Ben kept tromping over Caleb, to look out the window.

Craig was thankful for the warm spring days and grateful for cold nights that kept the ground firm. If the heavy vehicles sank into the mud, the party would be in real trouble.

Approximately two miles out, Craig rolled to a stop. He was approaching a slight bend in the road that trailed a rock wall. When he got out of his truck, Richard and Darren joined him.

"Is there a problem?" Darren asked.

Craig pointed at the wall. "I hope not, but it looks like the road may be narrowing."

Richard and Darren volunteered to check it out, and when they returned, Richard said that section was only an eighth of a mile long, but just around the curve he would be trailing a deep ravine.

"At one point there's about a three-foot clearance. You'll have to hug the wall—tight."

"Well, old buddy, it just keeps getting better and better, doesn't it?" Craig said. "I'll crawl through like a snail."

Richard said, "Yes, you will, and this may be the longest eighth of a mile we've ever experienced."

He leaned in the truck window. "Lois, you should move to one of the other pickups."

"Not a chance—I trust my son." She turned to Craig. "I *can* trust you, right?"

Craig smiled. "Of course you can. Mr. Trustworthy—that's me. But, I will not put you in danger. If I get stuck, I can open the sliding window and escape. How would I get you out? You need to listen to Richard."

"Not a chance. I'm getting used to these adrenaline rushes. They keep my heart pumping, and better still, they make me feel young and alive."

Craig stared at her for a moment then picked up his radio. "Okay, you guys, Mom's not getting out, but if you're not driving I want you to walk, and you other units hang back until I'm completely clear."

It didn't take long for Brianna, Chad, the mother hens and their chicks, to walk past Craig's rig and pass Richard. Joliene was holding Caleb and Sara's hand. Craig could tell Caleb was involved in a never ending conversation, but he was unable to hear what he was saying. Linda stopped at Craig's window and gave him a kiss.

She said, "Love you baby."

"Love you too. See you on the other side." *I hope the other side is this mountain and not heaven.*

As soon as the brood cleared, Richard waved Craig forward.

Craig said. "Here we go."

Craig rolled forward at a snail's pace, and in a few short minutes he began to feel the squeeze. Richard held up his hand, and his radio.

"Okay man, this is where the wall protrudes the most. You have no room to spare."

Craig said, "Just keep an eye on those tires, and watch for weak surfaces."

"You got it."

Just as Craig started to roll he caught a glimpse of Linda, along with the others, rounding the bend. He smiled then breathed a silent prayer. *Thank you Lord for my wife. She is the greatest gift You've given me. Please let us make it through . . . and I do mean, please.*

The radio squawked again and Richard said, "Sorry about this man. Wish we had another option. We should've used the SUV's and mapped this area. The smaller rigs couldn't have gone through first."

"Too late for should have's. Just keep an eye on all my tires. All you who are walking, don't get too far ahead. There could be wild animals in the area."

The screams of two little girls came through loud and clear. *"I probably should have handled that differently,"* Craig whispered.

He said, "Sorry girls. You other drivers hang back. I'll give you an all clear when I get to the other side." *If, I get to the other side.*

Craig pulled the mirrors in and began inching the big unit between the rock wall on the left, and the deep ravine on the right. When the radio squawked, he jumped.

Darren said, "Craig, how are you doing? Can you make it?"

"I'm totally committed. We're a little over half way through, but it's getting tighter. Richard, keep a close eye on the ravine side, would you? Have Linda come back and watch the wall. The mother hen brigade is up ahead somewhere."

Richard said, "Linda, did you copy?"

"Yes, I did, *and* his little crack. And just for the record, husband, I think walking is the safest option. I would rather face wild animals than what you're going through."

Lois looked down into the dark ravine. "I wish we could take wings and fly. It's a long way to the bottom."

"You had your chance. Do you still trust me?"

"I'll answer that if, and when we get out of this alive."

Craig smiled when he saw Linda come around the curve. She waved and the radio crackled with her voice. "You're in the narrowest portion right now. Once you're around this curve the road widens. There are no more large rocks sticking out."

Richard said, "Don't move until I make sure that outside edge is solid. We don't want it crumbling on you." Richard walked up and down the road, nodded, and gave Craig thumbs up.

"Darren here. Are you sure you can't let your mom out?"

"Only if I plan to drop her over the cliff. Like I said, we're committed. One good thing, if we make it, the others should do fine."

"And if you can't?"

"It's a little late to talk about that now. Okay, Linda's ready. Here goes."

Craig inched forward, scraping the side of his prized fifth wheel. He could hear windows popping, but refused to let it distract him. At one point, Richard held up his hand and yelled. "Hug the wall. The fifth wheel tires are pretty close to the edge."

"I'm scraping its side off now." Craig yelled. "Where's that three foot clearance you promised?"

With eyes glued to the road Craig said, "I'm sorry Mom, but I suppose you could look at it this way . . . if we go, we go together."

Lois piped back, "Just keep your eyes on the road, son. This is a little scarier than I thought it would be. We'll talk about this later before a judge when I put you up for adoption!"

"Now Mom, you know you couldn't live without me."

"The key word here is live. Just make sure I do, and I'm giving serious thought to the adoption thing!"

Lois took a quick glance in the direction of the deep ravine. "Well, I'll be. I see your dad. He's right down there. He's waving at me."

"That's not funny, Mom."

"Who knows, God could be letting him watch us."

"I hope not! If he sees the danger I'm putting you in, he'll be waiting for me in heaven with a big stick."

"I think—no—I don't think. I know he would understand the situation and trust you. Your dad loved a great adventure. He would have been right in the thick of this one. In fact, he would be driving this rig."

Craig caught a quick glimpse of a tear rolling down her cheek. "Sorry Mom—and you're right. He would love this venture."

Ten minutes later, which felt more like a hundred years, the road widened. Craig took his first deep breath, stopped his truck, and laid his head on the steering wheel. As soon as he felt he could talk, he announced over the radio that they were on the other side. Duane was next in line. He took over for Linda after the rest break.

Craig asked, "Duane, are you ready for this?"

"I'll try, but I'm pretty scared."

"Can't have that. Sit still until I get out of everyone's way. I'll take over for you. How about you Nathaniel? Are you going to be okay?"

"I'll be fine. Just guide me through when the time comes."

Craig had no issues taking the second unit through.

Darren was next. His voice came over the radio loud and clear. "You can take over for me anytime. Just kidding—sort of."

When all the units were safely on the other side, Craig noticed the road was gleaming with shiny mud. He suggested they take a break, eat a meal, and give frayed nerves a chance to settle.

While lunch was being prepared, Craig and Richard took a walk down the road. While they were talking, their boots began to sink. They hurried onto a grassy area, and rubbed off what they could.

"I think we stopped just in time," Craig said. "Let's make camp and leave early in the morning, and pray this road stays firm until we get to the valley."

Craig, Linda and Brianna spent a good portion of the rest of the day cleaning the area around the three broken windows, and covering them with plastic. As soon as dinner was over and the kids were settled, Craig undressed for bed. When his head hit the pillow he took a deep sigh. Linda lay down next to him, slipped her arm around his waist then snuggled into his back. Craig took another deep breath, and squeezed her hand. *I love this gal.*

At five o'clock the next morning, Craig woke up the whole party. "Grab a quick breakfast. We need to be underway by six."

The road appeared firm, and Craig was relieved, but his relief was short lived. A mile from where they camped Craig received the call from Richard, he did not want to get.

"My back tires just sank into the bog. It feels like a deep hole. The tongue of the trailer is right down there with them."

No trees were close enough to winch from, and no other unit could get back to him, so Nathaniel, Chad and Craig attempted to dig it out. With every shovel of mud they removed, twice that much oozed back in. Both back tires were suctioned firmly in place.

Craig looked at Darren and shook his head, "This is hopeless, and now the whole trail is soft. I'm afraid to risk it. We need to spend another night on the road. We'll leave in the morning at first light, and deal with the truck later. It's not like we're blocking traffic."

He walked across the clearing and turned. This small band of migrants reminded him an old west wagon train that came cross-country looking for a good place to settle. Thus far, the journey had been a significant accomplishment. He was thankful that God led them safely into Canada. He knew there were uncounted thousands, perhaps tens of thousands lying dead on the very route they travelled. He knew when they did arrive at the valley their journey had just begun, and perhaps only he and Richard had any idea of the challenges that could face them.

Craig sank down on a fallen tree. Twelve lives would be looking to he and Richard for safety and survival. He prayed they were up to the task?

"God help us."

PART II

CHAPTER 18

THE VALLEY

*A*t exactly seven forty-five the following morning, the caravan of weary travelers, rumbled over a rocky knoll, onto a large plateau. Craig let out a sigh, then shut off his engine. He stepped out of his truck, did a few stretches then made his way to the edge of the plateau. He crossed his arms, and drank in the scene.

Richard walked up, stood silent for a moment, then gestured toward two large sections of overgrown gravel. "Looks a little different up here, doesn't it?"

"Yes, it does. But wouldn't it be nice if helicopters were still sitting there?"

"It would, but we made it without them. In spite of all the odds—we made it."

Family members, except Lois, lined up next to the men. All eyes fixated on the panoramic view of vast wilderness. Directly below was a dark impenetrable forest—somewhat redeemed by the glistening lake that bordered its eastern border. Across the lake a glacier-laden mountain range framed both it, and the valley.

A lone eagle soared overhead, casting sweeping shadows over this silent group. For the first time, Craig understood how deafening *quiet* could be. The settlement was an eighth of a mile below them, but could not be seen from the top of the plateau, for which he was thankful. *One thing at a time. That's all they can handle. That's all 'I' can handle!*

Craig's heart began to race as his thoughts shot forward. *These are city dwellers—this is raw wilderness. Oh God, will they adapt? I pray they at least try.*

Part of his answer came when Linda whispered, "I don't know what I was expecting, but whatever it was . . . this is not it. Will we be able to carve out a home here?"

He slipped his arm around her waist and pulled her close.

Duane sat down on a rock close to Craig, put his head in his hands. "What were you thinking?"

Craig said nothing, but giant portions of regret flooded over him, until five-year-old Caleb asked, "Wow, Dad! Is this where we get to camp? Can I help you build a fire? Do we have any marshmallows?"

Caleb sees no problems—only possibilities. Craig smiled, wishing the rest of the family would catch some of this little guys enthusiasm.

Brianna moved next to her dad. "I don't mean to sound ungrateful, but now that we're here, what next?"

Craig took a few of steps back, and smacked the hood of the truck. "Good question. I've been wondering the same thing. I'll try to give you an answer tomorrow."

"Can I get out of this truck, please?" Lois yelled, sitting with the door open.

"I'm sorry Mom." He helped her slip to the ground as Brianna opened her walker. Lois walked a safe distance from the edge, leaned forward and drank it all in, as the others had done.

Craig gave her a few minutes then said, "We're all tired so let's get down the hill and check things out. All three Quonset huts face the woods. There's a large area behind. It should give us an ideal spot to park."

Duane said, "Ideal spot? Is there such a place?"

Craig turned his back and groaned, as he helped his mother back in the truck. *One of these days.* He led the caravan to the right across the plateau. He had them wait at the top until he was comfortable it was clear. He radioed an okay, told them it was rough, but reasonably short.

Thank God the huts are as large as I remember.

Richard backed the animal trailer close to the opening between the first two huts. He lowered the ramp, and let the two young calves out. The area was small, but at least it was confined, and reasonably safe. The corridor joining the two huts blocked the other end. He asked Chad to throw them some hay, and fill up their water container. The chicken coup would stay in the truck, and from all the squawking, the chickens resented it. He threw them some grain, cleaned their dirty water container and refilled it.

The other units parked in a U shape, approximately twenty feet behind the buildings. When they finished, Craig offered a tour of the huts.

Nathaniel helped his grandmother over the threshold, first. "Dad, the doors are not locked."

"I suppose they figured if someone needed shelter they wouldn't let a little thing like a locked door keep them out."

Lois said, "Good thinking, son."

The tour lasted approximately ten minutes, then the ladies—including Lois—went back outside, straight to the RVs, without saying a word.

Craig scratched his head. "I'm pretty sure they liked what they saw, then *zap*—they were gone. I even heard Joliene say the huts were nicer, and bigger than she expected. What's that all about?"

"I don't know," Richard said. "Give them time to adjust. Settling in, might feel like giving up."

Craig asked Chad and Nathaniel to place some rocks in a small ring for a fire pit then gather some firewood. He cautioned them to stay close.

"I have no idea what might be lurking just inside those woods."

When the fire was blazing, Craig handed Nathaniel a grill cover. Tracey pulled out roasting sticks while Lois and Joliene arranged hot dogs, marshmallows and chips on a camping table. There was a lot of chatter. Craig hoped it was a sign that moods were getting lighter.

~

The next morning, Craig, Richard, Chad, and Nathaniel worked hard to free the rental truck from the stubborn mud. At the end of the second day, Craig jerked the winch hook off the axle and threw it on the ground.

"This is hopeless. This thing is determined to stay where it's planted."

"What now, Dad?" Nathaniel said.

"We'll unload the other pickups, bring them all up here then lay boards out behind the rental . . . well, you can figure out the rest."

Nathaniel said, "I can hardly wait."

"At least we're close to camp," Richard said. "It could have happened farther out."

Craig ignored Richard's tolerance, climbed into his pickup and looked at his muddy boots. "What a mess!"

At camp, Craig called all hands on deck to help unload the trucks. "Put everything in the middle hut. We can't leave it outside."

As usual, Duane was missing. Craig was too tired to make it an issue, but the next morning at six, he rousted Duane without giving him an option. He *would* help unload the rental. Duane grumbled, but could tell Craig was in no mood to be argued with.

He asked Linda and Lois to stay behind with the younger children. Before he drove away he took his .22 caliber rifle out of the truck, and offered it to Linda.

She took a step back. "What do you expect me to do with that?"

"I expect you to shoot a bullet in the air if you need me. We're close enough to hear."

"I have never..."

Before Linda finished her statement Lois reached for the rifle. "Give me that thing. For crying out loud, have you forgotten how many times I've fired those? I'll give Linda a few pointers while you're gone. Now, get out of here."

Linda followed him out and said, "Sorry, hon. I don't mean to disappoint you."

Craig leaned in close. "It's not you who needs to apologize. I'm in a hurry and didn't take time to think. Please forgive me." He kissed her on the nose, turned and hurried away.

Two days later when the rental was finally empty, Richard jacked up the rear as far as it would go. This would be the final attempt to break it loose. Suction on the back tires held firm. Just as he started to relax the jack handle, an ear-splitting pop sounded throughout the region.

Craig took off running for his truck. "O, dear God! That's Mom!"

Richard yelled, "Craig! It's the tire. It broke loose. Everything's okay."

Craig took a deep breath then joined Richard. They packed the goopy hole with rocks then Richard climbed into the cab. He slowly released the brake while putting pressure on the gas pedal. Another loud pop and the big truck was finally free.

Before descending the hill, Craig tried calling Leon. The line rang more than twenty times. No one answered and voicemail was never an option. When he called the BLM line, he heard the same message Richard had relayed a few days earlier. Craig shuddered again at the gruesome report, and wondered how many of his family and friends were still alive.

CHAPTER 19

GETTING SETTLED

*R*ichard followed Craig into camp, and when the big truck came to a halt, the whole family clapped and broke out with whoops of joy. After getting a bite to eat the two men walked around the compound making a list of projects that needed to be done.

The chickens and cattle, unhappy with living conditions, made their feelings known. Between the squawking, and the mooing, Craig thought fried chicken and steak might be a good remedy. Big Ben was restless and curious about the new sounds and smells, yet to Craig's delight, the dog was Caleb's faithful shadow.

The huts faced north and south, and the lake sat to the Northeast, about a quarter of a mile away. Small groves of tall trees stood between the huts and the plateau. More were scattered throughout the area. The plateau and canyon road sat due west, less than quarter of a mile from the compound, and between those locations was a tool and storage hut, large enough to secure the animals in the night, or during bad weather. Craig suggested they build a corral and chicken coup in front of it. They would lay out long-term plans, if they were forced to be there when winter approached.

Richard rubbed his hands together. "That's a great idea. I've been itching to try out my new chainsaw."

Craig laughed, "Yes, and each night Tracey will count your fingers . . . Chad's too."

When the shed door was open they were pleased to see shutters with strong latches.

Craig pointed toward the woods. "There's plenty out there that would love to have our livestock for a snack."

It took a full week to finish constructing the corral and chicken coup. The cows frolicked from side to side, stirring up dust while the chickens flapped their wings, squawked, and frantically scratched the ground for bugs. Harsh winters discouraged insects, so any find was a treasure.

When the men reentered the middle hut Darren said, "All the critters seem happy, and nothing has fallen apart—so far. Good job guys."

"Now," Lois said, "I think its time for everyone to help clean and organize these huts."

Craig smiled. *Maybe, the initial shock and adjusting time was drawing to a close. Maybe this family is ready to move ahead.*

"Before we start cleaning," he said. "I want everyone to join me on a little tour."

Their first stop was the East side hut. Craig said, "The two outside huts are identical in every way—30 foot by 30 foot. BLM uses this lay out for large crews. Each have bunks with three drawers at floor level, plus a footlocker at the end. This is the unit we stayed in."

Richard pointed to the last set of the six bunks, closest to the back door. "I slept on the right. Craig was on the left. We liked being close to the bathroom. It's small, but there's a toilet, and a shower."

Tracey asked, "What powers the overhead lights?"

"Solar panels store some of it," Craig said. "A generator furnishes the rest. We'll get ours hooked up pretty soon. It runs on gas or propane. Let's pray we can keep some of both on hand."

He and Richard trailed behind the rest of the family toward the corridor. Craig said, "There's a different feel to this place, isn't there?"

Richard laughed. "Yes, we've gone from survey equipment, rock crushers and foul-mouthed men to lace, grace, poise and prayer."

Tracey yelled from the corridor, "Hey, I heard that, and it's going to stay that way."

Richard yelled back. "I'm not complaining."

Craig stifled a laugh then went to the kitchen area. He opened a pantry door and smiled. "They're still here."

On the middle shelf was a large collection of various types of rocks, including pieces of quartz. He called for everyone to come look.

"Most of these are the core samples Richard and I were testing."

"Was there any evidence of oil, or natural gas, Dad?" Nathaniel asked.

"Not as much as the BLM expected, but in that same area we did find some quartz with a few flakes of gold in them."

Sara said, "Ooh. That's amazing."

"How much is it worth, Daddy? About a million dollars?" A wide-eyed Caleb asked.

"I'm sure it must be. You guys can each have two, and here are a few for you, Mom."

Lois smiled as she rolled them around in her hands. When she finished, she asked Nathaniel to put them on the ledge above the sink then turned to Craig.

"Thank you, son. When you and Richard were out on a job, I often tried to imagine where you were, and what you were doing. Knowing you guys stayed in these huts makes it easier to make them my *temporary* home."

She turned and said, "Let's get busy. You can keep running in and out, and sleeping in your trailers, if you like, but let's gather here—often—as a family."

When Craig saw heads nodding an instant wave of relief swept over him, and from that point the work began.

Later that afternoon, Craig came through the door with additional cleaning supplies. Tracey and Joliene were in the center hut. Joliene was wiping down the wood stove. It was larger than the ones in the side huts. Not only was it the only source of heat for this building, it was the cooking range.

"We owned a stove like this when I was young," Lois said. "Mom used it every day, summer and winter."

"I've seen this type in old movies," Tracey said. "I never thought I'd be using one. By the way, Craig, I sure wish we had hot water."

Craig smacked himself in the forehead. "I'm such an idiot. We *do* have hot water as long as there's fire in the wood stoves. All three have stainless steel water lines running through them. As soon as you turn on the left faucet, it comes through. The problem is, it can be *too* hot so be careful, especially with the younger ones. Can you imagine the whining that would have taken place if a BLM crew was expected to shower in ice cold water?"

Lois laughed. "Yes, I can. By the way, what keeps the water source from freezing?"

"BLM places many crews in frigid conditions, so when this type of camp is set up, they bury both water and sewer lines several feet below the permafrost to protect them."

Craig thought of another water source in the area, but decided not to reveal it at this time.

As soon as the sleeping quarters were cleaned and stocked, Craig helped move Nathaniel, Chad, and Duane into the left unit. Joliene, Lois, and Brianna settled in the one on the right. Everyone sleeping in the RVs could capture the remaining space, when they were ready.

On one of his many trips, Craig saw his mom resting in a lawn chair close to the fire pit. She was wrapped in a deep purple, soft blanket. He unfolded a chair and sat down beside her.

"Are you okay, Mom, or just taking a break?"

She said, "Yes, I am. It's nice here by the fire."

They stared at the flames for a few minutes then she said, "I try not to think of all the horror that's taking place, but when I stop working, it floods my mind. We have family members scattered all over the states. I keep seeing their faces, wondering if they escaped."

Craig nodded, but said nothing. Lois went on. "On the other hand, as I sit here by the fire, I realize we have so much to be thankful for. It was God who provided this refuge for us, and in spite of my broken heart, I see beauty in that crystal clear sky, and those mountains. Overall, this is an incredible refuge, and we are blessed."

"Yes, we are. We tried to tell everyone we wouldn't be living like Neanderthals."

They sat silent for a few minutes as Craig stared at the fire, wishing he could hear from Leon. *Is he still alive? If not, what then?* He was thankful his mother interrupted his painful thoughts.

"Why was this spot so totally abandoned—in tact?"

"Well, you already know some of this, but it took BLM three straight months to build this site. They flew in a large crew, and a lot of equipment, to monitor and oversee the petroleum company—who was expected to be in the area for several years."

"What happened?" Lois asked.

"I'm not sure. The details have been hush, hush since the beginning. The company was given a decent amount of time to produce an oil reserves, but that didn't happen. Then they began to make negative impact on the environment. Canada's BLM contacted Leon to see if Richard, and I, were available. They wanted us on site as consultants. It was our job to confirm or deny BLM's suspicions. We visited pin pointed sites, gathered and tested samples. We got negative results for reserves, and positive results for damage. Canada gave the company a chance to withdraw then shut this whole site down. Leon told us that BLM walked away with their loose equipment, but it was too expensive to dismantle and move these huts."

"What a waste."

"That's what Richard and I said, but we've changed our mind."

CHAPTER 20

BLOCKING THE CANYON

*L*ater that day, Craig asked Richard to join him at the base of the canyon road. When they reached the site, Craig took a long look at the opening.

Richard asked, "What are we doing here?"

Craig said, "We've been so busy, today was the first time I've considered the shape of that drive. It's curved in such a way that an intruder, or anyone for that matter, could drive right into our camp. We would have no prior warning."

"I see your point, but what do you suggest we do?"

Craig said his plan might sound a little crazy at first, but he thought it would work. He recommended they strategically detonate a stick of dynamite toward the top, to scatter some moderate sized rocks. Locating dynamite was not an issue. They always carried it in the work truck.

"Well, you're the powder monkey, not me," Richard said. "But why do we want to seal ourselves in?"

"No worries my friend. We would only dislodge enough rock to keep someone from driving over it."

"Including us," Richard said.

"I have a plan for that too. Feel like taking a hike?"

When they reached the top of the ridge, Craig pointed out a thick grove of brush, surrounded by trees. It was near the outside of a cave entrance.

"We could hide two of our trucks under those. They could not be seen from any direction."

Richard said, "That should work. We just need to find a good detonation site."

Craig called Darren on the radio, and asked him to bring tools, on the 4-wheeler.

It took about an hour to finish trimming the grove. Darren volunteered to pack up the tools while Craig and Richard hiked back down the trail. When they reached the bottom of the incline a slight mist hung in the air.

Craig said, "Could we sit for a minute? I need to rest."

He motioned for Darren to join them, and when the engine was quiet, Craig said, "I need to talk to you guys."

They brushed damp pine needles off a couple of large boulders then sat down. Richard said, "So, what's on your mind?"

"To be honest, I feel like I'm in over my head. You guys keep telling me I'm the leader, but that lays heavy on me. I'm not afraid of responsibility, or hard work, but I'm a geologist, not a mountain man or a builder. You may have noticed I'm not very patient, and I'm not the most tactful person in the world." Craig grinned when he saw Richard nodding.

"Initially, I looked at getting here as an ending. That's what drove me, but I was wrong. We've barely started. We're stuck in raw wilderness, and if we don't get an all clear, we're likely to face the coldest winter we can imagine. After the first hard freeze we won't be able to use our RVs, and I'm afraid if we all try to live in the Quonset huts, as they are, we'll kill each other before spring. I want to get the whole crew together to make some short, and long term plans. If we don't, we could be in trouble."

Craig noticed Richard staring at him. "What are you looking at?"

"When did you get those dark circles under your eyes, and why haven't I already noticed them?" He gave Craig a little shoulder punch then said, "Don't worry. We'll help carry the load. Right Dad?"

Darren said, "Sure, but I will always recognize you as the leader, Craig."

"Me too," Richard said. "Truth is, Dad and I are too soft. We don't do well barking out orders. We might give under pressure, but everyone listens to you—well almost everyone. How can we help?"

"That's what I want to work out." Craig said. "I think we should take suggestions from the family, but I don't want a free for all, and I don't want to depress them with terminology like *long term plans*."

Darren said, "Don't forget, most of those guys have already proven they're pretty tough. We need to value their input, listen to their ideas and pass around the responsibility. The more vested we are, the less depression we'll have. Images of home will start haunting us as soon as we catch our breath."

Craig agreed. "Spoken like a true doctor. Thanks for the tips."

"On a lighter note," Richard said, "if we decide to build something, we won't have to get a permit."

Craig and Darren laughed then Craig said, "It's a good thing, because no one in their right mind would give us one."

"Remember my attempt to remodel the kitchen?" Richard asked.

"I remember it well. Your first mistake was thinking you could do it. The second was asking me to help you. How much did you end up paying that contractor to fix our mess-up?"

"Too much, not to mention dealing with a very unhappy wife."

Darren held out his hands. "Look guys, do you see any calluses? I'm a surgeon. Years ago, when I had time, I built a few pieces of furniture, but that was just for relaxation. If you're thinking we should attempt real construction, that's a whole different story. We would need to do some serious planning first."

Craig said, "Well, I for one am ready to plan. If we don't get to go home we need a barn right away. That tool shed is too small for our critters, plus, I don't want to step on cow piles and chicken poop to find my tools. We can construct it from lodge poles, and if it doesn't fall down, we'll keep on building."

"Those are great ideas," Richard said. "Sounds like we have a lot of tree cutting and slicing to do. I can't wait."

Craig and Darren laughed. Derek said, "Maybe you should have been a logger or a carpenter instead of a geologist."

Craig said, "Well, now is your chance. We need to partition off both outside huts to make separate bedrooms. Nothing fancy—just privacy walls."

Richard said they could handle that. Darren agreed.

"But," Craig said, "there may be a bigger job. I found the blue prints for the huts, and plans for a fireplace. They were on the top shelf above the core samples. The good news is, the pipe has already been inserted, which was the smart thing to do. The panels behind the hearth are removable, and they were going to build the rest out of rock."

"Well, if it doesn't work," Darren said, "I suppose we can put the panels back in. I'm willing to give it a try—if we're still here. Is that all?"

"Just about," Craig said. "They also had specs for a covered porch across that same end of the huts. I think that is a great idea. It would help keep the firewood dry, and give us a little shelter."

Craig waited for a response, but neither Richard or Darren said anything. They simply nodded, but when Craig said there's one more thing, they both moaned.

Richard looked at his dad. "And here I was afraid we might get bored."

"We need to take care of that entrance," Craig said. "We don't want to be surprised, do we?"

"Certainly not, but we better have a family powwow tonight, and get their input. You'll recognize me," Richard said. "I'll be the one standing right behind you and Dad."

After dinner, a heavier rain was falling, and the air was getting chilly. Craig waited until it was almost dark before turning on the overhead lights. The solar panels stored enough energy for several hours of lighting, in their battery bank, but he asked that it never be wasted.

He stoked up the wood stove then invited everyone to find a seat. The younger ones sat on the edge of the hearth. Craig wondered why this type of thing was so hard on him. He looked toward Richard and Darren for moral support then launched into his spiel.

There was a lot of excitement about building a porch and a fireplace, but when it came to blocking the road, Duane said, "Why can't you just build a gate with a lock? Why would you want to trap us in here? There must be some other way."

Craig's jaw tightened and Richard said, "I'll take this, Craig." Craig walked over to the door and leaned against it. "Help yourself."

"Duane, if we build a gate and intruders show up, they'll be certain someone or something of value is on the other side. Rocks look natural. They would appear to be placed where nature put them and alleviate all suspicion. People are in a survival mode, right now. That can bring out the worst in their natures. Do you get the point?"

"I guess. I just don't like the idea of being trapped."

"That's why we're hiding two trucks in the grove. Most of us can hike to the top of the hill in ten minutes." Richard gave Lois a quick glance. "The rest we can help, but if a vehicle drove down the hill— well—we would never know if they were friend or foe, until they were on top of us, but if a stranger *walks* down the hill, Big Ben will let us know. "

Craig took charge of the discussion again, suggesting they plant a garden, build a rock wall around the compound, and put together a green house. Specific assignments were given to everyone, including the children.

When the discussion was over, Craig said, "Great job everyone. Now that we've settled all that, after we get the truck in place, tomorrow, we'll blow up a few rocks. I'll let you know when the charge is set. If you want to, you can meet me at the bottom of the hill–just in case there's any final words, questions or concerns." He glanced Duane's way. "I'm sure there will be."

The next morning, Craig called Richard at 11:45. "The charge is set. Let everybody know. I'll wait at the bottom of the hill. Can you make sure Mom gets here, *if* she's coming?"

"No problem. I already have the quad ready. See you in a few."

While Craig was waiting, and out of earshot, he punched in Leon's number. There was no answer. He rubbed his stomach, hoping to remove the knot.

Craig watched as Richard drove behind a huge boulder with Lois, and smiled when he heard her say, "I could have used my walker."

I'm glad Richard insisted. Caleb ran up and grabbed his hand. "This is fun, Daddy. Will it be really loud?"

"Not too bad. You can plug your ears if you want to." He gave Caleb's little hand a squeeze then leaned down and kissed him on the forehead. "Right now, I need you to go stand by your mother, and keep your head down."

Craig held up his hand, motioning for silence. All eyes were fixed on him. "Please understand. We're doing this to make it difficult for unannounced, or unwanted visitors to drive straight through and surprise us. After the dust settles, we'll clear just enough rock, in a zigzag pattern, to drive a quad through. That way we'll have quick access to the pick-ups."

He was disappointed, but not surprised when Duane stepped forward. Joliene tapped her son on the shoulder, shook her head, and he stepped back. Craig narrowed his eyes, but said nothing. Duane had a right to express concerns, but Craig's daily prayer was, *Please God, help Duane get on board and stop spreading so much negativity.*

Craig took one last look at the area he was getting ready to restrict, then his knees became weak and his stomach queasy. As long as he was working with his hands or in his own field, he displayed the optima of confidence, but this was different. Once he set off the charge, a huge commitment was made. Two wires touching, followed by a moderate explosion, and this small band of survivors would be, for the most part, committed to a sea of wilderness. They could clear a path, but he still felt trapped. Perhaps he convinced the others, yet failed to convince himself. He whispered, *Oh God, will this be a valley of life, or a valley of death?*

He looked at the anxious faces. "Are you ready?"

There was some hesitation, but one by one, heads began nodding in agreement. "Stay behind the rocks, or go back to the campsite."

When the family was safe, he backed up a few yards and stepped behind a big rock. He started to pick up the detonating wires, but his hands shook so hard he could barely make himself touch them. His knees became weak and beads of perspiration popped out on his fore-head. *This is harder than I thought it would be. God, help me stay strong.* And, with that, he set off the charge.

The ground shook as rolling rocks were heard falling into place. Craig saw a small cloud of grey dust rising in the air just around the curve. Linda stood up and Craig looked her way. She gave him a thumbs up and a smile. He heard her say, "Come on, Caleb. Let's fix lunch. I'm hungry."

"Me too. Can we have macaroni and cheese?"

"Sure, but are you going to help me make it?"

"Yes, I am! Are you coming, Daddy?"

"You guys go ahead. I'll be right there. I'm going to take care of Grandma."

Richard walked up to him, "Are you okay man?"

"I am now, but when I knew it was time to set off the charge, I felt like someone punched me in the gut. A thousand pounds of reality fell on me."

Richard patted his friend's shoulder, then escorted his own family down the trail.

Craig sat down on the seat next to his Mom and she said, "I know that was tough, son, but it had to be done. Keep remembering you did it to protect us."

"I'll be fine. Just a bit overwhelmed. This is a huge undertaking, Mom." He barely finished speaking when quick footsteps approached from behind.

"You better be right, Craig! That's all I have to say! It will be very hard for us to get out of here now. You've sealed us in this God forsaken valley. Now what do we do? Tell me. What do we do? I don't plan to camp for the rest of my life!"

Craig's grip on the steering wheel tightened, and without turning around he said, "Duane. Go see if your mother needs help with your lunch."

"I mean it, Craig! I—"

Before he could finish Craig set his jaw, whipped around and said, "Now!"

Duane started to say something else, thought better of it, and stormed off.

Lois reached up and patted Craig's hand. "I would have punched him."

Craig put his head back and laughed. "I believe you. I've wanted to punch him many times, but I love his sister too much. Besides, she'd kill me."

Craig knew his contempt for Duane was growing deeper each day, and at times—moment by moment.

"He drives me crazy, Mom. He's thirty years old. I don't think he has a muscle anywhere on his body. If nothing else, maybe this elongated camping trip will help make a man of him."

"We can always hope."

CHAPTER 21

THE CAVES

*A*fter lunch, Craig asked Richard to take a walk with him. Craig tried to reach Leon again, but still no answer.

"I don't like this. What are we going to do if we've lost permanent contact with him?"

Richard shook his head. "I really don't know. All we can do is keep trying."

They sat on a rock for a few minutes then Craig said, "Let's get busy. We have a lot to do."

Craig wanted to look at the canyon first.

They stood for a moment, then Richard said, "I get a backache just thinking about moving those rocks. They're not that big, but there are so many."

"I feel your pain. I just hope it was the right decision to put them there."

"I think we had no choice, and it's done. Tomorrow lets get a crew together and formulate that zigzag path we talked about. But, right now let's go look at the caves."

Two caves, about twenty feet apart, were embedded under the canyon wall, west of the camp. A few scattered trees and tall patches of dry grass served as a welcome barrier.

Craig said, "I'm glad these are not visible from the huts."

The small cave sat to the left. The entrance was approximately six feet tall and four feet wide. When Craig stepped inside he smiled, and motioned for Richard to join him. They stood a moment listening to the soft sound of a flowing stream.

"Well, that's a relief," Craig said. "No matter what else happens, we know we'll have fresh water."

Craig walked around the stream, then an outcropping of rocks. In front of him was an opening. "I hope we never have to maneuver this corridor again, but at least it comes out close to where we hid the trucks."

Richard agreed.

As they approached the larger cave, Craig was first to hear the sound of breaking brush. An animal was running toward them from the direction of the woods. He raised his rifle and they both stepped back watching the area. Big Ben came bounding through the brush. He ran around their legs then sat down on his haunches panting.

"Boy! You don't know how lucky you are," Craig said, lowering his rifle.

When they peered into the large cave, Big Ben was hot on their trail. The opening was over six foot tall, and several inches wider than the small cave. The chamber was large with a natural chimney.

Craig took one step inside. "We can store a lot of stuff in here. We could even use it as a refuge, if the need arose." He took a quick step back and said, "What is that awful smell?"

A ridge of hair stood straight up on Big Ben's back. He hunched down and gave out a low growl. Craig patted him on the head. "I don't blame you. That's a terrible smell. Something must have died in here. When we have more time we've got to find the source or this cave will be useless."

Richard shined his flashlight in every direction, but saw no reason for the overpowering odor. Ben backed up until he cleared the door then took off running through a clearing in the woods.

"He acts like he's scared," Richard said. "I've never seen him run that fast."

Craig looked around. "Keep your rifle ready, just in case."

When they were comfortable no wild animals were lurking, Craig said, "Before we head back, I want to talk about the food situation. Mom says it's going way too fast. At this rate, she said supplies would be dangerously short in a couple of months. We have to stop the munching."

Richard suggested they select someone to be the food and supplies czar.

"What about your mom, Craig? She's tough."

Craig laughed. "How about your dad?"

Richard nodded his head. "That's a good idea, but I'm thinking, since you're the leader and all, you get to pick one, or at least ask them. I don't want that kind of fire."

"Coward! I'll ask Mom. She's always worrying about being a burden. This would be a good role for her. If your dad is willing to help, he could do the leg work."

"Sounds like a plan to me, now why don't you head back to camp, and ask them?"

"I have a better idea." Craig said. "We'll ask them together. If they accept, and if the smell is gone, we'll use our master craftsman skills and frame in the large caves opening first, then build and hang a door."

Richard laughed, "Sounds good—and so out of our skill level."

Lois and Darren were sitting by the fire ring when Craig and Richard arrived back in camp.

"Hey there," Craig said. "Just the two people we want to talk to."

"That sounds ominous," Darren said. "What did we do?"

"It isn't what you did, it's what we want you to do. We want you to take charge of distributing food and supplies."

He told them about the caves, the potential storage area, and how fast the food was being used.

Lois and Darren looked at each other. Darren said, "So what do you think?"

Lois said, "I think it's a great idea. I would love to help, but I'll have to do my work from here."

Darren said he would ask Joliene to partner with them, and he would check out the cave the following day. Craig warned him of the rank smell, and told him not to go alone.

"Don't ever go up there without your rifle. Both caves are out of sight of the camp," Craig said.

CHAPTER 22

ATTACK

*A*fter breakfast, Craig was standing by the campfire drinking coffee, when a loud scream came from the direction of the caves.

"Help me! Somebody help me!"

He ran into the middle hut, grabbed his rifle then fired one shot over the treetops.

Richard flung open his fifth wheel door. "What's going on?"

Craig yelled over his shoulder, "Grab your rifle. Sounds like some-one's in trouble near the caves."

Richard and Nathaniel caught up to Craig just in time to hear a fierce growl from what sounded like a large creature. It was running from the scene. They raised their rifles then heard again, "Help me. Help…"

Richard yelled, "That's Dad."

Darren was lying face down just outside the large cave with blood oozing from his head.

Richard fell to his knees and placed two fingers on his dad's carotid artery. "He has a pulse, but his breathing is very shallow. Nathaniel, help me roll him over. I need to see where the blood's coming from."

Craig stood over the two men, rifle ready, surveying the immediate area. If the attacker were a bear, it would not be easily intimidated.

Richard found two deep puncture wounds in the hairline just above the left temple. Darren's face was covered in blood and he was unconscious. Craig glanced down long enough to see Richard fumbling with the buttons on his flannel shirt.

Richard threw it aside, then pulled his undershirt over his head. He rolled it, then pressed it hard against his dad's wounds, "Can someone get my truck, please?"

Craig grabbed Richard's rifle and pushed it into Nathaniel's hand. "Keep this ready. The smell of blood may draw that creature back."

Nathaniel looked a little surprised but he couldn't stop a nervous grin from spreading across his face. "You bet . . . no problem."

Craig met all the family members, except Lois, running toward the cave. He knew it would do no good to tell them to go back, and he didn't have time to argue, but he did stop Linda long enough to tell her not to faint when she saw Nathaniel with a rifle.

Lois was sitting outside Craig's fifth wheel with her back to the woods, watching the rest of the family running toward the caves.

"I hate being so immobile!" Her walker was usually close by, but before all the excitement, Caleb was using it as a rocket launcher against invisible enemies. Even if it were close, she would not be able to maneuver the rough path to the caves. She sat helpless, craning her neck. Everyone was out of sight.

After what seemed like an eternity, but in reality was only a couple of minutes, she heard brush breaking from the area of the woods and felt a great wave of relief.

"Hey! What happened over there? Who was yelling? Is somebody hurt?"

The movement stopped for a second then she pinched her nose. "What is that awful smell?"

She heard a deep grunt, then heavy, shuffling footsteps, approaching from behind. When the portable barbecue crashed to the ground she looked over her shoulder and gasped. A large brown bear was rounding the end of Craig's fifth wheel. It threw its head to the left then dropped its chin. When it saw Lois it began a slow saunter in her direction.

She pushed hard on the arms of the chair, but her legs were too weak to lift her body. She lost her balance, fell to the ground, and watched in horror as the bear methodically made its way toward her, snorting and grunting. He circled her chair then positioned himself right in front of her. She knew he was satisfied that his prey was trapped then he moved in for the kill.

Lois covered her head and cried, "Help me God."

The bear laid his great head back, and split the air with a thundering, victorious, growl then looked right at her. Its breath touched her face then his monstrous claws swept the air in a simulated boxing match. Her pounding heart drowned out the rest of his threats. She barely heard the two rapid shots that rang through the air, reverberating across the hillside.

Lois peeked through her fingers just in time to see the great beast stumble backwards and fall with a thud. It lay motionless on the ground.

Craig poked at the still body, convinced himself it was dead then knelt in front of his mother. He could not tell which of them was shaking the most.

"Mom, I'm so sorry. Are you okay?"

Lois could barely speak. "I tried to scream, but my throat was frozen." She caught her breath, shuddered, and shook her head. "Did you see the size of those claws, and his teeth? He was getting ready to take me apart. I thought I was a goner."

He hugged her and said, "Not while I'm around."

"Its kind of funny—in a way. I was sitting here feeling sorry for myself because I was missing all the action. Crazy, huh? What happened up there?"

"It was Darren, Mom. He has a head injury and needs a ride. I'm pretty sure you were not the first person the bear visited. Thank God I came back to get the truck. I have to leave you again long enough to pick him up."

Lois grabbed his hand and squeezed it tight. "As long as you're sure it's dead."

"I'm sure. I'll let you hold my rifle, and I'll send Nathaniel right back." He pointed, "We're just over there by the caves."

Craig settled his mom in a chair, put the walker within reach then laid his rifle across her lap. Before he could start the truck engine Nathaniel ran into camp.

"What's going on, Dad? Why did you fire your rifle?"

"Hey! Who's guarding the cave?"

"Mom took my rifle so I could run back and check on you."

"Well, I'm glad you're here. I can't believe I'm saying this, but I killed a bear. It's lying right in front of your grandma. Please stay with her until I get back, but announce yourself. She's holding my rifle and might be a little trigger happy."

Nathaniel ran around the fifth wheel yelling, "Grandma, it's me. Don't shoot." Before Craig reached the truck he heard Nathaniel say, "Oh! That's a big one!"

Craig backed his truck up the hill around trees and through the stubborn brush until he was a few feet from the family. Darren was sitting up with Richard's blood-stained undershirt wrapped around his head.

Richard said, "We heard rifle shots. Is everything okay?"

"It is now. I got back to camp just in time." Craig took a deep breath. "There was a bear standing right over mom."

Everyone gasped in unison.

Richard said, "What? You can't be serious."

"Don't worry. I killed it. Those were the shots you heard."

Linda's eyes were wide. "Is she okay?"

"She is now. She may have a few bruises, but mostly she's pretty shaken up. Nathaniel stayed with her. Let's hurry and get Darren back to camp, in case the bear was not alone. I have no idea what we're going to do with the carcass."

Craig and Richard helped Darren into the truck bed. Richard and Linda climbed in next to him. Tracey demanded her three kids, and Caleb, climb into the cab and stay there, until *she* gave them permission to get out. Craig asked the rest of the crew to walk in front of the truck. He was pretty sure the bear was a loner, but not absolutely certain. Two dangerous surprises were enough for one day.

Craig and Richard helped Darren climb the three steps into his camper. The bear was not visible from this location, but they heard gasps from those who were seeing it for the first time. The smelly giant hump lay right in front of Lois. The parade of onlookers, frozen in place, stood in dead silence. Caleb escaped the truck, and ran to his mom. Tracey's kids were right behind him.

Nathaniel said, "It's okay guys, he's dead and Grandma's fine. Come take a look."

Tracey yelled to her kids, "You three certainly will not! Get in the fifth wheel!"

Lois said, "Tracey, let them look. They'll probably never be this close to a bear again."

Tracey put the back of her hand on her forehead. "Make it quick then get inside. Am I the only one who recognizes how dangerous this place is?"

Brianna and the three little ones crept forward and stopped behind Lois's chair. Sara put her hands over her mouth and her eyes were wide. She took several steps back then ran to her mother. Cassie asked if someone would take pictures of it.

Craig frowned when Tracey demanded her children get in the fifth wheel. Just as their door closed she heard Chad say, "Mom, why do I have to miss out on all the fun?"

"Fun? You call this fun? Not in my book."

Craig whispered, *"Poor Richard,"* then ran to check on Darren.

After Darren was settled in bed, Richard covered him with a blanket.

"Dad, you were not supposed to go to the caves by yourself, and you're not supposed to be the one getting hurt. You're the doctor."

"Sorry, son, but I'm sure my wounds are superficial. My right rib is sore. I must have fallen on something. My bleeding stopped pretty quickly. That's a good sign. Head injuries can bleed like crazy, and appear more serious than they are."

"As soon as you feel like it, can you tell us what happened?"

An involuntary shudder came over Darren, and he snuggled a little deeper under the blanket. "Actually, I think I'd like to talk about it now. After you asked me to make an inventory list, I decided to check out the caves. I never considered it could be dangerous. When I shined my flashlight in the larger one, I must have startled the bear. He came out with a vengeance and charged me. I started to run, fell backwards, and had just gotten to my feet when he swung me around. His claws sunk into my scalp, and I started yelling. He poked at me a few times. I thought I was done for. The rifle shot must have scared him. I'm sure that's the only thing that saved me."

"He didn't run far." Craig said. "I still can't believe he came into our camp."

Richard's eyes were wide. "I've got to see that thing. Your poor mom, she must have been terrified."

"She was. When she fell out of her chair she got covered in mud. She'll probably be sore for a while. Thank God, the bear didn't touch her, and in spite of her trauma, she was still concerned about you, Darren."

"Poor lady. Imagine how helpless she felt. Give me a few minutes then I'll check her out."

Craig stood up. "We'll keep an eye on her. If she needs to see you we'll bring her by. Lucky for us that bear wasn't in the cave yesterday! His scent was so strong we must have just missed him."

"I'll be back in a few minutes, Dad. Craig and I better take a look at the carcass and figure out what to do with it. I'm sure my wife has the kids in solitary confinement by now. I'm probably in for it too."

Darren said, "I'm sorry son. Tracey needs to lighten up. You might tell her, we can fight animals, but we were helpless against the virus."

"I like that. Can I quote you?"

"You go right ahead. By the way, how much experience do you guys have in dressing out bears?"

Craig looked at Richard. "Well, counting this one—none. There's always the possibility of winging it."

Darren laughed. "Sounds to me like, unless you're planning on eating the meat, or making a bear rug, you should haul it out of camp and burn it. You don't want the smell of blood drawing other animals here. Now, get out of here and let me rest a few minutes."

Richard handed him the hand radio. "Call me if you need anything."

When they opened the door, Joliene was just ready to knock. "How is he? Is there anything I can do?"

Darren heard her, "Sure come on in. I could use a good nurse, and a pretty one at that. These two sure don't make the grade. Is Lois still doing okay?"

"She's still pretty shaken. I think her only injury is a sore bottom, and I doubt she lets you look at that."

CHAPTER 23

DEALING WITH A CARCASS

On Craig's way to the fallen bear, Caleb ran out of the fifth wheel straight into his arms.

"What's wrong, son?"

"I can't find Big Ben. I thought he was with Nathaniel, but he's not. I can't find him."

"I'm sure he's around here somewhere." Craig said. "You keep calling. If he doesn't come back soon, I'll look for him, but you're not to search by yourself. Do you understand?"

"I promise. But what if he doesn't come back?"

Craig swallowed hard. "I'm sure he will. He's probably out investigating the area." Craig put his finger on the tip of Caleb's nose. "You stay in the camp."

Caleb said, "Yes, sir. I will."

Linda was a few feet away putting some wood in the fire pit. Caleb ran straight to her and buried his face in her lap. She looked across at Craig and nodded in agreement. When Caleb was out of earshot, Craig asked every family member if they had seen the dog. No one had.

"I haven't seen him since yesterday," Richard said. "Come to think of it, he wasn't here during all the excitement. I can't imagine him letting a bear get that close without warning us."

Craig whistled several times, but there was no response. Big Ben was the only pet they brought to the valley. He was a three-year-old King Chocolate Lab, and Caleb's constant companion. The dog's lack of response worried Craig.

"I hope he's not out hunting," Craig said, as he took a quick sweep of the woods. "He's fast, but no match for what *might* be out there."

Richard said, "Sorry buddy, but we better get down to business. We have a bear carcass to deal with."

Richard and Nathaniel helped Craig roll the giant creature onto a tarp.

"This monster must weigh five or six hundred pounds." Craig said. "I'm glad you guys have muscles."

Once it was evenly placed they put ropes through the grommets on all four sides. Craig threw two shovels and a pick in the back of the truck. Richard tied a knot on each end of the rope then threw one on each side of the tailgate before pushing it closed. A light rain began to fall again, and there was an instant drop in the temperature.

Craig took a quick glance at the dark clouds. "Nathaniel, would you grab our heavier rain jackets? Get the ones with BLM on the back. They're fleece lined. I think we're going to need them."

Richard drove through the tall grass and over the soft mud at a snails pace. Craig and Nathaniel walked alongside, keeping an eye on the tarp. When Richard stopped at the potential site, Craig grabbed the pickaxe and drove its tip into the ground.

"I think we're going to be here all night. It gives me a backache just thinking about it. It would be nice to have more help."

He glanced toward camp and said, "Duane is nowhere to be found, as usual."

"Let it go Craig. He would do nothing but complain, and irritate you the whole time. You know it. There's no reason Chad can't help. I'll be right back."

When Chad arrived he ran straight to the bear, and knelt down. He lifted its giant paws then ran his fingers across the claws.

"Wow, these could do some serious damage. Grandpa and Lois were very lucky."

"You got that right," Richard said. "By the way Craig, Linda said to tell you, Caleb cried himself to sleep at nap time. He's really missing his dog."

"Poor little guy." Craig stared at the dark woods, whistled, then listened. "I don't know where to begin to look. We can't do anything about it now. If he's not back by morning, let's do a *limited* search. I don't want anyone going deep into that forest until we get a better lay of the land, and what's inhabiting it."

It was dusk before the pit was finished. Craig cut away a thick layer of fur, then sliced off three large chunks of meat.

"We'll use this and try our hand at making Ben some jerky."

He took white gas from a container in the truck, and poured some into the pit. He twisted a large wad of grass, lit its end and dropped it. A flash of flames shot upward then quickly swept across the top before sinking into the deeper layers of wood.

They watched the flames for a minute then Craig said, "Listen boys, once we roll the bear into the fire, the smell will be hard to take. You guys should head back to camp. It won't be quite as pungent there."

Both boys assured him they would be fine and pleaded to stay. Richard nodded his okay so Craig said okay too. He did ask them to go back to camp long enough to grab bandanas, some food, and warn everyone what was getting ready to happen.

Richard said, "What about me? Can I go back?"

Craig looked his way and laughed. "Not a chance."

The boys returned with peanut butter and jelly sandwiches on biscuits, plus some water and coffee.

They ate first then Craig warned that rolling the bear in the pit would not be an easy task. He was right. It took determination, and muscle, but they did it. As soon as the fur began to singe the boys knew Craig had not exaggerated. The pungent smell was nauseating, and lingered in the air. They covered their nose with a bandana, and for a while, stuck their face inside their jacket.

At three in the morning, Craig looked into the pit at the display of charred bones spread across the glowing embers.

"Everything happened so fast. It was a magnificent animal, but I would rather be looking at its remains than grieving the loss of our parents."

Richard put his hand on Craig's shoulder. "You got that right. Now, let's go back to camp. We can fill in the pit later."

After a quick shower, Richard climbed into bed. He punched his pillows a couple of time, pulled the blanket over his shoulder then slipped his arm around his wife. She folded her body into his, gave his hand a squeeze then held it against her chest. Richard was exhausted, but he lay with his eyes open for a long time thinking about her. *This unrefined life might be more than she can handle. If only there had been another way—another place. If only I could keep her this close all the time.*

The following morning, Craig was happy to see his Mom and Darren standing by the fire pit, swapping bear stories. Darren said he was feeling okay except for a headache. Lois mentioned she had some bruising, but didn't state where it was. They both were thankful to be alive.

Before breakfast Craig took his rifle, and walked down by the lake. He worked his way up a small incline near the woods, whistled for the dog then listened. There was no response. He whistled several more times to no avail. He had no clue how to explain this to Caleb.

Craig temporarily gave up the search and called Richard. "Lets try Leon again."

CHAPTER 24

SEVERE CARNAGE

*W*hen Leon's phone rang the sixth time, Craig sighed. He was just getting ready to express his frustration when he received a call. It came from a number he did not recognize, but the voice was familiar.

Leon launched right in, and spoke so softly they could barely understand what he was saying. "I don't know how long I can talk, so let me go first, please. Are you at the destination we talked about, and are you safe?"

Craig put his phone on speaker and said, "Yes."

"I want to keep track of you as long as I can. If you're able to survive where you are, I recommend you stay put."

Richard started to say something, but barely got a word out when Leon whispered, "I need you both to listen for a minute. Every person in this facility had their cell phones confiscated except for the vice president, and his personal team. The rest of us were told our GPS might be compromised. We knew it wasn't true, but we didn't argue. That's why you haven't been able to reach me. One of my staff located a few of the untraceable phones in…well I better not say where. I'm linked to the same Canadian satellite you're using. It has an effective scrambler that hasn't been hacked, at least for now."

Craig felt his heart sink. "We're in the dark, Leon. You're the only outside contact we have. Can you tell us what's going on state side? Canada's news has been pretty sketchy."

"There's only one briefing a day," Leon said. "We meet with the vice presidents cronies at six o'clock in the morning."

Richard jumped in. "Who do they get their information from?"

"It isn't who, it's what. They monitor surveillance cameras twenty-four hours a day. There are approximately a hundred thousand active ones scattered throughout the nation, including a tiny camera called the *EYE*. The Department of Transportation installed those on every officially recognized speed limit sign. It was part of the Shovel Ready Program. It took two years. The project ended exactly three months before the initial attack."

"How is the *EYE* being used?" Craig asked.

"We were told it's used to spot movement. We found out the places it pin pointed were attacked soon after."

"This is crazy. Why are the attackers not being identified?" Craig was angry. "It makes no sense."

"I know. It doesn't make...hold on."

Leon's line stayed open, but all Craig and Richard could hear was muffled conversation. They could make out no words.

Five minutes later Leon came back, again speaking softly. "Sorry guys. I had to shove my phone in my pocket. Thank God I heard him approaching before he opened my door."

"Do you need to hang up?" Craig asked.

"Not yet. Let me tell you one more thing. Two months ago, in Los Angeles, five days went by without a drone sweep. On the sixth day a few people ventured out. On the seventh day a few more did the same. Stores began opening and people were excited to shop. On the eighth day the freeways were full. There was no all clear given by any government agency, but it was obvious that people were feeling relief."

"What happened?" Craig asked.

"At five in the afternoon, with the sun behind them, drones began sweeping the roadways. It was total carnage. I won't even try to describe what we saw. That's why I want you to stay put."

Craig and Richard were stunned.

"I'll communicate with you as long as I can, and try to find a safe place for you to relocate in Canada. It may take awhile. If they discover I have this phone I don't know what will happen. You can try me anytime, on the number that came up, but my phone will be on silent, including its buzz. Never leave a message. If I don't answer, there's a good reason. Take care my friends."

With that, Leon was gone. Craig and Richard looked at each other. Neither spoke a word as they walked back to camp.

CHAPTER 25

BALANCING THE BURDEN

*B*y early afternoon the next day, Craig and Richard finished framing both cave doors while Darren looked on, rifle in hand. The sky was a brilliant blue and the sun was warm. They were able to work in short sleeves, and by mid afternoon they were thankful for any shade. Craig was sure these days would be few and far between. When they finished their work, Darren pretended to do a close inspection.

"Not bad for a couple of geologists. I could have done better, of course."

Craig said, "Trust me, you'll get your chance. At least you're willing. Have either of you seen Duane today?"

Richard said, "I heard Joliene say he's sick. I saw her taking him his breakfast."

Craig laid his hammer down. "I've had enough of this. I'll be right back."

Duane was sitting with Joliene outside the middle hut. Craig walked toward them, said good morning then yelled over his shoulder, "Nathaniel, can you and Chad help your Uncle Duane build a smaller fire pit? Your grandma wants to start the jerky today before the meat spoils."

"Of course I will."

"You don't mind heading this project up, do you Duane?" With that, Craig turned and walked away.

Duane crossed his arms, and dropped his head into his chest. His wispy chin hair floated over the first two buttons of his jacket. After a few deep sighs, he pushed out of his lawn chair and slammed it shut. "Come on guys! Start gathering rocks. Let's get this over with."

When the smaller pit was finished, Duane disappeared again. Craig asked the boys to start replacing the larger, temporary fire ring, with a permanent one. Not only could the family cook and gather there, it would help illuminate the area. Both pits would sit on the West side of the huts toward the front. He hoped they would also help deter wild animals.

Caleb, Cassie and Sara pitched in. The rocks they gathered were much smaller than needed, but Craig was pleased when Nathaniel and Chad found a spot for each contribution. On the other hand, when he passed by the huts his insides boiled. He heard Duane complaining about his sore back and calluses. Craig wanted to say something, but kept his thoughts to himself. *Thank you God for the rest of the family. Even the children are on board.*

Craig asked Darren and Chad to take a shift turning the meat, until midnight. Darren put up a pup tent. The temperature would drop considerably, as it did every night. Chad told Craig he was looking forward to spending time with his Grandpa.

"We're going to play board games and talk. Grandpa has a lot of great stories."

At 11:30, Craig and Richard checked on them. Darren said, "I was not expecting blessings in this valley, but I was wrong. My grandson is quality all the way. I wouldn't trade the time we're spending together for anything. Why did it take a crisis to make this happen?"

"Thanks, Dad. I think all of us were caught up in the *good life*, traveling in different directions. Chad is a great son. I wish I could take credit for how he's turning out, but that belongs to Tracey. You know how much time I'm away."

In spite of his feigned illnesses and grumbling, Craig insisted Duane help Nathaniel with the night shift, beginning at midnight. At four in the morning, Craig went to check on them, and was surprised to see Darren sitting with Nathaniel instead of Duane.

"Nathaniel, where's your Uncle?"

"He didn't show up. Darren stayed with me and sent Chad to bed."

Craig took a deep breath then walked away. He saw Joliene sitting at the table working a puzzle so he knocked lightly.

"Hi, Craig. Is everything okay?"

"Well, not really. I'm looking for Duane. I want to ask him why he left Nathaniel alone to watch the meat?"

"Oh my goodness. I didn't know he did that. I'll go ask him."

He could hear a buzz of conversation, and about five minutes later she returned, fully dressed, coat in hand. "I'm sorry, Craig. He said when his alarm went off, he was so dizzy he had to lie back down. I'll take care of the rest of his shift. Just let me get my shoes. I can't sleep anyway. I'll stay until the meat's done."

"Weren't you planning to help Mom and Darren with the inventory after breakfast? How can you do both?"

"I'll figure it out. I'll just grab a quick nap later."

"That's too much. If you finish the shift with Nathaniel, I'll get someone else to help with the inventory. Tell Duane to come see me when he gets up. Okay?"

She hesitated, "Well...I guess so."

Craig clenched his fists, "Thank you Joliene." When he walked out the door, it took every fiber he had not to slam it.

He loved his mother-in-law, and respected her highly. Her husband abandoned the family when Linda and Duane were very young. She was a hard worker, and rarely complained about anything. She could handle both jobs, but why should she? Duane benefited from all the work others were doing, yet offered very little in return.

Craig walked back to his own unit, stomped up the stairs, and this time he *did* slam the door. Linda came stumbling out of the bedroom area. "What's going on?"

"If someone doesn't do something about your brother I'm going to. I'm so angry I can hardly see. He didn't show up for his night shift! He made no arrangements for anyone to take his place, so Darren stayed over so Nathaniel wouldn't be alone. Everyone was given a specific job, and now not only was Darren willing to do double duty, after being mauled by a bear, your mom volunteered to spend the rest of the night with Nathaniel, and then help with the inventory tomorrow . . . rather today."

"Calm down, sweetheart. Why didn't Duane show up?"

Craig told her about her brother's dizzy spell, and barely got the words out of his mouth when Linda's face turned crimson. She grabbed her coat, threw on her boots and said, "I'll be right back. Duane better be sick. One thing I won't let him do is dump his load on Mom and, he left Nathaniel alone in the night?" She headed out the door.

She stuck her head back inside long enough to say, "Stay in here. Caleb keeps waking up crying. Big Ben has been gone too long."

"I will." He felt bad about Caleb and the dog, but he could not stop the smile that was spreading across his face. Linda's hurried footsteps were crunching down the rock path. "Sure glad it's Duane, and not me."

Ten minutes later when Linda returned, her eyes were wild. "I'll be assisting with the inventory, and Duane will be joining us, as soon as the meat is finished, and the fire pit is cleaned. He's already taken a nice long nap."

Craig wanted to ask what happened, but knew better. He simply said, "Okay honey." He waited a few minutes then went back outside. When he walked by the fire pit Duane was sitting in a lawn chair, arms folded across his chest.

"Glad to see you're feeling better, Duane."

Without looking up, Duane grunted, stood, and turned a row of meat.

Later in the morning, with rifle in hand, Craig searched the area around the caves for Ben then made his way back to camp. Just before he reached the large fire pit he whistled. Off in the distance, from the direction of the lake, he heard two faint barks, which quickly turned to loud yelps. It was obvious Ben was headed for camp.

Craig could hear brush breaking. He knew Ben was running fast, but had no idea if the dog was being chased or doing the chasing. The family was scattered throughout the compound. He couldn't protect all of them if the dog was leading a wild animal into camp.

With his rifle ready, Craig yelled, "Heads up! Ben's running this way—fast!"

The dog broke through the woods, and to Craig's relief, there was nothing in front or behind him, but it didn't take long to figure out what the problem was. Ben's smell preceded him. He lost in an encounter with a skunk, and was running straight for Craig.

"No, Ben! No! Sit!"

Every part of the dog's body was moving. He struggled to be obedient, but was twitching all over.

"Ben, Ben. Now, what do I do?"

He pointed his finger at his pet. "Stay!"

He found the chain, cinched it and the dog to a tree then went to find Darren. Surely a doctor would know how to get the smell off.

Darren laughed, and told Craig the tomato juice theory. "It may be an old wives tale, but it's my best suggestion."

Craig sighed, "We can't afford to use our food to wash a dog. Surely there's something else we can do."

"Try liquid laundry detergent then rinse him with a strong vinegar solution. It might tone the smell down a little."

Craig did as Darren suggested without any help from the family. The smell was subdued, but that evening when he brought Ben to the campfire everyone scattered to the opposite side.

CHAPTER 26

PREPARING FOR WINTER

Craig hoped to be out of the valley long before winter, but knew he could not assume such a thing. Winter would come fast with an unforgiving vengeance, and last for a long time. To be unprepared would bring serious trouble, danger and potential death. He called Richard and Darren aside to finish working on plans, and timetables.

"First, the animal's dwelling has to be winterized and equipped with a simple heating unit." Craig said. "A small rock fireplace with good venting, similar to the large one we plan to install would work. If we keep large rocks in the bottom they will hold enough heat to make it through the night."

Darren said, "We can make bales from dry grass, and cover the stall floors with loose stuff. Its' crude—but it should work."

Because summer would bring extended sunlight, Craig knew a garden could be planted and replanted as long as possible. He also knew the largest projects would be the rock fireplace and porch.

Craig said, "We have a lot of able bodied people to assign tasks to. We need to get started. Cabin fever is very real. If it sets in, we'll all be looking for a hole to crawl in."

"I've been itching to start cutting the lodge poles and firewood," Richard said.

"Darren, would you stay with him just in case his fingers get in the way, or he forgets to duck?"

Darren laughed. "Funny! It's not *his* fingers and head I'm worried about. It's my own."

Craig said, "I think you have a point there. I'll have the boys do something safer. We have a lot of brush to clear and holes to dig. They can work close to the huts. I'll do the part closest to the woods. When you guys have a batch of trees ready, we'll start hauling them in. Be sure to take your rifles every time you leave camp. One shot will always mean *heads up* and we'll head your way. Two shots indicate a threat. We'll come running."

Richard laughed then said, "These are some lofty plans. I believe we can accomplish all of them, but when we're done, and a good wind comes up, you'll find me in the cave."

"No worries my friend. We've got this," Craig said. "Three of the brightest minds this side of Wilson Creek, are working on it. How could anything go wrong?"

Darren said, "Oh, so you're saying the ladies are building it!"

After enjoying more good laughs, they took measurements then inventoried the building materials. Craig wanted to avoid buying any from Wilson Creek if possible. He wanted no one asking what they were building or their whereabouts.

Craig was pleased with the progress the family was making. After clearing away more brush around the huts he asked Richard to walk with him toward the canyon.

"It's been three weeks since we talked to Leon. Let's see if we have any luck."

Leon answered after the third ring. He spoke in a very quiet voice, but this time, Craig felt Leon was forcing words. He knew something was seriously wrong.

Craig asked, "Leon, what's going on? Are you okay?"

Leon's voice was barely above a whisper, but every word he spoke was audible and full of agony.

"I haven't been able to answer our girls' calls all the time, but yesterday I did. My little one, Marie, was so excited. She said the rain had stopped so they were having a picnic on the porch."

Craig felt a knot growing in his stomach. "What happened?"

"My oldest told her to look at the tiny plane."

"I yelled at them to run inside."

Richard gasped. "Oh no."

"They said their noses were bleeding . . . then . . . we heard them die! Oh God! We heard them die. They were crying and asking us for help. They were gone in less than ten minutes. We were helpless. There was nothing we could do."

Craig's head dropped on his chest and tears rolled down Richard's face.

Craig swallowed hard and cleared his throat. "We are so sorry."

"They're probably still lying where they died. We can't even bury them. We're still under orders to shelter in place, and even if we could leave, there's no fuel available, and there's no safe direction to travel in."

Craig said, "I wish you could come to us. We feel pretty safe here."

"I hate to tell you guys this, but Canada is suffering more attacks too. They're not as far north as you are, but keep your eyes and ears open." Leon's voice dropped to a whisper.

"Someone's coming. I have to go."

And with that, the line went dead.

Craig sat down on a boulder, and put his head in his hands. "We complained about the rain all the way home from North Dakota and while we packed the rigs. We had no idea it was saving us. It all makes sense now. Poor Leon and Jeanette. How will they live with such pain?"

An involuntary shudder passed through Craig's body. He barely whispered. "If anything happened to my kids, I don't think I could take it."

Richard said, "We've tried to be straightforward with our family, since this thing started, but I think the loss of those children, and their grandmother is something we need to keep quiet about. Do you agree?"

"Yes, I will never get the pain in Leon's voice out of my head. There's no reason to put it in someone else's."

The following day, Craig went on line. He was happy to find a live broadcast coming from a small television affiliate in Spokane, Washington, until he heard the anchor, Bennett Wilson say, "Our broadcasts have been spotty, but this will be our last one. Until we meet again, may God be with you. Pray for the day He will bless, and restore this nation."

The next two days, Craig looked for other live communication from America. There was none. He did manage to find a Canadian station that gave the same report Leon had given. America was being destroyed, and Canada was facing limited, but deadly attacks.

Craig found Richard and gave him the unwelcome news.

"This is going to be hard for everyone, but we have to tell them. They have the right to know." Richard buried his face in his hands and wept.

Craig squeezed his shoulder. "You're right buddy. They do." Tears welled in Craig's eyes too, and his voice broke as he went on.

"Faces keep flashing through my mind. Our friends and family are scattered all over the nation. I wonder how many made it to safety? I have so many questions. Was there anything in the Bible about this? If there was why didn't we pay attention and prepare ourselves? Will the attack spread to other countries besides America and Canada? Imagine the depth of planning and intelligence it took to organize a terrorist attack of this magnitude."

Richard wiped his eyes. "I don't have any answers. I only know we're still alive. We didn't have much time to prepare, and here we are in the wilderness, unable to anticipate what's coming next. The bear attack proved that."

"All we can do is anticipate as many scenarios as possible. We can't cover everything, but the more prepared we are the better our chance of survival will be. Our family needs to understand how serious things have become without scaring them to death."

"I don't think that's possible, but maybe we can soften it a little."

Craig said, "They've gotten pretty tough. The more they know the truth, and help with the planning, the less fearful they'll be. Lets face it, buddy, we live in a state of survival mode."

"I can't argue with that."

"Richard, since we're talking, I feel I should tell you, Linda and I are worried about Tracey. She's very quiet and rarely speaks unless she's spoken too."

"I'm worried too. This is so hard for her. I think she lives in fear of losing more of her family. That's why I don't want her to know about Leon's daughters."

"I totally agree." Craig said.

"When her mother died, she was pregnant with Sara, and Cassie was only two. Can you imagine how painful it was when her dad committed suicide one month later? She lived a pretty sheltered life, but since those deaths, she's suffered with serious bouts of depression. Of all the people in our party, except Duane, she's probably the least equipped to face this hardship."

"Sorry buddy. I ask myself every day if moving here was the right thing to do, but neither you nor I could think of a better option. We would've lived in fear all the time. Just let us know if there's anything we can do."

"Thanks, I will. If you're patient, and keep giving her a little space, she'll come around." Richard stood up. "Are we ready?"

Craig took a deep breath. "As ready as we'll ever be. Let's wait until after dinner. You go first. Linda says I don't show much sensitivity."

"Okay, but I'm not looking forward to it."

CHAPTER 27

BREAKING THE NEWS

*C*raig and Richard waited until the evening meal was finished, then Richard interrupted the chatter by asking if he could have everyone's attention.

Duane muttered "What now?"

Craig did not respond to the comment, but his fists were so tight they left deep impressions in his palms.

Richard said, "We received some hard news today, and it's only fair we keep you guys in the loop. We hear very little from American broadcasters, but Edmonton reported attacks have now covered the width and the breath of our country—and expanded into southern and eastern Canada."

No one spoke or moved—except Tracey, who motioned for Cassie and Sara to sit next to her. Chad stood behind, placing both hands on her shoulders.

Richard scrolled the room. "If you have something to say, now is the time. In fact, we welcome it."

The few moments of dead quiet reminded Craig of a funeral parlor, until Darren asked what would happen if Wilson Creek became unavailable.

"Where will we get supplies, or prescriptions?"

Joliene was next. "What about propane and gasoline?"

The younger children said nothing until Caleb spoke up. "When can we go to Walmart? That's what I want to know."

Craig laughed, as did everyone else. "That's a good question, Son. I don't know, but as soon as we can—we will."

To the rest he said, "This I do know—we're not giving up. We'll face things as they come. In the immediate future we have a lot to accomplish that will keep us occupied, and everyone—and I do mean everyone, must do his or her part. We're in this together."

He made sure not to look in Duane's direction, hoping his lazy brother-in-law, who pushed every button, and rattled every nerve, was getting the point.

"We don't want to spend winter here," Richard said, "but if we have to we must be ready. Our largest and hardest project will be the new porch and the fireplace. It's a little—I mean a lot out of our area of expertise."

Craig said, "Parts of it will require hard manual labor. Tomorrow we start cutting and slicing more trees."

"Winter isn't all bad." Lois said. "Freezing food outside will be a real blessing, and we'll never be short of ice."

"Good thought, Mom. Maybe we'll build a cache."

Caleb asked, "What's a cache?"

"It's a small storage house high above the ground. It keeps animals out of the food. Maybe we'll have a chance to build one before winter —if we're still here."

Lois said, "There is one more thing I would like to say. I haven't been to the lake. Maybe someone could take me down there? I love to fish."

Caleb raised his hand. "I'll take you Grandma."

"Great! With your help, we can feed this crew. Now, speaking of food, if you men are finished with your report, we have several packages of marshmallows left. Lets go outside, sit by the fire and roast a few."

Craig looked around the room. "Is that it?"

No one spoke so he said, "Okay, come with me, boys. Let's build a fire."

As marshmallows were blackened and flaring, Craig noticed Richard was staring across the fire pit at Tracey.

Craig whispered, "Is she okay?"

"Watch her. Every sound that comes from the forest causes her to jerk in that direction."

Richard hit his forehead with the palm of his hand. "She's scared to death! It's hard for her to function, if she's not in a controlled environment. You know it's true."

Craig nodded then Richard walked around the fire and slipped his arm around Tracey's waist. "Let's go home."

She snapped, "We don't have a home!"

"I know, sweetheart, but we do have the fifth wheel."

She grasped his hand, began to quiver, just as her knees gave way. Richard caught her just before she fell, pulled her close and help her tightly in his arms. She buried her face in his chest and sobbed. He laid his head on top of hers, stroking her long silky hair. No one spoke, and the whole area seemed to honor the moment with an uncanny silence.

Tracey raised her head, looked toward the woods then stared into his eyes. "Every night this darkness engulfs me. I feel it penetrate my soul. Richard, it flows through our windows like a sea of black ink. I look where the woods should be, but there's only a dark shroud. I'm certain something is looking back. I'm afraid to let the kids out of my sight. I want to run, but where could I go? Sometimes it's so quiet the sound of my own heart is deafening."

She covered her face with her hands. "It's too much Richard. I can't deal with this."

He whispered, "I'm sorry, babe. If there had been some other way we would have taken it. We'll get the addition, and the fireplace built as soon as possible. I think that will help. The next time we go to Wilson Creek why don't you come too? I love you so much."

She whispered back, "I love you too. Let's go home."

Sara and Cassie were standing next to their Grandpa crying, and Chad's head was down. Richard said, "Come on girls. Let's call it a night. Mom will be okay. Chad, stick around and help with the fire, if you like."

Chad smiled. Craig knew he was yearning to be counted among the men—not viewed as a boy.

CHAPTER 28

PRODUCTIVE DAYS

*C*raig and Richard began assigning differing tasks to the family. They did not have to be hard taskmasters because every member—except one—willingly picked up the load. Even the children took responsibility for specific jobs and helped where needed.

Each time Richard used his chain saw, he became more efficient. He carefully selected trees good for firewood, and others for construction projects. A chain saw was not his tool of choice for slicing logs, but it was all he had. He soon learned his hammer, chisel, and sandpaper could make most boards usable.

The two older boys were his assistants. When Craig walked close to where they were working, Richard would wiggle his fingers, and say, "I still have all ten."

Craig's reply was, "The day is young."

For the most part, Lois prepared the meals. She was not only good at it, but it gave her a chance to keep a close eye on the supplies. She made daily adjustments on the inventory list. Craig loved the way she masterfully prepared the same foods in different ways. A family favorite was burritos. She made her own tortillas then spread them with refried beans. The way she seasoned the fish or meat, always made them tasty. If she had sour cream or cheese, it was an added treat.

Joliene and Darren helped her keep the inventory list updated and did the legwork, making sure supplies kept on the cave shelves were neat and orderly.

Craig never worried about the garden. Joliene, and Tracey loved working there, and others popped in to weed and check on growth, even the children. The fence was strong, and high enough to protect it from most intruders.

Everything was going smooth *except* for dirty laundry. It was piling up all around the washer and dryer, which sat at the back of the middle hut. Both machines were designed for efficiency, but it took electricity to run them. That power came from the generator. The washer was round like the old wringer style with a large agitator. It was designed for large crews, and could handle heavy loads. The dryer operated on 110 volts, similar to those in travel trailers. It did the job, but used a lot of energy and took twice as long.

While the BLM crew occupied the huts, they were privileged with large supplies of gasoline, and propane. They could run the generator anytime, and for as long as they wanted. This was not the case with Craig and Richard's crew. If they were unable to replenish their fuel in Wilson Creek, they would soon have a serious shortage, and none for the trucks, ATVs, plus limited generator use.

As leader, and chief taskmaster, Craig knew this problem had to be dealt with, so after talking it over with Linda and Lois, he gathered the family.

Craig decided not to beat around the bush, so he launched right in. "We can no longer furnish the fuel to operate the washer and dryer. From this point, everyone except for the little ones, need to hand wash their own clothes, starting today. Smaller things can be washed in the bathroom sink, and the rest in the kitchen sink."

Craig was not surprised when he saw Tracey shudder, and a wide-eyed Duane looking at his mother.

Craig did not respond to Tracey's reaction, but to Duane he said, "That means you too."

Duane grumbled a few words under his breath, but Craig ignored him and went on. "If weather doesn't allow us to hang clothes outside, hang them in your huts. The wood stoves should provide enough heat to dry them pretty quick. If the Wilson Creek Laundromat is still open, we can take some heavier stuff there when we go, but I don't want to hang around any longer than needed. So, keep your clothes as clean as possible, and wear most things more than once, but body odor will not be tolerated."

Tracey raised her hand. "I will probably wash most of my family's clothes. They're working so hard. Is that okay?"

Craig had to smile. Tracey would die before allowing her family to appear unkempt, so he gave her the go ahead.

Then he turned to Duane. "What I don't want is able bodied people pushing their responsibility on others." Before his irritation rose to the boiling point, he simply said, "That's all I want to deal with. Thanks."

He walked straight out the door towards the woods. He wished he could keep thoughts of Duane out of his head. How could any person, especially in the current circumstances, feel they deserve to be served rather than serve? *At least Linda makes him stack firewood. I'm sure she'll insist he does his own laundry. If she doesn't, I will.*

The next day, Craig asked Linda if she would drive Caleb and his mom to the lake. "In fact, would you take them at least twice a week, weather permitting? Just be sure to keep a rifle by your side. You can fish, but stay alert for unwanted visitors."

Linda said, "I know how to shoot the rifle—I just don't know if I could. I would probably fire two shots in the air then you guys better come running."

"Trust me. If the need arises you'll know what to do, or just toss the rifle to Mom."

Before they left the hut, Lois thanked Craig then told him she wanted to do some ice fishing, if they were still there in winter. He promised he would make it happen.

"Not only will we cut a hole in the ice, we'll build a little shelter to fish from."

~

On June 21st, there were fifteen hours of daylight. The weather was pleasant and reasonably warm. Craig walked next to his mom as she maneuvered her walker behind the huts.

"Son, I want to go to the garden a few times a week. It's producing faster than I expected, and everything's so big. The pumpkins are amazing. By the time they mature they'll be huge. I don't want anything to go to waste, so I want to start canning, and dehydrating—today, if possible."

Craig agreed, so he and Nathaniel carried thirty, one-quart jars and lids from the cave, and sat them on a table by the fire pit. All the ladies, and Sara, helped get the vegetables ready, and before long all the jars were filled. Lois set aside some for dinner then prepared the others for dehydrating. After the family admired the bounty, Craig, Nathaniel, and Chad took the filled jars to the cave.

Craig hoped to buy more jars in Wilson Creek.

~

Through the whole canning process, Lois noticed that Sara and Caleb kept an eye on every step. Cassie would pop by occasionally, but showed little interest. When the canning was finished, Lois sat down with them.

Caleb picked up a zucchini, and asked if he could cut the bottom off. His mother said, "Not until you're older. You might cut your finger off, too."

He crossed his arms and dropped his head. "I *do* have super powers, you know."

Lois, wanting to change the subject, said, "Well, at least we won't starve or get scurvy, huh Caleb?"

Caleb scrunched up his face. "Scurvy? What's scurvy?"

Linda laughed, "Yes, Mom. Explain that one."

"That's easy, Caleb. People must have vitamin C, or they can get very sick. We get that vitamin from fruit and vegetables."

"What does scurvy look like?" He asked.

"Well, I can't exactly tell you, but if you eat your fruit and vegetables you won't have to worry about it."

"I'm already strong. Want to watch me run?"

"Sure," Lois said. "But, first come give me a hug."

Cassie rolled her eyes, picked up her sweater, one of her many books then walked away.

Linda said, "Sometimes I think Caleb is just too much for her. She's happiest when he's out of sight, and she's found a quiet place to read."

"It's true, and her wire framed glasses are a perfect match for her personality. She's a lot like her mother," Linda said.

Sara was just the opposite. She was outgoing, friendly, and looked at each new project with positive anticipation.

Lois said, "Miss Sara, you stuck right by me through the whole canning process. Did you learn anything?"

"I sure did, and it was fun. Why doesn't everybody do it?"

"I think life has been too busy, and there were a lot of grocery stores. I'm thinking next year, if we're still here, you could head this up all by yourself."

"Thanks," Sara said, "but it wouldn't be any fun without you."

Lois smiled and gave her a hug.

There had been no recent calls from Leon, and Craig continued to be unsuccessful when he searched for media broadcasts from America. Canadian stations reported what they knew, but to Craig it felt like a dark blanket was covering *his* land. It let nothing in and nothing out. He knew some unknown, calculating force continued to call the shots.

CHAPTER 29

DUANE THE PAIN – A NIGHT IN THE CAVE

*A*s daylight grew progressively shorter the temperature began to drop. The first hard freeze came on September 30th. The RV's were winterized, but there would never be enough fuel to keep them warm enough to sleep in. The time had come for everyone to take up residence in the huts.

Four cords of firewood were stacked with precision on the new porch, and the solar panels were repositioned to catch the sun in its low arc across the sky.

After breakfast, Craig broke the news no one wanted to hear. "Today Richard, Darren and I, need to remove the temporary enclosure, and finish the fireplace. This whole area will be dusty, loud and cold. And when we build the first fire, we have to make sure it doesn't backdraft. If it does, it will fill all the huts with smoke. We want you to spend the next few hours in the cave, or until we're finished."

Groans and gasps filled the room. Tracey swung around and looked at Richard. "Are you kidding me? That place has a dirt floor, and—aren't you going to say something?"

"Sorry, babe, but Craig's right. It's the only logical place to go. The trailers are out of the question. They're shut down for the winter. Nathaniel and Chad can build a fire for you in the cave. It has a natural chimney. It will be warm, and we already put the lanterns, grill, portable toilet, and air mattresses in place. Take food, games, books or whatever. I'm sure we'll finish tonight. I'm sorry, but there's no other way."

"Work with us, guys," Craig said. "This is the final step." He pointed toward the partially finished fireplace. "You won't be *prisoners*, and you can check on our progress as often as you like. Just give us a heads up before you open the door."

Darren said, "I know this isn't what you want to do, but just consider this. I'm a surgeon, and these two knuckleheads are geologists. There's not a carpenter among us. We wanted to finish long before now, but had to make sure we knew what we were doing, so please cooperate. All of you will appreciate the extra heat when it's done."

Caleb grabbed a bag and started filling it with toys, "I've never played in a cave before. That sounds like fun."

Sara and Cassie gave Caleb a look that could kill, and Tracey just shook her head. "How much more? How much more do we have to endure?"

Duane put his hands on his hip, let out a loud sigh and whispered, *Neanderthals.*

Craig heard him, but decided to ignore the comment. *He'll never grow up. Duane the pain—a perfect title.*

After lunch Craig broke the bad news. "Okay guys. Its time to ship out. We'll get finished as fast as we can."

A troop of unhappy campers marched slowly out the door. Linda stopped and smiled at Craig.

"You guys are amazing men. I'm afraid we're a bunch of whiners. Thank you for doing this."

They all three smiled, and Craig said, "That's my girl."

When Linda entered the cave she thanked Nathaniel and Chad for building the fire. It was so warm she was able to prop the door half open. She helped Joliene and Tracey make the refuge as homey as possible by setting up chairs, a small folding table, and spreading toys and games over a large tarp.

Linda allowed Caleb to explore every crack, and cranny of the cave until a bat swooped his head. From that point he stayed close to her. Tracey asked Chad to go to the hut and find hats for everyone. The thought of a bat landing in someone's hair was not a tolerable idea.

When evening approached, a flotilla of air mattresses circled the roaring flames. Linda and Joliene played several games with the younger ones. Brianna, Nathaniel, Lois and Chad played trivia games. Tracey and Duane spent most of their time sitting by the fire, staring at the flames.

In the rear of the cave they kept hearing the unnerving swoop of bat wings.

Linda said, "I think they're trying to remind us who the real owners of this cave are."

At seven, she helped Joliene warm the pinto beans. The side dish was a peanut butter sandwich. Not a favorite, but it filled their empty spot. A little after ten, the younger children were sleeping as the three men continued to work. Duane was the exception. He sat in the warm cave snuggled up to the fire.

He said, "Is there anything to snack on?"

Lois pointed toward a box sitting by the door. "We have some peanut butter and pinto beans left. They're right over there. You can warm the beans over the fire."

He drew his knees up to his chin and buried his face. "This is ridiculous! We're being forced to live like Neanderthals by Neanderthals! How much more do we have to endure? You want us to eat beans and peanut butter as a snack? You've got to be kidding."

Duane held up both hands, and waved them in the air. "Look. Look at my hands. I have sore spots all over them from those logs. I'm not cut out to do manual labor! Sometimes I think we would have been better off in Seattle!"

Joliene put her hand on his shoulder. "Now, son—don't get all worked up, you'll make yourself sick. I'm sure things will get better soon."

"I can't stand it, Mom. Now winter is here. We'll never get out. I just want to go home."

She put her arm around him, "We all do, sweetheart."

Chad and Nathaniel entered the door just in time to see Linda stiffen. Her face was red and a surge of hot anger shot through her body. She stood up, walked over to Duane, and in a soft controlled tone pointed at his face. "Duane, do you know what time it is?"

He looked at his watch. "It's ten thirty-five. What does that have to do with anything?"

"Do you know what Chad and Nathaniel were just doing? They were getting us firewood. Do you know what my husband, Richard, and Darren are doing? Well, do you?"

"Uh, yeah. Why?"

"Why? Why?" Her tone was getting a little louder. She walked over to the cave door, opened it and said, "Get out!"

Joliene held on to Duane's arm, "Linda! What's wrong with you?"

Duane moved behind his mother.

"Mom!" Linda said. "Let me handle this."

She turned back to her brother. "Duane, put your jacket on and get out of here. Maybe if you spend the night outside, you'll know how to appreciate the fire. Maybe if you spend a night alone in the woods, you'll appreciate how hard those men work to keep *you* safe. Maybe if you get good and scared, you might appreciate the secure building you are allowed to live in. Better still, if you had offered to help, we might already be out of this cave."

Duane kept backing up, but Linda stayed with him.

"One more thing, little brother, I better not hear another negative word from you. Not one more—of any kind. Your bad attitude is contagious. We spend our time giving hope to the children, and each other, while you do nothing but spread a negative poison! No more, Duane! Do you understand?"

Duane grabbed his coat and stormed past his sister. When he got to the door, he hesitated and turned toward Joliene. "Mom can I at least have our flashlight?"

She handed him a red one. He slammed the door, and they heard his hurried footsteps crunching the frozen ground.

For a moment Joliene, Lois, Tracey and the boys, stood wide-eyed staring at the door. No one so much as looked in Linda's direction. This was a side of her few had ever seen. After a couple of minutes Joliene confronted her daughter.

"Linda, how could you treat your brother like that? What if something happens to him?"

"Mom, nothing will happen to him. He needs to understand we're in a very serious situation. Everyone has to pull his or her weight. Look how hard the *children* work. They don't complain. We've all shed our tears, but there's no room for weakness—at least not Duane's kind. You've got to let him grow up."

Linda turned toward the door. "Besides, better he freezes to death or has a heart attack than die by my hand."

Joliene snickered then burst out laughing. It was contagious. Tracey laughed so hard she was holding her stomach.

"What's so funny?" Craig said, entering the cave.

Linda gave him a firm hug then said. "I think we're all getting a little weird. Where are the rest of the guys?"

"They're coming. The enclosure is done. Richard is building a fire, and there's a lot of clean up to do. By the way, what got into Duane? He just passed me on the path and asked if he could help us finish."

Linda shrugged as Joliene and Tracey muffled their giggles. Lois smiled and turned her head.

Duane avoided Linda for the next few days, but she was pleased to see him cutting and stacking wood. She was sure he was walking a little taller.

CHAPTER 30

EMOTIONAL SURVIVAL

*C*raig struggled with an oversized load of firewood, and after he dropped it next to the fireplace, he pushed hard against the piercing wind to close the door. It was Halloween night, and the first snow flurry brought winter in with a vengeance. For three days the family suffered blizzard conditions, and no one was allowed to leave the porch area.

Craig, Richard and Lois were the only members who had dealt with such harshness. Before now, the rest of the family thought of snow as recreation used only for skiing or snowboarding.

Caleb was thrilled, and at least once an hour he asked, "Can we build a snowman, Daddy?"

"We will when the wind settles down."

On the morning of the fourth day, Craig looked out the window, and to his surprise the snow was floating slowing to the ground instead of flying through the air. He said, "Caleb, let's go build that snowman. Would you girls like to help?"

Cassie shook her head. "I don't like the cold."

Chad said, "I'll help. Come on Caleb. Let's go build ourselves a Frosty."

Sara jumped up. "Me too!"

By the time Tracey dressed her, covering all exposed skin, the little girl could barely move. When she ran out the door, she pushed the scarf off her nose and loosened it around her mouth. When her feet hit the snow, she dropped, and made a snow angel.

Big Ben ran like a young pup. He buried his nose, then snorted, swung around, and in a flash, ran over the snowman.

"Ben, get out of here." Chad threw several snowballs at him.

Craig came back inside and joined Linda at the window. They watched the frivolity, and smiled. Linda said, "You know, this almost feels like a normal day."

He nodded, but for the first time he wondered how they would get around if, or when, the snow got several feet deep.

Lois rolled her wheel chair next to the window. Linda put her hands on Lois's shoulders, and said, "The snow is beautiful, and the kids are having fun, but if we don't get an all clear to go home, we could be shut up in these huts for months. What are we going to do, Mom? The last time Craig spoke with Leon, the whole nation was in turmoil. Our work has slowed. How will we spend our time?"

"I've been wondering the same thing, but I'm developing an idea. Give me a chance to organize my thoughts before I pitch it. By the way, has anybody opened a Bible since we've been here?"

They both shook their head then Linda said, "Wonder why?"

"Well, I've been thinking about that too. Craig, can we have a family meeting after dinner? I should be ready to present my idea by then. Maybe you guys won't mind if this old lady has a word or two to say."

"If you can help us adjust and make this life work, I'm all for it," Craig said.

"Me too." Linda said. "Tracey keeps getting quieter, and Brianna cries a lot. Sometimes I feel like crying too, especially when I think about home, friends—and grocery stores. I close my eyes and imagine walking through rows of fruit and vegetables, not to mention cuts of meat, and cheese."

"I know," Lois said, "and this will sound rather trivial, but I miss *Jeopardy* and reruns of *Murder, She Wrote.*"

Linda said, "We took it for granted didn't we? And all the food we wasted. We ate what we liked, and let the rest spoil. It never occurred to me it would end."

"Me neither. But what if God is giving us a new chance at life, instead of robbing us? It wouldn't hurt to think along those lines for a while. We might even feel better. We need to be thankful for the quality things we've found here. The family has never been closer. Our former life can't be duplicated, but we must take a stab at learning, living and growing. We need an *intentional* search for genuine happiness."

"Sounds like a tall order." Craig said.

"Yes, it does, but don't you think it's worth a try?"

Linda gave her a hug, and said, "Yes I do, and I love you."

After dinner, Craig asked the whole family to go to the area around the fireplace, and find a place to sit. When everyone was accounted for he said, "Okay, Mom. What's on your mind?"

Lois was not sure how her observations, and suggestions would be received, but she jumped in anyway. "Something has been troubling me for several weeks now, but we've had so much to deal with I wanted to confront it at just the right time. I feel like this is it. I keep wondering, what have we done with God?"

The room was alive with gasps and head shaking. Everyone looked at her like she had slipped over the edge of sanity.

Richard said, "Excuse me?"

"I'm serious. No one mentions His name. No one opens a Bible. We don't even pray when we eat. What have we done with God?"

Tracey squeezed her arms together, and tapped her right foot. "To be honest, I don't think we lost God, I think He lost us."

Duane and Darren nodded in agreement.

Joliene said, "I don't read my Bible because frankly, I feel like the

Bible has ended. This has to be the end of the world. We must be living in the Great Tribulation."

A few heads nodded in agreement, and Brianna began to cry. "Grandma, I just can't understand why God is doing this to us. Why do we have to live *here*? I feel so isolated and claustrophobic. We can't leave, and I'm afraid I may never have a normal life. Its like life is over. Almost every night I have nightmares about my friends dying."

At this point, Brianna was not only sobbing, she was trembling. Linda walked over and put her arms around her daughter. "I knew you were suffering, but I didn't know how much. I'm so sorry."

Craig joined them. "I'm sorry too, baby. I buried myself in the work, focused on survival, and tried not to think, but I have not forgotten God."

He turned toward Lois, "Mom, I was about to get upset with you for causing this commotion, but I've changed my mind. Thank you. We've been discouraging this group from expressing themselves. Maybe because no one really has any answers. As far as your question, I think I'm ready to answer it."

Craig turned toward the group. "Since we first learned of the virus, I've been terrified I would let all of you down. Every evening, since I set off the dynamite, I've walked to the edge of the woods, looked into heaven, and begged God for wisdom. I'm convinced we would all be dead without Him. It's a miracle we survived the trip in, and I'm still amazed that we escaped with our lives."

Richard shook his head. "I haven't been praying. I've been too angry."

Tracey touched his arm. "You've been angry? You sure didn't show it. Why didn't you tell me?"

"You're having such a rough time that I didn't want to give you something else to worry about."

Caleb raised his hand. "I'm not mad at God. I tell him thank you for my food, in my head, every time we eat."

"Good job, Caleb. If we forget again will you remind us?"

"I will, Mommy."

"Well?" Lois asked. "We've heard from a few of you, but not everyone. Is there anything else anyone wants to say?"

Cassie dropped her head as her eyes filled with tears, "I just miss my friends."

"Me too," Sara said. "Do you think they're all dead?"

Richard motioned for both girls to come to him. He gave them a long hug then spoke in a soft tone. "We don't know who survived, and who didn't, but try not to dwell on it. I know it's hard, but don't torture yourself."

Both girls laid their head against his chest as he stroked their hair.

"I miss my soccer team and television," Chad offered.

"I miss a lot of things," Darren said. "But right now, I'm missing ice cream."

Everyone hesitated then laughed.

"Well, guess what?" Lois said. "I can't fix anyone else's problem, but I can help with the ice cream issue." She pointed toward the window. "See all that beautiful, clean white snow out there? As soon as this meeting is over let's make our own ice cream. We have the ingredients, plus some toppings."

"Is it safe?" Cassie asked.

"You bet, and the timing couldn't be better. It's been snowing steady for a couple of days so the snow is powdery. We need to gather some before it gets crusted over. We could still use it, but the texture wouldn't be very good. I'm glad you brought this up, Darren. Now, let's get on with our meeting."

Lois suggested from this point on, they acknowledge the Lord's Day by reading scripture, and singing. She thought it was time to quit focusing on the bad things and begin to have a grateful heart that God spared them. She asked the children if they would take turns praying at mealtime.

No one objected so she continued. "Now, for the second thing I want to talk about."

The room filled with groans, and Nathaniel said, "There's more, Grandma?"

"Yes, son, there's more. This will be a long winter. We need to use our time wisely, and creatively. And you children must continue your education."

This time, only the children moaned.

Craig knew his mom was right, but was curious to see how she would handle this portion of her talk.

Lois said, "Now don't get excited, we can add some good stuff to the traditional curriculum, if your parents will go along with it, and I think they will. We don't know how long we'll live here so what if we all begin sharing things we know or can teach? Everyone knows something that is exclusive to them, including Caleb and the girls."

Caleb jumped up. "Do I get to be a teacher, Grandma?"

"You bet. Think about what you are good at."

"All of you. What knowledge or special skills do you have? It can be something fun or serious. Just start thinking about it. Craig and Richard—you must have learned something new, every time you were on assignment. And Darren, imagine what you can teach us. I believe the more everyone shares the more things they'll think of."

Craig saw Caleb smile, and sit up real straight in his chair. It was obvious he had an idea.

Lois said, "I don't have exact details worked out, but I think we could have something prepared at least twice a week. For instance, Wednesday evenings could be used for class time, and Sunday evenings for entertainment. Just think, we could have music, games and maybe, someone could create a skit, a play or even a television show."

"This could work Mom. I like it so far," Linda said. "As long as we use our imaginations, life can stay fresh and fun. Plus, a little fantasy would give us a temporary escape from the long days."

Lois said, "Yes. It will be good for us." Then she turned toward Tracey, "If we decide to do this, would you consider heading it up?"

Tracey was wide-eyed. "Whoa! I'm not sure I'm qualified, but I love the idea. It would give us all something to look forward too, and I agree, we must continue the children's education."

Once again there were soft objections. They hadn't thought of school in several months.

"Don't worry kids. You won't be bored." Tracey turned back to Lois. "Who did you have in mind to write the plays?"

"Anyone who wants too. I've heard there's an author hidden in everyone. Let's find out and have some fun. Okay. Now bear with me another minute or two."

Craig said, "Okay, Mom, just another minute or two. Now that ice cream was mentioned, you're going to lose all of us."

Lois smiled. "I promise. I've been thinking. We've been through so much these last few months, and I have not recorded any of it. Have you?"

No one spoke a word. "I think I have my answer so—we have several reams of paper. Would you guys be willing to reconstruct this venture, then make frequent entry's—even if it's only a few lines. You could write it like a story, or just make a few notes."

"Isn't that a girl thing?" Duane asked.

"Yeah, Grandma, it doesn't sound very masculine to me." Nathaniel said.

Joliene spoke for the first time. "Lois, that's a wonderful idea. I'm excited, and you guys can certainly record some of the highlights, and your thoughts. You don't have to write a book. Think about it, when we leave this valley you'll have great—and accurate experiences to share."

Chad asked, "You mean like the bear attack?"

"Exactly," Joliene said. "Darren and I can hand out paper tomorrow."

Craig stood to put more wood on the fire just as the hair on Big Ben's back stood up, and he let out a low growl. He ran to the door, sniffed the cracks, then began scratching to get out. Craig patted his head and said, "What's wrong boy?"

Nathaniel started to open the door, but Richard yelled, "No Nathaniel! Don't! Turn off the lights so we can see what's out there."

CHAPTER 31

DANGER – JUST OUTSIDE THE DOOR

The window next to the fireplace was three feet by three feet, and the snow-covered ground was brilliant. Craig knew it was next to impossible for anyone or anything to hide. He reached for his rifle and gave Richard a nod.

Craig whispered, "Is this how the pioneers lived?"

No one moved as the men surveyed the area.

"Look there—to the right of that big fir." Richard pointed.

"I see two—no three," Craig responded.

Nathaniel asked, "What's out there, Dad?"

"Wolves, son. It's a good thing you didn't let Ben out."

Sara began to cry. "Daddy, I'm scared. Make them go away."

"Don't worry. Your safe in here."

Richard turned back to the window. "It looks like they're eating something. Don't tell me someone left food outside."

Darren responded, "We all know better than that. You guys have pounded it into our heads enough. Maybe they drug something in."

Craig shrugged. "They probably did. We'll see what it is, and let them know they're not welcome here."

He turned to Darren. "Would you keep everyone inside?"

Darren nodded.

Craig put his hand on the doorknob, and Richard was right behind him, rifle in hand. Caleb's eyes were wide, "Daddy, where are you going?"

"It's okay, son, we'll be right back. We're just going to scare them away."

When Richard opened the door, Nathaniel could barely control Big Ben. As soon as the door was closed they began yelling, but instead of the wolves running away, they lay back on their haunches, began creeping forward as deep guttural growls rolled from their throats. Blood was dripping from their mouths. They were not intimidated.

Craig and Richard stepped from the porch. Soft snow swallowed their boots as they advanced, but not to be outdone, the three predators lowered their heads and crept, breast to breast, toward the men.

Richard whispered, "I don't think they're afraid of us. Now what?"

Craig steadily raised his rifle, and looked down the sight. "Fire a few shots above their heads. I don't want to kill them unless we have to."

When the shots rang out all three wolves jumped, and ran into the woods. Craig and Richard stood perfectly still surveying the area. When Craig felt the wolves were no longer a threat, Richard turned on his flashlight. It was the carcass of a newborn baby deer with a severely deformed hind leg.

"Poor little thing, it didn't have a chance. The doe has to be close unless the wolves carried it here." Craig thought for a minute. "What are we going to tell the kids?"

Richard laughed. "Uh, I don't know. We sure can't tell them the wolves were eating Bambi. Right now, we better get this carcass out of here. It's small enough to fit in the fire pit. We can use kerosene to burn it up."

"We better douse the area as well, to disguise the blood smell, in case our friends are still hanging around," Craig said.

"When I was a little boy," Richard said, "I found a dead baby bird, at the base of a tree. I cried my eyes out, even with Dad's profound explanation of the balance of nature. I guess those wolves were playing the same role."

"I suppose, but they better play it somewhere else. We don't want them hanging around here. I'm surprised Ben's made it this long. He looks for a new adventure every day. He would be no match for wolves, although he would think he was. After what's happened tonight we better figure out a way to keep him in camp."

Richard glanced at the window. "We've got quite an audience over there. They haven't missed a thing."

Craig laughed. "Well, at least the wolves provided some of that entertainment Mom was talking about."

Darren was watching the action from the window. "Oh no," he said, in a loud whisper then grabbed a rifle off the rack. "Hold the dog. They're back."

He tore open the door, stepped onto the porch, and moved a few feet to the left just as Craig and Richard heard a low growl.

Darren yelled, "Stand very, very still."

He raised the rifle, gently squeezing the trigger, catching the wolf in mid air. Craig heard the whiz of the bullet pass close to his head. A shot whizzed by Craig's head followed by a loud yelp. It fell right behind Craig's legs. The other two predators took off at a dead run.

Richard looked at Craig, "Well, that wasn't too bright."

"No, it wasn't. I'm glad your dad was watching our back."

They both looked at Darren and nodded a thank you.

When the carcasses were burning they headed for the porch. Craig pulled back and let Richard go in first.

Richard asked, "Are you ready to answer questions?"

"No, that's why I'm behind you."

They were both laughing as they entered the hut.

"You two seem to be having a good time," Linda said. "Felt pretty intense to me." She whispered in Craig's ear, "You're in trouble mister. You scared me to death."

"I'm fine. You worry too much."

"Well, kids," Richard said. "I guess you saw the whole thing."

"Wow!" Caleb was wide-eyed. "Were those real wolves? Was that blood on their mouth? What were they eating?"

The men looked at each other, and Craig told Richard to go ahead.

"Well, guys, I have something kind of sad to tell you, but please listen to everything I say, okay?"

He saw several nods.

"It was a baby deer."

Cassie and Sara gasped.

"Now, wait a minute. I asked you to listen to everything. Wolves can be very dangerous, but God uses them in a special way—like tonight. The baby deer was born with a very bad leg. It couldn't walk or even learn to feed itself. When that happens, wolves are able to kill them. It's one way God feeds the wolves, and that, my children, is called the balance of nature. Do you understand?"

Sara said, "They killed a baby deer, Mommy!"

Cassie said nothing, but tears rolled down her cheeks.

Caleb glared at Richard, then buried his head in his mother's lap. Through his sobs he yelled, "It was just a baby, Mommy. It was just a baby."

Craig turned his back and fought hard not to laugh at the stunned look on Richard's face. When he composed himself he said, "Okay guys. I'm sorry about the deer, but right now I need you to listen. Wolves are territorial which means they usually live, and hunt in one area. We have invaded their area, so when Ben is not with us, he has to stay behind the fence. He's no match for wolves. Also, starting tomorrow, we'll begin the buddy system, including you adults. If you leave the fenced area make sure someone's with you, and you kids go nowhere without an adult."

"That's right," Richard said, without looking at his wife, he suggested other members of the family learn to use a rifle. "Nathaniel and Chad, I think we'll start with you."

They both nodded then Chad glanced at his mom. She said nothing, but her right foot was tapping.

Craig looked at Duane. "What about you? Do you want a few lessons after the boys?"

"Uh, that's okay, I don't mind being last."

Richard turned to Tracey, "Wouldn't you feel better if you learned to handle a rifle too?"

She asked for a few more weeks then laughed. "Besides, I have Linda to protect me."

Craig thought Tracey's laugh sounded healthy. Maybe Mom's plan was exactly what she needed.

Darren stood up and rubbed his belly. "Hey you guys. Did you forget about the ice cream?"

Lois said, "We're ready. Go get a few buckets of snow—but stay alert."

Craig was relieved that nerves were calming. The ice cream was a great success. He and Nathaniel put logs in all three wood stoves, turned down dampers and said good night. As they snuggled in their covers, Craig could never have anticipated what was coming next.

CHAPTER 32

TWIG AND SLICK ON THE MOVE

Twig shivered in the brutal cold as he and Slick approached a canyon ridge. They were tired, hungry, and burdened down with heavy backpacks. Twig made his way to a small grove of trees, set in an outcrop of tall brush.

"This here looks like a good spot, Slick. We can build a fire and warm up some of that soup. I'm freezing to death."

"Help me get this back pack unbuckled then set up that tent," Slick barked. "We'll stay here. I'll start us a fire."

They pulled dead grass, broke branches off trees, and after several attempts, their fire was burning. Twig dug around in the snow, found a few small logs then placed three of them teepee style over the flames.

In the glow of the fire, Twig saw a shiny reflection in the nearby trees. He pushed branches aside and was surprised, and delighted by what he saw.

"Slick. Look. There's trucks over here. They're just like the ones those nice people had in the park."

"Yeah! They sure are." *I knew they couldn't slip past us. Those were their tracks on the other side of that gate.*

"I hate to break into their truck, Slick, but I'm freezing. You know how to make it start. I've seen you do it before."

"There you go again being an idiot!" He hit Twig on the back of the head. "If they have gas, we don't want to run it out. We'll check out the tanks tomorrow. Those folks have to be around here close, but we don't want em to know we're here. We wanna surprise…"

Before Slick could finish his statement, two rifle shots split the night. Both men squatted and ran behind the nearest truck.

Slick whispered, "That came from right over that ridge. Wonder what they're shooting at? We know it ain't us. They don't know we're here … yet."

A few minutes later another shot rang out, and the brothers squatted even lower. When things were quiet Slick said, "I think we'll just hang out for a few days and look the place over. If those folks are living here, that means they have food and other things we need, if you know what I mean."

"Why can't we just knock on their door? They seemed real nice."

"Twig, you are such an idiot. We're going to look around first. Trucks may not be the only things we want to leave here with. Don't you dare do anything to give us away. We'll just explore, watch and listen. Now find some more wood for the fire so we can get some sleep."

CHAPTER 33

TEACHERS AND ACTORS

The whole family quickly took a seat, anxious and for the first night of entertainment, but Craig was a little surprised when Tracey offered to go first. She sang three songs from the Phantom of the Opera, using an accompaniment CD. Her high soprano voice rang clear, and beautiful, filling the hut.

Before she sang, *Wishing You Were Somehow Here Again*, she smiled, looked up and whispered, "This is for you Dad."

When she completed her last song, no one moved until Craig said, "That was beautiful."

Tracey smiled and said thank you. After everyone had a chance to breathe, she introduced Caleb. "He will be giving us a super hero demonstration."

Caleb's spent the next fifteen minutes explaining his every move. He fired invisible webs from his wrists like Spider Man, karate kicked and punched like Power Rangers then pretended to fly through the air like Super Man. His last feat was to distribute invisible cups of green juice to all the guys. He told them to drink it, and they too could have super powers. For the next twenty minutes the room rang with laughter watching the *boys* play their imaginary game. For a short time, worries faded.

When Tracey saw how much joy a night of diversion offered, Craig was pleased. She asked Darren and the girls to prepare for the following evening.

The next night after dinner, Darren went first—sharing a variety of emergency first aid treatments. "A good example of a pressure bandage is the one Richard used when the bear attacked me."

Cassie and Sara were next. Craig helped Joliene drape and pin a sheet over two chairs. Earlier, he and Richard had gathered branches for props.

When both girls were in position, Joliene invited the *audience* to take a seat, and enjoy a gifted, and *well-written Broadway production*. Sock puppets portrayed two little girls who became separated from their parents on a camping trip. They found themselves lost in the woods and threatened by wolves. After overcoming hunger and cold, they saw the light of their family's campfire. They were quite entertaining.

Craig whispered to his Mom, "This thing is working out great. Thank you."

She smiled and patted his hand.

When the presentations were over, Craig saw Linda put on her jacket, and boots then motioned for him to follow her. He stepped out on the porch and saw her looking up.

"I've never seen such a large moon," she said. "The way it glistens on the snow takes my breath away. I could read a book out here."

Craig put his arms around her. "It is amazing."

"This is the first time I've wanted to acknowledge beauty in this place, Craig. Maybe I'm finally adjusting?"

"Maybe you are. Today, I watched an eagle soaring overhead, wishing I could do the same."

Linda laughed. "Drink some of Caleb's green juice then you could get a birds-eye view of America, and tell us how things are going."

"That would be nice," he said. "I'm thinking we owe a lot to Mom.

She's given us a new lease on life. Everyone's working on something. I even saw Nathaniel and Duane, journalling. Let's go for a walk. We can see all the way to the lake."

Linda smiled, "I would like that. I haven't been on a stroll with my sweetheart for a very long time."

"Let me grab my jacket and boots—and my rifle."

"Well, that's a grim reminder."

Craig was laughing when he stepped back inside. Caleb saw him unlock the rifle case. "Are you going to shoot at wolves, Daddy?"

"No, Son. Your mom and I are going for a walk."

"Can I go?"

"Not this time buddy. I want to be alone with Mom for a while. Maybe I'll give her two kisses."

Caleb put both hands over his face. "That's gross."

Craig heard him tell Cassie the *disgusting* news. She wasn't impressed. Craig felt she was learning to love Caleb, but was keeping him on a lower rung of the human ladder.

Craig and Linda walked hand in hand, then arm in arm toward the lake. The air was cold, but not frigid. She laid her head against his shoulder, and whispered. "Welcome back."

"What do you mean, welcome back?"

She turned and faced him. "I think you know."

Craig put his finger under her chin, lifted her face, and for the first time in months, they actually kissed. "Wow! I like that! You're right. I *have* been away." He wrapped her in his arms, and held her close. "I love you baby. How did I get so lucky?"

"I feel the same, and I love you too. No matter what happens, I can face anything with you by my side."

"Thank you, and that's my favorite place to be. It ranks right up there with smelly old bears, and blood-soaked wolves."

She smacked the side of his head. "Thanks a lot."

"Just kidding."

They stood, staring at the moon, drinking in the moment, then Craig broke the silence. "Our life certainly took a strange turn."

"Yes, it did. But without you and Richard, I shudder to think what would have happened to us. Imagine all those poor people who didn't have men like you."

"Don't give us too much credit. We are literally living day-to-day. But come to think of it, isn't that how we were living before all this happened, except in more comfort?"

"Yes, and I do miss some of the comfort, but it's been years since we've spent this much time together. I like that."

"Me, too—and in a way it's a strange answer to prayer—or at least my wish to be home more. Richard said *his* mother told him to be careful what he wished for—it just might come true. It did, but in a strange way."

"That's for sure. Shall we head back?"

They held hands, slowly retracing their path. At one point, he lifted her hand and kissed it. "Are you my baby?"

"Yes, and you will always be my prize."

As they approached the huts, Richard came out the door, and picked up a shovel. Craig cocked his head, and Richard smiled then put his fingers to his lips. "I'm going to help Duane pile snow against their hut, for insulation." He smiled and walked off.

Craig said, "What's that all about?"

Later, when Richard came back inside, Craig asked him to take a short walk. "So what's this shoveling thing?"

"Well, I heard something hit the hut. I went to see what it was. Duane was shoveling snow *away* from the outside wall. When he saw me he leaned on his shovel, and smiled ear to ear."

"Away from the hut?"

"Relax. I was so happy to see him working, I pretended not to notice. I told him what a good job he was doing, and how important it was to keep snow *next* to the hut for insulation, then asked if I could help. He looked a little surprised, but nodded his head, so we shoveled snow."

"You're a good guy. Glad it was you who saw him. I don't know how I would have responded."

Richard patted Craig's back. "I think I do."

"I'm sure you're right."

The following day, Craig and Chad were carrying a load of wood into the kitchen area, just as Lois was getting ready to make corn bread for dinner. She opened the tin of meal, scooped out something very small, then dumped it in the trash.

Chad asked, "Is that a bug?"

"It could have been, but probably just a piece of black grain."

"Where did it come from?"

"It was in the cornmeal."

"You're throwing the rest away, aren't you?"

"No, I'm not. It's not uncommon, and we can't waist our food. That's why I use this old fashioned tool. It's called a sifter. Now, please don't say anything. Keep this as our little secret. Okay?"

Craig laughed out loud when Chad said, "But, can I tease Sara and Cassie?"

"No, you can't."

"How about Brianna?"

"No! But since you're here I could use some help. Will you set the plates and silverware out, please?"

Chad hated anything to do with domestic work, but he did as she asked.

"Next time," he said, "I'm staying out of here at meal time."

Craig was washing his hands, caught Chad's eye and winked. "What about me, Mom? Can I tease the girls?"

She threw a dishtowel at him. "Here! Dry your hands and find someone else to harass."

At dinnertime, Craig rounded up the family. Darren was first to the table. "Wow, Lois, this is quite a spread."

She had prepared a pot of pinto beans, cornbread, and baked a wild huckleberry cobbler for dessert. Craig was sure his mom felt like celebrating, and it was her way to thank the family for accepting, and implementing her idea.

Craig shot a quick glance at Chad. They both grinned, then looked at Mom. She said nothing, but her narrowing eyes spoke a thousand words.

After the family was seated Lois asked if she could have just a moment.

Duane laughed. "You're not going to make us sing for our dinner, are you?"

"Keep talking and I might. What I really wanted to do was thank you for taking part in the family night programs, either as audience or performer."

She noted how fun it was, plus it gave everyone something to look forward to. She closed with, "That's all I wanted to say. Caleb, would you say our prayer?"

"Just a second, son," Craig said. "Mom, all of us need to thank you. I admit I wasn't overly impressed with your ideas, but look at us. There's been a marked change in this family. Everyone is happier, and we have something to concentrate on besides our situation—and work. Now, if you don't mind, I think its time I start leading this family back to God. Caleb, you go first then I'll pray too."

Lois was overcome with emotion and unable to speak. She swallowed hard then took a deep breath. "Thank you, son."

After dinner Lois gave Darren and Nathaniel a list of supplies to get from the cave.

Twenty minutes later Craig, and Richard jumped to their feet when Nathaniel burst through the door, with Darren right behind him. Lois swung her wheel chair around. "What's wrong?"

Nathaniel didn't answer. He yelled, "Dad! Can we speak to you and Richard outside—like—right now!"

CHAPTER 34

UNWELCOME VISITORS

"Son, what's wrong? You're white as snow."

"Wait until we get outside—please."

Darren led the way to the porch, and shut the door behind them.

Craig asked, "What's going on? Did you spot another bear?"

Darren answered. "No, it's something a lot scarier. When we got to the cave I started to open the door, but Nathaniel stopped me."

"Yes, the moon was really bright. I saw them as clear as day."

"You saw what?"

"Footprints. I saw human footprints. There were two sets—around both caves."

Darren said, "That's not the worst part. Both doors were pried open."

Craig and Richard looked at each other then Richard said, "I'm not surprised someone found us, but this is not the way I wanted it to happen."

Craig opened the hut door, "There's not a second to lose. Everyone stay inside."

His face was so intense Linda whispered, "What's wrong?"

He didn't answer her directly, he just barked, "Get everything locked down as quickly as possible. Go!"

When the hut was secure they gathered by the fireplace. Craig said, "You guys are to stay in this room, away from the windows, and keep all the lights off. Both caves were broken into. There were at least two sets of footprints. We're going to check it out. Nathaniel, put Ben on his leash, and come with us."

Linda snapped. "Leave Nathaniel here. I'll take the dog."

Craig handed her a rifle. "No, you need to stay. Keep this handy. Okay?"

Her hands shook as she stammered, "Of course."

Tracey called Cassie, Chad and Sara to her. "Richard, what if they're still here—in the valley?"

"We're not sure where they are, but it makes me nervous that they didn't knock on our door. Keep your eyes and ears open."

With rifles in hand, Craig, Richard, Darren, and Nathaniel walked out the door.

Their footsteps sounded like drum beats as they broke through the crusted snow. There was no quiet way to approach the caves.

Linda asked Brianna to sit on the floor next to her and hold Caleb. Joliene and Duane sat next to them with their backs against the wall.

"Duane," Linda said, "post yourself at the East window and keep watch. I'll stay here on the West side. These are the only two without shutters."

He groaned, but knew better than to argue with his sister. Twenty minutes later the men came back. The only visible light in the hut came from the fireplace's dying embers.

Brianna whispered. "Dad, how did they get into our valley?"

"They may have already been here. This valley covers a lot of miles. They could have migrated this way from the other side. The third option would be, they came through the smaller cave."

"Cave? What cave?" Duane asked.

"Part of our job, when we worked with the Canadian BLM, is to search out and explore caves at projected drilling sites. That's how we discovered the corridor in this smaller cave. It twists, turns, has low spots, and dead end off-shoots. Only one corridor goes all the way through. It's not that long, but it takes about forty-five minutes to maneuver. The cave exits behind boulders, close to where our pickups are parked. That opening is not easily seen."

"And just why didn't you tell us?" Duane demanded.

"We saw no need to tell you, Duane, and we certainly didn't want anyone checking it out. Once the door was in place it wasn't an issue."

"That's for sure, and it still isn't," Darren said. The intensity of his stare caused Duane to back up two steps. "Right now we need to focus."

Darren turned to Craig. "So how do we handle it from here? Whoever they are, they weren't very discreet. I hope that means they're gone."

Richard spoke up, "Fortunately, because they were on foot, they couldn't have gotten away with much."

Linda said, "Craig? What will you do if you find them, and what if they're armed?"

"Try not to worry. If someone's in this portion of the valley, we'll find them. They can't hide as long as there's fresh snow. Their footprints will give them away. Ben picked up their scent, but we didn't go into the corridor. If that's the way they went, we can look for them there. Everyone needs to stay calm. We're not going to let intruders get the best of us."

Tracey suddenly became very angry and pointed to the gun rack, "Richard, hand me your rifle! Now!"

He looked a little confused, "Why, honey?"

"Because I was a fool. You tried to teach me how to shoot and I refused. I know there isn't time to give me a lesson, but would you at least show me how to load and fire? You guys can't be every where at once."

As soon as the front windows were covered, and the area could be lit again, Richard took Tracey, Joliene and Duane to the kitchen. He went over the basic steps of loading, unloading, firing and keeping the barrel of the weapon down when not in use. When he finished the brief instructions, he unloaded the rifle and insisted all three take aim, and fire. The final step was showing them how to reload.

Craig gave Lois the extra key to the gun rack, which she put on a chain and hung around her neck.

"We've had enough talk," Craig said. "Big Ben will let us know if they come close to the hut, but just to be safe, each of us men can take a two-hour watch, and I'll go first," Craig said.

❧

On the other side of the canyon, Slick was pacing wildly. "Why didn't we just knock on their door?"

Twig popped up, "Because you said we would sneak in and look for supplies."

"Shut up you idiot! I wasn't really asking a question. I was thinking out loud."

"Well, it shore sounded like a question to me."

"Be quiet! I've got to think." He started pacing again. "We're going to die without food. We could've grabbed more if it hadn't been for that man and that boy! Should've shot 'em."

"Then we would've been caught and maybe killed. It's only midnight. Let's go back. Then we can get out of here."

"Yeah, right. They know we're here. Sounds like you're asking to get shot."

"Why don't we just give ourselves up?"

"Give up? What's wrong with you? Sometimes…" Slick put his hand on his chin. "Wait a minute, I got a better idea. I'm sure they'll track us tomorrow. We'll be waiting. I keep thinking about those pretty women. If we can get those men out of the way we'll have those gals all to ourselves. Get some sleep little brother. I think tomorrow will be a good day."

"What if they shoot us first?"

"We're going to die anyway. Getting shot would be the easiest way to go."

CHAPTER 35

MANEUVERING THE CAVE

*a*t first light, Craig said, "Let's take time to eat breakfast. This could be a very long day."

When the last hurried bite was consumed, he and Richard grabbed their coat and rifle. Craig gave quick hugs, hoping they could get out the door without too much drama. Brianna took his hand. "I love you, Dad. Please be careful."

Tracey clung to Richard a moment, but neither she nor Linda said anything. Just as Craig opened the front door, Duane rushed in from the kitchen and grabbed his coat. "I'm going too."

Craig almost fainted. "Duane this could be very dangerous. Are you sure?"

"Yes, I am. I need to do this, and yes, I know its dangerous, but I couldn't sleep last night. It hit me just how much I owe you guys. I'm alive because of you. You've got to allow me to prove myself."

"The cave will be dark, and we'll be in it for a while. If you quit on us, we won't be able to bring you back."

"I understand, but I still have to do this."

Craig looked at Richard. "What do you think?"

"I say give him a rifle, and let's get going."

They chose to hug the edge of the forest rather than cross the low brush. When both cave entrances were in sight they surveyed the area.

"I don't see any new footprints, do you?" Craig whispered.

It was obvious there was no quiet way to open the broken cave door, so Richard grabbed the edge and yanked it toward him. They stood behind it for a moment listening for unusual noise or activity. When there was none, they moved forward in a low squat. Richard did a quick sweep with his flashlight, and Craig's trigger finger remained steady.

There was no sign of intruders in this part of the cave, but in the midst of the existing, internal turmoil, the peaceful flow of the calm spring, felt more like a contradiction.

Craig placed a finger across his lips, letting Duane know to be quiet, then motioned him inside. They moved around the rock wall leading to the inside corridor, and were instantly swallowed in a surreal, suffocating sea of darkness that wrapped itself around them like a shroud. Craig took several deep breaths and suggested Duane do the same.

He stopped to listen, but the deafening quiet distorted his hearing, as did the pounding of his heart. When it calmed, and he was comfortable there was no one in the area, he turned on his LED headlamp, as did the others. Craig had temporarily forgotten how restrictive their light beams were, and how well the darkness protected itself.

Craig shuddered, and briefly recalled the lost world of caves he and Richard had already experienced. They were assigned to explore many, by order of the BLM, plus he and Richard discovered many others on their own. They were at least familiar with this one, but at the moment it offered little comfort.

Four sets of distorted footprints were visible in the dusty earth. Two sets belonged to him and to Richard, still in place from their first visit. He could only assume the other impressions belonged to the intruders.

The deeper they penetrated the darkness the heavier the air became. It was difficult to take a deep cleansing breath. A screeching bat flew out of the darkness, and hit the top of Richard's cap. He ducked then pulled it down as close to his ears as possible.

"I'm glad you're the tallest," Craig whispered. "It keeps the bats off of us."

Richard started to respond, but Duane interrupted. "Uh . . . Craig? I think I'm in trouble."

"What do you mean?"

"I'm wet with sweat, and my heart is racing. Give me your hand."

Duane placed Craig's hand on the left side of his neck over the artery.

Richard whispered, "What's going on?"

"Duane's heart is a little excited. Are you just scared, or is it something else?"

"I'm embarrassed to tell you." He could hardly catch his breath.

Richard said, "Come on man. Spill your guts."

"I have claustrophobia really bad."

Craig put his hand on Duane's shoulder. "Everything is fine. Sit down here with your back against the wall. We can take a break. The air is very tight in here, so close your eyes and take some slow, deep breaths."

"Shall I tell him about our first cave experience?" Richard whispered.

Craig said, "Are you trying to embarrass me?"

Duane asked, "What happened?"

There was a muffled laugh from both men, then Richard continued. "The first time Craig and I explored a cave, I had to carry him out. He passed out on me."

"I did not," Craig said in a low, but forceful whisper. "Look at him and look at me. He may be taller, but he couldn't carry me if he wanted too. I did pass out, but it was from the heat. The cave was near a volcano. At least I never ran from a few harmless cave bats!"

"A few harmless cave bats? There were hundreds of them, and they flew right for my head. I simply ran to another cavern."

Duane placed his hands over his mouth to suppress his laugh.

Craig said, "So, have we blown our super hero image?"

"Not really. You guys are pretty great. Hey, my heart's slowed down, and I'm not sweating anymore. We better get going and find those intruders before they find us."

"Are you sure you're okay?" Craig checked Duane's pulse again. It was beating at a slower, more steady pace.

"I really am. Thanks. Thanks a lot."

"That's okay," Richard said, "but if you ever tell anyone what we just told you, we'll bring you back in here, and leave you without a flashlight."

"Don't worry! Your secret is safe with me, but it will make a good journal entry, just in case I ever need it."

They both popped him on the head.

Craig said, "Lets get moving. We have a ways to go. If I remember right we're going to hit a series of slight inclines and descents. It can make you feel a bit unsteady, especially in this dark."

The next thirty minutes the only sound they heard, in the deathly quiet cave, came from their muffled footsteps, until Richard stopped. He turned, put his fingers across his lips then turned off his light. Duane and Craig followed suit. A few feet ahead, they saw a small glimmer of light coming through an opening.

Craig passed Richard, reaching the exit first. It opened off to the right. Just before stepping out he whispered, "There's a lot more brush here than before. Our intruders must have found it by accident. Duane, hang back while we look around."

CHAPTER 36

CAPTURED

*D*uane took several steps back then heard a slightly familiar voice. "Welcome gentlemen! We've been expecting you. Lay those rifles on the ground, real slow—and that pistol."

Duane saw Craig and Richard lay their rifles at their feet then the man said, "Give up the .44 too, boy. I can shoot the tail feathers off a crow a hundred feet away. I've done it many times."

Another voice said, "He ain't lying! I've seen it!"

"Shut up and get their guns!"

"What do you want with us?" Craig asked.

"Now that's real funny ain't it Twig? Twig?"

"You told me to shut up, Slick." Twig whined.

Duane's knees shook. He kept backing up without making a sound, and managed to hold his breath until he rounded the first bend. He turned his headlamp on then kept his eyes on the existing footprints. He moved at an accelerated pace. The air was close, and the fact that he was alone in the depth of this darkness, made him shiver.

Duane's thumping heart sounded like drums pounding in his ears. His chest grew tight—he struggled to catch a deep breath. *Come on. You can do this. It all rests on you. You have to warn the family.*

Twenty-five minutes later he reached the end of the corridor, and stumbled around the rock wall. A streak of light breaking through the edges of the broken door was a welcome sight. As he pushed it open, a single rifle shot reverberated in the cave behind him.

"Oh God. No."

Duane raced across the crunching snow toward the settlement. His breathing was so rapid, white clouds of frigid air formed around his face. His lungs felt like fire, but when he reached the rock wall it infused him with a burst of energy. He stumbled up the porch steps, dropped to his knees, fell against the locked door while tightly clinching his rifle.

In a breathless plea he said, "Let me in. Please."

Joliene yelled, "That's Duane."

She flung open the door and squatted down beside him. "Son, what's wrong?"

"They got Craig—and Richard! There's two of them—they've got guns."

Darren helped him inside then locked the door, "Duane. Take some slow breaths then tell us what happened."

When he could speak without gasping he said, "They got Craig and Richard. I heard a gun shot. It came from the cave."

Linda buried her face in her hands as tears welled in her eyes. "Thank God Tracey's in the back with the kids. Duane, tell us the rest. Who has them?"

"When we got to the other side of the cave, Craig and Richard stepped outside. Those two longhaired guys—the ones we met at the park, Slick and Twig, were waiting for them." He stopped to take a few more breaths.

"They took Craig and Richard's guns. The one called Slick said they were expecting them. They didn't see me, so I walked backwards until the cave made a turn, then I took off running. Maybe I should have stayed and fought."

Darren patted his shoulder. "You did the right thing. If they captured all three of you we wouldn't have a clue what was going on. This way we're not caught off guard."

Duane took another deep breath. "Slick was bragging about being a crack shot. They talk like they're straight from the hills. I mean, not very educated."

Darren covered his forehead with his hand. "They're probably coming through the cave right now. We've got to move fast—and be prepared in case someone's injured."

Tracey walked up behind Darren. "Why do you think someone got injured?"

"We don't know what happened, exactly. Duane heard a shot just as he exited the cave."

Tracey stared ahead for a minute then moved in the direction of the bedrooms. She called over her shoulder, "Let's hurry and get everyone to safety."

Darren said, "Chad grab some blankets. Everybody else grab a coat. I want all of you in the supply cave. We'll take the path closest to the woods. If they beat us to the area, they won't be able to see us on that trail, then we'll go to plan B— as soon as we can make one. Lois, the boys and I can help you with your walker. Duane you bring the lanterns."

Lois said, "I'm staying here. I will just slow you down. I'll hide in the shower if they show up. Now, get going."

Linda started to object but Lois raised her pointer finger and said, "I'm going nowhere. Get yourselves and those kids out of here."

Darren frowned, but didn't argue. He turned to Duane who still had a rifle in his hand. "Under no circumstances are you to allow anybody to get close to the family. Do you understand what I'm saying?"

Duane did understand, but couldn't stop his hand from shaking.

Tracey reached toward him. "I understand too. Give me that gun." He didn't argue.

Darren said to Nathaniel, "We'll work on a plan, as soon as we escort these guys to the cave. Since they don't know about Duane, we may have a chance."

Linda spun around. "No! Not Nathaniel. I'll help you."

"Mom, listen. I'm not a child, I know how to use a rifle—and Dad would want me to do this. You know I'm right."

Linda hesitated a moment. "I wish that wasn't true, but it is." She hugged him tight then said, "Let's go."

~

After Slick and Twig confiscated Craig and Richard's weapons, Slick told Richard to go first followed by Twig. Craig would be next, and Slick would bring up the rear. Craig wasn't scared, but was ready to explode with anger. *How is it possible I let these two hillbillies get the drop on us?*

Fifteen minutes later Slick said, "I can't wait to see your pretty ladies again. There's three or four of 'em, isn't there?"

Craig clinched his fists, and gritted his teeth. *I'll kill him long before he gets close to our family.*

They needed to stall, so when they were about a fourth of the way down the corridor, Craig jammed the toe of his boot firmly in the loose dirt, which caused him to stumble past Twig. When Richard reached down to help him up, Craig whispered, "Your dad will try something. Be ready."

Slick struck Craig in the back of his head with the butt of his rifle and yelled, "What are you two whispering about?"

Craig hit the cave wall as he fell, this time for real. First, to his knees then on his face.

Slick leaned over him. "Get up or I'll hit you again."

Richard reached for Craig. "Are you okay?"

Slick lunged passed Craig toward Richard. "Shut up or your next!"

Craig, seizing the opportunity, punched Slick behind his right knee. Slick lost his balance and fell forward. His rifle dropped at Richard's feet. Richard kicked it down the path. Twig seemed frozen in place, doing nothing.

Richard spun around, grabbed the barrel of Twig's rifle, and twisted it, unaware that Twig's finger was on the trigger. When it fired, the bullet hit the opposite wall, ricocheted down, and Slick cried out. Twig's rifle fell next to Craig.

Twig yelled, "Slick. What's wrong?"

"You shot me you idiot."

"No, I didn't. The dang gun went off."

Craig checked Slick's wound, after retrieving the .44 caliber.

Richard yelled, "Drop your backpack, Twig, and remove your brothers."

He separated the men from their backpacks, then told Twig to keep his fingers locked behind his head.

"Yes, sir. I will. Please hurry and help my brother."

Craig handed Richard the .44 then shined his light on Slick's blood-soaked jeans. Craig cut away enough cloth to expose a bullet hole just above Slick's knee. Blood was oozing from the wound in a slow but steady stream. Craig yanked off his belt, wrapped it around Slick's leg then cinched it tight enough to slow the bleeding.

"We've got to get him out of here," Craig said. "Darren will know what to do."

Craig unloaded Twig and Slick's rifles then strapped one on each of Twig's shoulders. The backpacks would be left behind.

Slick cried out when they lifted him to his feet. He tried to hop on his good leg, but only made ten steps before he passed out. It took almost an hour for them to drag his dead weight to the end of the corridor. When they reached the spring, Craig breathed a sigh of relief. Twig and Richard laid Slick down close to the door.

When Craig pushed the broken cave door open he took a couple of deep breaths then saw Nathaniel standing a few feet left of the door. Darren was on the right. Both were ready to fire.

"Everything's okay!" Craig shouted. "We're safe, but one of the intruders was shot. I'm afraid he got it in an artery. You better check him out."

"Where's Richard?"

"He's right behind me. He's okay."

As Darren rushed past, Craig looked at Nathaniel. "Good job, son. Would you let the family know we're fine?"

"Sure will, Dad. They're in the other cave, except Grandma. She made us leave her behind. Can I let them out?"

"Yes, but tell them to go to the huts and stay there. You go with them and take charge for a while. Keep the doors locked. I'll be there as soon as I can."

Nathaniel tried to keep a straight face, but a small smile escaped. "Yes, sir, I will. Glad you're okay, Dad."

Craig wasn't okay, but tried to play it off. He wanted no one to know he his vision was blurred and his head was throbbing.

Before Nathaniel got away, Darren stepped out long enough to yell, "Have Chad bring me my bag. I need to do vitals."

Nathaniel gave thumbs up as he ran, without missing a beat.

CHAPTER 37

TAKING CARE OF SLICK

*T*en minutes after Craig re-entered the small cave, Joliene came through the door. Linda was right behind her.

Craig said, "You two are supposed to be at the huts."

Linda hugged Craig tight. "We thought you might need some help. Nathaniel told us what happened. He said it was safe, and took the kids back. They'll be fine."

Craig started to respond, but he stumbled backwards, and fell against the rough wall. Linda dropped to her knees and took his hand. "Craig, are you all right? Are you hurt?"

"Slick hit me in the back of the head with his rifle. I'll be fine in a few minutes."

She rubbed her fingers over the bump, which made Craig wince a little.

"Darren, he's got a pretty good sized lump here. Can you check him out?"

Darren said, "As soon as I can. Don't let him fall asleep, and don't give him any food until I can get over there. This guy's breathing is very shallow."

Chad ran through the door with Darren's bag. Twig was sitting at Slick's head, running his fingers through his own stringy, dirty hair, watching every move. When Darren lifted the stethoscope he closed his eyes a minute then sighed.

"What's wrong, mister? Will my brother be okay?"

"I'm not sure, but I have to be honest with you, it doesn't look good. He's lost a lot of blood. His pressure is low, and his breathing is shallow. My medical supplies are in the other hut, plus there's more room. I want to get him moved before I loosen the tourniquet."

Darren asked Joliene and Chad to go ahead of them, fix Slick a bed, and make sure the fire was still going. When they were ready, Richard and Twig helped Darren carry Slick's dead weight over the beaten path. Tears were running down Twig's face.

Craig's legs were weak, but his dizziness had subsided. Linda helped him to his feet and he stumbled his way to the larger cave.

Joliene held the light as Darren cut away more of Slick's jeans. When he loosened the belt, blood rolled freely over Slick's leg. Darren quickly cinched the belt back in place.

Darren said. "I'm afraid I don't have the right set up or supplies to help him. He needs a transfusion, plus that bullet needs to be removed. I don't have the right clamps or a lot of other stuff. His artery is completely compromised."

Twig covered his face. "I'm sorry, Slick! I didn't mean to do it!"

"I'll try to save your brother, Twig," Darren said. "But I have to be honest with you. He's in bad shape."

Darren turned to Richard and pointed at the far wall. "Would you pull that trunk over here? I need to start an IV, and give him some morphine, *if* I can find a vein."

Darren busied himself with Slick, and without looking up he asked, "So where did you get the name Twig?"

"My brother named me that cause I'm so tall and skinny."

"Do you know if Slick has any allergies?"

"I ain't heard of none."

Twig began to tremble. "If something happens to my brother, what are you going to do with me?"

Through gritted teeth Craig said, "Twig. Come over here."

"Yes, sir."

Twig squatted down then Craig put his finger on the end of Twig's nose. "That's a *very* good question, and right now, we don't have an answer, but you and your brother threatened our family today. You're lucky I don't take you to the woods, and shoot you. As of right now consider yourself under house arrest, and it will be a *very* good idea if you do exactly what you're told. Do I make myself clear?"

Twig dropped his chin on his chest for a moment, then looked Craig straight in the eyes. "Yes, sir, I do. But I promise, I would never hurt your family."

"That may be true, but one of those gun barrels poking us in the back belonged to you. I have no reason to believe or trust you, so stay close to Richard. He *will* use that rifle if he has to."

Twig dropped his head. "I will, and I'm very sorry, sir."

Craig fell to the cave floor, let out a long sigh, and rubbed his temples. Linda leaned over him. He said he was fine, and asked if she would get a wet cloth for his head.

Twig was quiet for a long time then asked. "If it's not too much trouble, could I have just a bite to eat?"

Linda looked down at Craig for approval. He said, "Go ahead."

Linda fixed Twig a peanut butter sandwich, which he ate as if he was starving.

"You'll be able to have more later, Twig, when we have dinner," Linda said.

He smiled and said, "Thank you, ma'am. That's very kind."

As soon as Slick's IV was dripping, Darren checked Craig's vitals, including the dilation of his eyes. "Your eyes are responding like they should. That's good news. Have you had any nausea?"

"No, but I'm starting to have hunger."

Darren laughed. "Well, we can remedy that later, but for now, I don't want you to eat or sleep. You may have a slight concussion. That's a big lump. It's a good thing you have such a hard head."

A slight smile spread across Craig's face. "I guess I'll be on guard duty tonight since you won't let me sleep, but I want some food pretty soon."

~

Late in the afternoon Richard accompanied Twig, Linda and Joliene to the huts. Chad stayed with his grandpa and Slick.

Richard sent Linda and Joliene in first. He wanted Tracey to take the three younger children, and Brianna to the opposite sleeping quarters until Twig had bathed, and was wearing clean clothes.

When he got an all clear Richard took Twig inside, and straight to the shower. Linda offered an outfit of Nathaniel's.

Richard said, "Twig you can wear socks, but I'm taking your shoes for the night."

Twig nodded and asked no questions.

When they moved to the living area, Twig sat down in front of the fireplace and never moved, even when Lois gave him a plate of dinner.

Tracey motioned for Richard to follow her to the kitchen. She whispered, "Is it safe to have him in here? Wasn't he ready to kill you?"

"To be honest, I don't think so, but find something for the kids to do and keep them away from him. Let's get through this night. Tomorrow we'll figure something out."

Richard looked in Twig's direction. "He doesn't seem to be anything like his brother. It will be good to hear his story."

He gave Twig a twin sized blow up mattress, blankets and a pillow. Twig chose to sleep as close to the fireplace as possible. Richard would stand guard until two in the morning then Nathaniel would take over. Richard didn't think Twig would try to escape, especially without shoes, and nowhere to go, but he wouldn't take a chance.

When Twig climbed into his covers he smiled. "I ain't been warm or slept in a real bed for a long time. Will you folks keep that fireplace going all night?"

Richard said, "We will, but you be sure you stay in bed. Someone will be guarding you. I haven't forgotten you were ready to shoot me."

Twig shuddered, "Honest mister, I ain't never shot nobody. My brother, Slick, he's real mean. He makes me do whatever he says. If I don't, he hurts me bad. It's been like that since I was a kid."

He rolled over facing the fire. "But, I don't want him to die. He's my brother."

"I'm sure you don't. Now get some sleep. We'll wake you if anything happens."

"Thanks mister. I really mean it. Thanks."

"You're welcome. Now go to sleep."

CHAPTER 38

BACK FROM THE DEAD

*E*arly the next morning, Richard woke Twig, and handed him his shoes. "Put these on. I'll get us some coffee then we'll check on your brother."

Twig rubbed his eyes. "Will we get to eat some breakfast?"

Lois said, "Yes. We'll feed you when you get back. Don't worry."

Tracey followed Richard to the kitchen area and said, "We've faced harsh weather and wild animals, but next to these two men those incidents seem almost tame, and not nearly as frightening. Where would we keep two criminals?"

Before Richard could answer, Linda came out of her sleeping quarters. "Have you heard from Craig and Darren?"

"Not yet," Richard said. "We're getting ready to head up there."

Linda thanked him, and said they would get breakfast started. This morning Lois was preparing oatmeal with brown sugar.

Linda walked to the front window, and looked in the direction of the caves. "I just want the family all in one place."

Craig didn't move a muscle when Twig pulled open the cave door.

209

Richard closed it, not expecting to be met with Slick's weak voice. "Hand my brother that rifle, and be quick about it. Believe me . . . I'll shoot you."

Craig wanted to shout out a warning, but Richard would have no chance to retreat. He knew what this man, Slick, was capable of.

Craig, and Darren had been living this nightmare since four in the morning. Most of the night, Slick appeared to be taking his last breaths. Neither Craig nor Darren thought he posed any type of threat—but they were wrong. The IV fluid gave Slick's vital organs a charge, and in spite of his grave condition, he woke up.

At 3:00 a.m., Craig's head was splitting, so he took two, over-the-counter pain relievers then shut his eyes, hoping they would take affect. He did not intend to go to sleep, but he did. His rifle slipped out of his hand, over his leg, and onto the cave floor. Darren was sitting near Slick, with his back against the cave wall. He too was dozing.

While they slept, Slick had apparently scooted until he reached Craig. He must have gently pulled the rifle until he got a firm grip then scooted back into position. The tourniquet rolled, relaxing the tension on his wound and it began slowly oozing out. When Darren awoke, even in the dim light of the lantern, he saw that Slick's blood was pooling on the mat.

Craig woke to Darren's voice. "Wake up. We've got problems."

Craig reached for his rifle, then heard a weak laugh. "Don't bother. I got it right here. I sure appreciated you fellas taking such good care of me. Now, fix this bandage and tell me—where's my brother? Where's Twig?"

"He's in the huts sleeping." Darren said. "What are you doing?"

Craig remained seated, not wanting to further antagonize the situation.

"What does it look like I'm doing? I'm taking over this camp."

Darren said, "You're too weak to take over anything. We've been trying to help you. You're bleeding to death. You can't walk out of here, Slick, and you certainly can't fight all of us."

"I ain't planning to walk outta here." Slick winced in pain. "Believe me, I've got a plan. This is going to be my new home. Now, one of you fellas get up and get me some grub then sit together where I can see ya.'"

Darren offered him crackers and peanut butter then sat down next to Craig. Slick scoffed them down, as Twig had done, but unlike Twig, Slick vomited them right back up. Darren started to help him, but Slick grunted, "Stay where you are. We'll just sit here, and wait for your friends to arrive, then we'll decide who we're getting rid of. We have to even the odds a little. You know what I mean? You got yourself a real sweet setup, and some pretty women too. I got plans for them, especially the younger ones."

Craig's blood was boiling. He felt like the top of his head would explode. He started to lunge at Slick, but Darren held his arm tight. This man was a monster. He wasn't human. His insides were burned out, and in spite of his condition he was still in charge. Craig hoped he would pass out before anyone else showed up. Unfortunately, he didn't.

Craig wanted to yell out a warning when the cave door opened, but he knew Slick would certainly shoot one of them. He whispered, "How could I have been so careless?"

Craig thought, *one false move, Slick. One false move and we'll bury you. God, save us from this maniac.*

"Give Twig that gun," Slick yelled to Richard, "or you'll be the first one I shoot!"

"Slick, what are you doing? These people saved your life." Twig said.

Slick gave a weak, but firm order. "Get that gun you idiot. It took us too long to get here to change plans now. They got everything we need to survive, and more. They even got women."

Twig slowly took the gun from Richard's hand.

"Now, little brother, let's see how much of a man you really are. Take your friend there and this big guy, right outside the door and shoot 'em. We'll keep the doc. He may come in handy."

"Slick, you know I ain't never killed nobody, and I don't plan on starting today. Let's just get some supplies and get out of here."

Slick slowly set his sight directly on Twig. He slanted his eyes, set his jaw and whispered loudly, "Do as I say or I'll blow your fool head off. You hear me boy? Two rifle shots, that's all I want to hear."

Craig's eyes met Richard's. They understood each other completely. One of them would undoubtedly die, but they would not let these maniacs have access to their families.

Twig motioned for Craig to stand up. He did not move so Slick pointed his rifle right at Craig's belly.

"Stand close to the opening. It will be easier for me to see you fall."

Craig and Richard backed up as instructed, but before Craig took one step out, a shot reverberated through the cave. Craig spun around, expecting to see Richard fall. Craig could see the same relief in Richard's eyes.

Slick lay slumped to the left. His head was on his shoulder, and his rifle lay across his chest. The bullet hole, placed directly between his eyes was oozing a trail of blood down his nose, across his cheek.

Twig stared at his brother, put his head down then handed the rifle back to Richard. In a quiet, but audible whisper, he said, "I should've done that a long time ago."

CHAPTER 39

WE HAVE TWIG – NOW WHAT

*C*raig rushed to Slick's side and recovered the rifle from the dead man's hand. Richard stood stunned. Darren felt for a pulse. There was none. In the city they would call 9-1-1, and the legal system would take over, but they were not in the city. In this valley they *were* the legal system.

The cave door swung open. Nathaniel stepped in, and Craig told him he could lower the gun.

"Are we sure he's dead, Dad?"

"Oh, he's dead all right. No doubt about that."

Craig said, "Darren, Richard and I need to talk. Would you take Twig to the lodge? They'll ask you about Slick. Just tell them he died, and give Twig some breakfast. We'll fill you in later. Okay?"

"Sure, do you want me to keep a rifle on him?"

"No, there's no need for that. I think he showed us where his heart is—in a most profound way."

He turned toward Twig, "Am I right, or do we need to keep a gun on you?"

"No, sir, I ain't going nowhere unless you send me." Tears were streaming down his face. "Sir, Slick's my brother. I'd like to be the one to bury him."

"Well, that can be arranged, but right now Richard and I need to talk. Go with Darren, and don't either of you tell them what just happened. We'll be along pretty soon. But Twig, Slick said he could shoot the tail feathers off a crow at a hundred feet. You agreed with him, but said nothing about yourself."

Twig's head was on his chest. "I guess I should have told you—I can split a crow's feathers from a hundred feet. Shooting was the only thing I could do better than my brother."

When the cave door closed, Craig said, "Well, what do you think? Did we witness a murder or a justified homicide?"

"Let me put it this way, if things had gone the way Slick planned, one or both of us would be dead. That makes me shudder. I think we owe Twig a lifetime debt of gratitude."

"That's what I think too. Twig's not a robber, or a killer," Craig said. "Most likely, he's been on this rampage because he was forced into it. Today, he chose us over his brother. I don't think I'll be forgetting that soon."

Richard said, "Still, we can't ignore the facts. Should we load him up with supplies, take him through the cave, and threaten to shoot him if he comes back? Although, I would never want to be in an actual shootout with him."

"I wouldn't either! Let's pray it never happens."

Richard started to push the door open then turned back to Craig. "Are we ready to face the family, and how much do we tell them?"

"Well, after we remove the three younger children, I think we should start, and end with the truth, without the gruesome details. That way we can stay out of trouble."

Everyone was eating when they walked through the door. Linda hurried to Craig, and Tracey to Richard. Linda was first to speak, "Are you okay?"

Craig said, "Actually, everything is great, but we're starving. Let's have some breakfast then we can talk."

"Why all the mystery?" Linda asked.

"No mystery, just intrigue," he said as he kissed her on the forehead.

After breakfast, Craig asked Duane to take the children for a walk. Twig was told to sit in the bedroom quarters until the family finished talking. Craig told the story without gory details, but he was confident everyone got the point.

He said, "What we're planning is a long, serious talk with Twig. We want him to understand we know what his intent was when he came here, although we believe he was constantly threatened by Slick. We men will become his probation officers." He turned toward Nathaniel. "That includes you."

Nathaniel sat up straight, "Sure Dad, I'll keep an eye on him. He better not think about hurting anyone."

Richard spoke up "Make sure your rifles are locked up until we know he can be trusted. Things seem to happen really fast around here."

Tracey was pacing. "This makes me very uncomfortable. How could he shoot his own brother in cold blood?"

"Tracey!" Richard was stern. "He made a choice. His chose to shoot Slick instead of Craig and me. Think about that. We're standing here alive because of him."

"I know!" She held her face in her hands. "I just can't imagine such a thing."

Joliene said, "I kind of go along with her. It's hard to imagine, but what if Twig did what Slick ordered, we would be burying you two, and God only knows what would have happened to us."

Linda shuddered and slipped her hand into Craig's.

Nathaniel asked, "Dad, how can you bury Slick in frozen ground?"

Craig opened his eyes wide for a moment. "That's a good question, son. I hadn't thought of that. How *do* you bury someone in frozen ground?"

"Well," Lois said, "I heard about some Eskimos who kept a fire going, then dug out each section as it thawed. They didn't have caskets so they wrapped the body in cloth then covered it in pine branches. The pine smell helped keep animals from digging it up."

"I think that will work," Craig said. "We'll let Twig do most of the digging. He asked if he could be the one to bury his brother."

Lois wheeled her chair close to Craig. "Son, could I speak to you and Richard in private?"

"Of course. Let's go out on the porch."

Lois's wheelchair thumped along the logs then she spun around facing the two men. "I'm really worried about allowing Twig to be part of the family. He and Slick might have been on a robbing binge all the way from Tennessee. As much as I hate to say it, I think others in the family need a turn at questioning him."

Craig was a little taken back. "Are you talking about some type of a trial? Are we qualified to do that?"

"Why not? Maybe its time we become legally organized. Who knows what will hit us in the future. Wouldn't we be better off to have a plan in place? I think we have a right to question Twig. The first question is, have you ever killed anyone else?"

Craig said, "I don't think we can get *legally* organized, but as far as Twig is concerned, we heard him tell his brother he'd never killed anyone. I feel like he was telling the truth."

Lois pressed on. "Maybe so, but it seems like we're assuming Twig's role in their crime spree was an innocent one. We have to make sure he's safe around our children. For that matter, is he safe around the whole family?"

Craig was too tired to argue. "Okay, Mom, we'll have a family meeting, and get everyone's opinion. If the family wants a trial, we'll have one."

"Don't get me wrong, I like the young man, but we need to hear what he has to say. Tracey is beside herself. She probably has a pistol strapped to her leg."

Richard and Craig doubled over with laughter, but composed themselves before going inside.

Craig said, "Okay, everyone, we need you to gather over here by the fireplace. We have to make some decisions regarding Twig."

He moved his neck in every direction, and asked Linda for a pain reliever before he started the meeting. His head throbbed, and he was still a bit woozy, but thankful to be alive.

"Everyone here knows about the latest sequence of events. Mom is under the opinion we need to put Twig on trial. What do the rest of you think?"

Tracey spoke first, which was no surprise, but what she said—was. "I've been giving this issue a lot of thought. If we put Twig on trial, wouldn't that be like a slap in the face? I mean . . . my husband . . . the father of my children, is here with us because Twig had the guts to fire a bullet at the *right* target. We should be giving him an award!"

Chad said, "You can tell he isn't a bad guy. He had a bad brother."

"I agree, but I think he has some questions to answer," Joliene said.

"Okay, let's do this," Richard said. "Spend some time thinking about your questions, write them down, and we'll talk again tomorrow night."

Craig nodded. "Sounds good to me. So if we have no more questions or comments, Nathaniel, would you get Twig? It's only fair we tell him what's going on."

Twig was white as a sheet when he came back into the room. Craig knew this hillbilly had no idea what to expect.

Craig motioned for him to sit down. "Twig, I'm sure you understand we had to have this meeting, and it was about you."

"I understand, and I can't say I blame you, but can I just ask one question?"

"What is it?"

"Are you gonna send me out on my own? If you are, could I talk you into just locking me up somewhere? I'm scared to death to face all that cold and hunger again."

"Twig, we aren't plotting against you, but we do have some questions. We would do anything to protect our family. You believe that, don't you?"

"Yes, sir, I do."

"Tomorrow night we're going to meet again, so be prepared. Everyone, even the children, will be allowed to ask you questions. We expect you to tell the truth. After the meeting is over we'll make a decision as to whether you stay or go."

Twig said, "If I had a family like yours I'd be real careful too."

Craig knew the next twenty-four hours would be an agonizing eternity for Twig.

CHAPTER 40

LAYING SLICK TO REST

*A*fter breakfast, the following morning, Craig helped Twig find a satisfactory spot to bury Slick, a quarter mile from the huts. He thanked Craig for the help, but wanted to do the rest by himself. He would take Lois' suggestion, build a fire, and as the ground thawed he would dig. The rest of the guys offered to help, but Twig said no. He wanted to do it by himself.

Joliene and Linda volunteered to wrap Slick's body in a white sheet, and suggested it remain in the cave until the grave was ready. Darren thought the gunshot wound would be a little traumatic for the ladies, and everyone else, so he covered it with a small bandage then wiped Slicks body down. Lois asked Twig if he would like to have a brief graveside service.

"That would be real nice. Thank you Miss Lois."

Craig asked Nathaniel and Duane to check on Twig until the grave was finished. "Make sure he's fed, and has something hot to drink."

After the second trip, Nathaniel told his dad that both times they approached, Twig wiped his eyes before facing them.

"In spite of the circumstances," Craig said, "he's grieving the loss of his brother. Slick chose to live a vile, wicked life, but he was still Twig's flesh and blood."

Twig turned the final shovel of dirt about 4:00 pm. Craig and Richard laid Slick's wrapped body across the four-wheeler, and plowed through the snow to get it to the gravesite. Craig went back for his mother, and the rest of the troop followed on foot as a funeral procession.

Darren read Psalm 23, and to everyone's surprise, Brianna asked if she could say the prayer.

"Heavenly Father, we don't know if Slick is with you or not, but would you please be with Twig now that his brother is gone? Thank you so much that we are not burying my dad or Richard here today."

At that point in her prayer, several gasps, and amens were heard.

Brianna continued, "Please help Twig make good decisions for the rest of his life, no matter where he lives, and help all of us to make a good decision at our meeting tonight. And God, please let this be the last person we have to bury."

Twig wasn't the only one weeping silently. Craig could see the death grip Tracey had on Richard's hand as tears streamed down her face.

Craig asked, "Twig, is there anything you would like to say?"

"Thank you all very much. You didn't have to do this, and my momma would be real proud. She was a church going woman, and I can tell y'all are too. I used to go with her, but Slick and Dad stayed home. They said I was a sissy, but Momma said God is looking at your seat every Sunday to see if you're in it, so I went."

Lois said, "Twig, would you please come over here a moment?"

He leaned down in front of her, and she wrapped her arms tightly around his neck. He wept openly against her shoulder. Caleb ran over, hugged Twig's leg and said, "I'm real sorry, mister."

Craig knew everyone was deeply moved, so he stepped back, a few respectful moments before saying, "We better head back. You don't want your tears to start freezing. Take Twig to the huts while Nathaniel and I put pine branches over the grave. It won't take long. Richard, would you drive Mom back?"

At dinnertime, Craig smiled when the ladies served moose steak, pinto beans and corn bread. In times past, a dinner like this would have enlisted a few groans, but now it was enjoyed. Richard shot the moose on their initial hunting trip, right after the first heavy freeze. Processing was a learning experience, but it was done. Chunks of meat were individually wrapped then kept inside Craig's smaller trailer away from predators.

CHAPTER 41

QUESTIONING TWIG

*C*raig asked Richard to join him on the porch after dinner. They pulled up their coat collars, and turned their backs to the frigid wind.

"I'll make this quick. Do you have any new thoughts on Twig? Are we ready to accept him as a family member, if the family agrees? Are we satisfied he can be trusted?"

"I'm going to reserve my judgment until I hear his answers to the barrage of questions he'll be bombarded with. I think he's been bullied all his life, and doesn't seem to have his brother's characteristics, but we can't make any snap decisions."

"I agree, so let's get it over with. I'm tired of this constant drama. Are things ever going to settle down?"

Richard smiled. "I sure hope so, but I think the drama helps divert our attention from the virus, and home, if such a thing is possible."

When they reentered, the family was seated in a semi-circle in front of the fireplace—except Twig. His chair was placed in the middle of the floor, facing those who held his future in their hands. He was cleaned up, shaved, hair slicked back, wearing Nathaniel's clothes, and squirming as if he were sitting on a colony of fire ants.

Craig said, "All right. Let's get this thing started with prayer. We need all the wisdom we can get, but first—for crying out loud make room for Twig in our circle. Give the man some dignity."

Nathaniel and Duane were on the end so they moved their chairs apart, and Twig placed his there.

Craig looked around the circle. "Cassie, would you say our prayer, and ask God to help us make good decisions?"

"I never prayed in front of a bunch of people before, but I'll try." She bowed her head, "God, here we are again. I think we're just not smart enough to figure out what to do by ourselves, so would you please help us? We like Twig very much, and we want to keep him so would you let everything go okay? Amen."

Tracey slipped her arm around her daughter, and said, "Amen."

"Thank you, Cassie. Now, who has the first question?"

Lois said, "I do. Twig, I feel the same way Cassie does, but Slick was bragging about robbing stores, and killing a young clerk. How could you possibly go along with that?"

Twig faced her squarely, "Miss Lois, I didn't want to rob that boy, and I ain't never killed nobody—well, except Slick. Slick shot that kid and he wasn't even sorry. I told him I was going home, and he said if I did, the next thing I would see was our Momma's face in heaven. I knew he meant it. He was as mean as a snake. I want you to know I ain't no thief. Why I even told Slick we should walk right up, and knock on your door. He wouldn't do it."

Darren was next. "Twig, has Slick ever hurt you?"

"Yes, sir. Can I show you something?"

"Well, I suppose that depends on what it is, and where it is. Should we send the children and the ladies out?"

"Yes, sir. That's a good idea."

Twig waited until the others disappeared, then proceeded to unhook his jeans. He dropped them to his knees then pointed to his left cheek. Two large mounds of pink scar tissue were visibly portrayed against the stark white surface.

Duane stared in amazement. "What happened?"

"Slick stuck me with a pitchfork when I was sixteen. He could get real mean sometimes, especially after Momma died. We were working in the barn, throwing hay to the cows. Slick yelled, *run!* So I did, but before I got out the door I slipped on a cow pile. He threw the fork and it stuck me. I tried to pull it out, but I couldn't. My daddy came home about that time and pulled it out for me. He just laughed, and said I should watch out for cow piles. I almost couldn't walk for a few weeks."

He raised his shirt to show some deep stripes. "My daddy did this. He said he was making a man of me so he beat me real good with his whip. I was scared not to do what they both said. I know that ain't no excuse, but honest, I ain't a bad guy. I don't want to hurt nobody, and I'm a real hard worker."

"Put your clothes on so we can let those guys back in." Craig was sure their curiosity was killing them.

Caleb came bounding in first. "What did he show you? Was it real gross?"

Linda said, "Caleb! That's enough. Use your manners."

"I'm sorry, Mom." He turned to his dad and whispered, "Was it real gross?"

Craig screwed up his face and whispered back, "Yes, it was."

To the rest of the group he said, "Twig has shown us some pretty impressive scars. He had reason to be afraid of his brother, however we're going to continue with the questions, so who's next?"

Cassie raised her hand halfway, put it back down then raised it again. Craig nodded her way. "Go ahead Cassie. It's okay if you ask a question."

"My brother drives me crazy, but I couldn't kill him. How could you do that?"

Twig turned to face her as he spoke. "I knew one of you would ask me that. I've been thinking real hard on it. When we were in the cave he told me to take your dad, and Craig outside and kill them."

Sara gasped. "He told you to kill my daddy?"

"Yes, little girl. He said if I didn't, he was going to shoot *me*. I knew

224

he meant it. I also knew if your dad and Craig were dead, Slick would treat all of you real bad. He never thought I'd shoot him or he would have dropped me on the spot. I just spun around and got him first. I don't know what else to say. Craig told me to speak the truth. That's what I'm doing."

Caleb raised his hand, "Mister, why do you talk so funny?"

Linda rose to her feet, "Caleb! You apologize right now."

Caleb put his hand over his mouth.

Twig came to his defense immediately. "It's okay, Miss. I do talk different than y'all. Maybe Caleb could help me learn better, that is if I get to stay."

Cassie spoke up, "Can I help too?"

Everyone laughed, including Twig.

In Lois's usual peacemaking manner she said, "Twig is just fine the way he is, but I think everyone is thinking the same thing. Twig, do we have anything to fear from you?"

"No, Miss Lois! You have been so good to me. You gave Slick a real nice service. I owe you a bunch. None of you have to be afraid of me!"

"Anyone else?" Craig asked.

No one said another word.

"Okay. Sorry, Twig, do you want to wait on the porch, or on the bed?"

Twig stood up, put on his coat, and walked outside to wait for the verdict. Would he stay or would he go? He sat on a rough-hewn bench, head in his hands then raised his eyes. The moon was bright and reflected off the snow. Twig could see deep into the forest. "God, thank you for the bright moon. Its real pretty out here. I sure am sorry for not talking to you more often, but can I ask you a favor? These are real nice people and all, but if they decide to lock me up, could it be in the cave so I can have a fire? I know they'll give me food."

When the door closed, Craig faced the family. "So, what do you think?

Can we accept Twig as a family member or do we give him supplies, and send him back through the cave?"

Duane said, "I think we need to keep him. He's just a kind, uneducated country boy who's been used, and abused. I'm not afraid of him."

"What about the rest of you?"

Tracey said. "Craig, why don't we just put it to a vote?"

"Good idea. Who wants to send Twig away?"

To everyone's surprise, Darren raised his hand.

Craig asked, "Darren what's your concern?"

"I don't necessarily want to send him away. I like the guy, but will we have to watch him all the time? Can we really trust him? And there's no way we can keep the guns out of his reach. I'm willing to let him stay, but only if we put him under close observation . . . a type of probation, like you mentioned earlier. Is that unreasonable?"

Joliene was next. "That's not unreasonable. At least we'd be giving ourselves an option if, God forbid, something went wrong."

Craig said, "Let's have a new vote. Who wants to keep Twig with this stipulation—and we keep the fire arms locked?"

Everyone raised a hand.

"So what time frame are we talking about?" Craig asked.

Nathaniel offered, "How about three months?"

Lois gave Craig a long look. "Could we break the probation part to him gently?"

"Well, I'm not known for my tact. Darren, you're the doctor. Aren't you trained in giving people bad news?"

Darren laughed. "Sure, bring him in."

Twig's head hung low when he reentered. Darren asked him to sit down then said, "Twig this whole family likes you, and all of us want to keep you here. But, you know what your past few months have involved."

"Yes, sir, I do."

"Well, we voted unanimously to offer you a place in our family with one condition."

Craig and the rest of the family watched as Twig brightened up. "You just name it, sir. I can do it."

"For the next three months you'll be on probation. In addition, and I'm taking some liberty now, we'll be watching to make sure you're a man of integrity and good character. You will need to set a good example for the children, and treat the ladies and everyone else with the utmost respect. We expect you to work hard, and let us know if you have any special abilities that can help us survive here. Craig has been elected as head of this clan, and even though we practice some democracy he will always have the final word. Do you have any problem with these conditions? Can you live within them?"

"I can do what you say. I just want to tell you thank you, thank you, thank you."

Darren said, "That's all I have to say, so welcome to the family." He stood and shook Twig's hand.

Craig took over. "Well, guys let's make our new family member welcome." As hard-nosed as Craig was, he was pleased with the family's decision, but hoped this uneducated farm boy would not require a large amount of instruction or monitoring.

As each person welcomed Twig, his eyes became moist, and a smile spread across his face from ear to ear. Nathaniel and Darren worked on sleeping arrangements, and Lois filled him in on the Friday night routine. She asked him to take a turn sharing when he was ready.

Twig said, "I would love to ma'am, but I don't reckon I know anything you folks don't already know."

"Just think about it. I'm sure you'll think of something."

CHAPTER 42

A WORD FROM LEON

The next few days were free of danger, drama and family problems. Craig could live with uneventful for a while, and so could everyone else. He and Richard were desperate for a word from Leon, which usually came on Friday mornings between six and ten. He and Richard liked to take the calls away from the huts. That way, if the news was bad, they had a chance to absorb it before delivering it to the family.

Leon's next call came November 15th, at eight o'clock in the morning. He offered no glimmer of hope, except one, but the bad news came first.

"I'm still talking in a sealed room. I know you're hungry for news so let me talk first in case we get cut off. Everyone outside the vice president's inner circle is always under suspicion. I think I'm still okay because I have clearance to attend all level two meetings. I don't want to lose that. This takeover is well backed. Military and law enforcement agencies remain under Federal control. When uprisings pop up, the drones make a sweep, and when people start dropping, compliance is immediate. We know the virus is spreading deeper into Canada, and the Canadians are hopping mad. The problem is, they don't know who's behind it, so there's no target for them to launch an attack against. It's an overt act of war, and so easy, and quiet."

Leon took a deep breath. "The next portion of my news was worth waiting for. I made contact with your Canadian BLM supervisor, Jacque. I didn't give away your location, just that you were on the western side of the country, in a wilderness area. He said when its safe to travel, he will not only give you sanctuary, he is offering both of you a position in Canada's BLM. You would work for the same division you're in now, except Canada will be paying your salary."

Craig was itching to ask questions. He knew Richard was too, but they listened to every word Leon spoke saying nothing.

"He said you guys always gave a 100 percent. He can place you in the northeastern section of Canada, but in order to get there you would have to dip south. That could potentially expose you. He recommends you continue to shelter in place until one of us tells you its safe to travel."

Craig was stunned, and thanked Leon profusely.

Richard said, "I feel like you've given us a chance to breathe. A call like that will be worth waiting for. Take care of yourself, Leon. When and if you're able, fill us in on how you and your wife are doing."

Leon offered nothing personal, just, "I'll get back to you as soon as possible. Stay safe."

When he hung up Craig said, "So what do you think. Do we tell the family everything, or . . . what?"

"I'm thinking we give them the whole spiel—both good and bad. They deserve it, don't you think? Let's do it right after breakfast."

CHAPTER 43

DEATH FOG

*A*s soon as the last bite of food was consumed, Craig called for everyone's attention, then shared Leon's news. Whoops and yells of excitement bounced off the walls. Craig felt it was their first ray of real hope since leaving home. It was a joyous time.

Craig said, "But, don't start packing yet. Like Leon said, we can only travel when its safe."

Later that day, still basking in Leon's good news, Craig was playing a game with Caleb and the girls. He invited Duane to join them. When Duane walked past the window, he stopped, backed up and stared.

"Look guys! That's the weirdest thing I've ever seen. A thick fog is rolling in. It's already covered the woods, and it's settling right down on the ground."

Several members joined him, and watched as the consuming mist wrap itself around every familiar landmark—in every direction. The outside world was becoming invisible.

Twig moved to the fireplace and began to shiver. Lois asked, "What's wrong, Twig?"

"It's the death fog, ma'am. I ain't seen it since I left Tennessee, but I've been expecting it."

"Twig," Tracey said. "You'll scare the children, and you aren't doing much for me either. Remember, you're supposed to be setting a good example."

Before he could answer, a spine tingling cry came from the direction of the woods, closest to the lakes.

"Never heard that sound before," Richard said. "Have you?"

Craig shook his head. He'd heard the cry of many animals while on BLM assignments, but nothing that raised the hair on the back of his neck like this.

Without speaking, Lois handed Craig a key for the gun rack. He removed the cord then took a 7 mm and a .22 rifle down. He leaned them against the door then glanced Richard's way. Nothing he could say, at this moment, would lesson the impact of the terrifying cry.

As Craig was slipping on his boots the second cry came. It seemed to linger, as if resting on the encroaching darkness. Involuntary chills shot down his spine. *It's just an animal with a scary voice.*

As if orchestrated, all eyes floated back and forth between he and Richard.

Richard whispered to Tracey, "Where's the flashlight?"

She took it from a shelf by the fireplace then held it out to him. His hand was shaking so hard he could barely hold it.

At the beasts first cry, Big Ben ran behind Lois's wheelchair and haunched his body. The hair on his back stood straight up. Craig thought he was ready to attack, but would rather not.

Craig said softly. "Listen guys, no matter how it sounds, it's just an animal. Let's turn off the lights and see if we can pick it out from another window."

The whole family, except for Twig and Lois, trailed behind Craig and Richard to each location. They stared as if they were getting full view of *something*, but heavy fog—an impenetrable wall—wrapped their buildings. The windows were nothing more than grey holes.

Twig was standing with his back to the fireplace shivering. He turned to Craig and said, "It ain't no animal, sir."

Joliene snapped, "Well, if you know what it is, tell us."

"It's a banshee, Miss Joliene. The devil done called it up to take Slick's spirit out of this world."

Duane said, "What in the world is a banshee?"

Cassie narrowed her eyes and looked at Twig, "A banshee is a mythical creature. It's a legend from Scotland. They supposedly show up to announce the death of royalty. They're not real."

Twig persisted, "Yes, they are. Plenty of them have come around in Tennessee. There ain't no royalty there."

"Twig," Lois shouted in a loud whisper. "Stop all this death talk!"

There was no stopping Twig. He was on a roll. "I ain't kidding. Slick was real mean, so his soul is leaving this world kicking and screaming. That's why Satan is using that banshee, and I bet he has a dozen death demons out there too. Just be glad you can't see what's going on."

In spite of the seriousness of the situation, Craig grinned. "Twig, thanks for your input, but I promise. What we have here, is a real flesh and blood animal. It's checking us out under the cover of fog. The problem is, we don't know what type of animal it is. Richard and I are ready to go outside if we need to. Now, everyone back to the fireplace, and try to calm your nerves. Put the lights back on. The animal will be gone soon, and I'm sure the fog will be gone tomorrow."

Craig thought, *At least I hope so.*

"I'm going to make some popcorn, and hot chocolate," Linda said. "Who wants to help me?"

Duane, always first in line for a snack, followed her to the kitchen area. "I will, and I hope that animal—or banshee—or whatever it is, leaves."

Craig looked at Big Ben. "I bet if that dog could talk he would echo Duane's sentiment."

The creature cried out for the next three hours. Big Ben ran back and forth between Lois's chair and Nathaniel's bed. He found no place to settle.

"Great watch dog we have here," Craig said.

The rest of the family, except for Lois and Twig, was stretched out on a massive bed, in front of the fireplace. Each time the creature cried, Brianna yelled in a loud whisper, "Dad! Did you hear that?"

Craig gave up trying to sleep. He stoked the fire, warmed up the leftover coffee then sat down facing the door. Richard joined him, followed by Darren, then Twig.

Craig said, "I wasn't too concerned as long as we knew that creature was in the lake side woods, but it's circling around."

"I noticed." Richard said. "It won't be light for another few hours, and the fog is still hugging the window. It hasn't thinned or lifted—at all. There's not much we could do out there."

The words barely left Richard's lips when the creature screamed again. This time it was close to the hut, somewhere near the edge of the porch. No one moved. A portion of their woodpile fell with a thud, then the creature bumped hard against the door.

Craig and Richard grabbed their rifles and pointed them at the door. The creature cried out again, waking the three younger children. They began sobbing with their faces buried in their pillows. Big Ben yelped then began a frantic bark. Craig had never heard such a sound come from his dog.

Craig whispered to Richard, "I hope he's not taunting that creature. I'm sure Ben would be no match—for whatever it is."

Darren took charge of the big dog, patted his head and held his collar, but could not control Ben's low growls.

Nathaniel whispered. "Can I have a rifle too?"

Craig whispered back. "Not yet. If he breaks through, Richard and I will handle it. Right now, our friend is checking us out. He'll probably leave soon."

Caleb popped his head up, "Should we just yell real loud and scare it away?"

"No, son. We might make it angry. You must stay very, very quiet."

Craig searched the whitest faces he had ever seen. He whispered, "Darren, I think its time to move most these guys to the bedroom. Take the other Magnum with you. Keep them back there until we give the all clear. We have to be ready to fire."

It wasn't Craig's nature to be so blunt in front of the kids, but this was not the time to hold back.

Cassie and Sara continued to cry silently. Chad squatted down, took Sara in his arms then gently led his mom and Cassie to the designated area.

Darren slipped his arm around Joliene, and followed Duane and Lois out. Linda took Caleb's hand, but he refused to budge. His feet were glued to the floor, and he swung his shoulders back and forth in total defiance. His cheeks were as red as his hair, and his eyes darted around like a bird of prey . . . but not from fear.

In a forced whisper he said, "Dad, hand me a rifle."

Craig nearly dropped his own, and chuckled under his breath. "Well, not tonight son. Grown-ups have to take care of this, but we'll talk about it later. Right now, you have to do what I say. Take your mom and sister to the safe room. I'm counting on you to take care of them."

Linda smiled, and Craig smiled back. "I wish I could stay here with you," she said.

"I know, but I think you better get this little man out of here before he takes over."

Linda nodded, guided Caleb by his shoulders, and backed him out of the room.

When they were gone, Richard whispered, "It's too quiet out there. I think it's listening to us."

Twig whispered to Craig, "It ain't found Slick yet. It's still looking."

Craig leaned back, looked at Twig, but said nothing. He must stay on course—ready for whatever was to come.

After what seemed like an eternity, the creature stirred. It brushed the door again, causing the handle to move ever so slightly. Both rifles raised, ready to fire. Big Ben stiffened and offered another low growl.

There was total silence for a few seconds then a sniff, a snort and shuffling toward the end of the porch. They heard a grunt, and a thud when it hit the frozen ground. It began crunching away, in the direction of the caves.

Craig grabbed his coat and threw Richard's toward him.

"Let's go out on the porch and listen."

Before they left, Craig opened the bedroom door. "You guys can come out now, but under no circumstances are you to leave this hut. The creature jumped off the porch. Richard and I are going outside. We want to try and figure out where it's going."

Tracey pointed her finger at Craig. "You can't see that beast any better out there than you could in here."

Richard said, "It's not that we can see it—we can hear it move across the frozen ground."

As family members migrated to the living area, Darren moved from the fireplace to the front window straining to catch a glimpse of Richard and Craig. He couldn't see them, but heard them walking back and forth the length of the porch.

Just as he turned from the window, a muffled sound floated through the air. Darren knew it was not the pesky creature, but what ever it was, it enticed Craig and Richard to run off the porch into the abyss of the fog.

Darren paced like a caged animal. "Did you hear that? They left the porch? Why would they do that? We can't protect them out there. We couldn't see them, even if there was no fog."

Linda said, "Did they take the radios?"

"I don't think so," Chad said.

She gritted her teeth, and just as she turned to face the fire the creature cried out then shortly—cried out again. "I think its by the barn. Oh, God, please keep them safe."

The next minutes felt like an eternity as the family paced and listened, then Nathaniel caught Darren's eye, and motioned toward the door. Without saying a word they started dressing for the cold.

Twig moved in front of Darren and said, "I'm the one to go, sir. I won't have no trouble getting around out there. Slick and I ran into this kind of fog lots of times, besides, at least one of you needs to stay here with the ladies, and the little ones."

Duane spoke up, "Hey! I'm here!"

Chad said, "So am I!"

"Sorry fellas. I didn't mean to offend you, but I'm down right sure I'm the one who needs to go."

Nathaniel looked at Darren, "What do you think?"

"He's right. So you stay here and I'll go with him."

"Good try, but I think we better keep our only doctor available."

"I'm tired of hearing that, Nathaniel. You are no more dispensable than I am, and if anything happened to you I would never forgive myself. Plus, your parents would kill me."

Twig put on his winter gear and said, "Don't worry, mister. I won't let anything happen to him. Now, please hand me a rifle and some cartridges."

Darren started to hand Twig the old, reliable Mauser, then hesitated. Giving Twig a weapon was a direct violation of the family's probation decision. He turned toward Twig.

Twig said, "You can trust me, sir. This is just a small way I can pay back some of your kindness."

Darren handed him the rifle, and ammunition. "Don't take any chances. Here's a radio for each of you, and don't forget to use the rifle signal if necessary. Nathaniel knows what it is."

Linda touched Nathaniel's arm. "Son, please..."

"Mom, I'll be fine. Don't worry."

He gave her a quick hug as Twig opened the door. They descended the stairs, and in less than five-seconds were swallowed by the fog.

Darren bolted the door then took the last rifle off the rack and made sure it was loaded. Just as he closed the bolt, three rapid rifle shots came from the area of the barn, followed by a single shot.

Darren's face drained, and Joliene hurried to his side. "What's going on?"

Darren said, "Three rapid shots mean they're in trouble, but no one is to come to them. The single shot had to be fired by Twig or Nathaniel, letting them know they got the message."

"Yes, but Nathaniel or Twig's shot was fast," Tracey said. "Craig and Richard will surely know they're already outside."

She moved from the window and stared into the fire. "How many more will that fog swallow tonight?"

Joliene hugged her and said, "They'll take good care of each other."

Darren slapped the wall, sending shock waves pulsating through the family. "I have to do something! I can't just sit here!"

Lois asked, "What could you do? We'll tie you up before we let you go out by yourself. I think you're forgetting how capable those four men are."

Darren laid his face on the glass. "You're right. They are. I just wish I could see what's going on. I guess there really isn't anything else I can do. Twig knows his stuff, and Nathaniel won't do anything foolish."

Joliene asked, "Why would they get a signal to stay away?"

Darren said, "I can't imagine. I just wish it was me out there instead of Nathaniel."

Joliene joined him, and laid her hand on his arm. "Calm down. Its like you said, Twig knows his stuff. He's a mountain man through and through. He'll take good care of Nathaniel, that is, if he doesn't scare him to death with his stories. Besides, I'm glad you're here with us."

Darren reached out and touched her cheek with the back of his hand. They stared deep into each other's eyes.

Lois perked right up. She was the only one who saw their exchange. *Wow! Is a little romance blooming right in the middle of this drama?*

Tracey said, "We're putting a lot of confidence in a man we just met, but for some reason, I do feel better he's out there. What about you, Linda?"

Linda took a minute to answer. Caleb was on her lap and Brianna snuggled close.

"I agree, but it's not easy having any of them in that ungodly fog with a creature lurking about, whose cry sets our hair on edge. I don't like it, but I know Richard and Craig will watch each others back and we all agree, Twig will certainly protect Nathaniel."

She turned toward Lois, "Mom, how are you dealing with this?"

"I'm fine, but it's a good thing I don't have two working legs. I swear I would run off the porch to find them myself. This type of situation brings home how isolated we really are. There's no one to call on for help except God—what am I saying? There's no one *better* to call on than God, so who wants to do that?"

After a moment of silence Duane said, "I think it's about my turn if you don't mind." He clasped his fingers behind his back, bowed his head and said, "God, there's been a lot of crying and praying going on around here lately. Once again we need your help and you're the only one who can see through the fog. Please keep those four guys safe. We'd be lying if we said we aren't scared and worried. Thank you very much, and amen."

Duane's amen was barely out when the creature screamed again.

Lois saw Chad lay his hand on Tracey's shoulder, and put his arm around Sara while Cassie stayed near the fire. Linda held Caleb, and Brianna sat on the floor in front of her.

Tracey said, "What else is going to happen to us? Last year at this time we were making plans for the holidays. Who could have guessed our lives would take such a weird turn? I swear, when Richard gets back he's never getting out of my sight again."

Big Ben squatted and let out his deep growl.

Darren said, "Every time Ben makes that sound it sends shivers up and down my spine. He may be warning us. That creature could be heading this way, again. I want you guys to go back to the bedroom area. It's safer there."

CHAPTER 44

CONFRONTING THE CREATURE

*W*hen Craig and Richard were on the front porch, they shined high-beamed flashlights in every direction, but their light bounced back as if the fog were a mirror. Then from inside the barn, they heard a crash, followed by mooing and squawking.

Craig said, "That creature's trying to get to the animals."

Both men ran off the porch toward the small barn, stumbling over the invisible terrain. As they neared the gate they heard movement directly above, accompanied by a quieter, more ominous growl. A small limb fell close to Richard, bouncing off the top of the fence.

"What...?" Richard started to say.

Craig touched his arm. "Get inside, quick!"

Together they pushed open the heavy corral gate, then Craig ran ahead and unlatched the sturdy door. Once inside, he dropped the bar in place as Richard switched on the LED lanterns.

The chickens and cows were in a state of fright. Two of the cage doors were open, and the chickens were squawking, plus taking short airborne trips. One landed on the back of the young bull, and was quickly bucked off.

Craig checked the gate in front of the stall, then spoke in a loud whisper. "Settle down, boy. We're all scared." He turned to Richard, "I feel like we're actors in a horror movie. All we're missing is the eerie music. I think these animals would like to head for the hills."

"I don't blame them—what's going on? They're suddenly quiet," Richard whispered.

Craig raised his rifle in the directions of the door. Richard spun around looking at one window then the other.

"I believe that creature is carefully calculating a way to get in here," Craig whispered.

At that moment another spine-chilling growl floated throughout the area. Craig leaned close to Richard. "What kind of animal makes that sound, and climbs trees?"

"I don't know, but we're going nowhere until we can at least see it."

"From the sound of that growl, I'm not sure I want too—and not in this devilish fog."

"We're only about a couple hundred feet from the tip of the porch, but at this moment it feels like a hundred miles," Craig said. "You know those guys are sick with worry. If they didn't hear the animals going crazy they don't even know why we ran off the porch. Why didn't we grab a radio?"

Craig glanced around. The barn was strong, and latched from the inside, as well, with a heavy log laying between to upright slots. Two 3x3 windows were shuttered with the same type of closing. The whole set up *should* offer safety, but at the moment, safety seemed only an illusion.

Directly above the barn a large branch broke and plummeted to the roof.

"It's climbing down." Richard said. "Can't wait to see what its got in its bag of tricks."

"Yep, can't wait." Craig said.

They stood side-by-side ready to fire as the creature hit the crusty snow just outside the fence. For the moment the cattle and chickens made no sound.

"I think the animals are waiting to see what's coming next— just like we are," Craig said.

They didn't have long to wait. The unknown intruder rammed the corral gate with a heavy thud. The chickens went crazy.

Richard took a quick glance around. "I wish they'd be quiet. I can't keep track of our visitor."

No sooner did he get those words out of his mouth than the bull began lunging in every direction, shoving the cow into the wall. Craig turned in time to see her hunker down in a corner, trying to avoid her partner's hoofs.

"That bull is going to kill her if he doesn't settle down," Richard said.

"I know, but there's nothing we can do about it right now. He'll feel worse if that creature gets in. It sounds like its ramming the fence. It won't be long until he figures out he can climb it."

There was quiet for a few minutes then as Craig predicted, the heavy creature hit the ground with a thud. Craig knew most animals would approach an unknown enemy with caution, but not this guy. He sauntered toward the barn with a steady stride and stood just outside the door as the animals cried in terror.

Craig said, "Their natural instinct is correct. They know they're in grave danger, but have no exit plan, just like us."

Richard whispered over his shoulder, "If those chickens don't stop flying around, they're going to kill themselves, and that bull will eventually break out."

The creature stood quiet for a few seconds then lunged at the door. The whole barn shook. On the fourth attempt Craig said, "That door is strong, but it does have its limits."

Richard whispered, "I don't think he's very tall. I'm guessing about four foot or less."

Craig scrunched up his nose. "What is that awful smell?"

"It has to be our friend."

"That's worse than a skunk!"

Craig yelled, "Get out of here! You're not getting in!"

The animal was quiet then responded with its familiar yet spine tingling growl.

Richard said, "I know one thing for sure, if it gets in, it will tear us to shreds. We have to get it first."

Richard stood next to Craig, ready to fire. The creature made two more attempts then exploded with a loud grunt. It slowly and methodically began circling the whole corral area, which went half way around on both sides. Craig and Richard turned in conjunction with the creature's every move. It stopped several times to ram new areas then its movement stopped.

Craig whispered, "What's it up to now?"

Suddenly, it changed directions, lumbering away at a quick gait. They could hear it climbing back over the gate. It was heading in the direction of the wooded area that lined the path to the huts—then branches, and twigs began breaking.

Craig said, "The only tree big enough for it to climb in that direction is right on the edge of the path."

Craig's heart began to race. "You realize what this means, don't you? It's between us and our family."

"You know what, Craig? I think I figured out what it is."

"Well, tell me."

"I think it's a wolverine! That makes sense. They're unbelievably mean and incredibly strong. It checked us out first then moved to the barn. It thought our animals would be easy prey—before we got in the way."

"You may be right, but I didn't think they lived this far north."

"They don't actually live anywhere. They roam, and if my memory serves me right, one species, probably our friend, has a large range and many nest sites. It usually doesn't chase or stalk prey. It actually jumps out of trees on top of something, or lets another animal make the kill then swoops in, chases the animal away, and steals the carcass."

"How do you know all this stuff?"

"You're forgetting who my daughter is. At home we call her Miss Walking Encyclopedia. She always has her nose in a book."

"Will the creature go away on its own?"

"Not likely." Richard said. "Especially if it's hungry. It'll stay close, waiting for an opportunity to strike."

"You know someone will come looking for us, eventually. We've got to use the *stay away* signal before they leave the porch. If the creature attacks, we might not get there in time."

Richard said, "I say fire the gun."

Craig walked to the side window nearest the trail, and fired three shots straight up in the air. Both men were startled at the rapid reply. One shot meant the message was received except it didn't come from the hut.

"Oh, dear God." Richard said. "Whoever fired that shot has to be close to the tree that creature's in."

They listened for a second then Craig shouted, "I can hear them on the path! You know *it* hears them too." He ran to the door and yanked off the bar.

They both ran outside shouting, "Go back! Go back!"

Craig yelled, "There's an animal in one of the trees close to you. It may jump. It's probably a wolverine. Don't come any closer!"

The steps stopped, and the creature didn't make a sound.

Richard shouted, "Go back to the hut!"

They dared not breathe, and even the animals were quiet.

Twig started to respond, but a shrieking growl, and a falling limb broke the silence.

He whispered, "Be quiet, boy, and start backing up. It knows we're here."

The words barely escaped his lips when a loud thud, accompanied by a pungent odor, filled the air. The animal was on the ground. A ferocious growl split the night to their left.

Twig spun and yelled, "Get behind me, boy."

"I'm not a boy." Nathaniel said, as two shots rang out, splitting the darkness.

They heard a slight cry, a muffled grunt then the foul-smelling beast fell at their feet.

Twig yanked a flashlight out of his pocket, and shined it on two entry points that pierced the creature's skull. Both were right between its eyes.

Craig yelled, "Did you get it?"

"Yes, sir." Twig called. "I believe we did."

"Dad! Are you okay?"

When Craig heard Nathaniel's voice he stumbled over himself getting through the gate. "Nathaniel, what are you doing out here? Twig, what were you thinking?"

"Ain't my fault. He would have come alone. This here's a good boy, sir—I mean a good man."

Craig took a deep sigh. "I'm sorry. Thank you Twig for killing that beast, and keeping him safe. I mean it. Thank you."

"I didn't kill it, sir. It was Nathaniel. He beat me to it. It wasn't even twitching. Yes, sir, it was right in front of us. Two shots. That's what he fired. Both of them right between its eyes."

Craig took two stumbling steps back. Richard grabbed his right arm, and when Craig was stable, Richard put his big hands on Craig's shoulders. "Everything is fine. Twig's right, or have you already figured it out? Your son is a man, and he's acting just like you. He would give his life for this family. It's how you raised him. Take a deep breath, and let it go."

Craig hesitated a second then turned back toward Twig and Nathaniel. "Let's lock this place down, and make our way back —together."

Nathaniel said, "Dad, are you okay?"

Craig placed his hand on Nathaniel's shoulder. "I'm fine, but you scared me to death, son. I'm very proud of you. You do understand when your Mom finds out about this we're both in trouble?"

"Maybe we better sleep in the barn, Dad. Give her a night to cool down."

"Or you could give her your *need to know* routine, then tell her you'll fill in the blanks later," Richard said.

Richard asked Twig, "Was this your first run-in with a wolverine?"

"Yes, sir. But how did you know what it was?"

"Well, I would like to say it was part of our training, but it was my daughter Cassie. She told me all about them, including their awful cry and roaming patterns."

Craig said, "I hope it's the last time we encounter one. I'm going to be nervous about walking under trees for the rest of my life."

Twig said, "Me too. And thanks for warning us. Tomorrow, if this fog lifts, and if he ain't been drug off, I want to look him over real good."

"I do too. I want to get a better look at the animal that planned to have us for dinner," Richard said.

The four men stayed close together as they made their way back to the lodge. They were welcomed with tears, laughter, and just a bit of anger.

Linda's finger was on Craig's nose. "Whatever possessed you to leave the porch? Why didn't you take the radios? Believe me, we don't need that kind of scare."

"Linda, when we heard the animals going crazy, we had to check it out. It seemed like the right thing to do at the time. We had no clue what we were facing, but we were rescued." He winked at Nathaniel.

"That's my point! You had no idea, and *we* certainly didn't. By the way, what was it?"

Nathaniel couldn't contain himself, "It was a wolverine, Mom. We'll get a closer look tomorrow, and you won't believe the smell. It's ten times worse than a skunk, or that bear that tried to kill Darren and Grandma."

"Thanks, son, I think I'll pass—and let's change the subject. At least it wasn't a banshee, huh Twig?"

"No, Miss Linda, I guess not, but it sure sounded like one."

Craig looked over the room at the large family. *Well, we've made it so far, but I can't help but wonder what's next.*

CHAPTER 45

SNOW MACHINES

*M*uch to Lois's dismay, after the night of terror the chickens quit laying eggs, and for a solid week the cow gave no milk. When they started producing again, she made an omelet for breakfast, and later in the day tried her hand at making butter. It was so simple she wondered why she hadn't tried it before.

The lack of snack foods was always an issue, but in spite of complaints, Lois and Darren remained frugal. Jerky and popcorn were usually available, and little niceties such as melted butter over the popcorn, once overlooked, was something to be thankful for. Pots of soil sat in various spots throughout the huts, in an attempt to grow herbs, zucchini and yellow squash. Fish, wild fowl and game were also plentiful. Craig and Nathaniel switched off with Richard and Twig when it was time to restock.

It became apparent to Lois that Nathaniel and Twig were the sharpest shooters, and brought down most of the game. On occasion, when Chad was allowed to hunt with the men, Lois was glad. Chad, like the other men, took the roll of supplier and protector very seriously. Tracey was not happy when he left camp, but Richard would stand firm. He insisted Chad be given a chance to mature, and develop his survival skills. Lois often heard them debating in the bedroom, and was happy when Richard won. She had become very fond of Chad.

At the break of dawn, Craig walked with Richard and Twig up the hill to the plateau. It was Richard's turn to make the monthly trip to Wilson Creek. The air was crisp and every puff of breath created small silver clouds. The truck had to be started, filled with gas, and stocked with survival and travel equipment.

Craig asked, "Who's going with you?"

Richard laughed. "Well, if you don't mind, I'm taking the *muscles*, Nathaniel and Twig. That way I can creep along in the warm truck while they shovel."

Craig glanced Twig's way and smiled. "Sounds like a plan, but I don't know how *they'll* feel about it."

A big grin spread across Twig's face. "I don't mind, sir."

The truck engine grumbled a few times before turning over, but soon it was running smooth. Twig dug a path to the snow-covered road, and they were under way in about an hour.

Wilson Creek businesses had been receiving small amounts of merchandise on a weekly basis. Craig hoped this time would be no different. The sweeping policy of the whole town was—no one would be allowed to *clean* them out. Several owners boldly declared their primary loyalty to the local residents. In spite of this policy Craig and Richard had always been allowed to purchase staples and a few specialty items such as candy, sodas, extra flour, sugar or oil for bake goods. Their BLM credentials, in relation to their attachment to Canada, helped keep doors open. No matter how many times they were asked where they were living, their rehearsed answer was, "We found a place off road, past the state park."

When Richard and the two young men pulled out, he was forced to keep the truck in four-wheel drive low range, for most of the way. Twice, Nathaniel and Twig had to dig out large, frozen snow banks. Six hours later they made their first stop at the hardware store. While there, Richard spotted a three-by-five card on the bulletin board.

*For Sale – Two Four Stroke POLARIS SNOW MACHINES – Great Condition – $200 Each – For Details Call...*followed by a phone number.

Richard said, "They're probably pieces of junk, but on the off chance they're not, the price is too good to pass up. In fact, it's a steal."

Mr. Strasser, owner of the store, gave them directions.

The young woman who had the machines lived two miles north of town. Her name was Tia Fowler, and looked to be in her late twenties. When she showed him the machines, he was taken back. They looked to be in perfect condition. She explained they had belonged to her father. He passed away two years earlier, and they had been in her garage ever since. Richard was skeptical. *Those prices cannot be right. I think somebody dropped a zero.*

Tia explained the price was so low because every family in the area already owned one. To ease his mind he had her repeat the price, and was astounded when she said they were truly $200 each.

Both machines started with little effort, and the engines purred—loudly—but purred. Richard took both for a spin. They floated across the snow with such little effort, he grinned. *This must be a dream. Please don't wake me up.*

Richard told her he would buy both. "Can I pick them up when we're done shopping?" She said, "Sure," and thanked him for taking them off her hands.

Before leaving Wilson Creek, Richard reached Craig on his cell. "Hey there. The boys and I will be *roaring* into camp so don't be alarmed by approaching noise. Oh, by the way, I spent $400 of our cash. See you later."

Craig had no idea what Richard could spend so much money on. They were not short of money when they arrived at the valley, but had no way to replace what they were spending, but he trusted his buddy. He would say nothing to the family. They would all be surprised together. Leon had the fore sight to suggest they exchange their American cash for Canadian money as soon as they got to Canada, before no exchange would be permitted.

It was well after dark when a loud, unfamiliar *roar* approached the valley. Craig, Chad, and Darren hiked to the top of the canyon to look at the noisemakers, and help carry supplies back to camp. Craig was astounded at the low cost. These machines would open up the whole valley, not to mention the ability to glide across the frozen lake.

Richard noticed that Craig was unusually quiet as they descended the hill. Before they entered the huts, he asked Craig to hang back. "What's bugging you, man?"

"I reached Leon this afternoon. His source told him the whole nation is under Martial Law, but the curious thing is— no attacks are taking place where squads of special troops are. As of yesterday, all power grids were placed under Federal Government control. He said drone flyovers have increased over the northern borders and are coming deeper into Canada. Incoming and outgoing movement is being controlled. He says for us to continue sitting tight."

"I'm having a hard time accepting what I think I'm being told," Richard said.

"Me too—but facts are facts. We know who's behind the attacks, but I just can't make myself say it. Leon is laying his life on the line every time he calls us. He truly is *sleeping with the enemy*. Where would we be if it wasn't for him?"

The following morning, Craig accompanied Nathaniel and Chad to the larger cave. The boys built two, three foot-by-three foot sleds, equipped with large, removable wooden containers for the snow machines. Craig looked the area over for unwanted visitors then helped the boys gather the necessary tools.

Shortly before five o'clock the following afternoon, they roared into camp pulling the sleds behind them. The sturdy runners were made from the curved branches of a fir tree. The boxes were screwed on and reinforced with straps made from deer hide.

"Why don't you boys draw up blue prints and present them on family night?" Craig said.

"That's a great idea, Dad," Nathaniel said. "It was easy and it was fun. We'll be glad to share, and who knows—maybe somebody will give us a project...one we can build, that is."

CHAPTER 46

HOLIDAYS

*N*ot long before the holidays, Lois was looking over some recipes in the kitchen area. Tracey, Linda and Joliene were sitting by the fireplace. She paid little attention to their conversation until she heard Tracey's comment.

"Thanksgiving will be so depressing this year, and it breaks my heart to think about how disappointed the kids will be when they don't get any Christmas presents."

Joliene said, "If I had the right material I could make them a quilt, but I don't."

"My two older ones will understand," Linda said. "It's Caleb I worry about."

Lois's cheeks grew hot. This conversation was one she dare not ignore. A few deep breaths quelled her anger as she put the recipes away.

"Ladies, I didn't mean to eavesdrop," she said, "but please help me understand why you're talking this way?"

"It's the kids, Mom," Linda said. "We're afraid they're going to be really disappointed with Thanksgiving and Christmas. They've always been such special days."

Lois hesitated a moment then said, "It's not the kids I'm worried about, it's you three ladies. You're anticipating disappointment. The children will be fine. This may be the first time this whole family celebrates the right way. The real meaning of Thanksgiving has been buried with decadent meals, and Christmas is insane. There are so many gifts they won't even fit under our tree. We have given these holidays lip service and that's all. This year we may have a chance to celebrate them right—celebrate with meaning. We can take them back to their roots."

There was dead silence in the room until Linda spoke up. "You know what, Mom, I think you're right. In my mind I was missing a big fat turkey, pies and the rest of the trimmings, but I need to remember the grace that God has shown us. We've faced dangerous and terrifying situations and never once has He abandoned us. We've always had enough food to fill our bellies. I would still like all those trimmings, but—what I really need, is a grateful heart."

Joliene nodded her head, and took Linda's hand. "Me too."

Tracey continued to look down, and said nothing. Lois asked, "Tracey, are you okay?"

"Not really. I know what you're saying, but I don't have your kind of faith. I don't know if I can portray a positive front. I need you to pray for me."

Linda and Joliene gave Tracey hugs, and Lois took her hand.

Lois said, "I know it's hard, but we can't change it. We don't want to accept it, but we must—at least for a while. Let's talk to God right now."

After she prayed she said, "Now, let's work together and make these holidays meaningful with *new* traditions."

Tracey said, "Thank you, Lois. While you were praying I got an idea. Let's ask the kids to write a Thanksgiving and a Christmas story. They can make them into plays or puppet shows, or just read them. That will give all of us something to look forward to."

Joliene said, "Great idea. I'll help where I can."

"Good job ladies." Lois said. 'Life keeps throwing us curves, but our Heavenly Father straightens them out. I am most thankful that we have each other. If the virus would have reached Seattle before we escaped—well, things would be different."

From that point, Lois noticed the holidays were anticipated with modest joy. On Thanksgiving, she baked three loaves of coffee cake, topped with cinnamon and sugar. Dinner consisted of corn bread, moose roast, fried rice, seasoned zucchini, and was eaten without complaints. When everyone finished, Lois asked if each family member would share something they were thankful for.

When it was Caleb's turn he said, "My whole family, and Twig."

Twig smiled. "Thank you little man. I am thankful for you too, and the rest of you kind folks. You've been real—well you know."

"Now," Lois said. "I think our kids are going to entertain us with a puppet show, so let's move to the living room."

Two weeks before Christmas Craig popped through the door and said, "Watch out! Incoming."

Richard was right behind him, and almost knocked him over with a fresh cut Christmas tree. He stood it against the wall next to the front window. Around Craig's neck were two strings of Christmas lights.

"I bought these a couple of months ago."

Lois said, "Well since we have such a lovely tree, we better decorate it."

She popped corn then handed out needles and thread to Chad, Nathaniel and Brianna. She gave paper, scissors, glue and glitter to the younger kids. They could make paper chains while the older ones strung the popcorn. Darren contributed some small pinecones and acorns.

Craig saw Twig watching their every move so he gave him a nod. "Go help them. I may make a few chains myself."

Tracey played prerecorded Christmas music from her computer, and when the craft items were finished, the whole family decorated the tree.

For the first few days, the tree sat bare of presents then Craig noticed gifts, wrapped in decorated copy paper, began showing up. It was clearly the work of children. He encouraged everyone else to ask no questions, but laughed when reports of missing items were brought to his attention.

"Wait until Christmas morning. I'm sure the lost will be found."

He was right. On Christmas morning, every adult family member had something to open. Craig thanked the kids for the return of his warmest gloves, and everyone else said thank you when a prized, and necessary item was returned.

At six o'clock on Christmas night, Craig asked everyone to join him by the fireplace. "I'm going to read the Christmas story from the Bible. To make it more special, Mom suggested you close your eyes, and try to imagine what it would have been like to be there the night Jesus was born. After that, Tracey said she would lead us in some carols."

"Great ideas," Linda said, and asked Caleb to come sit next to her.

When Craig was finished, he asked the kids to read the stories they had written. Cassie wrote about spending Christmas at Disneyland when she was five. Sara told about getting a kitten for Christmas when she was four. Caleb was different.

"*This* is *my* favorite Christmas. We get to spend it where there's snow with a really big family."

When the children finished, Craig gave a nod to Richard and Twig. When they stood up and put their coats on, Craig said, "We'll be right back. We need to get something from the cave."

"It takes three of you to get something from the cave?" Tracey asked.

The snow machine's roar filled the room, and fifteen minutes later the men returned, toting three large garbage bags. They didn't say a word as they carefully removed wrapped gifts and placed them under the tree. All three of the younger children clapped their hands.

Sara said, "Those are really pretty. I didn't know we were getting presents like that."

When they finished, Richard took one package at a time, read the tag and handed it to the appropriate person.

Craig knew his mom wanted a new lap robe. She rubbed it against her cheek and said, "This is so soft. Thank you."

When Tracey opened a *Three Tenors* CD she was speechless, and Linda laughed when she unwrapped her 2-liter bottle of Pepsi. Craig laid three more in front of her. She also received a new pair of warm insulated mittens.

Joliene's gift was a scarf, gloves, and some dark roast coffee—her favorite. The older boys held up pocketknives, and much to Linda's chagrin, Caleb did too. Cassie's gift was three used books from the library, and Sara was thrilled with her art material.

Brianna jumped up and hugged Craig and Richard when she opened her new hair products. Darren and Duane received Hershey chocolate bars, warm gloves, and hats that folded down over their ears. In addition to the gifts, there was a large bag of mixed candy, popcorn kernels, and fruit-flavored powder drinks.

Craig shook the bag, looked surprised then grinned at Richard.

"Hey! There are two more presents in here. Wonder who they belong to?"

Craig turned each gift over a few times, pretending to have difficulty reading the tags. "Oh, I see. These have your name on them, Twig."

Twig swallowed hard then stumbled over his words. "Me, sir? Well, thank you."

One package contained two black and white flannel shirts. The other was a hat similar to Duane's and Darren's, and a pair of gloves lined with rabbit fur.

Twig swallowed hard. "I sure didn't expect a thing. These are the nicest gifts I ever got."

Craig pretended to toss the bag aside then said, "Wait, I think there's something else in there." He reached in and took his time pulling out four DVD's.

"Richard reserved these at the library the last time he went to Wilson Creek."

"He got *It's a Wonderful Life* and *The Christmas Carol*," Craig said. "They didn't have the Grinch. Sorry kids, but he did get *Frosty the Snow Man,* and *Rudolph*."

Sara said, "Can we watch them tonight, Dad. Can we?"

"You bet we can. We'll watch the others when you go to bed."

Richard said, "I had to put down a pretty hefty deposit on these, and Mr. Barker was still apprehensive about letting me have them."

Lois said, "This is great. Let's pop some corn, whip up some powered drink and watch movies."

There were no gifts for Craig and Richard—except the ones confiscated by the children, but this would be an evening Craig would never forget.

Richard said to Tracey, "Every time I went to Wilson Creek I tried to find music for you. I was about to give up then on the last trip, I found that one in the sale bin."

Tracey walked across the room, and without shame, gave him a very passionate kiss. Sara smiled, Cassie covered her eyes, and Craig looked away.

Tracey touched Richard's cheek with the back of her hand, and said, "Thank you."

∼

Three weeks later, Craig and Nathaniel returned from a scouting trip, searching for game tracks. Just as they shut down the snow machines, Craig felt his phone vibrate.

"I have some updates," Leon said. "Is Richard with you?"

Craig said no, but asked Nathaniel to run and get him. "Go ahead, Leon. He won't be long."

"I have to keep this brief, as usual. Are you still doing okay?"

"We are. Some interesting things happened. When we have a chance we'll fill you in on our new family member, Twig."

"Twig? Sounds interesting, but I better fill you in while I have a chance. Attacks continue in Canada, mostly over the border areas and the north-south highways that join our two countries. Both bases in Anchorage were hit again, and large gatherings are still being controlled."

Richard came running up the path just in time to hear Leon's final news.

"I have something important to tell you, so listen carefully. I can't go into details, so ask me no questions."

Richard said, "Go ahead, Leon."

He whispered so low the men strained to hear him, but soon understood his caution. "A militia has been formed, and growing in number. The general heading it up is a seasoned powerhouse. I don't know how successful the movement will be, but its good news, and thank God, it's a start. I was able to reach him—Sorry, someone's coming. I'll call when I can."

Craig scratched his head. "These interrupted phone calls are driving me nuts."

Richard said, "At least we're getting them, even if they do keep us guessing."

"I don't know what hope a militia has, but we need to keep them in prayer."

"You got that right," Richard said.

CHAPTER 47

SPRING THAW

$\mathscr{E}$ach time Craig drove one of the snow machines, he was thankful. They were less expensive to run than the trucks, and made trips to Wilson Creek a lot safer. They also enabled him and Richard to keep abreast of the road conditions to and from the valley. Miles and miles of new territory had been opened to them, and for the first time since winter started, he dreaded the thaw—but it came.

On March 25th, he cringed when his mother said, "Look, son. There's water dripping off the porch. Maybe there is such a thing as spring. I was ready to give up!"

On April 10th, Craig watched gentle streams flow down the hillside next to the caves. The snow machines were already useless. He and Richard solemnly placed large tarps over both machines.

As daylight and warmth increased, spurts of greenery popped up everywhere. Snow that rested between trees, and in full shade, stubbornly took several more weeks to disappear.

Craig noticed the family's demeanor was improving every day.

There was more conversation and laughter—except for Brianna. She was helping her grandmother make dinner when he walked through the door. She spun around and snapped.

"Dad, will we ever have real food again? You know—the kind we buy at the grocery store. I know you guys love hunting, but aren't you sick of eating the same things over and over again?"

Her comment caught him off guard, but there was no sensible way to address it, so he shrugged his shoulders and kept walking.

Later that day, Craig happened to be on the porch when Caleb and Cassie were getting wood for the fireplace. He saw Caleb stiffen then heard him whisper, "Don't move. Brianna's coming. If we hold very, very still, maybe she won't yell at us again."

One more time, Craig let it go, but now his hackles were up a little.

At dinner, Richard said, "Hey guys! Before long, the ground will be ready to till. Why don't we get some seeds started? It will be nice to have fresh…"

Before he got another word out, Brianna stood up. "What are we doing?"

Craig said, "What do you mean?"

"I mean, why is he talking like we're planning to live here another year?"

"You are being disrespectful, young lady. You—"

She put her hands over her ears. "I just want to go home, Dad. Sometimes you act like you don't even care. I know you enjoy this wilderness stuff, but I don't. I used to have a life. I want to finish college, and get married someday."

Linda turned to Brianna and said, "Are you finished?"

"I can't believe you're going along with this madness, Mom. Why can't you talk Dad into getting us out of here?"

Linda's jaw tightened. "Brianna, its time for you to stop. We're alive because your dad and Richard had the courage, and foresight to make a difficult plan and carry it out. If we had gotten close to that virus, we would be dead. No chance at life. Just death. Now, you need to apologize to Richard and your father. Do I make myself clear? We have to look forward. There is nothing to look back to."

Brianna's knees buckled, and Darren jumped up and guided her to a chair. She was crying hysterically. "Oh, Momma. I'm sorry. I'm sorry."

Just before she reached the chair she turned, and ran straight into Craig's arms, and almost knocked him over. "I'm sorry, Daddy. Please forgive me."

Craig held her against his chest. "To be honest, I've felt the same way many times. I'm sure we all have, but we make it work because this is where we live, not just exist. It is the only way to survive mentally and emotionally."

Craig saw many nods of agreement.

He went on. "Just do all of us a favor. Before you get to the point of a melt down, will you talk to someone?"

She nodded against his chest in agreement, and in a muffled voice she said, "I really am sorry. For several days I felt like my insides were exploding. I tried to turn my mind off, but I couldn't."

Richard stood and said, "Let's postpone the planning meeting until tomorrow. I think Tracey and I will take a walk."

Brianna walked over to Richard. "Will you please forgive me for talking to you like that? It wasn't fair. I'm sorry."

Richard hugged her, kissed the top of her head, and said, "Of course I will. I think you may have just said out loud what most of us have been thinking. I hope you feel better now since you got it all out."

"I do, but I'm still sorry."

Craig was happy to see that exchange. Richard was his best friend. *The last thing I want is a riff in the family.* He started to stand up until another exchange caught his eye. *What's that all about?*

Joliene and Darren were sitting side by side at the table. He saw Darren slip his arm around Joliene's waist, and pull her to him. Her grin was—well—interesting.

Caleb jumped up. "Anybody wanna play Power Rangers?"

"Sure," Chad said. "I'll play. What color are you?"

"Red," Caleb said. "I like to be the red guy."

CHAPTER 48

LOVE IS IN THE AIR

*D*aylight hours grew longer, and the sun gave off more warmth, but heat was always needed inside the huts. After Craig, Darren and Richard finished stacking firewood on the porch, Craig sat down on a log.

"I need a rest, how about you guys?"

Darren said to Craig and Richard, "I want to address the family after dinner tonight, before our talent show. Is that all right?"

"Sure," Craig said. "Is everything okay?"

"Yes, things are pretty good in fact, but if you don't mind, I'd like to talk to everyone at once."

"You got my curiosity up. It'll be hard to wait," Richard said.

Darren laughed, and hit Richard on the shoulder. "You'll make it."

As soon as dinner was over Linda and Tracey started to stack the dirty dishes when Craig said, "Would you mind waiting a few minutes to do that? Darren has something he wants to say." He turned to Darren, "Okay, Doc, what's up?"

"Well, what I have to say concerns everyone, but in all fairness I really need to address my first comments to Richard, Duane, and Linda. As some of you may have noticed, Joliene and I have been

261

spending a lot of time together. In fact, this may shock you, but—we've fallen in love."

He stopped for a moment to give this first announcement a chance to sink in.

Joliene stood up, walked over to him, and took his hand. "What we're asking for is your blessing."

Duane said, "What do you mean by blessing?"

Joliene smiled. "He means, he asked me to marry him, and I said yes."

Linda and Duane were speechless for a moment then looked at each other and laughed.

"Is that what you really want, Mom?" Linda asked.

"It certainly is. I've never been more sure of anything in my life."

Duane stumbled over his words, but managed to say, "I guess if you're that sure, you have my blessing. What about you sis?"

"Well, yes, of course. I'm just a little surprised...but happy."

Twig looked like his buttons would burst. "Well, I think this here's the greatest thing I ever heard of."

Linda hugged her mom and Duane shook Darren's hand.

Richard wasn't saying anything until Darren said, "What about you son, can we have your blessing?"

Richard reached out and shook his dad's hand then grabbed him. The two men embraced, and patted each other on the back.

"Of course, you have my blessing, you just took me by surprise, too. We've been so busy, how have you had time, or presence of mind to court her? You never showed any interest in dating, but here you are holding Joliene's hand looking like you could pop your buttons."

Darren laughed, "I know our announcement has to be a surprise. Who would have thought, under these circumstances, anyone could find love."

Craig was quiet until Linda gave him a little nudge.

"I guess congratulations are in order, but I have just one question. Who's going to perform the ceremony?"

Darren said, "Why you, of course."

"Me? I'm no preacher," Craig said.

"You don't have to be a preacher. We voted you in as the head of this community. You're like a mayor, a judge, a governor, a…"

"Keep talking and I'll resign all the above positions. Besides, I wouldn't have the slightest idea what to say."

"Don't worry about that," Joliene said. "We're writing our own vows."

Twig made everyone laugh when he said, "Dearly beloved, we are gathered—is all you have to say."

Duane asked, "Have you set a date?"

Darren squeezed Joliene's hand. "Actually, we have. It's two weeks from today."

"Isn't that kind of quick? What's the hurry?" Craig asked.

Darren said, "My question is, why wait? And, I promise, we will not let our personal plans interfere with our duties, so mark your social calendars. We're getting hitched, two weeks from today."

Joliene gestured toward the window and added, "Just think, in two short weeks I'll have someone to snuggle up to when I'm cold—and when I hear those scary sounds coming from the woods."

Darren laughed. "Oh, so that's what this is all about?"

She looked in his eyes. "It's not the only thing. I've had my eye on you for a while."

"Okay, okay, I've heard enough mushy stuff," Duane muttered.

"Wow," Brianna said. "This is exciting. We've got a wedding to plan."

"I want everyone to settle down a minute. I think you two need to gather up some identification, go to Wilson Creek, and find a pastor or a judge and ask them to marry you. Under normal circumstances that would not work, but since you cannot get married in America they may do it. When you come back, we'll have another ceremony and celebrate."

"What if they say no?" Darren asked.

"Then I'll do it here. I want to be sure to the best of our ability we obey the law. Are you willing to try?"

Darren and Joliene left the area for a while and when they came back they both agreed Craig was right. The following Tuesday,

Richard went with them to Wilson Creek, and with much pleading, a local judge performed their wedding. He gave them an official document with a Canadian stamp on it. Two days later the family had a celebration with cake and handmade decorations. They insisted Craig officiate another ceremony. He kept it simple, but when they looked in each other's eyes, and said their vows, it touched everyone's hearts.

CHAPTER 49

A LIGHT IN THE WOODS

*A*fter the wedding celebration, Craig and Linda descended the porch steps, arm in arm.

"When your mom volunteered to help Darren with the inventory," Craig said, "I thought something might be brewing, but I didn't pay much attention after that. I'm very glad that judge agreed to marry them."

Linda started to answer, but before she could, Craig stiffened and stared past her. He put his hands on her shoulders, and said, "Let's go back, right now."

Linda whispered, "Craig, you're scaring me, what's wrong?"

He didn't answer. He just kept her moving, up one step, then two. Linda groped for the doorknob, and they both pushed through. Craig closed, and locked the door in one swift motion.

"Now tell me, what did we just escape from?" Linda said.

Richard rose to his feet. "What's going on?"

"Turn off the lights, and spread out the fire. Is everyone accounted for?"

Richard nodded. "I believe so. What's wrong?"

"I saw a light in the woods."

Linda asked, "Was it a fire?"

"No, it wasn't a fire. It looked more like a high beam flashlight."

"How far away?" Richard asked.

"In that open meadow near the lake, about a mile from here. It looks like we have company. Let's pray there's not another Slick among them. Sorry Twig, nothing personal."

"That's okay, sir. I understand."

Richard turned to Chad and Duane, "Fasten every shutter except the one left of the door."

As was customary, the mother hens gathered their chicks. Tracey put her arm around Sara and Cassie. Caleb climbed onto Linda's lap.

Brianna crossed the room and stood next to her dad. "What are we going to do?"

"I'm not sure. Give us a few minutes to think. Just keep your eyes and ears open. They may be hunters. I can't think of any other thing that would draw them here, but I can't be sure."

Craig was quiet a moment then said, "You're not going to like this, but I want you to get ready to move to the cave in a moment's notice. Start getting things together and no arguing."

Brianna said, "Just tell me what to do."

"Thanks. You know the routine. Just get ready and pray we don't have to go."

Twig positioned himself by Lois and patted her shoulder. Craig heard him whisper, "Don't worry, Miss Lois, we'll be okay."

She touched his hand, "Thanks, Twig."

Lois handed Richard the key to the gun cabinet. He handed Twig his rifle, passed one to Craig then took one for himself. "If they haven't already spotted us, they may pass us by. The part that makes me nervous is—how did they get in the valley? They didn't come through the canyon."

Caleb took Craig's hand. "I'm not afraid, Daddy."

"I'm not either." Lois piped in. "God has taken good care of us so far. No reason to believe He's going to abandon us now."

"That's true, Mom, but I think there's a verse which says something about the strong man guarding his house, isn't there?" Craig laughed a little.

"You bet there is, and you guys are the best."

The closing of the front door was barely audible, but still heard.

Richard spun around and asked, "Who went out?"

Cassie said, "It was Twig."

"What does he think he's doing?" Duane put his hands on his hips. "He'll get us all killed."

Joliene pointed her finger at her son, "Stop it, Duane, you know better than that. Twig would die first."

Craig said, "That may be, but he shouldn't go off on his own. He needs to work with the rest of this team."

Richard was pacing, "Give him a few minutes. You've seen how he moves."

"Yes," Lois said. "Just like a cat . . . quiet and sure-footed."

Linda said, "Let's just hope he has nine lives."

About an hour later, Twig showed up at the door. Craig let him in, "So who is it?"

"It's hard to tell. I'm sure they don't know we're here so we need to be real quiet. If you all don't mind, I'll go back and keep an eye on things."

Richard asked, "How many?"

"I only saw two. One was a lad about twenty, and the other one was older. It might be his pa."

"Could you hear what they were saying?"

"Yeah, they said they were tired of hunting for food. While I was watching, the man went to the lake and caught a fish. After they ate, they put a tent up. I'm thinking we shouldn't build up another fire."

Craig said, "You're probably right. How many guns could you see?"

"Each was carrying a rifle. That's all I saw." He headed for the door.

Lois said, "Twig."

"Yes, Miss Lois."

"Take some water, and a snack. And Twig, be careful. We've gotten kind of attached to you."

After Lois fixed his snack, and gave him a container of water, he headed for the door, again. He called over his shoulder, "I like y'all too."

"Okay family, I hate to tell you this, but we better get you to the cave." Craig said.

The room rang with moans. Tracey looked at Richard, "Do we really have to do that again? We hate that cave."

"I know, but you're a lot safer there. Besides, it will get way too cold in here without a fire."

Duane was pacing. "Why can't we just walk right up and talk to them? They might be just passing through. Everybody can't be out to get us."

Craig started to speak, but Linda beat him to it. "You don't exactly pass through this valley by chance, Duane, so they didn't get here by accident. They may be trying to escape the virus, just like us, but on the other hand they may be desperate, and desperate people do desperate things. We can't take a chance, so get on board here. And just for the record, we all hate being in that cave."

"Sorry, sis. It's just one thing after the other. Don't you ever get tired of it?"

"We all do, but we're not on an extended vacation. We have to deal with what life hands us, and right now we're being served another helping."

Lois was already scurrying around in her wheel chair adding to the pile of things Brianna had gathered. "Actually, the cave isn't that bad. We'll be able to cook, read and play games. I'm looking forward to beating someone in a game of Trouble."

"I'll play, Grandma," Caleb said. "It's my turn to win."

"Your turn to win? You always win! You're too good for me."

Richard had his hand on the doorknob just as two powerful rifle shots rang through the air.

Crag jumped, "Now what's that all about?"

"I don't know, but it sure sounded close. You don't suppose...?" Richard said.

Craig stopped him. "I think we need to get these guys settled so we can check things out. Duane, you and Nathaniel go through the brush to the cave. Check for blankets, firewood, food, etc. You know where the list is."

Duane stomped his foot, "Oh, man, I hate that place. It's too dark in there and the air is so close."

Craig was standing watch at the window then swung around. "Duane! Are you starting again? The cave is well ventilated, and fortunately, the smoke filters away from the valley. I've heard enough of your whining. Would you rather take a rifle, and join Twig?"

Duane set his feet in motion, and grabbed his jacket and gloves. "No, sir! Come on, Nathaniel."

Richard called Craig off to the side. "Do you have a plan?"

Craig said. "What did Twig do when we were in trouble?"

"Okay. Gotcha."

As soon as Duane and Nathaniel returned, and a few more items were gathered, they ushered their reluctant family to the cave.

Craig, Richard, and Darren settled in a thicket between the hut and the cave. They could barely catch a glimpse of the intruders' fire through the trees.

Craig said, "They don't seem to be headed this way, so Richard, why don't you stay here while your dad, and I find Twig?"

"Not on your life. You seem to forget, Dad is our only doctor, so I need to go, and he needs to stay."

"Craig's right, son, and quit talking about me being a doctor. You two need to stay separated. We can't afford to be without a leader."

"I don't like the sounds of that. Are you planning on coming back?"

Craig spoke up, "Don't be ridiculous. Of course we're coming back, but if on the off chance something did happen, you'll know what to do."

Richard muttered a few unintelligible words then said, "I'm staying planted right here. At the first sign of trouble, I'm joining you."

Craig nodded then he and Darren began a quiet trek toward the lake.

CHAPTER 50

INTRUDERS

When Twig approached the area he saw two men about twenty-five yards ahead. They were camped between the woods and the lake, sitting next to their fire. He squatted low, close to a tall pine tree, to watch and listen, but before he could catch himself, his foot rolled on a rock causing dry leaves to rustle.

The younger man jumped up, and grabbed his rifle. "Did you hear that?"

The older man said, "I didn't hear anything. Relax, son. Sit down by the fire. We've been wondering in this wilderness for a long time. Nothing's harmed us yet. It was probably a ground squirrel."

Twig tried to scoot behind the tree, without making another sound, but the foliage was dry. The young man heard him, and jumped up. "There it is again."

Before Twig could take another breath two bullets whizzed past his right ear. He hugged the ground, thankful to be alive.

"Man, that was close," he whispered.

"I think I got something," the young man shouted. "Let's go look."

"Like heck we will. Hand me a couple of logs. We need a big fire in case you wounded a bear. And, don't do any more firing. Save your bullets."

Twig watched the young man stoke the fire, sit down by it, while never taking his eyes off the wooded area. A few minutes later Twig heard a sound that caused his heart to race. Faint, muffled footsteps were heading his way.

He scooted backwards on his belly, thankful the crackling logs drowned out the noise of his retreat. *I know who that is.* When he felt safe he walked toward the sound, stopped behind a large spruce tree, and whispered, "I'm over here."

The footsteps stopped, then proceeded a little faster.

Craig reached him first. Twig cautioned him to speak softly. The strangers camp fire cast a dim light—enough to make each other out.

"Are you okay?" Craig whispered. "You've got stuff all over you."

"I tripped once, then had to dive for cover when that fool kid fired at me. There's two of 'em, and that younger one is down right trigger happy, so hug these trees. He already thinks he's killed something. That would be me. I couldn't believe it. He had no idea what he was firing at. A bullet whizzed right past my ear—like a darn mosquito."

Darren leaned in, "What should we do?"

Twig said, "I better stay and keep an eye out. They seem just like normal folk. When its daylight I will try to talk to them. If they're headed toward our place, I have an idea."

He shared his plan, then Craig and Darren backtracked toward the compound.

Twig moved into position, careful to keep shelter behind large trees. The strangers appeared to be sleeping soundly, so he took a nap, too. Just before sun up, he walked toward their camp, intending to call out an introduction, but the toe of his boot caught in a vine. He fell head long into a dead limb, and struck his right shoulder on a rock.

"Well, that'll wake 'em up," he said under his breath.

The boy jumped. "I knew somebody was out there!" He pointed his rifle toward the woods, "Who are you? Come out with your hands high."

"I'm coming. Don't shoot me." Twig stumbled over more brush before breaking through to the make shift camp, then found himself staring down the barrel of *two* rifles. Leaves, and mud were stuck to his clothes, beard, and hair. He looked the part of a mountain man.

The older man stood steady. He had a full beard, shoulder length hair, as did the boy, but neither was straggly. He said, "Stoke up the fire, Jeremy," then addressed Twig. "Who are you, and where did you come from?"

"My name's Twig. When the virus hit, my brother and I high tailed it here. It seemed like a safe place to wait it out. You know about the virus?"

The man with the rifle looked all around, "Yes, we do. Where's your brother?"

Twig looked at the ground, "He's dead, sir. He had an accident with his rifle."

"Sorry to hear that. My name is Ralph, and this is my son, Jeremy. A bush pilot flew us in for a week of hunting, fifty or sixty miles from here. He never came back, and no one has come looking for us. We followed the virus news on our radio, until the battery died. Now, we don't know what's happening. We don't know if our family survived, or if its safe to go home, or what. Do you have any news?"

"No sir, I ain't. I just figured it would blow over in a few months then I'd head back to Tennessee. I think it's worse than I thought, though."

Jeremy jumped in. "Why?"

"Cause there ain't no airplanes flying overhead. Seems like they'd be up there, if everything was okay."

Jeremy raised his rifle again. "Where's your camp, and what do you want with us?"

Twig shrugged his shoulders. "Nothing. I don't want nothing. I saw your fire and just wanted to talk to you—but you dang near shot me last night. Figured I'd come back in the daylight. My camp is a ways from here in the woods, so put your gun down, boy. I won't hurt you."

Ralph motioned for Jeremy to relax, but kept his finger on his own trigger.

Twig brushed himself off, and moved closer to the fire.

"If you don't mind me asking, where you folks headed?"

"Out of this valley," Ralph said. "We want to find some civilization."

"Well," Twig said. "Maybe we can help each other. I could sure use something hot to drink, then I'll catch us some fish. Is that okay?"

They both nodded, and before long the three men were sharing a cup of hot cranberry tea, and chatting in a friendlier manner, but Ralph's rifle lay touching his leg.

When he relaxed a little he said, "It took me awhile to believe we were really abandoned. The hunting camp was equipped with plenty of supplies, but there was no cell service—which was one of the big drawings. They offered a complete break from the outside world, and that's what we got—a complete break."

Twig threw another log on the fire and let Ralph continue with his story.

"On the tenth day, we left a note for the pilot, telling him which direction we were headed, loaded our packs, and took off walking. When we didn't find civilization, we knew there was food at the camp so we went back. We headed out again the first of March. We've been on the move ever since."

Twig asked, "Do you still have food?"

"Yes," Ralph said. "Not a lot, but we're thrifty. We eat a lot of fish, and picked a lot of berries before winter set in. We dehydrated them as good as we could, each time we built a fire. If we reach civilization before too long, we'll be okay. Right now, I would give my right arm for a good home cooked meal. Heck, I wouldn't even care if it was good."

Twig flinched. He could certainly identify with that, and was so thankful things were different now.

Jeremy said, "You're the first human being we've seen since we got here. How can you stand being alone? Don't you get lonely? Don't you get scared?"

"That's a lot of questions, boy. Yes, I get lonesome, and I sure do get scared. Once, there was this wolverine. We—I mean I couldn't see it because of a thick fog. I could hear it though, and I was plenty scared."

Jeremy surveyed the woods. "There are wolverines here?"

"I've only seen that one, and it's dead."

"Well, I hope no more roam this way. We're almost out of bullets."

Twig pointed at Ralph's fishing pole. "If you'll loan me that, I'll see if I can catch us some of those fish, I promised."

Thirty minutes later they were roasting trout over the fire on willow sticks, and Ralph continued to share his story. He told Twig he had been a bank manager for ten years before this hunting trip. Jeremy was a college student. Jeremy cried when his dad mentioned his five-year-old sister, Beth, and his mother.

"We weren't there to protect them," Ralph said. "We adopted Beth when she was two. I promised I would always be there for her."

"Maybe they're okay," Twig offered.

Jeremy yelled, "They're not okay! Dad told you we listened to the radio. Everyone in our area is dead. Mom said God would always take care of us. Where was He when all this happened?"

"Son, we've been over this a thousand times. I can't answer for God. I just know *we're* alive. We've got to keep it together and get out of here. Are you still with me?"

Jeremy nodded, then Ralph turned to Twig. "Would you walk with us to the base of the canyon? Better still, why don't you come along?"

"Yes, I will walk with you, but I'm staying in this valley a while longer. Hang on a minute while I get my gun."

"Dad?" Jeremy started, "I like this guy, but…"

"Young fella, I watched you all night, and could have dropped you anytime I wanted. Tell you what, if it makes you feel better, go get it for me."

Ralph said, "Don't be silly. Go get your gun. It's true. If you were going to harm us, you would have already done it."

"Listen, I've got some fruit leather and jerky in my lean-to. When your ready to leave, let's go by there. Made it myself."

When Twig saw the lean-to, he was relieved. He climbed inside and brought out a backpack, but when he reached inside to pull the jerky and fruit leather out, he hesitated, fumbled a moment, then handed them to Ralph.

"Thanks, man—this looks good. When this mess is over, come find us. We would love to put you up."

Twig didn't want to linger too long in case something caused suspicion. "We better get on the move. You don't want to be scaling that rocky incline after dark. Go the direction I told y'all. You'll come right out in the park. If you go left on the highway, it will take you to Wilson Creek."

Jeremy said, "I'm ready, and no matter what we find, I think I can handle it better than this."

Craig, and Darren were crouching behind a large boulder when the three men approached. They hoped Twig's site was ready, according to his instructions, and were happy to see he was carrying his rifle. When the three men walked away, Ralph, and Jeremy were bent low under the load of their packs. Ralph stumbled, caught himself then rubbed his chest.

Darren whispered, "Did you see that? His pack is way too heavy."

"I did, but he has obviously been carrying it for a long time."

When the three men disappeared, Craig and Darren headed back toward their settlement. Craig said, "You don't suppose Twig will go with them do you?"

"No, he's part of us now."

"That's true. He seems to make everyone feel safer," Craig said. "I almost think the family would rather get rid of me than him."

"Yeah, right. You know better than that."

Richard was walking out of the cave when Craig and Darren walked up. "Where's Twig?"

Craig laughed. "See what I mean?"

Darren nodded. "I think I do," then turned to Richard. "He's leading them away from here, but making sure they can find the road."

Craig knocked on the cave door, and Lois let them in. "Where's Twig?"

Craig laughed again then relayed the whole story, including Twig's willingness to accompany Ralph and Jeremy to the canyon base, closest to the road.

Lois said, "I'll be glad when our family's together again."

Craig said, "Me too, but in the mean time, I'm hungry."

Lois said she forgot to grab the leftover roast, so Darren and Joliene volunteered to get it. Craig and Richard stayed posted a few feet from the cave entrance to listen for Twig. Craig stared at the two lovebirds walking arm in arm, giggling like school kids.

Richard said, "I remember when Tracey and I acted like that. I'm glad they found each other, and she makes Dad happy, but it does hurt a little to see him with another woman."

"I'm sure," Craig said. "But, does it help that death separated your parents, not divorce."

"It does. Thanks for the reminder."

Linda came out of the cave, and stood beside Craig. She stared at the woods and said, "You don't suppose Twig would consider leaving us, do you?"

Craig said, "Not on your life. He knows we would kill him."

"We've received a lot of gifts from God, and Twig is right at the top," Linda said. "I hope we see him soon."

CHAPTER 51

AN ILL FATED FAREWELL

$\mathcal{N}$inety minutes later, Craig saw Twig exit the woods. When he was comfortable that Twig was alone, he hurried to meet him, and slapped him on the back.

"Great job, Twig. Glad you're back."

Richard said, "You handled that situation like a pro."

Twig grinned from ear to ear, and when he entered the cave he was welcomed like royalty.

Craig smiled. It was true. Twig was a gift.

"You almost caught us," Darren said. "We were trying to make it look well used, but we're lacking in lean-to building skills. And, there was an issue with the back pack." Darren looked at Lois.

"What?" Lois asked. "What was wrong with the backpack? I put it together myself."

"You did a great job, Mom. They'll have enough food for at least a week. It was your wrapping job. Fruit leather and jerky neatly enclosed in plastic wrap—and tied together with red ribbon?"

Lois's face became a little red when everyone laughed. "I'm sorry Twig, I wasn't thinking."

"That's okay, Miss Lois. You didn't do no harm. I kept the ribbons inside my pack. Those guys didn't see 'em, and they're on their way. They said a bush pilot flew them in last year and never came back."

"Wow!" Caleb said. "They got to ride in an airplane?"

Craig rubbed Caleb's head. "People pay lots of money to fly into places like this, to hunt and fish."

Twig said, "Ralph's the dad, and Jeremy's his boy. Ralph was sure tired. He kept stopping before we barely got started. He was sweating too."

Darren perked up, took his eyes off Joliene and said, "What else was he doing or saying?"

"He wasn't saying much except, he was breathing real hard." Twig said.

"What's wrong, Dad?" Richard asked.

"It sounds like he's in trouble. I saw him rubbing his chest when they were walking away. I thought it was because his pack was too heavy. I'm not so sure now. He may be having heart problems."

"That boy will never make it without his Pa." Twig said. "He jumped at every sound. He told me all about his five-year-old sister and his mama. He sure cried a lot."

"I don't mean to come across as calloused, and I'm sorry they've got trouble, but how can *we* help them?" Craig asked. "We struggle to take care of the family we have. We work darn hard for everything we eat—except meat. Twig pointed them in the right direction. When they get to the park they'll find help. Now pack up. Let's get back to the hut."

When Craig and Linda stepped outside, Twig was standing very still and looking toward the top of the ridge.

"Don't even think about it," Craig said.

Twig laughed, grabbed supplies, and headed for the hut. Darren started to follow, then turned and stared in the same direction.

"Twig!" He yelled. "We have to go after them. They don't have much of a head start, and I'm sure they're not making good time. If Ralph's in trouble, and if we don't help him, I'm afraid he'll die. I'm going to gather a few things. Will you help me find them?"

"Sure will. I've been real worried too."

Craig had started down the trail, but when he heard the latter part of Darren's comment he turned around. "What are you doing?"

"Twig and I are going after those men. I'm convinced Ralph's in trouble."

"Darren, we've been over this. Don't you think it's a family decision?"

Darren crossed his arms and faced Craig. "Yes, I suppose it is, but there may be a man out there in serious distress. I can't stand by and do nothing."

"Well, you've obviously made up your mind."

"I'm sorry, Craig, but I have. I'm very aware of our situation. Believe me I am, but I'm also a physician, *and* a Christian. That boy will die without his father. I hope it's not too late already. Are you going to back me up?"

Craig turned to walk away, and said, "You're not giving me much choice. I guess you have to do what you have to do."

Richard walked up. "Hey, what's going on here?"

Craig turned to him. "Your dad is going after Ralph and Jeremy. He thinks Ralph might be having heart trouble. I just don't know how we'll handle two more mouths to feed."

Richard looked at Craig, pursed his lips, but said nothing.

Craig hesitated then said, "What's on your mind?"

"Right from the beginning, Twig told us those men were ordinary people caught in a desperate situation, yet *I* went right along with our plan to hide. Why didn't we *start* by asking them to stay? If we've forgotten our responsibility to humanity, the virus didn't defeat us— we defeated ourselves."

Craig's face turned red. He started to point at Richard, thought better, and turned toward Darren. "We'd better get you two ready to go if you want to catch them before dark."

Twig shuffled around a minute, looked at Craig—then Darren. "Okay, sir—but I don't want no trouble."

"There won't be any trouble," Craig said. "I'll talk to the family, and as much as I hate to admit it, you guys are right. We can't turn our back on decent people. If they come back here, we'll figure out a way to make it work."

Nathaniel came running up. "Dad, Mom wants to know what's holding you up. Is everything okay?"

Craig said, "Darren and Twig are going after Ralph and Jeremy."

"I'll get my stuff together," Nathaniel said.

"You better stay here, buddy," Darren said. "Twig and I can handle this, but I could use some help putting my supplies together. I'll get the nitro and IV setup. Will you get the hand-held radio from the hut, and some water and a little food? Will you ask Chad to get that hammock out of my camper, just in case we have to carry him back?"

Craig went with him to the huts, and was bombarded with a flood of questions. He walked back up the path with Joliene. She grabbed Darren by the arm, and pulled him a few feet away. Their conversation was private, but Craig watched Darren wipe her tears before they embraced.

When Darren and Twig were ready to leave, Craig and Joliene walked to the edge of the woods with them.

The backpack was the heaviest piece they were taking. Twig insisted on carrying it and led the way. Soon the two men were swallowed by a maze of brush and groves of trees.

Craig said, "We'll just have to wait and see what happens. No sense in borrowing trouble. I'm sure we'll be okay. What do you think, son?"

"We'll be fine," Nathaniel said. "Twig and I can always bunk in the cave. We can bat the bats for entertainment."

Craig laughed. "Sounds like fun. I may join you."

Linda took his hand. "Not in this lifetime, mister."

CHAPTER 52

A LONG WAIT

*C*raig paced back and forth between the porch and the edge of the woods. Linda took his hand, and they walked together, in silence. On each pass they saw Joliene standing at the front window, wringing her hands. Tracey and Brianna took the younger kids to the bedroom area so they could play games.

Nathaniel and Duane asked if they could post themselves near the caves with a radio. Craig was happy for them to do it. Chad played with Big Ben and stayed outside, just in case the radio wasn't picking up a signal, as it so often did not. He knew Big Ben would hear Darren and Twig first.

A light drizzle began to fall, as did the temperature. Craig took Linda back to the porch, and Richard joined them.

"We've made a mistake, Richard," Craig said. "We let our two men leave without any backup plan. It'll be dark in a couple of hours. Should we try and find them?"

Richard crossed his arms. "No, I don't think so. They both know to fire a rifle if they need us. I'm not really expecting them back tonight, anyway. If Ralph's in trouble, Dad will make sure he's stable before moving him. They'll build a big fire and hunker down. They'll be okay."

"I'm not sure Joliene would agree with you. She's a wreck," Linda said.

Richard said, "I'll talk to her."

When Richard entered the door, Joliene was nowhere in sight. He found her sitting on a large stump, just outside the back door. Her head was down, and her eyes were closed. She appeared to be oblivious to the light rainfall. He started to say something, but realized she was praying, so he just took her hand, and closed his eyes. Joliene looked up long enough to see who joined her, then bowed again. After a moment or too she said, "Amen."

"I really needed this time, Richard. I needed to talk to the Lord. He and I had a lot of things to settle. Do you realize I haven't stepped foot in a church since my husband died?"

Richard kept his eyes on the ground and said nothing.

"I blamed God for his death, and I've been so angry. Now, I realize my husband's stubborn nature played the largest part. No matter how bad he felt he wouldn't go to the doctor. He blamed his symptoms on stress, and anything else he could think of, for a solid year. When I finally talked him into making an appointment, he was diagnosed with colon cancer, and it was too late for treatment."

"I'm sorry, Joliene. I had no idea."

"Many people were praying. I was sure God would heal him. In fact, I wouldn't take no for an answer. I expected him to recover—until it was time to turn his life support off. After that, I buried myself in my job, but since we've been in this valley my relationship with God has changed."

"I'm glad to hear that. Mine has too," Richard said.

Joliene sat quiet for a moment staring off into space. Without looking down she said, "Millions of people died, and thousands are trying to survive, but look at us. We escaped the virus, we have wonderful shelter, and we've never gone hungry. In spite of a few conflicts, for the most part everyone gets along. I'm back on track, and ready to put all that anger behind me. Now, your sweet dad has come along."

She began to shake so Richard slipped his arm around her. "I'm terrified of losing him, Richard, but I won't stand in his way. He is being true to his profession, and to his Lord. I should expect nothing less."

She buried her head in his shoulder and wept.

"I'm glad he's found you, Joliene. You're good for him—and for me. It may not be until morning, but he'll be back. Mark my words."

CHAPTER 53

THE ENCOUNTER

Twig and Darren shoved their way through heavy brush, tromped in sloshy bogs, and climbed over fallen logs before reaching the canyon wall. It was a decent slant to climb, but the wet rocks were slippery. Twig noticed Darren was slowing down, and suggested they take a five-minute break.

Darren said, "I'm already tired. That heightens my concern for Ralph. Tackling this type of terrain would be hard on anybody's heart. I'm glad you're leading the way, Twig. Once we left our familiar surroundings, I was lost. This is not like the movies. There are no trails or informative signs showing us the right path. I don't know how you do it, but keep it up. I trust you can get us home, too?"

"Don't you worry none. I can."

Darren said. "I'm still struggling with why we sent those guys away in the first place."

"It's a hard one, sir, but you chose Craig as leader, and he's a good one. He's tough too."

"That's for sure," Darren panted. "He and Richard make a good team. They've been friends a long time."

Darren stopped again. "Can we rest a couple more minutes?"

"Yes, sir. Take your time."

"Thanks, Twig. My lungs are beginning to ache."

Twig watched as Darren took deep breaths to compensate. "Tell me more about those two fellas."

Darren leaned back on the wall, and smiled. "They went to high school and college together. In fact, Richard dated Linda before Craig did."

"You're kidding me. I can't imagine Miss Linda with anyone else."

Darren closed his eyes for a minute then said, "Twig you didn't send those guys up this steep incline, did you?"

"Oh no, sir. They were north of here. It was steep, but a lot of trees to hold on to. I knew if we got south of 'em, we could head 'em off. Five more minutes, and we'll be at the top."

"Thank God," Darren gasped.

Just as they were leveling out onto flat ground, Twig stopped. "Did you hear that?"

"Hear what?" Darren whispered.

"Sounds like somebody's crying."

"You're right. Must be Jeremy. They're pretty close."

Twig cupped his hands to his mouth. "Jeremy! Ralph! Where are you?"

"Twig, is that you?"

"Yes, it is, boy. We're coming."

They followed Jeremy's voice to a sparse grove of trees on top of the plateau.

"Hurry, Twig. Something's wrong with my dad. I don't know how to help him."

"We're here, boy," Twig said, as they broke through the brush.

Jeremy was cradling his father's head in his arms. At first glance, Darren couldn't tell if Ralph was dead or alive.

Jeremy looked at Darren. "Who's that?"

"He's a doctor."

"A doctor? Where did you find a doctor?"

Darren extended his hand, "Hi, I'm Darren. I'm here to help your dad. We'll explain everything later."

Darren took out his stethoscope, and moved it around on Ralph's chest. "How long has he been like this?"

"For an hour or more—I don't know! It seems like forever. Is he going to be all right?"

Jeremy dropped his head, and his words were barely audible. "I can't lose my father, too. Please mister. Help him."

Darren took a small bottle from his bag, and put a nitro pill under Ralph's tongue.

Jeremy said, "Dad was having trouble breathing, but he wanted to get to the top of the rise before we stopped. When we got to this spot, he grabbed his chest, and fell to the ground." Jeremy wiped his tears. "Will he be okay?"

"Let's see how he reacts to the nitroglycerin, and I'll start an IV drip too. Why don't you guys help me get him onto a sleeping bag, then build a fire?"

"I don't want to leave him. What if he dies while I'm finding wood?" Jeremy held his dad's head all the tighter.

Darren listened to Ralph's heart again. "Actually, his beat is steadier now. He probably had a heart attack, but Jeremy, not all heart attacks kill. Let's give him some time. I think he'll come around pretty soon. We'll have to spend the night here, so how about that wood?"

"Okay, but I'm not going far." Jeremy lowered Ralph's head then he and Twig circled the area for firewood. When they had a nice pile, Twig cleared a spot, dug out an area, lined it with rocks, and started a fire. He helped Jeremy tie ends of a small tarp to nearby trees to cover Ralph. Darren's tent was placed on the other side of the fire pit.

Twig took food from the pack, then tried to explain to Jeremy why they deceived him and his dad. Jeremy listened for a moment then flew off his log. He grabbed a branch, tackled Twig to the ground, and tried to hit him in the face.

A faint voice said, "Jeremy stop. These people were right in what they did."

"Dad!" He stumbled off Twig, and crawled over the muddy, rough ground to Ralph. "Thank God you're alive."

Darren gave Twig a hand. "Are you okay? I thought you were going to get clubbed."

"Would be no more than I deserved. Nothing I was telling that boy sounded good—even to me."

"I know exactly what you mean," Darren said then turned to Ralph. "How are you feeling?"

"Like a tractor ran over me. What happened?"

Darren listened to Ralph's chest again. "I think you had a heart attack. We plan to take you back to our camp so I can monitor you."

Ralph offered a weak laugh. "I take it you're a doctor, or am I dreaming?"

Darren stuck out his hand. "I'm Darren. You've already met Twig. We got worried about you guys when you left today, so we came after you."

"Good thing you did. Jeremy couldn't make it by himself. If things get worse, will you promise to take him with you?"

"I promise, but I think you're going to be fine. Rest for a while. If you have more symptoms let me know right away so I can give you nitro. If you're stronger tomorrow we'll head to our camp, unless you want to keep going. I wouldn't recommend it though. I don't think you'll be strong enough for quite awhile to climb a mountain."

"Sounds good to me," Ralph said, as he drifted off.

Jeremy sat staring at the fire, speaking to no one, until he heard Darren's last remark.

"You guys are really something. What happened? Did you get a touch of conscience? Did you start feeling guilty? Why *did* you come after us? What do you want?"

"Look son…"

"Don't call me son. You don't care about me."

Twig stood up. "You need to watch your mouth, boy. This man is here to help you, and that's all."

Darren held up his hand. "It's okay, Twig. I don't blame him for being angry. We would feel the same." He turned to Jeremy again.

"Jeremy, all I can say is, I hope you can forgive us. We were trying to protect our family."

"Oh yes! We sure fit the image of a couple of crooks. We were a real threat to you. I can see why you wouldn't want to help us."

"Jeremy, that's enough. You apologize right now." Ralph's voice was barely a whisper.

"Apologize for what? They don't care about us."

"Come here, son. Get your sleeping bag, and lay down next to me. We'll talk about this tomorrow. Twig, Darren, please be patient. Give him a little space. He's been through a lot."

Darren told Ralph *that* was not a problem then he listened to Ralph's heart again. "We're not upset with the boy. We're the ones in the wrong. Get some rest. Things will look brighter in the morning."

Twig and Darren took turns keeping watch and stoking the fire. Darren checked Ralph throughout the night, and knew the man would not be walking anywhere for a while.

Just before dawn, Twig said, "I've been thinking. The road ain't far from here. Let me have that radio. I'll keep calling those guys until they hear me. One of them can drive that ATV pretty darn close. We can carry Ralph to it and give him a ride back to camp."

"Good thinking, Twig. That would be easier on all of us."

Ninety minutes later, the roar of an engine echoed throughout the area.

Twig, Richard, and Nathaniel broke through the trees. Darren looked at the men and said, "Thank you, God. What a relief."

Ralph was awake, and Darren said. "This is Richard, my son, and Nathaniel. Guys, this is Ralph and his son Jeremy."

Ralph stuck out his hand. "Sorry about this. We'll try not to be a burden to you, and as soon as I'm strong enough, we'll head out again."

Richard knelt beside him. "Ralph, we acted like jerks. On the surface, our motives appeared to be justified, but right now they're looking pretty lame. Let's just get you back to camp to a hot meal and a real bed."

Jeremy shuffled his feet toward Richard, stuck out his hand, and gave a limp attempt at a shake, but said nothing.

By eleven-thirty, Craig and Darren had Ralph resting comfortably in a lower bunk. Craig laughed at the barrage of women turned nurse. Lois served pinto beans, corn bread, and moose steak for the midday meal. At first, Jeremy refused to eat, but with a little coaxing from Tracey, he sat down at the table next to her.

Joliene and Darren volunteered to stay with Ralph. She said she would spoon-feed him bean broth.

Ralph asked, "Is Jeremy eating?"

Craig said, "Yes, he's doing fine."

Darren said. "Don't worry. We have a house full of mother hens. They'll take good care of him."

"Thank you for everything. I think I'll sleep awhile." With that, he rolled his face to the wall. Darren and Joliene were deeply moved when they heard his soft sobs. Joliene laid her hand on his shoulder. Ralph laid his hand on hers—then whispered, "Thank you."

After Craig realized how serious Ralph's condition was, and witnessed the anger in Jeremy's eyes, pangs of guilt surged through his chest. *We must do everything we can to remedy the wrong we did to these two men. God forgive me, please.*

CHAPTER 54

TWO MORE TO FEED

*C*raig was amazed to see how quickly Jeremy became Tracey's protégé. She gave him a haircut, mended his clothes, listened to his fears, and seemed to feel his pain. His mother and sister were most likely dead. At times he boiled with anger, focusing most of it toward Craig. On the fourth day, following their rescue, Craig walked by the porch where Jeremy, and Tracey were talking.

"How about helping me cut some firewood?" Craig held out an axe handle to Jeremy.

"Not right now. I think you can see we're talking."

Craig turned the axe around, raised it over his shoulder then buried it with a resounding thud in the ground. He lowered his brow and stared right into the lad's eyes. "Come with me, boy, we need to get some things straight."

Jeremy looked toward Tracey for help, but she shrugged her shoulders. "You better do what he says. He's the *big* boss."

Craig led Jeremy on a brisk walk toward the cave. He wanted to cool down before he said something he knew he would regret.

"Look boy, how many times do I have to say I'm sorry, before you let this thing go? You're here now. Your dad is improving every day. So, unless you want a few days of total isolation you better stop your whining. Life is too hard to tolerate an attitude like yours. You don't have two options. Your one choice is to buckle under, and become a team player. And, you better start showing some respect for everyone in this camp. Am I getting through?"

"Yes, sir. I'm sorry, and I'll try to do better."

"Did I hear you say *try*?"

"I meant I *will* do better."

Craig gave him a little punch on the shoulder, and said, "Well good. Welcome to the family. I'll take care of the wood. You ask around and see if anybody else needs help, and tomorrow I want you to work with the other guys. Our survival depends on all of us working as a team. Do you understand?"

"Yes, sir, I do."

Craig walked behind Jeremy into camp. He saw him start to run past Tracey, but then he stopped. "Is there anything I can help you with, Miss Tracey?"

"I can't think of anything right now except, do you have a special talent, or ability you could share with us? Twice a week we give members of the family a chance to teach, or entertain us. Wednesday is the teaching time and Friday the entertainment. We have great fun learning from each other, and both nights give us something to look forward to. We would love you to share something unique to you. It doesn't have to be world changing. And your dad—what about him?"

Jeremy said, "Can we have a chance to think about it?"

"Sure. Talk to your dad and let me know when you're ready. You guys are going to be a great asset."

"I know one thing my dad is great at. He's a hunter. He even knows how to tan animal skins. Is that what you mean?"

Tracey laughed until tears poured down her cheeks.

"What's so funny? Isn't that what you meant?"

"Yes, yes it is, and I'm not laughing at you. It just reminds me of an incident we had when we first got here. We could have used him then. Thanks Jeremy. I needed a good laugh. Why don't you go see if Lois needs help with dinner?"

~

When Ralph was stronger, Craig asked him to go for a walk. "What kind of work were you in, Ralph?"

"Nothing too exciting. I am . . . rather *was*, a bank manager. My hobbies are hunting, fishing and working with leather. I was a scout leader until Jeremy out grew it. Did I mention anything you can use?"

Craig patted him on the back. "Believe me, we need help everywhere. I'm sure Tracey will be signing you up for our weekly class time. I was never involved with Scouts. Maybe she'll have you teach us more survival skills."

"I'll do what I can, but from where I stand, you're doing fine. I can't believe how well you've provided for your family. It's really helped Jeremy to be in civilization again."

"Civilization? Man, I can't wait to share that observation with the ladies."

"Well, you guys have sure treated us good." He turned to shake Craig's hand. "I can't thank you enough."

Craig took his hand. "You're welcome, but I wanted to talk to you alone to apologize."

"Apologize? You don't owe me an apology for anything. I would be dead if it wasn't for your family, and my son would be wandering alone in the wilderness."

"I feel bad we weren't honest with you in the first place. It was my fault, not the family's. I can be pretty stubborn, and bad-tempered at times. I thought I was doing the right thing, but it almost cost you your life. Can you forgive me?"

"Craig, no one can change their yesterdays. Of course, I forgive you. Let's just move forward from here, okay?"

At that point, Ralph dropped his head.

"What's troubling you man?"

"I owe some apologies myself, which I'll probably never be able to give. Do you have any idea how much I would like to tell my wife and little girl how sorry *I* am? I left them alone to face this terrible horror. If only..."

"Ralph stop. Remember what you just said about yesterdays? No one knew an attack was coming. You were stuck in this valley with no way out. It's not like you ran out on them."

"I know you're right, but it's hard. Jeremy has nightmares every night and cries way too often. What about you guys? Were you together when it hit?"

"We were in Eastern Montana, many hours from Seattle. We felt just like you, and had no guarantee we'd make it home. We were shot at—by convicts—when we ran through their roadblock."

"We talked a state trooper into letting us pass. I think our federal government plates and IDs made the difference to him."

"Why do you have government plates, and what happened with the prisoners?"

Craig shared a large portion of his family's adventure, and ended with the trip to the valley.

"By the way," Craig said. "We never told the whole story about the convicts to the family, so keep it to yourself. We made it home safe. That's all that matters."

"I understand." Ralph stuck out his hand. "Thanks Craig. Thanks for everything. Jeremy and I will work hard to do our part. That's a promise."

"I know you will. Let's head back. I still have a few chores to do before dark."

"What can I do?"

"Why don't you go inside and sit down for a while? Your day is coming, believe me."

By the end of the week Ralph was getting stronger. Craig assigned him minor chores, as his strength allowed. Jeremy was doing better every day.

Craig asked Tracey to question Jeremy again about his skills or special training. He said, "Nothing. I can't think of anything I do well."

Ralph laughed. "Ask him to show you how to tie a fly."

Jeremy put his head down. "Dad, no one cares about that. I think she means something important."

"Are you kidding?" Tracey said. "We've been taught how to suture wounds, make quilts, crossword puzzles, dehydrate jerky, not to mention smoking fish, tying knots, and so on. Oh yes, I almost forgot. We found out how to gain super powers by drinking invisible green juice. I think tying flies would be a welcome change."

Jeremy laughed. "I can guess who served the green drink. Okay, I'll do it. When will it be my turn?"

"Why don't you go next?"

Tracey asked Lois to help him gather thread, hooks and the younger children searched for feathers. On Wednesday evening when Jeremy presented, Caleb was fascinated and caught on fast.

The following Saturday, Craig took Nathaniel, Jeremy and Caleb fishing to try out the new flies. They hiked to a creek about a mile from camp. Twig went along too, only he sat on the shore with rifle in hand. The stream was filled with a series of large boulders.

Craig said, "We're fishing for Grayling. They stay close to the rocks. We need to sneak up on them, or they'll scatter. This is the perfect place to fly fish, so be very quiet."

They hopped across the rocks, casting their newly made flies into the deep pools. Craig fished with his rifle strapped to his back, keeping his eye on the opposite shore. He spotted a large brown bear scooping up fish, a hundred or so yards to his right. It was paying no attention to the humans. Craig looked back at Twig, and motioned in the direction of the bear. Twig nodded.

Craig and Nathaniel caught five fish each. Caleb caught seven plump ones, and Jeremy, six. They headed back to camp early afternoon, but before they got there Craig saw Richard hurrying through the woods toward them.

CHAPTER 55

A NEW AMERICA

Craig said, "What's up man?"

"I need to talk to you. Take a walk with me."

Nathaniel asked, "Can Twig and I come too?"

Craig looked at Richard and he nodded. "Sure. Its time we let you guys in on everything. Let's get the fish inside first."

After giving the Grayling to a thankful Lois, they walked in the direction of the caves. When out of earshot, Richard said, "Leon called. He wants us to call him tonight after ten our time. He left us the number for one of the *burner* phones. He said no one else should have access to that phone except him, so if anyone else answers, hang up and don't leave a message. He'll get back to us as soon as he feels safe. He also said to keep our phones with us at all times."

Craig said, "Sounds intense."

"You would really think intense if you heard the urgency in his voice. And there was something else. He said look at the new Federal Government website. It came back on line yesterday. He said it's just being built, but will give us a snapshot of what's going on in the country."

Craig pulled up the site on his phone. "Listen to this." Craig read it out loud while the others tried to view the small screen.

Welcome to the New America – If you are viewing this page, you are connected to your federal government. It is your lifeline and the only search engine available. To receive life-preserving benefits every citizen **must** register on this site. That form is available below. Once your registration has been received—and approved, you will have access to food banks, medical care, medications, limited fuel locations, and other benefits, in your area, **if available**. Your password is your Social Security number, or your thumbprint. Follow the instructions. Until this crisis is under control, and for your protection, city-to-city and state-to-state movement is restricted. More detail on all categories is available below. Post questions in the designated areas. Follow the directions carefully. This website will be monitored twenty-four hours a day, and will post current conditions concerning attacks, closed areas, new benefit locations, etc.

Craig stared in disbelief. "I feel like we're living in a science fiction movie."

Richard pointed to the familiar face of the president. "He is supposedly making this announcement, but I think whoever's in charge is just using his face to comfort people. He may be dead or held hostage."

Craig said, "I don't know, but this is not the America we left. I can't wait to talk to Leon."

Nathaniel said, "How could a takeover like this happen, Dad? Isn't anybody fighting back? I sure would."

"I'm not sure, son. If our government is behind the terror attack, they were successful in bringing the country to its knees."

Craig shut down the site and continued to stare at his phone. "This all came to fruition in one year. That means it's been in the works for a long time. We were living in a virtual time bomb and didn't know it. We were making plans for a non-existent future."

Richard was pacing up and down the path. "Should we fill everyone in as soon as we get back, or wait until after we talk to Leon?"

Craig thought for a moment then said, "We need to wait until we have the full scoop. It's starting to rain. Let's get inside."

∼

Craig choked his dinner down, which tightened the knot he already had in his stomach. At times he felt it would double him over. Linda touched his arm and started to say something, but he shook his head. He knew she understood what that meant.

When Caleb was asked to give a fly tying demonstration, and a report on his first fly fishing expedition, Craig began feeling better. Caleb asked Jeremy to stand by him. After every twist, turn and knot, he waited for a nod of approval. When he finished Jeremy patted him on the back.

"You're doing a great job. Pretty soon I'll be taking lessons from you."

Caleb laughed. "Really?"

"You bet."

∼

At exactly nine forty-five, Craig gave Richard a nod. He simply told the others they were taking a walk.

"In the rain?" Duane asked.

"Yes, in the rain," Craig barked over his shoulder then grabbed his coat and walked a few yards away from the huts.

At ten sharp, Craig punched in Leon's number then put it on speaker. It rang six times before a soft voice answered, "Hey, Craig."

"Hey, Leon . . . glad to reach you. We looked at the site. Welcome to a New America?"

"You were witnessing web control at its finest. I know you guys are eager to move out of the valley, but this is not the time, unless—let me get to that later. Sit tight for a little longer."

Craig said, "That's what we were afraid of. Can you fill us in? We need some facts so we can quit speculating."

Leon spent the next twenty minutes giving details, which were so horrific, both Craig and Richard sank onto a boulder.

Leon said, "Nothing was as it appeared to be. The virus was real, for sure, but the invasion didn't come from a foreign radical terrorist group—it was home grown, and get ready for the next part guys. It's not pretty."

Craig said, "We're ready . . . I think."

"Members of our federal government, linked with home-grown terrorists, are behind the attack."

Craig said, "After seeing the website, that's what we suspected. How can the president fool so many people? How can he sell out his own country?"

Leon said, "Hold on. The president hasn't been seen or heard from in almost eleven months. His official seal is being used everywhere, but not by him. The only people barking out orders are those who made up his inner circle—his close-knit cabinet—those who just happened to be absent when the attack on Washington took place. My crew has been gathering proof for months."

"Why is the president's face on the web page?"

"Because he's loved by a large mass of people. If messages come from him, they're trusted. People feel safe and do what they're told. If you were able to see a graphic of the exact viral attack areas, and compare them to the areas that weren't hit, you would understand. I think he's dead. No, I'm almost certain he's dead. They wouldn't dare let that news get out. If they did, the areas in submission would explode . . . then they would die too."

Craig shivered and dropped his head. "This is crazy."

Leon said, "They're promising protection, and a smooth transition, but drones are still flying to areas of unrest. Fear of death brings submission."

Richard said, "Surely, counter measures are in the works —someplace."

"Yes, they are, and I'll get to that in a minute, but let me give you some details. This takeover didn't happen overnight. It was well thought out. I don't know how they pulled it off, but can you imagine how much control they have now?"

"How can they be so heartless? How can they have such little value for human life?" Craig asked.

"They believe they're on a holy mission. Unless they're stopped, Sharia law will soon rule America—and there is so much more. I have to hang up soon so listen carefully. I received a message from a high-ranking general. He has a stellar reputation—tough as nails, and carries a lot of weight. He may be contacting you . . ."

Leon's voice became so soft they could barely make out his words. "The counter offensive has begun. Recruitment and training are going great, but no one knows the geography of this nation better than you two. Would you guys be interested in coming back, and taking up the cause as consultants?"

Craig and Richard looked at each other. Craig spoke first. "Leon, we have a huge family, plus a few more we've collected. We live under extreme, rugged conditions, and we're scraping the bottom of the barrel for some of our supplies. Before we could even consider a commitment like that our family would have to be secure. Here in the..."

"Don't say anymore. Better if we keep locations secret."

Leon's voice dropped to a whisper. "Someone's coming. I'll call tomorrow evening—if I can."

Craig looked at his phone for a moment then at Richard. "And what if he can't? What then?"

Richard punched Craig's shoulder. "Well, here we go again. Are you feeling the heat? How are *you* going to break this great news to the crew?"

"I really don't know, but if I could do things over, *you* would be the leader of this ever-growing band of isolated misfits."

CHAPTER 56

CALMING THE FAMILY

*A*s soon as Craig's and Richard's feet touched the first step, the hut door swung open. Nathaniel came running out with a mob right behind him. "Okay, Dad, what gives?"

"Let's get inside and we'll tell you."

When they settled he said, "Well guys, I might as well get straight to the point. There's no way to soften this."

Craig relayed Leon's message just as he received it, and when he finished he sat down. "Are there any questions?"

Richard glanced around the room. No one moved. The faces of the adults were frozen. He glanced Craig's way, and said, "Nothing like getting to the point."

Tracey gasped. "In America? This is happening in America?"

Richard said, "I'm afraid so. Those who are pretending to be fighting for us are in control. Leon will try to call back tomorrow night with more details."

Craig was glad he didn't mention Leon's request that he and Richard join an insurrection.

He said, "Apparently, the virus is being spread using American terrorists with radical ties. It's not a safe time to go home."

At this point everyone's demeanor fell. No one said a word. Craig let it go a few minutes then said, "I know you're disappointed. We are too. But what good does it do to fall apart unless you're all planning to give up? Leon will update us as often as he can."

Craig and Richard waited, but Leon did not call back the next night, or the one after that. After a full week they were getting nervous. The stress weighed heavy on them. They resisted calling their friend for fear of exposing him, or disclosing their own location.

Craig did not know what to do about the widespread, corporate depression. It was even deeper than the one experienced when they initially arrived in the valley. For a solid week, meals were eaten for the sole purpose of survival. Plates were taken to bedrooms, porch steps, stumps and so on. No one fished, and family night was not mentioned.

He went to the woodpile, and split one log after the other. Every blow of the axe echoed his frustration. He wanted to give the family words of encouragement and comfort, but what would he say? He too thought of his former life, his friends, his work, but he did not have the wisdom to make sense of these new facts. Normally, he would turn to Richard, but one look at his friend's demeanor told him Richard was struggling too.

Craig looked to heaven and said, *"Help me God. I don't have a clue what to do."*

Lois and Caleb were in the living area playing a game when Craig brought a load of wood in and stacked it by the fireplace. He gave them a nod, then went back outside.

Caleb watched him go. "You know what, Grandma? Everybody's so sad. I asked God to make them feel better. Do you think He will?"

Lois was taken off guard. "I . . . of course He will. He's our God."

"I think I better go talk to Him some more."

"Caleb, what would I do without you? Before you go, would you please ask your dad to come see me in my bedroom?"

"Sure," he said, slamming the hut door.

When Craig entered, he gave her a hug and said, "What's up?"

"You know that old saying, 'Out of the mouth of babes?'"

"Yes, I do."

"Well, I just experienced it. Caleb is being affected by this family's low mood. He said he asked God to make us all feel better. We, including me, need to pull ourselves together, and make a plan."

"I agree, Mom. I'm trying to figure out a way to do that."

"Well," she said. "One of my favorite scriptures goes something like this: If a man lacks wisdom, he needs to ask God for it and God will give it to him. I think that's what we *all* need. We need a good dose of God's wisdom. We're powerless to change these circumstances, but we can't give up."

"That's exactly right, but Mom, there's something we didn't disclose. A resistance force has been formed, and troops are being enlisted. Because of Richard's and my expertise, they want our help as consultants."

"I had no idea. Have you made a decision?"

"No, we haven't. On one hand we feel an urgency to go, but on the other, we can't walk away, and leave our family unprotected. Leon will want an answer the next time he calls. By the way, we haven't told our wives, so please don't say anything."

"Don't worry. I won't, but I can see Richard keeping your dilemma from Tracey, at this initial stage, but not Linda. Have a little confidence in her judgment."

"I'm sure you're right. If I had half her wisdom I would already have an answer. What else did you want to talk about?"

"Son, this family has shut down one more time—except Caleb. We have to fight the depression. I'll make a special dinner tonight then afterwards, would you read from the Bible? John, chapter seventeen, would be a good spot."

"Okay, but why that chapter?"

She said, "Look it over and you'll see. You do a great job as head of this clan. You've taken us through good *and* bad times, so get your rear in gear then give *us* a kick in the pants. Get us moving. None of this is taking God by surprise. Have some confidence that He's in charge even if it looks otherwise—and dinner will be served at six sharp."

"Yes, ma'am. I'm going."

CHAPTER 57

RALLYING THE FAMILY

*C*raig's first move was to rally all the men. He sent some to fish, some to cut wood, and some to clean the barn. The small army marched with reluctance toward their individual assignments.

Craig yelled after them, "Hey, Mom just took me to the woodshed, and I'm sure she has all the ladies lined up next. You're getting off easy."

At dinnertime, Craig and Lois were pleased to hear a little friendly banter, and teasing.

She smiled and whispered to Craig, "Funny how a little boy and a little work can remind us to go on living."

After dinner Craig asked Richard to join him outside. When they were past the steps, Richard asked, "What's up?"

"I think its time we tell the family the rest of the story. You and I have to make a decision before Leon calls. We sure can't *dump* it on them. I didn't want to say anything without running it by you first, so what do you think?"

Richard paused for a few seconds, then said, "They have the right to know. I say go for it."

When they reentered the hut, Craig said, "There's something we need to tell you. Leon had a few things to say we haven't shared."

"What's going on, Craig? What did you keep from us?" Duane asked.

Craig told them about the volunteer resistance militia then dropped the bombshell. "Because of our familiarity with the lay of the land, Leon asked if Richard and I would be interested in taking part."

Tracey gasped. "Richard, you're going nowhere. I can't survive this place without you."

"Craig, that's how I feel too," Linda said.

He walked over to her, and slipped his arm around her waist. "I wish it was that uncomplicated."

"We're not making a commitment right now. But, we're needed, and the stakes are high. We're waiting for another call from Leon. Right now we're in the dark, and it's about to drive us crazy. Mom said I needed to read from the Bible tonight. She suggested John seventeen. I already looked it over. It's Jesus prayer for Himself, His disciples, and He even mentions us."

Cassie's eyes opened wide. "He did? What did He say?"

"Well, when I'm ready to read that part, I'll point it out."

When he got to the third prayer he winked at Cassie. "Just listen to this."

When he finished reading, Cassie said, "Wow!" Craig smiled and launched right into prayer.

"Father, Your Son prayed for us a long time ago. I want to thank you for His prayer. He knew days like these were coming, and how hard they would be. We don't know what to do, and we don't want to make wrong decisions so we're asking for your help. Do we go, or do we stay? Please give us a sign. In Jesus name—Amen."

Brianna sat down next to her dad, wrapped her arms around his neck and whispered, "I don't think I could survive without you. I know I've been a brat and I'm sorry. Please don't go."

Craig gave her a hug, but said nothing except, "I love you too."

Twig slowly stood up and moved in front of the fireplace. "Well, I don't know much about no militia, but I do know how to fight. Seems to me, I'm the logical person to go. You fella's got families to take care of. When you find out how to report, let me know."

Nathaniel stirred a minute then joined Twig. "I can go too. It's my country, and I'm willing to fight for it."

Craig and Linda gasped, and Twig's face turned white. "Now see here boy, your mom and dad need you right here holding this place together. I think I need to go by myself. I'll give it a look-see and report back, that is, if you'll loan me one of those cell phones."

Jeremy gave Ralph a quick look and Ralph shook his head. "Don't even think about it."

"But Dad, maybe I could check on Mom and sis."

Craig stood up. "Okay, okay. Relax. Nobody's going anywhere. We need a lot more information—and details. We don't even know where the militia is based."

Darren said, "How do we get more facts with such limited access to the outside world?"

"That's a good point. If we don't hear from Leon soon, we'll start formulating a plan. We can also visit Wilson Creek, and see if they know anything. What do you think, Richard?"

"Sounds like a plan to me."

Craig turned to Twig and shook his hand. "You're a good man. We've already said this so often, but I'll say it again. In spite of the circumstances, you coming to this valley was one of the best gifts God gave us. Let's get together later and hash some of this out. Okay?"

"Yes, sir. Thank you, sir."

Craig walked back to Linda, took both her hands and said, "Let's take Ben down to the lake, and see if we can catch our breath."

He led her to the door and stopped long enough to take his rifle off the rack. He saw Duane start after them and shook his head. Duane retreated. When they reached the lake, Linda crossed her arms and stared over the calm water. Some geese were flying overhead in perfect formation, honking to each other as they made their way south.

Craig turned her around, and she buried her face in his chest. She could not control her sobs, so he laid his head on top of hers and held her tight. After a few minutes she took a step back. Craig wiped her tears with his finger.

She said, "Our son is a man."

"Yes, he is."

"If he decides to go, we can't stop him, can we?"

Craig took her hand. "Don't worry, sweetheart. Both of us won't go. If, or when that decision needs to be made, I'll make sure he stays here. He'll do a great job taking care of this family."

Linda jerked her hand back. "Is that what you think I want—a choice—a choice between my husband and my son? I would rather go myself than have either one of you leave. It just never occurred to me life would come to this."

She spun around and stared into the darkening sky. "Nathaniel was supposed to go to college, get married, and provide us with grandkids—not volunteer to join a mysterious militia. It seems only yesterday he was Caleb's age."

"I know. My insides are torn up too. Why don't we do what Mom said, and pray for wisdom?"

Big Ben's common practice at the lake was to run, sniff and bark, but tonight he sat on his haunches at their feet, looking first to Craig then Linda. Craig patted his head. "We're okay, boy." The dog whimpered and stayed in place.

Linda smiled at Ben then hugged Craig tight. She turned toward the long row of mountains that bordered the East side of the valley. Glistening streams of ice was trailed up their sides. They presented an illuminating presence, even in the darkest night.

"What are those ice movements called, again? I forgot," Linda asked.

"They're rock glacier velocities. A pretty spectacular sight, aren't they?"

"Yes, they are. You know, Craig, even though my heart is heavy, I'm stronger than I've ever been. Life in this valley has been insanely difficult, but it's provided all of us with a chance, as you guys say, to man up. I think I could face anything—except losing a member of my family."

Craig smiled and looked Linda over from head to toe. "It's hard to imagine you as a man."

Linda lifted her eyes to heaven. "I don't know how we'll make it through this without God's help."

Craig placed both hands on her shoulders. "He may get tired of hearing from us."

CHAPTER 58

THE GENERAL

wo days later, Craig stood on the porch drinking coffee when his cell phone rang. He walked a few feet away then said, "Thank God. Leon, where have you been? We just about gave you up."

"Sorry, Craig. I've had no opportunity, and I have to keep this short. It's still hard to tell the good guys from the bad ones. Listen, General Stokes, the head of the militia, wants to talk to you guys. Write down his number."

As Craig prepared to write on his hand he said, "General Stokes? General Ethan Stokes?"

"Yes, he wants you to call him as soon as possible. He'll ask for a code. Its *dust in my eyes*. He should be the only one answering the phone, but if someone else answers, and doesn't ask for the code, say nothing and hang up."

Craig stared across the lake, as he placed the call. The morning sun was just beginning to peak over the mountain range. He knew General Stokes well. He served under him in Desert Storm. The general was as tough as they came, one hundred percent American, and the perfect man to head up a militia. He wondered if the general would remember him? He did not have long to wait. His call was answered on the first ring.

"What's the code?" A gruff voice said.

Craig gave the expected answer. "I understand you want to talk to me."

"You do know who you're speaking with—right?" He gave Craig no chance to answer. "I understand you and a buddy were in North Dakota when the first attack happened?"

"Yes, sir."

"This is a secure line. Feel free to give me your name."

"It's Craig . . . Craig Michaels."

"Craig Michaels? That sounds familiar. Wait! Were you with me in Desert Storm?"

"Yes, sir, I was."

"Well, I'm glad it's you. You're a good man—a great member of my team."

"Thank you, sir, and thank you for forming the militia. Things looked pretty bleak until now."

"You're welcome. I don't know how far we'll get. The vice president, and his cronies think they've turned America's lights off. We plan to turn them back on. I could sure use a man of your caliber, and your friend. Leon says good things about him too."

"Thank you, sir. We would love to join you, but in our camp we have the young, the old, and every age in between. Survival depends on all of us working together. We can't leave them to fend for themselves."

"I thought as much, but would you consider being my consultants?"

"Of course, if we can do it from here." Craig said. "Is there something specific?"

The general paused. "We're looking for a lab. For several years it's rumored that DHS commissioned a private lab to experiment with deadly virus's, and how to eradicate them. If there is such a lab, the mountains around Denver would be a perfect, and logical place to hide. As soon as the attack broke out, I tried to find it on my own—maxed out my level of clearance, then made the mistake of approaching John McIntyre at DHS. I've always liked the guy . . . "

Craig heard heavy breathing, but the general was not speaking. When he did speak again, Craig moved the phone away. The generals tone had always been commanding, but this time it was filled with rage.

"McIntyre laughed at me. Then he said—loud enough for everyone in the area to hear—'General! It's a conspiracy theory. There's always one floating around. I can't believe someone with your experience fell for it.'"

"I wanted to grab him by the throat. I wonder how he views it now?"

The general took another breathing break then continued. "He knew just how to shut me down—for the moment—but there's a good chance we've caught a break. I may have been right about the Denver area, all along."

Craig asked, "Why is that sir?"

"I was in the mess hall and overheard a conversation. One of our volunteers was talking about his friend, Mrs. Heileich. Her husband was doing a top-secret assignment for Homeland Security, shortly before the first attack. He took a train to Denver and never returned."

"How does that relate to the viral attack?"

The general said that Mrs. Heileich knew very little of her husband's assignment, but when she was clearing out his dest she found a scribbled note. It said to meet Brock in Denver . . . take the 6:30 morning train. She retrieved a graphic from his deleted file—a map of the United States. WESTERN FLOW CHART was written across the top. Since the DHS had no record of her husband working for them, she did not give them this information.

"It got me thinking," the general said. "Leon told me how to access the personnel files from the 'back door.' I found a few Brocks, but only one who worked in a lab with a supervisor named Dr. Savi who has expertise in viral eradication, and antidotes. That is all the information there was, but enough to convince me . . . that lab is somewhere close to Denver."

"Well, that's some good work," Craig said. "So, how can we help?"

"Would you search your maps, and see what you boys can find?"

Craig said, "Richard's your man, sir. I'm good, but he's a topographical expert. We'll get right on it."

"Great! Sorry you guys can't join us, but I understand."

"There is one more thing, sir." Craig hesitated, and felt he would choke before he could get the next words out.

"We do have a couple of men who want to come your way. One of them is my son, Nathaniel. He's only twenty, but he steps up to the plate and carries his weight. He's grown up in this valley, right in front of our eyes. The other guy came straight from the hills of Tennessee. He's a crack shot, responsible, and a team player. He would be a real asset. They both would."

"We can use them. You work things out on your end. Call me if you find anything suspicious, otherwise, I'll get back to you in a couple of weeks. If your men still want to join us, we'll pick them up close to where you are."

"You do realize where we are, don't you?"

"Yes, the Canadians help us cross their borders. They like our new technology. We can talk about that later."

"Sir, before you hang up, can you help us understand how this happened? Where was our intel? How did they sneak up on us?"

"It didn't sneak up on us, Michaels, and it didn't happen overnight. The signs have been in place a long time. Any country that embraces tyranny, anarchy, and disrespect for authority, makes itself fertile ground for such a takeover. It's a big fire, but we plan to give them a run for their money and put it out. We're going to crush their mission and put this country back on its feet. That's about all I can offer right now."

"Whoa!" Craig said. "It all makes sense, but it sounds like a monumental task."

"We're a monumental people, Michaels. Gotta go. Call me when you get something."

Twelve days later, Linda was working in the kitchen with Lois. She walked by the window, then began to shake. "Oh, no."

Craig and Nathaniel were walking up the path toward the caves. Craig's head was down, and his hand was resting on Nathaniel's shoulder. When she saw them stop and embrace, she was afraid she would pass out. When Nathaniel became a teenager, he and his dad expressed affection with shoulder jabs and knuckle punches—not hugs. She suspected immediately what was taking place. *No God—no. Not my son, please.*

Lois said, "Linda. What's wrong?"

Linda's throat was restricted—reducing her voice to a mere whisper. "I'm afraid it's happening. I'm afraid Nathaniel is joining the militia."

Lois's face grew white, and she began to weep. "I didn't want this day to come, but I'm not surprised."

Craig and Lois were so similar. Both were stalwart—towers of strength. It was disconcerting to see these two strong ones so distraught.

Linda took a handkerchief from the folded laundry, placed it in Lois's hand, then sat beside her. They wept together—fearing the unthinkable was now a certainty.

Linda whispered, "Why my son?"

Lois said, "Why would Nathaniel enroll in such a dangerous venture?"

Lois wiped her eyes, and cleared her throat. "I'm sorry, sweetheart—I hurt for myself, and for all of you, but we can't let them see us like this."

"You're right. We have to pull it together. Craig is a strong man, but if his son is leaving, it has to be killing him. When you feel better, would you send one of the guys to find Mom? I'm going to join my men. I believe they're at the lake. This will hit her hard too."

"Sure," Lois said.

"I'll be right back." Linda gently closed the outside door, and walked up the path. She slipped an arm around each of their waists. Two minutes later a fourth person joined them. It was Twig. Sweet Twig. An unexpected son, delivered in such a strange way.

CHAPTER 59

A LONG GOODBYE

*J*oliene was surprised when she saw Chad approaching.

"What's up, son?" she asked.

"Grandma Lois wants you guys to come back to camp, but she didn't tell me why."

"She's not sick is she?" Joliene asked.

"No, nothing like that. There's something she wants to tell you. I think it's about Nathaniel."

Joliene turned pale, and grabbed Darren's hand. He drew her close, and they hurried up the path, arm in arm. Chad ran ahead. Lois was no where in sight, but Nathaniel met them just inside the hut door. He smiled at his grandma, and asked if she would walk with him.

As soon as they closed the door, he got right to the point. "Twig and I are signing up for the militia. We've given it a lot of thought—and prayer. America is our country, and we want to fight for it."

She choked back tears before saying, "I'm proud of you—and Twig. It sounds like you both know what you are doing, but it breaks my heart to think of you in harms way, but I'll support you both, in every way I can."

They hugged then she turned him around, and gave him a little shove. "Go! Spend some time with your sister and little brother. I don't want to start blubbering all over you."

Nathaniel ran inside long enough to grab the football. He yelled, "Brianna, Jeremy, and Caleb, you be on my team. Now, who thinks they can beat us in a game of flag football?"

Chad yelled for his sisters and Twig. They came running. "We'll take you on anytime, anyplace."

Nathaniel said, "We'll see about that. Games on!"

Joliene, and Darren watched from the porch, listening to all the laughter, and watching the three younger ones breaking all the rules—and getting by with it.

She turned loose of Darren's hand, and said, "I'll be right back."

Duane was on his bunk reading, when she walked through the door. "Duane, there's a game of flag football going on out side. You need to help Nathaniel's team."

"No thanks. Football's too rough for me."

Joliene stared at her son as if she was seeing him for the first time. "Duane, your nephew, and your friend, are joining the militia. They are willing to give their lives for our country, and you think a game of flag football is too rough? Get off that bed and get out there. It might be good for you to get scratched up a little."

Duane was shocked on both accounts, but didn't argue. He jumped up and ran out the door. "I'm going."

Craig noticed his mom's eyes were puffy, and she was abnormally quiet. She prepared a dinner of fish, fried cornbread, and jars of seasoned tomatoes, from last years crop.

When the meal was over Craig called the family to the living area. A small fire burned in the fireplace, pushing back the coolness of the evening, but cheery flickering flames did nothing to comfort breaking hearts.

Nathaniel and Twig's type of enlistment was unfamiliar territory. Their movements could not be tracked, and their would be no contact with home. Days of open communication was a thing of the past. This new militia would be outnumbered, undermanned, and always—in danger of being eliminated—but Craig would never say those words out loud.

He said, "When I was a boy, my mom insisted I look her in the eye when she talked to me. When I was in the military they required the same. Right now I'm asking you to do the same."

He waited for every head to lift then said, "Nathaniel and Twig made this decision on their own. It hurts all of us, but we need to respect it, but—its time to dry up our tears, lift up our chins and give them a good send-off. Are you with me?"

While heads were nodding, Brianna wiped her tears, walked across the room and hugged her brother.

"I'm so proud of you, but I wish you weren't going. We're twins. Half of me will be missing." She punched his chest with her fingers. "You be careful. You hear me?"

Nathaniel nodded. He was able to keep it together until Caleb ran across the room, scooting himself between him and Brianna. She stepped back, and Nathaniel picked him up. Caleb buried his face in Nathaniel's neck—sobbing. Nathaniel turned his own face away from the room, but Craig could see his tears dropping on Caleb's head. Jeremy let them have their moment then laid his hand on Caleb's back.

"Hey, buddy. I know you're going to miss your brother, but Chad and I will be here. We need you to help us tie flies and catch fish. What do you say?"

Caleb shook his head, and after a few more sobs, Nathaniel put him down. Caleb ran straight to Jeremy and climbed up on his lap.

Craig saw Nathaniel mouth, "Thank you." Jeremy smiled and nodded back.

Richard stood up, opened the front door, fanned it a few times, and drank in the cool fresh air.

"Okay everyone. Do what I just did and breath deeply! We've had our tears. Time to pull it together. We need to enjoy these men. Just think of all the stories they'll have when they return."

Craig heard Darren whisper, "I like that word *return*."

Craig knew the pangs of war . . . the adrenaline rush as enemy soldiers closed in. Whizzing bullets screaming past his head, only to find the temple of his buddy. He still suffered pain from the shrapnel buried in his side, and still felt the suffocating mask—wrapping his face when chemical weapons were threatened. He wished none of this on his son . . . or Twig.

At eight o'clock, the following morning, the dreaded call came from General Stokes. Nathaniel and Twig would be picked up in three days at the State Park, around 1900 hours.

When the day arrived, both men were up a little after five. The trucks were prepared for travel the night before. Ralph and Jeremy would follow Craig in the second truck, and make their first trip to Wilson Creek.

Craig joined the two recruits, drank coffee with them at the fireplace, and talked about nondescript things. Lois came in at six, and prepared omelets and biscuits for breakfast. She opened a jar of Current jelly and mixed it with peanut butter then spread it on leftover biscuits for the trip.

After breakfast, Craig said, "Well guys, are you ready to hit the road? We never know what we might face before we get there."

"Yes, Dad," Nathaniel said.

"How about you Twig?"

"Yes, we are. And don't you worry. We're going to watch out for each other. Ain't that right boy?"

"You bet." He said, "I want to take a walk with Dad, Twig. Do you mind?"

"You go right ahead. Take all the time you like."

Craig and Nathaniel walked a short ways in the direction of the lake. There was a slight breeze and a few waves rolled into shore. Five baby ducks were trailing their mother rocking up and down in the unsteady water.

They watched them for a moment then Craig said, "What's on your mind, son?"

"Dad, when we're ready to leave, would you help me keep the goodbyes short? I want to beat it for the ridge as fast as possible. I don't want us blubbering all over each other."

"I'll do my best, but you know who we're dealing with here."

Nathaniel laughed. "I won't hold you responsible—I promise—so let's get this party started. Twig and I are ready."

"Your Mom and Brianna are riding along. Hope that's okay. We're leaving Caleb here."

Nathaniel nodded without speaking.

After breakfast, Craig asked Richard to drive Lois to the bottom of the canyon on the ATV. Caleb held Nathaniel and Twig's hands the whole way. Linda snapped several pictures on her iPhone. After all the hugs and handshakes were given, Nathaniel knelt before Caleb, then pointed at Cassie and Sara.

"It's your job to take care of those two girls. They need a good man like you to watch out for them."

Cassie crossed her arms and gave Nathaniel a look that made him laugh.

He ruffled Caleb's hair, gave him a knuckle punch then squatted before the girls. They almost knocked him over when they came flying into his arms. They began crying with loud wails. He hugged them tight, gave each a kiss on the forehead then Linda lifted them off.

Craig smiled and said, "Its time to go."

When the crew got back to the hut, Richard made sure Lois was settled. Tracey suggested they put together a picnic lunch, and take the kids to the lake.

"The chores can wait," she said.

"Sounds like a plan to me."

Everyone joined them except Lois and Duane. Lois said she wanted to read a little while then rest before dinner. Tracey went back inside to grab some water, and heard her sobbing. When she told Richard, he turned around, but Tracey stopped him.

"Leave her alone, sweetheart. She's a proud woman. We'll see if she wants to talk later."

The ride to the park was rough, but without incident. After the gate was secured, and branches put in place, Craig chose a spot close to the entrance, but not visible from the highway. Nathaniel built a fire, and after eating the food Lois prepared, Linda removed a bag of marshmallows from the truck.

"If someone would cut a few long sticks we could roast these."

Twig and Jeremy did the honors. Then, at exactly 1900 hours, they heard a vehicle leave the main highway and turn into the park. Craig's heart skipped a beat. He looked in the direction of the sound, following the steady rotation of its tires. Linda and Brianna sat perfectly still until the vehicle wound its way to where they were sitting.

Linda whispered, "I was hoping they wouldn't come at all."

Nathaniel stood up. "I think our ride is here."

A dark Humvee with tinted windows, and four swaying antennas backed into the parking spot next to Craig's. The driver nodded at Craig's crew as three other soldiers dismounted. Before approaching Craig's family, two soldiers in the back seat laid rifles on the floor, and unbuckled their belts laden with numerous items. Craig recognized the belt. He knew it contained a baton, pepper spray, brass knuckles, ammo, a knife, a pistol, and more. He also remembered how heavy it was.

The driver was the first to approach. "I'm assuming two of you gentlemen are waiting for a ride?"

Nathaniel and Twig walked out to meet him and said, "Yes, sir," at the same time.

Craig followed them, but instead of shaking the sergeant's hand, he saluted him. The sergeant quickly snapped to attention and saluted back.

He said, "Its good to meet you, sir. Our general has nothing but good things to say about you."

Craig thanked him, then introduced the family. All four soldiers were together now and seemed especially happy to meet Brianna. Sergeant Fowler introduced himself first, then Sergeants Nelson, Lopez and Wagner. He explained they would do all their travel in darkness. He offered no coordinates, but did say the trip would take three and a half nights.

Linda said, "Would you gentlemen like to roast a few marshmallows before you leave?"

Sergeant Fowler said, "Thank you ma'am. We have a few minutes. We appreciate your hospitality. Marshmallows over an open campfire remind me of my family's camping trips in the California redwoods..."

He stopped abruptly. His unspoken pain spoke louder than any words he could say. Craig knew it could be multiplied thousands of times over. So many stories . . . so much loss.

Twenty minutes later Sergeant Fowler gave a ten-minute warning. Nathaniel said they wanted a moment with their family, if that was okay. Sergeant Fowler nodded, so Craig took Brianna's hand, and Nathaniel took his mom's. Twig walked with them a few feet away out of earshot.

"I want you to remember we're doing the right thing, and try not to worry. Twig and I are in God's hands, and God is always in control. You guys take care of each other. We love you."

Nothing else was said. Linda squeezed Nathaniel's hand, and they walked back to the fire for the final goodbye, and one more hug.

Nathaniel and Twig were assigned to the middle seat. Sergeant

Wagner and Lopez took the seat facing the rear. When the Humvee door was opened, Craig caught sight of two huge weapons, along with multiple rounds of ammunition. Sergeants Nelson and Fowler were in the front, Nelson in the driver's seat.

When the engine started, the dashboard came alive with a multiplicity of gauges. Now Craig knew why so many antennas were needed. This war required technological instruments he was unfamiliar with.

When the sound of the Humvee's tires moved from crunching gravel to the whine of the open highway, emptiness filled the space. They sat a little longer by the fire, ate a few more marshmallows, but tasted nothing. Brianna laid her head on her mother's shoulder, and cried.

The following morning, Ralph and Jeremy followed Craig to Wilson Creek. Ralph entered a small bank and tried to exchange his American currency, but was turned down. Craig paid for all the purchases, including new boots, jeans and some personal items for Ralph and Jeremy.

Craig gave Ralph fifty dollars to buy groceries from Lois's list. Do to individual quantity restrictions—mostly on food items—they would be able to purchase more.

Craig allowed a couple of hours to just walk around. Jeremy and Ralph were delighted. On their way back to the valley they stopped at Rosie's diner. Craig treated them to a small lunch.

Rolling over the hundreds of bumps, and the narrow road was exhausting. Craig said, "I'll be glad when we make this trip for the last time," Craig said.

"Me, too," Linda replied.

CHAPTER 60

ANOTHER LONG WAIT

raig was aware that Nathaniel and Twig carried a large workload, but not until he began to spread it around did he realize just how much. The only person who did very little was Duane. There was not one callus on either of his hands. His attitude was better, but his willingness to volunteer for physical labor was lacking.

Craig asked Duane to join him by the outside fire pit then broke the news. "Duane, I need your help. With Nathaniel and Twig gone we have to spread the jobs they were doing among the rest of us. I have two specific things I want you to take charge of. One is splitting wood. The second is fishing."

Duane gasped, "I don't mind splitting logs, but fishing? I'm not very good at that."

"Don't worry. Jeremy is a natural. He will teach you, and it also gives you a chance to spend some time with Caleb. I would love to see you two get closer, and he loves to fish."

Duane was quiet for a moment then, to Craig's relief, he smiled. "I'll do my best. I promise. When do I start?"

Craig was taken aback and pleased. The last thing he needed was a confrontation.

"Well, good. Go talk to Richard first, then see Jeremy. I'm sure they'll get you set up. And Duane—thanks."

Craig and Richard not only did their portion of work, they spent hours pouring over their BLM maps looking at the Denver area for any possible lab site. On their third day of searching all their new maps, Linda stopped and watched them for a minute.

"Do you guys have any of your older maps to use as a comparison?"

Richard hit himself in the head with the back of his hand. "I am such an idiot. We're looking for something to pop out at us. We need to be looking for changes. Don't ever tell anybody I'm an expert again."

He stood up and hugged Linda. "You're the genius. And yes, we do have older maps. We also have some satellite imagery, which we rarely look at. Tell Tracey I'll be back in about forty-five minutes. Those maps are in the work truck up in the grove."

Craig said, "Good job, hon. I'm going with him."

An hour later, old and new maps were spread out on the floor. Both men used magnifying glasses looking for changes between the two.

Two more hours passed and nothing had popped out at them. Craig walked away and spent his frustration on the woodpile—again. He struck with such force he drove the axe deeply into the wood with every blow. It felt good. If only he could use this same force to rid his anxiety over Nathaniel and Twig. If only the general or Leon would call.

"I wonder if I would feel better if I cut the whole forest down." He sunk the head of the axe deep in the ground, sat down on a stump, and buried his head in his hands. He didn't hear Richard approach, and was startled when his friend touched his shoulder.

"Come with me. I may have found something."

Craig wiped the sweat off his brow and turned around. "I sure hope so. I could use some good news."

Richard spread the map over a large log then pointed to an area he had lightly circled. "Tell me what you see."

Craig took a few minutes while wishing Richard would just tell him what he was looking at . . . then he saw it. "It looks like a small road. A road to nowhere."

"Yes, and notice how it curves to the backside of the mountain," Richard said. "There are no facilities of any type listed there. Now look at the satellite imagery. This one was taken just before dusk."

Craig traced the image with his finger. "Well, I'll be darned. It disappears into the side of that mountain."

Richard said, "I compared this area with two of our old maps imagery. It was not there. Our map is not detailed and simply shows the road begins and ends in Denver. The satellite imagery shows it begins and ends at a large building. Looks like a warehouse."

"I hate to call the general, but this news is too important not too, and with any luck, he'll tell us how our guys are doing."

"Sounds good to me."

After figuring out the exact coordinates, Craig and Richard sat down on their familiar boulder. Craig reached the general after a few rings, and gave the same password, hoping it had not changed. They told him what they found, and pinpointed the location. The general was elated.

"I know just how to check it out. Thank your friend for me. I'll let you know what we find, when I can. Oh, and about your men."

Craig's heart dropped until General Stokes finished.

"They're still in boot camp. You should see some of the wimps and sissies we have. Your boys put almost everybody to shame. Good job teaching your son how to be a man, and that country boy is a force to be reckoned with. Talk to you soon, and thanks."

Craig didn't want tears to well up in his eyes, but they came anyway. He and Richard rushed back to the huts to share the general's news with the family. Lois made popcorn, and they had a celebration. At least for now, their men were safe.

∾

On July 12th, at seven in the morning, Craig and Richard hiked the canyon road to prepare both trucks for a trip to Wilson Creek. Just as they reached the crest, Craig's phone buzzed. It was Leon, and as usual he launched right into the conversation, but this time, it was a bit cryptic and caught the two men a little off guard.

Leon spoke in a loud whisper, but they understood every word. "Hey, guys. A gentleman friend you spoke with a while back said to tell you—*spot on.* He said if he goes hunting in the future, he hopes you will be his guide."

Craig thought for a moment then said, "Of course. Tell him we would love to."

"Now for the news you've been waiting for. It appears you're safe to travel. Positions are being held for you, and residences for your crew. Jacque said take your time. Travel only after dark as a precaution. There've been no drone strikes for a week, but you can be sure it's not over."

"I don't know what to say, Leon. Thank you." Craig looked at Richard.

Richard said, "I echo that. We can't thank you enough. We could never have made it without you."

"Glad to do it, but Jacque said, do not call him. Just go straight to the facility when you get there. I will let him know when you leave your site."

"What's going on there?" Craig asked. "Is there any progress?"

"Yes, the militia keeps growing. Our friend says red-blooded Americans are coming out of the woodwork to join while the drones are quiet. Hundreds of trained soldiers that were forced to stand down have joined him. He says this is a battle between the good guys and the bad guys—his words."

"Do we dare think that things are finally going in the right direction?" Richard said. "What about where you are?"

"I'm not sure. There are a lot of closed-door meetings, and the strangest thing has happened. The vice president hasn't been seen in four days. There's a new man in charge with a foreign accent. This facility has filled up with his men. When he learned about the general's successes he was very angry. I saw him push several people to the wall while his cronies stood by with weapons. Everyone's afraid of him—including me."

"Have you been under suspicion?" Craig asked.

"Not so far, but I keep Jeanette in our quarters. Listen, I've been on here too long already. Start packing up, and try to be out one week from today, and linger at the park until you hear from me—or the general. We *will* figure out a way to get back to you."

Craig's heart was pounding so fast he could barely catch his breath. "Why the general?"

"I'm not sure. It's just what he told me to tell you when you were able to move."

"Thanks again, Leon, and please stay safe."

When Craig and Richard ran onto the porch, a startled Linda met them at the door.

She said, "What's wrong? Are you being chased?"

As soon as they stepped inside, she slammed and locked it.

Craig laughed which earned him a punch. "We aren't being chased, but we have some great news. First, get everybody in here then we'll share it."

It felt like an eternity to Craig, but finally everyone was accounted for. He stood in front of the window and said, "General Stokes was able to destroy the chemical lab that was producing the virus—from the coordinates *we* gave him. Leon said the drone attacks have stopped for the time being, and General Stokes is gaining a lot of recruits."

Darren said, "Thank God for his leadership."

Craig pointed at Richard. "But, the best part for *our* family is yet to come. I'm going to let Richard tell you."

Richard looked surprised, but happy. "Well, folks, this has been a long time coming, but we can finally leave the valley."

At first the room was quiet, then whooping and hollering bounced off the walls—until Duane asked a question.

"Does that mean we get to go home?"

Craig said, "I'm sorry, Duane, but the recovery of America has just begun, and will take a long time to accomplish. Richard and I have jobs waiting for us in Eastern Canada—in fact the Canadian BLM Bureau Chief has been holding them for us."

"Leon said we even have temporary living quarters until we get on our feet, and we always have our camp trailers," Richard offered. "Leon wants us to leave the valley one week from today."

Craig said, "The first thing we have to do is clear the entrance and…"

Before he went any farther Duane said, "I'll help."

"Thank you," Craig said. "We will need a big crew for that job, but right now, let's take a deep breath, and start packing. Leon said we are to stay at the park until we hear from him or the general. If anything is new they will let us know."

Jeremy moved closer to his dad and asked, "Will there be any way to check on people?"

Richard said, "I'm not sure, but if there is, Jacque will know. We'll sure try."

Ralph whispered, "Thank you."

"What about Nathaniel and Twig, Daddy?" Caleb asked. "Will they be able to find us?"

"Don't worry son, we'll make sure they know where we are."

Six days later, Craig led the caravan of survivors up the bumpy canyon road. When they got to the top he pulled onto the plateau. Lois stretched to take a final look, as he walked to the edge of the tall hill. The rest of the family joined him, and stood in silence drinking in the scene. The sun reflected off the glistening lake in direct contrast to the impenetrable dark forest. Glacier velocities trailed down the side of the distant mountains.

Big Ben whimpered a little—perhaps—Craig thought, *a whimper of objection?* He patted the dog's head. "I hear you, boy. I have mixed emotions too."

As Craig turned to continue this long awaited departure, a lone eagle floated above, casting a moving shadow over the family. It was a bittersweet departure from this valley of life—and death. In spite of hardships, he felt certain every family member was taking away memories, deeper values, and an appreciation for life they would never have gained in their former life.

The trip to the state park went without incident except for grumbling cows, squawking chickens, and rough, narrow portions of road. This time Craig's fifth wheel took deep scrapes on the passenger side, but unlike the first trip, his mother was riding with Darren and Joliene.

Once again, Richard followed up the rear in the overloaded rental truck. Craig thought of wicked Slick, left behind in a grave that would never receive a visitor.

When they reached the park, Craig led the family to a group site, while Richard and Chad took care of the gate. Craig wondered if this was a dream or were they really heading for civilization? Would they even *like* civilization?

As the ladies began to prepare dinner, Craig's phone buzzed. It was Leon.

"Hey, Leon, we're at the National Park. What's up?"

"I wanted to check your progress, and I have a message from the general."

Craig's heart sank. Why would the general call Leon unless he wanted a friend to break bad news?

Leon said, "I told him about your plans, and how many vehicles and trailers you have. There's been no drone attacks for a few weeks, but he's afraid you'll attract too much attention. He's sending you a military escort. They'll meet you in the park. "

"We didn't expect that," Craig said. "If you talk to him again, tell him thanks."

Three days later as night fell, Caleb ran up to Craig. "Look, Dad. Look what I found."

Before Craig could turn he heard the distinct sound of Caleb's treasure. It sent chills down his spine. Images of little Tommy rushed through his head. Caleb was holding a bell—a small gold bell. It made only a quiet tinkle, but to Craig it was a gong. *Oh God, please don't let this be an ominous sign.*

Caleb startled him back to reality when he said, "Listen, Daddy. Someone's coming."

Craig heard the sound of two vehicle's transition from the smooth surface of the highway onto rough gravel. He was not surprised to see two black Humvee's, each with four swinging antennas. Their escort had arrived.

When the first two doors opened simultaneously, Sergeants Fowler and Nelson embarked. When the second set of doors opened the two men who stepped out were not sergeants. Their ranks were private first class, and—they were Nathaniel and Twig.

EPILOGUE

*N*athaniel and Twig stood at attention within arms reach, but no one moved, they just grinned. Craig wanted to shake their hand and welcome them, but out of respect, kept his place. Caleb, unaware and unconcerned about protocol, ran straight into Nathaniel's arms. Nathaniel shot a nervous glance at Sergeant Fowler, who smiled and nodded.

"Go ahead, folks. Welcome your men."

After hugs and introductions were made, Nathaniel asked permission to take a short walk with his dad and Richard.

When the others were out of earshot, Nathaniel said, "I have a message for you from General Stokes. He asked me to give it orally in case—well never mind. You know what I mean."

Craig said nothing, but the knot in his stomach yelled a resounding, *Yes.*

"First, your destination has changed. It's now Saskatoon. Leon and Jacque have both been notified, and the BLM office is expecting you. However, our escort will be leaving you twenty miles west of there. We have to drop south on Highway 4."

Craig said, "Why is that, son?" Twenty miles wasn't far, but having an escort all the way to the BLM office was appealing.

Nathaniel said, "Six sleeper cells, equipped with drones, have been spotted close to Montana's northern border. The general needs our Humvee's. Each has software that detects drones anywhere in a five-mile radius. We can also power them off."

Craig said, "That explains why drones kept sweeping the border, and venturing deeper into southern Canada. They were trying to keep that cell from being exposed."

"That's exactly what the general said. He also said, when we're finished in Montana we're heading straight to Washington, DC, and sweeping the—" Nathaniel stopped and cleared his throat. "Well, he used his most colorful language, but basically he means to do a thorough job of sweeping the White House, Capitol, and Pentagon. It wouldn't be possible without Leon's inside tips."

Craig had a vivid memory of the General's colorful language.

Richard said, "Maybe Leon and Jeanette will be able to leave —finally."

"The general also said to tell you thanks," Nathaniel said. "The spot you pinpointed was the exact location of the lab. He wiped it off the map, and—there's no evidence another viral-producing lab exists."

Craig smiled and said, "We have your mom to thank for that one."

Richard nodded.

"Son, has he figured out how the attack covered so much of America so quickly? That puzzles me."

"Yes, he did, Nathaniel said. "The group that is behind it, bought a large portion of land in Northern Kansas, as their hub. They farmed the land until everything was ready, then they launched the attack. They could reach most of America quickly from that location—except where there was heavy rain. Other sites, such as the one on the Montana border, are in play now, but Kansas was headquarters."

"That makes sense. When the attack began, and we were headed home, I wasn't thanking God for the rain, but I am now."

"Me too, Dad. Now let me tell you the last thing he wanted you to know—and I better get it right—He said, 'America has been on her knees a long time, but she's rising. Her lights are coming back on, and maybe in a year or so, you can go home.'"

Craig looked stunned for a moment, then punched Richard on the shoulder. "Did you hear that, man? The good guys are finally winning. Thank you, son, and tell the general we heard him loud and clear. I feel like I can finally breathe."

Richard placed his hand on Nathaniel's shoulder. "I want to thank you, too. You're part of a great movement, and because of guys like you—and probably some gals too—this thing may finally be drawing to a close. I'm going back to the campsite. I'm sure your Mom wants a few minutes with you, too. Take care of yourself."

As Richard walked away, a wave of emotion flooded Craig's heart. Undisciplined tears rolled freely down his cheeks. He turned and hugged his handsome son, and prayed.

"Father, bring Nathaniel and Twig back to us, please."

To Nathaniel he said, "I love you, son. You've made me very proud."

AUTHOR'S NOTE

Devastating terrorist attacks are frequently taking place on American soil, with no regard for human life. The possibility of a crippling nation wide attack is not only possible, it is probable. Should such an attack occur and render our government and municipalities useless, are we prepared to survive on our own without daddy government's help?

When drones came on scene they were harmless, expensive toys, but quickly evolved into silent machines that are able to conduct surveillance, carry payloads, and act with silent precision. (*Something to think about.*)

THE VALLEY is a work of fiction, and most named locations do not exist. The premise, however, is real.

Should you find a mistake in my book, please feel free to let me know by sending a message to: nlbailey6282@gmail.com

FOR YOUR BOOK CLUB, SMALL GROUP, OR PERSONAL REFLECTION

- Could you pick a terrorist out in a crowd?
- Would you find it hard to believe your next door neighbor, or other associates might be terrorists?
- If you consider the unrest, violence, insurrection, and tyranny, already present in our country, how long before a nationwide attack happens?
- If America was attacked and your government could not help you, where would you go?
- What would you take?
- Who would you take?
- Would you wonder how God could let such a thing happen?

These questions are poised for the express purpose of raising awareness, and perhaps to evoke us to become more vigilant. No one wants to believe such a devastating attack could happen in America, but from what we are already witnessing, we know it is possible. Perhaps not on a broad scale, as this story depicts, but how widespread would it have to be to interrupt your life?

ACKNOWLEDGMENTS

It took many hours of research, floor pacing, and hard work to write this book—but that was the easy part. I knew it must be written to the reader, so feedback was critical. Thank you Lois (Mom), sister-in-law Jeanette, husband Richard, good friend, Carol, and my supportive children for their constant encouragement.

My manuscript would still be resting in my computer without the publishing skills of my friend and mentor, suspense author Rich Bullock – www.perilousfiction.com. Thank you for the many hours you invested.

Thank you Rob Henslin for the beautiful cover art.

Rob Henslin at www.rhdcreative.com

www.ingramcontent.com/pod-product-compliance
Lightning Source LLC
Chambersburg PA
CBHW061322170626
46817CB00001B/267